D0626914

"Are you afraid of the mighty Crush Taylor?" She took another step closer. "He's not as bad as he seems, you know."

"I'm not afraid of him." He placed his hands on her shoulders to keep her from coming any closer. Her warmth carried into his skin, into his being, as if it was igniting him from within.

"And I'm not afraid of *you*." She ducked underneath his hands in a quick move right out of the NBA. He took a step back and his calves hit the bench situated next to the lockers. She reached out in apology and suddenly they were right smack against each other, chest-to-chest.

Fire flashed down his spine, hot and urgent. He hauled her against him—oh, sweet Lord, she felt good. Soft and firm and shapely and alive and fresh and . . . then her mouth was under his, her lips parting, her breath warm, her flesh lush and sweet. It wasn't a kiss so much as a head rush.

By Jennifer Bernard

Love Between the Bases
DRIVE YOU WILD
CAUGHT BY YOU
ALL OF ME

Bachelor Firemen
IT'S A WONDERFUL FIREMAN: A BACHELOR
FIREMAN NOVELLA
THE NIGHT BELONGS TO FIREMAN
FOUR WEDDINGS AND A FIREMAN
DESPERATELY SEEKING FIREMAN: A BACHELOR
FIREMAN NOVELLA
HOW TO TAME A WILD FIREMAN
SEX AND THE SINGLE FIREMAN
ONE FINE FIREMAN: A BACHELOR FIREMAN NOVELLA
HOT FOR FIREMAN
THE FIREMAN WHO LOVED ME

Drive You Wild

A LOVE BETWEEN THE BASES NOVEL

JENNIFER BERNARD

AVONBOOKS

An Imprint of HarperCollinsPublishers

Excerpt from *All of Me* copyright © 2015 by Jennifer Bernard.
Excerpt from *Caught by You* copyright © 2016 by Jennifer Bernard.

First Avon Books mass market printing: July 2016

ISBN 978-0-06-237220-8

Avon Trademark Reg. U.S. Pat. Off. and in Other Countries, Marca Registrada, Hecho en U.S.A.
Avon, Avon Books, and the Avon logo are trademarks of HarperCollins Publishers.
HarperCollins® is a registered trademark of HarperCollins Publishers.

16 17 18 19 20 OPM 10 9 8 7 6 5 4 3 2 1

For my wonderful husband Scott, whose
love and support mean everything.

Acknowledgments

Thanks are due to Kristy, Steph and Lizbeth for helping this story grow. To my brilliant editor, Tessa Woodward, I can never send enough gratitude, though I'll keep trying. Without Alexandra Machinist, I might not be writing these words. Thanks for your constant support. The Avon team—Tom, Pam, Kaitlyn, Elle, Jessie, Shawn, Dana, and so many more—continues to amaze me. Thanks to one and all. Lastly, thank you to Wendy and the Hot Readers for making this writing gig so much fun.

Drive You Wild

Chapter 1

IT'S A RARE baseball game that ends with the star slugger being chased with a BB gun. But no one who knew Trevor Stark would have been surprised by the news. The Kilby Catfish left fielder had a certain way about him, a way that made women lose their minds and men lose their cool. It had been that way his whole life. One of these days, people often said, Trevor Stark was going to run into trouble he couldn't get out of.

If that day had come, on a Saturday in July, Trevor had no inkling of it when he stepped onto the field at Catfish Stadium. The banks of lights aimed at the diamond lent a haze of lavender to the early evening sky. A friendly sort of roar drifted from the bleachers, a mixture of lazy chatter and cracking peanut shells. The sound system was playing some country song Trevor didn't recognize, and the heady scent of dust and grass and leather made something inside him settle into place. He loved baseball. Loved every second on the field, and merely endured the seconds off it.

On the mound, the pitcher was warming up, the *thunk* of his fastballs drilling into the catcher's mitt. Heading for his spot in left field, Trevor deliberately stepped on the chalk line between foul territory and the infield. Touching the line was known to be bad luck—unless you were one of those players who believed the opposite. Trevor believed in facing bad luck head-on, armed with cleats and a cup.

"Hey Trev." Bieberman, on his way to his spot at shortstop, popped up next to him. Bieberman, whose real name was Jim Leiberman, looked enough like Justin Bieber to allow his teammates to torment him with that nickname. "Did you hear the news about Crush?"

Crush Taylor, former pitching legend, owned the Catfish and had been riding Trevor's ass since last season.

"You lost me at 'Crush.' I break out in smallpox when I hear his name."

"Smallpox was eradicated in 1980," chirped Bieberman, a former med student who had all kinds of random facts at his disposal.

"I'm bringin' it back."

Dwight Conner, the center fielder, jogged past. Dwight was his closest friend on the team. Trevor still didn't know how that had happened; normally he avoided friendships, along with relationships in general. "Bringing what back? Forget that, did you hear about Crush?"

Bieberman answered quickly. "I was just saying that he went on TV and promised to win the Triple A championship. He said if we don't, he'll sell the team to the jackass Wade family. His words."

Trevor glanced at the owner's box, where Crush Taylor spent most games drinking from his ubiquitous silver flask and flirting with his lady-of-the-moment.

"By the time that happens, I'm going to be outta the Catfish into the Friars," said Dwight with a grin. "Fried Catfish, that's me."

As usual, the mention of the San Diego Friars, the major league team that held his contract, made Trevor's gut roil. Most players lived for "the Call," but not Trevor. If he had his way, he'd never get permanently called up to the Friars. He'd stay right here, where no one knew him. He wanted one thing—to keep his sister Nina safe and anonymous, which would *never* happen if he played in the majors.

But he couldn't let anyone in baseball know his true situation, so he continued with his usual act. The legend of Trevor Stark, selfish, arrogant bastard. "Why should I care who buys the team?" he said to Dwight. "I care about Trevor Stark only. Trevor Stark should not be stuck here in Limbo, Texas. Hell, I don't even like barbecue. And I can hit these Triple A pitchers with my eyes closed."

"Hey, Gossip Girls," yelled Duke, the manager. "Shut up and get your butts on the field."

With a gesture of apology, Trevor sped up to a jog, parting ways with Dwight, now headed toward center field.

"Buy me a Lone Star after the game and I won't bust you on the barbecue thing," Dwight called as he settled into position. "That could get you shot around here."

"You're on." Trevor faced the infield, where the first Albuquerque Isotope batter was just leaving the on-deck circle. He adjusted his cap to shield his eyes from the glare of the lights, and that's when he caught sight of the homemade sign in the stands. Kilby fans were known for their expressiveness at the ballpark.

Trevor Stark, it read, but the *Trevor* had been crossed off and replaced with *Traitor*.

Traitor? That seemed like a stretch, even though Trevor knew he wasn't a popular player like Dwight. Everyone loved Dwight; Trevor tended to inspire the opposite emotion. Let Dwight be the charmer. Let Bieberman be the cute and cuddly one. Trevor Stark was all about mental toughness, mystery, and intimidation.

Block it out. The guy was probably an Isotope fan trying to rattle the competition.

With two outs, someone finally made contact. A sharp *crack* carried across the field, accompanied by a rising roar from the crowd. A fly ball was heading toward the outfield.

"It's all you, baby," called Dwight.

Trevor loped left, then slowed to a gentle drift, tracking the ball on its spinning descent. He jogged back, back, back, until he knew the outfield wall was just behind him. The ball was taking forever up there, as if it had caught a wind current headed to the Gulf of Mexico. As it finally headed for the ground, he leaped into the air and got a glove on it. It bounced off, and he had to lunge in a kind of split-leg pirouette to snatch it back into the webbing. The crowd roared.

He held up his glove with the ball nestled inside.

"Trevor, Trevor!" In the stands, a teenage kid selling peanuts waved to him. Trevor ignored him. He knew Brian pretty well from the Boys and Girls Club. Good kid trying to bring in some extra cash for the family. But when he'd gotten Brian the job here, he warned him that was the extent of his help. What was the kid doing grinning at him like that?

Instead he tossed the ball to a little boy jumping up and down next to a pretty blond woman. "Come find me after the game and I'll sign it," he called to the boy—and his hot mother—as he and Dwight jogged off the field. On the way to the dugout, he caught sight of another homemade sign.

Trevor Skank. You suck.

Trevor shook his head. *Bring it on, hecklers.* That sort of thing just fueled his drive.

In the dugout, he left his glove on the bench and pulled on his batting gloves, since he was batting third. Duke, the manager, called over to him. "Message from Crush. He says stop flirting with the ladies in the stands and get your pretty face on base."

Trevor gritted his teeth. "Crush can kiss my ass. Times three. Triple into right field, coming up."

The other Catfish jeered and scoffed, which made sense because this wasn't pool, this was baseball.

But now that he'd made that statement, he had to do his best to make it happen. The "legend of Trevor Stark" constantly needed more material. He was a big guy, with lots of power in his arms and shoulders, but his biggest weapon was his ice-cold manner at the plate, the way he refused to be intimidated, the way nothing rattled him. Nothing on a baseball field fazed him because off the field he'd faced the worst already.

When it was his turn at bat, he carefully worked the count. On the ninth pitch, the pitcher threw way inside, so close that he felt the movement of air milliseconds from his face. An attempted brushback. He stepped closer to the plate, defending it like a barbarian with a spiked mace. Will versus will. Stamina versus stamina.

Pitch number ten was a too-slow curveball, weighed down by the pitcher's disheartened fatigue.

Trevor drilled it into right field. Stand-up triple.

In the dugout, Dwight flipped him the bird, while the rest of his teammates jumped up and cheered. Truth was, he'd gotten lucky, but hell if he'd tell anyone that. Mystery and intimidation. Name of the game.

The game ended in a win for the Catfish. On the way to the clubhouse, he paused to sign the baseball he'd tossed to the kid. The boy's sexy mother mouthed something to him, but he just gave her a wave and continued into the clubhouse. Honestly, some nights he preferred quiet and a good book.

After his shower, he'd barely gotten his shirt on before Sean Richards, a reporter from the local cable station, stuck a microphone in his face.

"Trevor Stark, you're the Friars top prospect, but you've only played two games in San Diego. They spent a record amount on your contract, you broke two hitting records back in Double A, but once again you're back in Kilby. What's the reason for that, in your opinion?"

Trevor hated this line of questioning. Each year, he made it impossible for the Friars to call him up. A well-timed scandal, a DUI arrest, an injury. But that information was locked in the vault.

"You know what?" he said. "I don't think about that kind of thing. When I'm on that field, I'm there to do my best and help my team. Right now my team is the Catfish, and I think we have a good shot at the Triple A championship this year."

Richards, a lanky kid right out of college with a soul patch and gauged ears, brightened. "So you support Crush Taylor's mission?"

Trevor suppressed a grin. Distraction accomplished. "Of course I support it. Just like the Catfish fans support us. We want to bring it on home for the fine people of Kilby."

Across the clubhouse, Sonny Barnes was making the universal sign for blowjob, and Dwight Conner was doing the "slow clap."

Trevor shot them a below-camera-level finger while continuing to gaze earnestly at the reporter. "Us Catfish, we play our hearts out every single game, and hopefully it shows."

"Heart? That's not usually a word associated with Trevor Stark. People say you're made of ice out there. You never get rattled, never show emotion."

"Well, Sean, I have a heart. I just try not to let it affect me on the field." He paused. "Or off." He winked at the kid and clapped him on the shoulder.

Sean grinned and lowered his camera. "Thanks, Trevor. Good game tonight."

"Thanks, dude."

All in all, Trevor was feeling pretty good about things as he shouldered his gym bag and ambled down the tunnel that led to the exit.

Stepping outside Catfish Stadium, he drew in a long breath of warm, exhaust-scented air. The parking lot was nearly empty; he'd taken his time getting dressed, putting off the moment when he had to leave the ballpark. In the far corner of the lot, Ramirez was wrapped so tightly around his wife that the two of them could barely walk. Trevor wondered briefly what that kind of intimacy might feel like, then dismissed the thought, since he didn't expect to ever find out.

As he reached the edge of the parking lot, a man stepped from the shadows, his hand in the pocket of his bulky military jacket.

Gun.

A cold rush of adrenaline flooded his system. This was it. His past coming back to stalk him. He'd feared this day since he got out of juvie. Being hunted, found, punished.

He dove behind the nearest car, using it as a shield.

"You'd better run, Trevor Fucking Stark, 'cuz I got a BB gun and I'm going to hurt you!" The man spoke in a high, whiny voice, like he'd had a few six-packs too many.

The death grip of fear around Trevor's lungs loosened. This wasn't anyone from Detroit. If those guys came after him, they'd have real firepower, and they wouldn't be wasted. They'd mean business. Crazy local dudes, on the other hand, he could handle.

Trevor scanned the parking lot. He'd parked his Escalade in the usual spot, but there was no way he could reach it without giving the guy a clear shot at him. Behind him lay the shadowed corner where kids sometimes snuck under the chain-link fence. If he could crawl backward without the guy seeing him . . .

He glanced at the players' exit. He needed a distraction. But the shadowed double doors offered no help. If only he could grab his bag, with his cell phone and a couple of baseballs. But it was just out of reach, where it had fallen when he dove for cover.

The man was striding toward the car, a Jetta which he was pretty sure belonged to Terry, the physical therapist. If he hurt her car, he'd never hear the end of it. *Talk to the guy. Talk him down.*

"Look, sir, can we talk about this before you get yourself in trouble?" Trevor called. "There's gotta be a way we can work this out."

"Did you bother to talk to me before you screwed my girl?" the man shouted.

Oh, hell. "If I did that, I apologize. I would never screw someone else's girl. If you know me at all, you know it's true."

Silence. Trevor peered under the car. The dim outline of cowboy boots a few yards away reassured him that at least the man wasn't right on top of him.

"Listen, man. I know my reputation, and there's a few things in my past I'm not proud of, but I think there's a chance this might be a misunderstanding. I'm not sure I know who we're talking about here."

Wrong move. "I guess she just slipped your mind, then, dickbrain." The cowboy boots moved forward. "Aisle six at the Walgreens? She gave you a neck massage. Now she says you're her soulmate. Fucking asshole."

What the . . . ? Trevor remembered his headache, and the shy girl in a baggy denim dress who'd told him about her acupressure classes. "Nothing happened, man. Of course I remember her, but we didn't do anything more than talk."

"That ain't what she says. She says you *connected*."

"Well, sure, maybe on a friendly level. She's a sweet girl. You're a very lucky man to have a good woman like her. Do you think it's going to impress her if you get arrested? It won't, I guarantee."

In answer, a spray of BBs glanced off the trunk of the car with light metallic pings. *Holy fuck, this guy is serious.* Ironic that he was going to get shot over a completely innocent encounter at a Walgreen's, when he'd done so many worse things in the past.

Well, maybe he deserved it. It wouldn't exactly be a big loss to the world if Trevor Stark wound up dead in the parking lot of a nowheresville Triple A stadium. Duke would be pissed. Dwight would miss him in the outfield. A large number of women would be sad for a moment, then decide he probably had it coming.

If he was gone, Nina would be safe. No one would ever find her or hurt her. At that realization, his body relaxed into the pavement as if it belonged there.

"Trevor Stark." Judging by his gloating tone, the man had him in his line of sight now. "Not so ice cold now, are you? If you want to live, you'd better start begging."

Did he want to live? The weight of his life pressed against his heart, all the pain and danger and abandonment. Was this his life flashing before his eyes in the moment before it ended? Based on the sound of the pings, the BB gun didn't have much power, but at close range it could probably do some damage. Was it for the best?

A shadow of movement told him the man was raising his gun. *Do something, do something.*

But he was frozen, paralyzed. His father's face, fearful and vacant, stole into his mind. Why, of all images, did he have to go out with *that* one? He'd rather end with the only perfect thing in his life—baseball. A home run singing across a blue sky, the satisfying *crack* of his favorite birch bat hitting the sweet spot of a fastball. Nina, leaping across broken beer bottles and dandelions, chasing a fly ball in the vacant lot where they used to play.

The sound of an engine gunning broke the moment. Trevor caught a glimpse of a white car speeding toward him across the parking lot, the passenger door swinging open.

"Get in," a female voice called out.

The man shifted—oh hell, the lunatic was going to aim at the oncoming car. He was going to shoot an innocent bystander.

Trevor's paralysis snapped. He dove for his attacker's ankles and jerked his feet out from under him. The gunman toppled over and landed with a hard crash on the pavement.

Trevor scrambled to his feet and flung himself toward the open car door. He crawled in and the vehicle took off before his feet were even inside.

Pulling his legs into the car, he slammed the door shut, then lunged for the wheel, brushing against the warm, slim body of a woman.

"Get your head down," he ordered. "I'll drive."

But the driver swatted his hand away. "I don't think so, mister. This is a rescue, not a carjacking."

Awkwardly crammed into the passenger seat, he gaped at the woman behind the wheel. He saw a tumble of wild hair, a set jaw, a fine profile. His right arm throbbed painfully. She shot him an impatient look. "Would you please buckle up? That crazy man is still shooting, and this is a rental."

Chapter 2

For a wild moment Trevor wondered if he would have been better off taking his chances with the BB gun. The girl didn't seem to be the best driver, zigzagging all over the parking lot. She hunched over the wheel, peering out the front windshield.

"*What are you doing?*"

"I'm trying to confuse him so he doesn't have a steady target." She veered to the right.

"Don't worry about that, just head for the exit. We're faster than him because *we're in a car.*"

"I know we're in a car. How else would I be able to rescue you?"

"*What?* Just . . . go that way, that's the exit." He pointed toward the opening that represented safety and freedom—or more moments of lunacy in the company of this strange girl. He saw his Escalade off to the side and wondered if he'd be better off jumping out of this car and into his.

Before he could act on the thought, they were practically on top of the Escalade. "Watch out!" he yelled.

She jerked the wheel to the left, but not before she'd shaved off the sideview mirror, which went clattering onto the pavement. She winced, but didn't seem too worried.

"That was my car you just maimed."

She shot him a scathing look, her eyes glinting like sea glass in the light from her dashboard. "Are you seriously worried about your car when we have a man with a gun after us?"

He groaned. "It's a BB gun, but never mind. Just get us out of here."

"That is the general idea."

Snapping his mouth shut, he sank lower in his seat. Probably best not to engage in any conversation with this girl, at least until their physical safety was ensured. There was a strong possibility that knocking her out so he could drive would be the safest option of all. But he couldn't bring himself to do that.

After another near-miss with a Camry, she finally reached the exit that led onto Catfish Way, the feeder street from the main road. He swiveled his head to see if the man was still following, and found himself staring into one glowing blue eye.

"*What the fu—*" The eye disappeared as whoever it belonged to dove to the floorboards.

"Don't yell, please," the girl said in a stern voice. "Jerome isn't used to car chases."

"*Jerome?*" Who—or what—was Jerome? Who was this girl?

On the bright side, he could now see through the rear window. The man with the BB gun was standing next to his Escalade, aiming little BB bullets into his tires. Well, better the car than him.

He swung back around and let out a whoosh of relief. "He stopped shooting at us. You can drive normally now. If that's possible."

Now that the danger had passed, the aftermath of adrenaline overload had him shaking. He tightened his fists and made his body rigid, then forced himself to relax. Air in, air out. The same way he'd handled all the traumatic situations he'd faced in the past. It was over. Deal with the next moment. Then the next.

The girl headed down Catfish Way. "I was really afraid he was going to shoot you. I was in the middle of calling 911 when he aimed his gun. I didn't think the police would arrive before he pulled the trigger. I just tossed my phone away and slammed on the accelerator."

"That took a lot of guts, but you shouldn't have done it. He could have shot you. You can't just go barging into dangerous situations like that."

She shook her hair away from her face in an offended gesture, and he caught a light, sweet fragrance, like apple blossom. "Is that your way of saying thank you? Because it needs some work."

"Look, strange girl, I'm grateful, but I don't want to encourage you to ever, *ever* do anything like that again."

She aimed a scowl at him, and now that they were driving down a well-lit street, he finally caught the color of her eyes. Blue. A pure, deep, starry blue, like sapphires. The skin around them looked puffy, as though she'd been crying. "Are you all right?"

"Sure, I've just been going through a lot lately."

Oh, even better. There was an emotionally unstable girl behind the wheel. Again he contemplated diving out the door and taking his chances.

She sniffed. "But I'll get through this, just like everything else. Can you make sure Jerome is okay?"

"I don't even know what Jerome is."

"You're a very odd person, aren't you? Didn't you just look right at him? Jerome is a cat, of course."

Trevor twisted around to squint at the backseat. He ignored the jumble of clothes and textbooks and shoes and glanced at the floorboards, where a massive pile of white fur nearly overflowed a pet carrier. "That thing is a cat? I only saw one eye. He looks more like a white shag foot stool."

"Is he all right?"

The cat stared up at him, unblinking, through the open door of the carrier. "Aside from the obesity? He looks okay to me."

"I'm letting your insulting comment slide because I'm used to it, but he's a large breed, that's all. He's a cream point Ragdoll, and very sweet-natured. He only has one eye, but that's the way I found him, so I don't know why. See what happens if you try to pet him."

Trevor eyed the creature, who looked even more wary than the Isotope pitcher from earlier that night. "You want me to try to pet him?"

She sighed. "You must still be traumatized by the incident. You seem a little slow on the uptake. It's completely understandable. As I mentioned, I too have been going through a lot lately, although no one's gone after me with a gun until—"

"I'm not traumatized," he said through clenched jaws. To prove it, he reached a hand toward the cat, which jammed his huge head against Trevor's hand. "I think he's trying to head-butt me out of the car."

"Good."

"Good?"

"He wants you to pet him, so he must be fine. Jerome is a very loving and affectionate cat, but he's not a fighter. He's a gentle giant. He's been with me through a lot, though this is officially our first car chase."

"Well, tell your gigantic cat that I mean you no harm. Hell, five minutes ago I didn't even know you existed, Miss . . ." He left the end of the sentence open.

"I'm Paige."

"I'm Trevor Stark."

She nodded, showing no particular reaction to that information. Yet one more strange moment of this night. Kilby was a small town, and the Catfish had been in the news a lot lately, thanks to Crush Taylor and various other circumstances. She should at least recognize his name.

Then it clicked. A cute girl—and she was most definitely that—waiting alone in the stadium long after everyone else had left. Of course she didn't have a reaction to his name, because she *already knew* it.

She'd been waiting for him. She was a groupie, one of the Trevor Stark fandom the other guys mocked him about.

"I have to hand it to you, you caught my attention," he told her.

She laughed, a sound as bright as a waterfall. "I suppose barreling straight at you in a car would do that."

"You definitely beat out the woman who sent her kid to the railing. Oldest trick in the book, that one."

"Excuse me?"

He eyed her outfit, which consisted of black leggings and a loose V-necked top that screamed comfort. "You didn't want to dress up for the occasion?"

She turned her face toward him, and he saw she wore not a stitch of makeup—pretty unusual for the girls who went after him. "Are you saying I should have changed before I rescued you from the crazed gunman?"

"I'm talking about the part before. When you were waiting for me to come out of the stadium. What were you planning to do? Whisk me off for a romantic . . . uh . . . yoga class?"

She stopped at a red light and twisted to face him full on. Her sapphire eyes brimmed with amusement. "Just for the sake of argument, let's say that I was. I was parked outside Catfish Stadium just longing for you to appear so I could lure you into my extremely messy rented Chevy Cavalier. What would happen next?"

It was starting to sink in that he'd read the situation wrong. Understandable, since it wasn't uncommon for girls to lie in wait for him at the stadium. But still—he didn't like looking like an ass in front of this girl, with her sparkly blue eyes and wild mane of hair that looked like she'd just rolled out of bed. She'd knocked him off his game and now he had to get the upper hand back.

"Well, Paige, despite my reputation, I'm not that kind of guy. So I'd probably do this next."

In one smooth motion he stripped off his Kilby Catfish T-shirt. Her deep blue eyes went wide. He felt her swift, sweeping inspection like a wave of heat across his skin. Her quick intake of breath was supremely satisfying. Better yet, she was momentarily speechless.

He dug in his duffel bag for a Sharpie and signed his T-shirt with a big flourish. *Trevor Stark,* the T and S the only legible letters.

With a flourish, he presented the shirt to her. "Thank you for being a loyal fan."

Still speechless, she accepted the T-shirt, just as someone honked behind her. The light had changed. The energy between them snapped, like a rubber band breaking. It suddenly felt as if a pressure valve had released. She tossed the shirt into the pile of junk on the backseat, then turned back to the steering wheel.

He let out a long breath. He hadn't realized how caught up in the moment he'd been until she looked away from him. In the short time he'd known Paige, he'd been more off-balance than with any woman since the age of twelve. Then again, getting threatened with a gun might have had something to do with it.

"You know," Paige mused as she steered her car into the intersection. "You'd think that rescuing you from an armed gunman would get me more than a T-shirt. Like, say, your jockstrap. Do you ever give those away?"

"I might consider it, but it was just a BB gun."

"I guess you have a point. The greater the risk, the more ridiculous the reward." Before he could get in a comeback, she continued. "Well, Mr. Shirtless Stranger, what would you like to do now? I don't want to drive back to the stadium until we're sure the police have arrived."

"There's no way in hell I'm letting you drive back there. Besides, the dude shot out the tires on my Escalade. I'll have to get it towed." He thought for a moment. "Can you drop me at the Days Inn on Alamo Drive?"

"Sure. But don't you want to give a statement to the police? I can take you to the station."

"I'll call it in." Trevor never willingly went near the police. Back in Detroit, some of them had been on the payroll of the syndicate that had destroyed his family. Even though Kilby was a small town with a completely different atmosphere, his mistrust ran deep. "I'd rather get back to the hotel. Afternoon doubleheader tomorrow."

She steered toward the street that would take them to Alamo Drive, which told him that she knew Kilby well enough to find her way around. Was she from here? But she'd said her car was a rental, and it definitely had the lived-in feel of a long road trip.

"Are you an out-of-town player?" she asked him.

"Nope. I'm a Catfish. Go Kilby." She reacted to that information with an almost invisible flinch. Interesting. "I live at the Days Inn. I rent by the week and own a bunch of take-out menus. Home sweet home."

"Wouldn't it be cheaper to rent an apartment?"

"That's a big commitment." Not only that, but he'd be easier to find. Motel rooms worked just fine for him.

"Oh, please. Let me guess, you're one of *those*." She tossed her tangle of hair away from her face. "The 'don't fence me in with your pesky apartment leases or marriage contracts' types."

"Maybe. And you're the 'give me two minutes and I can slap a label on you' type."

Surprised, she looked over at him, and he caught a glimmer of respect along with the laughter. "Touché."

As she turned the car onto Alamo, the neon Days Inn sign loomed ahead, illuminating the misty night with its yellow glow. The sight brought an odd sense of reluctance—surprise, surprise, he didn't want this encounter to end. Paige didn't seem one bit intimidated by him, or awed, or flustered. The change of pace was . . . well, like he'd said, she'd caught his attention.

He looked at her sideways, wanting more details impressed into his brain. Now that he got a good look at her, he saw that she was on the quirky side of beautiful, with lean lines and a wide mouth. Her hair tumbled around her shoulders and halfway down her back, the curling strands picking up glints of light, copper and red and gold. She wore a pendant on a leather thong around her neck, and woven bracelets marched up her wrist. Her yoga-ish outfit might be casual, but she had a sexy body under those leggings, he could practically guarantee. Whoever Paige was, she was suddenly front and center on his radar screen. It made no sense, considering the craziness of the past ten minutes, but he wanted . . . well, more. More conversation, more of that sweet apple fragrance, more of those looks she shot him.

He wanted to hear her laugh some more. It made him feel halfway human.

She pulled into the driveway of the Days Inn and stopped under the overhang at the entrance. "Nice place you've got here," she said, all cheeky.

"Thanks. It's even nicer inside. Why don't you come in and tell me all about Jerome, or why you were at the stadium, or where you learned to drive? I have a fully stocked kitchenette. My specialty is midnight snacks." He unleashed his most potent weapon—his smile, which had slayed every woman he'd encountered since the age of twelve.

Not Paige. She tilted her head, giving him a long, serious survey. "Anonymous sex with a stranger is not the right way to process a trauma."

The word "sex" on those full, upturned lips amped up the strong attraction he already felt to her. "What makes you think I was talking about sex?"

Her gaze immediately flashed to his bare chest, and she pulled her bottom lip between her teeth.

"I get it," he said. "*You* were thinking about sex."

When her cheeks went pink, he bit back a satisfied smile. Now that the word "sex" had been spoken aloud, it sounded like a great idea to him. "Besides, there's nothing like a near-death experience to make you want to live life to the fullest. Shouldn't that include sex? Or at least a midnight snack?"

He offered another smile, aiming for charming this time. She drummed her thumbs on the steering wheel, looking at him from under her lashes, the garish Days Inn glow sliding across her skin. Had he tempted her? Finally she shook her head. "I'm supposed to be somewhere right now. I got sidetracked rescuing you, but I really need to go."

"Wherever you're going, I bet there isn't a famous baseball player ready to satisfy your every desire."

Her head jerked back and her eyes went wide with an expression of horror. "You . . . no . . . um . . ." Clapping her hand over her mouth, she gave a peal of laughter that raked at his pride like a burning torch.

"Say no more." An unfamiliar emotion coursed through him—the humiliation of rejection. Girls didn't turn him down. Most often, they came after him in the first place. He opened the car door and swung himself onto the pavement. "Do me a favor, Paige. Next time you see a man with a gun, drive the other way."

"Wait, I didn't mean to laugh. It's just that—"

He held up a hand to stop her right there. "Thanks for the ride, and the rescue. Appreciated."

She opened her mouth as if she had something important to say, then changed her mind and pressed her lips together. Perfect, curving lips. And damn if he didn't want to kiss her, even if she had just laughed at him. Light spilling from the hotel entrance fell across her face, turning her skin luminous.

He wanted her.

Not going to happen.

He turned away and stepped into the shadow cast by the overhang. Idiot that he was, he'd given her his shirt. This close, she might see the damning marks on his back. He needed to put some distance between them, so he walked quickly toward the hotel's front doors. Beyond the glass he saw the familiar check-in counter, the coffee setup, the dusty ficus tree in a planter.

"Thank you for the T-shirt," she called after him.

Without turning around, he flashed a peace sign.

"Stay out of trouble," she added wryly, as if she knew trouble was part of Trevor's DNA. Smart girl.

Oh. My. God. That was one *extremely* potent male. Paige put a hand to her heart, feeling it gallop like a runaway horse. The amount of adrenaline coursing through her system right now would fuel an entire squad of sprinters.

On autopilot, she drove away from the hotel, barely

noticing the familiar terrain of Kilby—tidy little stucco homes, the restored brickwork of the downtown area, strip malls, and, as she reached the outskirts of town, the ranch lands. Her destination.

"Jerome, I had no idea a baseball player could be like *that*."

Not even her ex-husband, a professional basketball player, had prepared her for the sight of Trevor Stark without a shirt.

"Did you hear what he said about a famous ballplayer waiting to fulfill my every desire? I swear, Jerome, I almost lost it. He probably thought I was nuts. Do you think he did? I guess if he saw me talking to you he'd really think I was nuts. No offense, kitty-cat."

Her cat gave a soft meow. Now that the interloper was gone, Jerome lurched out of his carrier onto the backseat, then climbed into the passenger seat and curled up in his usual spot. They'd been driving this way for three days, ever since her Alitalia flight from Rome had landed at John F. Kennedy Airport. She hadn't even stopped for a visit with her two college roommates who lived in New York. She'd gone right to the car rental counter and booked this Cavalier. A more sensible idea would have been to fly to Houston, but she needed the time to acclimate to the United States. To her American self. Her old self, before she'd crashed and burned.

Out on Highway 60, she peered through the darkness in search of the sign for her father's ranch. Her stomach tightened when she spotted it. She'd been hoping to surprise him at the stadium because he was always in a better mood there. Or at least that had been true three years ago, when she'd last seen him.

But she'd waited too long in the parking lot, trying to screw up her courage, and then a man with a BB gun and a ballplayer with incredible green eyes had ruined that plan.

Spotting the sign for Bullpen Ranch, she turned off the highway onto the private road that led to the ranch. The car rattled over a cattle grate. In five minutes she'd be at her father's door.

For a desperate moment, she contemplated turning the car around and taking Trevor Stark up on his invitation. He was beautiful, like an avenging angel, with those slashing cheekbones and sensual mouth, his eyes the clear light green of the Caribbean on a crystal calm day. But he wasn't calm, not underneath. She sensed turmoil behind his controlled exterior. Maybe that's what made him so magnetic and compelling.

The sight of his muscled back, wide at the shoulders, lean at the waist, powerful everywhere in between, was still branded on her eyeballs. A massive tattoo filled his entire back and shoulders, although she hadn't been able to make out any details before he disappeared into the lobby. His physique had stunned the breath out of her, the perfection of each muscle and bone gilded by the hotel lights.

Her father's big circular driveway was packed with the usual array of vehicles. Inside the ranch house, a sprawling glass and steel structure, lights glowed. For better or worse, he was home. "Moment of truth, Jerome," she told her cat.

She got out of the car and took a deep breath of Texas air, cooler here than in Kilby proper, flavored with mesquite and alfalfa and a hint of cow manure.

Delaying the inevitable, she picked Jerome up from the passenger seat. As usual, he went floppy as the rag doll his breed was named after. He loved to be carried like a baby. "You keep quiet and let me do the talking."

She put him into his carrier, where he went right back to sleep.

Heart beating like a bongo, she hurried up the steps. She put down Jerome's carrier and knocked on the oversize wood-planked door. Footsteps sounded inside. *Please be happy to see me. Please don't be a jerk.*

The door opened and Crush Taylor stood before her, his tall, rangy frame as fit as ever, squinting at her with bright hazel eyes. He blinked a few times, as if he didn't quite believe what he was seeing. "Paige?"

She burst into tears.

Chapter 3

AFTER A LONG moment during which Paige fought to get a grip on her sobs, Crush finally opened his arms and pulled her in for a hug. "Aw, kiddo. Come on. You know there's no crying in baseball."

"S . . . sorry." Crush hated tears. All his ex-wives and their children knew that. Paige knew it more than anyone, because she'd always been the sap in the family. "It's been a long trip." Through her hiccuping sobs, she breathed in the familiar smell of her father, a mixture of tobacco and grass and bay rum.

"From Italy?"

She nodded against his chest.

"Hudson?"

"We're getting divorced. I mean, we are divorced." She pulled back and wiped the tears off her cheeks. "And if you say 'I told you so,' I'll get right back in the car."

He made a sound that could have been a chuckle or a protest. With his hands on her shoulders, he scrutinized her face. "When did this happen?"

"A month ago."

"You never said anything."

"We haven't exactly been communicating." A few strained emails over the past three years barely counted.

"Jenna didn't mention it either."

"She doesn't know." Telling her mother she was divorced at the age of twenty-four . . . Yeah, she was not looking forward to that conversation.

"Well, you'd better come in, honey. I bet you're hungry. Divorce can give you a real appetite. I ate like a farmer after all three of mine."

Crush's caustic sense of humor came in handy sometimes. Her entire body relaxed, all the anxiety about her homecoming released in a long exhale. She'd done the right thing, coming here. Despite their epic battles over Hudson, Crush would never turn her away. And he wouldn't interrogate her the way her mother would. She wasn't ready to answer her mother's inevitable million and five questions.

"So . . . uh . . . you planning to stay awhile?" Crush asked when she was through the door, car carrier in hand.

"For now, if that's okay."

She saw concern simmering behind his curious gaze, but he merely nodded and walked with her up the stairs to the bedrooms. In the upstairs hallway, she stopped short. Both walls were lined with Kilby Catfish posters, each featuring a different player, along with the bold blue Catfish logo with its curving, jumping fish.

The poster next to her old bedroom featured none other than Trevor Stark. Trevor, in full Technicolor, wearing a Catfish uniform that hugged the muscles of his thighs and arms as he held a bat on his shoulder. Those killer crystal eyes stared into the distance with a look of pure distilled intimidation. You could put that look in a bottle and win a war with it. He looked epic, legendary, fearsome.

And yet, in the car with him, she hadn't felt intimidated. Not for a second.

"Trevor Stark," Crush said, eyeing the poster with an expression of extreme animosity. "Sorry, I'll get the housekeeper to move the posters."

"Don't bother, I'll consider it homework. I should get to know your players, right?"

"Wrong. Especially that one." He gestured at the poster of Trevor. "Stay very, very far away from that one."

She bit the inside of her cheek. Should she mention that it was already too late for that? No, she had more important information to unload first.

Inside her bedroom, she put Jerome's cat carrier on the floor and opened the door. He prowled out and sniffed his new surroundings.

"Cardio for this one." Crush squatted down next to the enormous ball of white fur. "At least an hour a day. Maybe two."

She laughed, bending down to pet Jerome, who immediately began to purr with a sort of voracious joy. "Leave Jerome alone. I'll be down in a second, Dad. Let me just get him situated."

"Does he need his own room? His own kitchen?"

Affectionately, she shook her head at Crush. She'd missed his sarcasm.

Crush left to put together some snacks, while she got Jerome set up with his litter box and some food and water. He only bumped into the wall a couple of times while exploring the room. His missing eye made him more awkward than most cats—maybe that's why she'd related to him the second she'd spotted him in a side alley in Rome. She curled up on the bed, still covered with the same lily-patterned coverlet from her teen years, and petted him for a while, soaking in the comfort of home.

Home. Until a month ago, home had been the little

apartment in Rome. What was Hudson doing right now? It was nearly morning in his time zone, so he was probably snuggled in bed. Maybe on the road, maybe with Nessa.

The familiar headache gathered, the aftermath of all the arguing and tears and *upheaval* making her shake on her old bed. She had no one but herself to blame. She should have stayed in college instead of trailing across Italy with Hudson Notswego. Hudson needed someone to decompress with after a game. He needed a back-rubber, a hand-holder, a dinner-preparer and complaint-listener. He needed someone to wear cute clothes with the other players' wives, to look emotional when the camera turned her way, to cheer him on through all the ups and downs. He needed someone to root for him while he labored in the Italian League, hoping to catch the attention of the NBA. He needed *her*.

Until he'd met Nessa.

Ugh, she didn't want to think about Hudson. She'd spent enough tears on him. She was back in Kilby for one reason only. Make a fresh start. Get her own life back, before it got hijacked by Hudson Notswego's basketball career.

Starting now.

She jumped to her feet, startling Jerome, and hurried down the wide, curving stairs that led to the expansive living room.

Paige was on the tall side, having inherited her father's rangy pitcher's build, although none of his hand-eye coordination. But even she felt dwarfed by the cavernous open space that formed the main living area of the ranch house. All the furniture was immense, most of it covered in some kind of animal hide. The center of the room featured a stone hearth so vast a toddler could stand inside it.

She found Crush pouring himself a root beer at the polished teak bar. A plate of cheese and sliced bread awaited her. "You're drinking root beer?"

He gestured with the tumbler, inciting a clink of ice against glass. "It's my new crutch since I quit drinking."

"I fully support that habit. It's a lot better than the last one." He rarely drank around her, but she knew that partying had been one of the things that ended all three of his marriages.

"Hell on the waistline. I've been spending a couple hours in the gym every day just to keep up with the young sprouts."

The young sprouts . . . did that include the much too fascinating Trevor Stark? She realized that the ball-player hadn't left her mind much since she'd first laid eyes on him striding arrogantly across the parking lot. Just the mention of his name brought back the feel of his presence in her nerve endings, like the aftermath of adrenaline.

On the other hand, there was the actual adrenaline of the attack and the car chase. That's probably what this was, she told herself, not interest in another pro athlete. Because she was never, *ever* doing that again.

She folded a slice of cheese around a chunk of bread and chewed for a moment. But she hadn't been very hungry since things fell apart with Hudson, so after a moment she put it down.

Crush cleared his throat. "So, Paige, you might as well let me have it. Was it a clean break?"

"A clean break? What exactly does that mean?" She busied herself scanning the options in the small fridge under the bar. Basically root beer or root beer. She went with root beer, and pulled out a tray of ice cubes while she was at it.

"Mutual, amicable, no collateral damage. Don't

forget you're talking to an expert on breakups here. Scale of one to ten, how finished is it?"

"It's completely over, but I don't know how your scale works. Would that be a ten or a one?"

"Nine is divorce. Ten is divorce with no chance of sex with the ex."

In the midst of cracking the tray of ice cubes, she pressed too hard and sent ice cubes bursting out of the tray. Crush, his reaction time still lightning quick, managed to catch one of them. She lunged after the others before they skidded off the bar. "Can you please try to remember that you're my father?"

"Hard to forget, with you following in my footsteps so soon."

She bristled as she plopped the runaway ice cubes into her tumbler. She'd entered into her marriage with complete determination *not* to get divorced. But maybe divorce was a genetic flaw, one she'd inherited from both parents. "It wasn't my intention, believe me. I've been lecturing myself the entire trip from Rome."

"Aw honey." He leaned forward and patted her knee. "Skip the lectures. I'm not sorry to see Hudson gone."

Hot and immediate, her usual resentment flooded to the surface. "That's because you had a problem with his—" Color, she was about to say, since Hudson was black. But Crush smoothly finished the sentence for her.

"Sport. How the hell did you think it would work out with a basketball player? Even football would be a stretch, but basketball?"

"If you're trying to make me laugh, don't bother. There is nothing to laugh about here."

"Sorry." He slouched back onto his bar stool and sipped from his root beer. "What happened? Did he cheat? There's a lot of temptation on the road."

"You could say that. As a matter of fact, he's already engaged." The humiliating words felt like dirt in her mouth. "To Nessa Brindisi."

"The cooking show chick? *Cooking is Easy with Nessa Brindisi?* The one with the big baz—" He sketched a large bosom in the air in front of his chest.

"Yes! God." She dug her hands into her hair. "You're. My. *Father.* Can you *please*?"

"Sorry. Paige, I'm sorry, I'm sorry. Bad habit, you know me."

Still simmering, she took a long swallow of her root beer. Sweet, but missing something. Would it be tacky to look for something stronger? *He'd* quit drinking, she hadn't. "Hudson was a guest on her show. You know that steak rub he's so proud of? With the rosemary and thyme and all? She invited him on TV to share that recipe."

"I suppose he rubbed more than her steak."

She surged to her feet. "That's it. I'm going to bed. It's been a long trip and I'm exhausted." She'd been dead wrong, after all. Coming to Kilby was a terrible idea. Crush never took anything seriously.

"What? What did I say? No, honey, sit down. I want to hear the whole story. Come on." Crush slid off his bar stool and snagged her arm as she charged past. She felt tears gathering at the corners of her eyes. God, hadn't she cried them all out already? "Want the truth?"

Paige nodded, blotting the tear with her thumb.

"I'm cracking jokes so I don't try to murder the asshole. He was never right for you. Ever." Crush's hazel eyes drilled into her, stealing her words. "Selfish, self-absorbed, willing to take whatever you'd give and offer nothing in return, except the privilege of being married to a star athlete. You deserve better."

Wow. That was the most passionate, sincere thing she'd ever heard her father say to her. It took her a moment to recover from the shock. Blotting more tears, she managed a smile. "Better? You mean a point guard instead of a small forward?"

Slow delight spread across Crush's face. "Aw honey. You cracked a joke." He swept her into a big hug, the sweet scent of root beer and his usual bay rum cologne flooding her with comfort. Right at that moment she could have fallen asleep, right there in her father's arms, and rested for a month.

The phone rang. Of course it did. The business of being Crush Taylor never ended. She stepped away so he could answer.

"Yeah." His face darkened. "Are you fucking kidding me? How bad?"

After a long moment of listening, his expression hardening as the caller spoke, he ended with, "I'll talk to him tomorrow."

"What's going on?"

"Trevor fucking Stark. Biggest pain in the ass player I've ever had on the team. Mother-effing Christ, it's just one thing after another with that guy."

Oh my God. She'd bet anything the call was about the attack in the parking lot. But that wasn't his fault, was it? She opened her mouth to explain that some stranger with a BB gun had gone after him and she'd impulsively driven her rental into the midst of it, risking her own safety, then spent the next fifteen minutes verbally sparring with Big Bad Trevor Stark . . . yeah. No. Best to keep all that to herself.

"Anything you want to share, Dad?"

"Not right now. Go to bed, honey, we'll catch up more in the morning. Got some calls to make." He squeezed her arm, but the familiar absent look in his eyes told her he was mentally already far away. Dealing with Trevor Stark.

Funny, her mind was also filled with Trevor Stark at the moment. For the first time, she wondered what exactly Trevor had done to earn the ire of that BB-gun wielder. Maybe he'd deserved those BBs. Given the intensity behind his flirty manner, she wouldn't be surprised.

The next morning, Paige woke to the smell of coffee and bacon. She took a few deep breaths, inhaling the scent. The food in Italy was amazing, but the coffee didn't smell the same and they didn't eat bacon for breakfast. She stretched, head to toes, nearly knocking Jerome off the bed. Good thing he weighed about as much as a bag of cement.

A big part of her wanted to sleep for another day or so. It had been so hard to drag herself out of bed the past few months. But she was here to make a new start. That was the whole point. And it had to begin with getting out of bed.

Once upright, she pulled on a pair of shorts and an *Olimpia Milano* T-shirt—the biggest rivals of Hudson's team, so there. On her way down the hall, she paused at the poster of Trevor Stark, still aiming that crystal gaze into the distance, still posing with those tremendous muscles. With a flash of searing heat that went straight to the pit of her belly, she remembered the moment when he'd stripped off his T-shirt and handed it to her. His manner hadn't been fearsome then. It had been teasing, playful, sensual, but still with that dark edge underneath. What would a man like Trevor Stark be like in bed? Powerful, relentless, teasing, focused . . . she shivered.

She had no business thinking about that.

In the kitchen, Crush, still sweaty from his morning workout, plopped a mug of coffee and a plate of bacon and eggs before her, then slid a fork and knife across the breakfast bar.

He propped his elbows on the granite surface. "So, Paige, what's your plan? Something tells me you don't have one yet. Very understandable, and it works out well for me. I have a proposal for you."

She groaned, tempted to turn around and go snuggle with Jerome again. "Can I drink my coffee first?"

"Nope. I called Jenna. She said it's best to approach you first thing in the morning while you're still vulnerable, like a sleepy gazelle in the savannah."

"You called *Mom*? I haven't even talked to her about any of this yet." Head beginning to pound, she slid onto a stool and poured about half a carton of cream into her coffee. Her mother, Jenna Jarvey, had been the first of Crush's three wives. He'd met her when she was interning for a newspaper. She was now a newscaster in Philadelphia. Paige often wished those journalism skills could stay at the news station. Being grilled by her mother was nothing to look forward to.

On the other hand, Crush's parenting style was one step away from "do it yourself, kid." He'd tell her inappropriate road trip stories, take her to the stadium, let her run around and play with the vendors and the other players' kids. His intense focus on baseball didn't leave much room for a daughter. Sometimes she'd hated the game because it consumed so much of his attention.

She wished baseball would consume his attention right now, as a matter of fact. No such luck.

Crush shrugged. "I did you a favor. Now you don't have to call her, though she invited you to see her as soon as you're ready. You don't have to worry, Jenna's glad you dumped him too."

"I didn't dump him." If she had, maybe she wouldn't feel like such a failure.

He waved that off with a forkful of scrambled egg. "You should have. You would have, if you weren't such a loyal, caring, and all-round spectacular human being."

She nearly choked on her mouthful of French roast. Crush didn't normally shower on the compliments unless he wanted something. And when he wanted something, he used every weapon in the arsenal. Carefully, she placed her mug on the table, preparing for battle. "About this plan of yours . . ."

"I'm glad you asked. Because if you don't have a plan of your own—"

"I do. I want to finish my college degree. I had two years left when Hudson signed with Virtus Roma. I can get my credits transferred to wherever I decide to apply."

Crush opened his mouth, but she forestalled him. "In the meantime, I was thinking of doing some volunteer work here in Kilby."

Again Crush tried to interrupt, but she could have taught a course on "How to Handle Crush Taylor."

"There's something else too. I went to a counselor to help me deal with the divorce. Did you ever wonder why I chose to marry a pro athlete, when my own father is one? Don't you think that just screams 'daddy issues'? I was figuring we could work on that while I'm here. Together, like family therapy. What do you think?"

At his horrified expression, she wanted to high-five someone. Three marriages and three divorces had made Crush dread couples counseling. His hatred of therapy was no secret. Next, he'd mumble something and check his phone and find some important e-mail to answer. After that he'd leave her alone and let her grieve in peace.

But this time her father surprised her. "Fine," he said, gazing at her coolly over the rim of his mug.

Her jaw dropped. "Fine? You heard me, right? The part about working through my daddy issues?"

"I get it. I'm a famous, eccentric, impossible, part-time alcoholic, full-time misanthropic prick. Why wouldn't you have issues with me?"

"Bonus points for self-awareness," she murmured into her coffee.

"I heard that." He took the cast-iron skillet to the sink, adding it to the pile of other dishes awaiting the housekeeper. His domestic side only went so far. "Paige, I think my plan is going to suit you fine."

"Okay then, lay it on me."

He leaned his rear against the enamel sink and folded his arms. "As you know, you're my oldest progeny and the only one who can stand me."

She pulled a dubious "sometimes, maybe, I suppose" face that he ignored.

"The Catfish isn't just my team. It's your legacy."

"My 'legacy'?" Shouldn't a legacy be something good, like an art collection or a kingdom? A Triple A baseball team with a wild reputation didn't qualify, did it?

"I want you to work with me at the stadium, learn the ropes. You'll be a sort of intern, going from one department to the next, watching, learning, helping out. No pay, but you will have full room and board here at Bullpen Ranch. And you'll get lots and lots of daddy time." He offered a wolfish grin, the sort that women fell for all the time.

She knew better. "I hate baseball."

"No, you don't. You sucked at it, but you didn't hate it."

"I broke my nose twice in Little League."

"Your fielding needed a lot of work, that's true."

Paige stuffed a strip of bacon into her mouth to stop herself from arguing. After her fourth time tripping over first base, her mother had laid down the law about her Little League career.

"Anyway, it doesn't matter. You won't have to play. That's what the players are for. It will be strictly front office stuff, behind the scenes. You'll be sharing my world with me. The Wild and Wacky World of Crush Taylor."

"I don't know, Crush, baseball brings out very conflicting feelings in me—"

He held up a finger. "Daddy issue number one. Daddy was always busy with baseball. He was on the road, up late at night, entirely immersed in the life of a major league pitcher. Therefore, his child grew to hate baseball. That the gist?"

"I suppose."

"Now you can immerse yourself right along with me. Daddy issue, solved." He brushed his palms together, then spread them apart.

"It's really not that simple." But her voice trailed away, because in fact the idea sounded like just what she needed. She could spend her summer at the ballpark the same way she had as a kid, pestering the cotton candy vendors and running errands for the ballplayers.

The ballplayers.

The image of Trevor Stark, all intensity and power and clear crystal eyes, entered her mind. She shivered again.

As if he'd witnessed her inner movie screen, Crush held up a hand. "One condition. No fraternizing with the players. I don't trust a single one of those guys. Maybe Mike Solo, but he's gone. Maybe Jim Leiberman, because he's harmless. The rest, no. Promise me."

"Dad, do you think I'm nuts? I got divorced *last month.* You don't need to warn me away from rowdy ballplayers."

"So you'll do it?"

"Yes." She gave a slow nod and bit off more bacon. "Maybe it will help heal the abandonment issues that make it difficult to feel secure in my relationships."

He groaned and dragged a hand through his hair. "You're going to torture me with this crap, aren't you?"

"You know it." She grinned around her mouthful of bacon. Even though she was teasing, maybe it would be good to spend some time with Crush. Their falling-out had been horrible. She'd always been the "good girl," anxious to please whichever parent she was with. When it came to grades, she'd done fine. Sports, not so much. Career obsession, even less. When she'd dropped out of college to marry Hudson, both her parents had been furious.

Working with her father could be interesting . . . or it could be a disaster. On the plus side, it would allow them to reestablish their relationship, as her counselor had suggested. On the minus side, Crush was . . . well, he could steamroll right over her if she let him. She'd have to start off on the right foot.

"I have a condition too," she told him.

He raised a wary eyebrow.

"I don't want to be just an intern. I'm twenty-four, I've been married, I've lived in a foreign country, I have half a college degree. I'm not a kid anymore. I'm familiar with athletes and their personalities. I want to contribute. I want to take on real, meaningful tasks, not just 'pat Paige on the head' jobs."

Crush offered his hand. "Fair enough."

They shook on it. Funny—Crush totally missed the fact that she'd made no promises regarding "fraternizing" with the players.

Oh well.

Chapter 4

"**TREVOR STARK! CRUSH** wants you in his office."
The clubhouse attendant broke the news with an evil
grin on his face. "Sounds pretty bad. Three F-bombs
and a C-word."

Oh, hell. Trevor shoved his gym bag into the open
wooden cubby of his locker. He should never have
called Duke to report the BB gun incident. His protective instincts had kicked in and he'd finally decided to
call it in for the sake of his teammates. While he could
handle an armed asshole, most of these guys hadn't
grown up the way he had. "Right this second?"

"Five minutes ago."

The other Catfish, at varying points in their dressing
process, perked up to listen.

"Thought you and Crush signed a mutual avoidance
pact," called Sonny Barnes from his locker.

Dwight chimed in as he wrapped an ace bandage
around his wrist. "Heard it was signed with the blood
of a virgin." Trevor glared at him. The guy was supposed to be his friend.

"Isn't being around Trevor automatically devirginat-
ing?" Ramirez wondered out loud as he pulled on his
sliders.

"That's not a word," Trevor growled. He'd already changed into his jersey. He always put it on first to avoid showing his back any longer than absolutely necessary. But his legs were still bare, and he hadn't put on his cleats yet.

"Riiiiight," said Dwight, who had clearly gone over to the dark side. "I think they call it 'Starkinating' now. Saw it in the Urban Dictionary."

Shaking his head, Trevor decided to book it to Crush's office right away and get it over with. Pants or no pants. That would teach the domineering owner to call him in so close to game time. He strode past the gape-mouthed attendant, ignoring the hoots from the other players.

Crush's office was located on the upper floor along with the rest of the management offices, except for Duke's, which was the same level as the clubhouse. The management wing was filled with private, glass-door offices, cubicles and computer desks, and a blur of faces that all swiveled in his direction.

Crush's door was open, so Trevor stalked right in. He'd never seen Crush actually sit at his desk like a normal person. The man usually propped his boots on it, leaned one hip against it, or ignored it completely. Today he leaned one shoulder against the plate-glass window that overlooked the field.

Crush Taylor inspired respect in every ballplayer with a sense of history. That included Trevor, who knew every detail of his record. The man was a legend. A living icon. And now Crush was staring at him as if he were an earthworm crawling across the infield grass.

"I came as soon as I got your message, sir," Trevor said in his most mockingly subservient voice, the one he'd perfected in juvie after one too many infractions.

He could have sworn that he saw one corner of Crush's mouth lift in a smile. "No pants, I see."

As always, they launched into a sparring match that rivaled Ping-Pong for speed.

"It sounded urgent."

"So are pants."

"I'm decent."

"That's not what they say."

"Listening to gossip?"

"Listening to my manager. Apparently someone went after you with a BB gun."

"I handled it."

"According to the security tape, someone in a white car handled it."

That made Trevor pause. If the mysterious Paige was on tape, maybe he could locate her. By license plate or something.

"This isn't a problem."

"Videotape says your arm got nicked. Your five million dollar arm."

"Just a bruise."

"Bend your elbow."

Trevor tried, but truth was, he had some swelling and it wouldn't close all the way.

Crush cursed freely. "One of these days someone is going to hit a vital organ."

"I wear a cup."

Someone snorted from the corner of the room to his right. He wanted to see who but was too locked into his glare-down with Crush to turn away.

"Paige, stay out of this," said Crush, not looking away either. "Observation only today. I didn't think you'd be observing someone without pants, of course."

Slowly, the words penetrated. Paige. Trevor swiveled to the right.

Paige.

She sat with her long, long legs crossed, her wild hair in a ponytail, her eyes bright with laughter. True blue, deep and sweet, like the petals of a delphinium. She wore tomato red shorts, a T-shirt with some Italian words on it, flip-flops, and electric blue polish on her toenails. A composition notebook was propped on her lap, as if she was taking notes on this conversation. She wore a charm bracelet around one ankle; crescent moons alternating with stars.

Not that he noticed every detail or anything.

"That's my daughter, Paige."

Ho-ly. Shit. She was Crush's daughter? He had a daughter? No one had ever mentioned a daughter. Especially one so . . . so . . . He tried to drag his gaze away from her but couldn't.

Crush kept talking. "She's going to be working around here for a while. Remember her face so you can make sure to leave her alone."

Eye roll from Paige. From his brief experience with her, Trevor figured the chances of Crush being able to control her were pretty much zero. Her gaze traveled down his body, stalling somewhere around his bare thighs.

Right. No pants.

Well, now she'd seen just about the whole package—no shirt last night, no pants today.

"It's costing me good money to fix the fence and install extra security cameras around the parking lot," Crush continued. "For some reason, none of that was necessary before you came to Kilby."

"Safety first. A wise choice."

Crush rubbed the skin of his forehead as if smoothing out five decades' worth of wrinkles. "I ought to report this to the Friars."

As always, mention of the Friars gave Trevor a rush of anxiety. He knew a call-up was inevitable, but for his sister's sake he wanted it to take as long as possible. "That ought to be a fun conversation."

Crush ground his teeth. "Do you have anything to say that isn't a waste of my time?"

Trevor maintained his stony facade. He respected Crush, unlike most authority figures. But there was no way Crush would believe he hadn't done anything to merit being chased with a BB gun. "Sorry."

"Don't go overboard." Crush stopped him with an upraised hand. "I don't need you to grovel."

Grovel? Trevor felt a muscle jump in his jaw as he fought to keep it clamped shut.

Crush turned to Paige. "Yesterday I stood in front of the entire sports media and announced that I intend to win the Triple A national championship."

She plucked a pen from behind her ear and made a note in her little book. "There's a championship in Triple A?"

"Yes, but there's a reason you've never heard of it. No one cares. This year, I do."

He turned back to Trevor. "If there's one thing I hate, it's looking like an ass. If there's another thing I hate, it's losing." He ticked the items off on the fingers of one hand. "And if there's yet another thing I hate, it's watching a talent like you fuck up his life."

"I'm not—"

Crush stopped him with another gesture. "Something else I hate. Getting interrupted. Know what else I hate?"

Paige spoke up. "Is this open for anyone, because I've been compiling notes all my life."

Trevor glanced over and their eyes met, the sparkling sapphire of hers filled with sexy mischief. Once again the fact slammed him in the face. Daughter. She was *Crush's daughter*. And he'd come on to her outside his hotel about ten minutes after they met.

Crush snapped his fingers to regain their attention. Just the sort of thing Trevor hated. "Now, I didn't report this fiasco to the Friars. So I figure you owe me. And I know exactly how you can pay me back."

"Yes, sir."

"Yes, sir, what?"

"Yes, sir, I'll help you. Win the championship. That's what you want, right?"

Crush gave a brisk nod. "It's a win-win, really. You play well and help the team, the Friars *will* be calling."

That wouldn't be a win for him, but no need to reveal that. In the meantime, he'd be here in Kilby. He'd get another season of anonymity. Nina would be that much safer. *That* was a win-win.

He'd also get to torment Crush for another season. Win-win-*win*.

"It's what I would do anyway." He called on every ounce of shit-eating media experience he'd acquired. "I always give my best for my team. Every game. Every play. Every at-bat. Every pitch." He could just imagine the blow-job gesture Sonny Barnes would be making right now.

Crush narrowed his eyes. "If you're trying to impress my daughter, forget about it."

"I never *try* to impress. It just happens."

Paige rose to her feet, clearing her throat. She waved at the plate-glass window and the field beyond. "Um . . . not to interrupt, but it looks like the players are coming onto the field for the National Anthem."

"Uh-oh, and me without my pants," Trevor deadpanned.

He caught Paige's suppressed giggle . . . and so did Crush. He pointed a finger at his daughter, then at Trevor.

"Paige, you and I are going to the owner's box. Stark, take the next two games off. I want you to rest your elbow from that bruise. The championship is important to me, but the Friars own you. Your future comes first."

Trevor's heart plummeted. He needed that time on the field, time when he could block everything out and channel all his rage onto little cowhide-covered spheres of cork. "Duke has me in the lineup."

"Not anymore."

Trevor spun on his heel and stalked out of the office. *Bullshit.* There was absolutely no need to take him out of the game. Once again, every eyeball turned his way as he went marching past. Christ, it's not like they could see anything—his jersey covered everything. Deploying his most intimidating, stony-faced look, he ignored the stares and headed for the clubhouse. He *hated* being out of the lineup. Damn Crush Taylor for being the most interfering team owner he'd ever seen. What was he supposed to do with himself now?

Footfalls raced after him. *Paige.* It had to be. Blood boiling, he stopped at the head of the stairs and intercepted her, grabbing her wrist and pulling her down the stairs after him.

"What are you doing?"

"Rescuing you," he growled.

"From what? I'm perfectly fine."

"I haven't decided yet."

"What . . . that makes no . . . sense . . ." She continued to squawk as he hauled her down the stairs into the clubhouse. He knew it would be completely empty during the National Anthem. Even the clubhouse attendant would be out on the field.

Once inside the smelly, towel-strewn locker room, he spun her against the wall and braced his hands on either side of her head. "This," he ground out, "is a bad idea."

She stared at him with a bewildered expression. He seized the opportunity to gaze his fill of her in the daylight, up close. Close enough to notice the outer rim of purple surrounding the sparkling blue of her eyes and the light spray of freckles across her cheekbones. A long strand of honey-brown hair clung to her neck. Fresh and alive, her apple fragrance lured him closer; he sensed the racing of her heart.

He eased off, in case it was fear causing her heart to beat so fast. "Why didn't you tell me who you were?"

A crease appeared between her eyebrows. He clenched his hands to keep from smoothing it away. "I told you my name."

"*Part* of your name."

"We didn't exactly meet at a formal tea party," she said. "I don't remember how I introduced myself."

"I do. Paige, you said."

"Well, it's Paige Mattingly Austin Taylor, since you seem to require the whole thing."

"The only part I'm worried about is the 'Taylor.' Your father despises me."

She held his gaze. "He doesn't like seeing talented players waste their gifts."

As if she'd suddenly caught fire, he released her. He wasn't wasting his gift, he was using it to protect his sister the best way he could. He paced away from her, rubbing his hand across the back of his neck.

"So you were in the parking lot waiting for Crush?"

"Yes. But I must have missed him, and then I saw you. And that man."

"Does he know that was you on the security tape?"

Her eyes widened in alarm. "No. And please don't tell him. He'd kill me. Or you. Maybe both."

"I won't tell him as long as you promise not to put yourself in danger like that again."

She pushed away from the wall and sauntered toward him. "Um, I'm alone in an empty clubhouse with Big Bad Trevor Stark." On that word, she tilted her head back and swept past him. "Apparently danger is my middle name."

He followed her as she advanced farther into the clubhouse, peering curiously into the lockers. "I've never been in here before. It was always off-limits."

"Is that why you turned me down? No sleeping with the players?"

Outside Ramirez's locker, she turned to face him, folding her arms over her chest. With a mighty effort, he fought to keep his gaze away from the pretty curves of her breasts under her T-shirt. "I turned you down because our acquaintance consisted of about ten minutes of conversation while fleeing a man with a BB gun. Also because I was headed to see my father. Not only that, I'm not in the habit of sleeping with men I've only met once. I can probably come up with a few more good reasons. Is it really so strange?"

"In my life, it's unusual," he said simply. What the hell, it was the truth. Girls came on to him all the time.

A distant thumping sound told him the pregame ceremony had finished and the Catfish were taking the field. Normally, he'd be pissed as hell that he wasn't out there with them. Not this time. Talking to Paige in the empty quiet of the clubhouse, he didn't miss the baseball field. Strange.

Paige had scrunched up her face at his mention of his love life. "I think we can both agree that it's a good thing I turned you down, given who my father is. I hope your feelings aren't still wounded."

He shot her a sharp glance. "You know, suddenly I see the Taylor family resemblance. Crush always irritates the hell out of me too."

She bit her lip, amusement filling those big blue eyes. "I picked up on that."

"My *feelings* don't get wounded, so you can just put that worry out of your mind."

"Just like that, huh?" She flicked her fingers in the air. "What are you, some kind of emotionless robot?"

"Not at all. I have emotions. I get horny."

He used crudeness deliberately, to get a rise out of her. But it only made one corner of her wide mouth lift, as if he'd issued a challenge. "Could have fooled me. We've been alone all this time and you haven't once made a move."

Narrowing his eyes, he closed the space between them. "Your taunts won't work. You rejected me, remember? That ship has sailed."

"Really? Where's the ship going?" She stepped forward. *Olimpia Milano,* that's what her shirt said, and damn him for not being able to keep his eyes off her. Those curves made the palms of his hands twitch, so he closed them into fists.

"Nowhere," he said firmly. This girl was trouble with a capital T—for Taylor.

"Are you afraid of the mighty Crush Taylor?" She took another step closer. "He's not as bad as he seems, you know."

"I'm not afraid of him." He placed his hands on her shoulders to keep her from coming any closer. Her warmth carried into his skin, into his being, as if it was igniting him from within.

"And I'm not afraid of *you*." She ducked underneath his hands in a quick move right out of the NBA. He took a step back and his calves hit the bench situated next to the lockers. She reached out in apology and suddenly they were right smack against each other, chest-to-chest.

Fire flashed down his spine, hot and urgent. He hauled her against him—oh, sweet Jesus, she felt good. Soft and firm and shapely and alive and fresh and . . . then her mouth was under his, her lips parting, her breath warm against his mouth, her flesh lush and sweet. It wasn't a kiss so much as a head rush.

Her breasts pressed against him, soft and enticing. He growled and walked her backward, pinned her against a locker. Lifted her legs to wrap around his waist. Pressed his sudden, extreme erection into the warm space between her thighs. His lack of pants meant the bare skin of her legs slid against his, a smooth friction that sent more blood to his groin.

She trembled in his arms and grabbed the back of his jersey. "Touch me," she whispered wildly. "Just touch me."

Her urgency threw fuel on the fire driving him. He adjusted her on his thighs and slid his hands under the edge of her shorts, her skin like warm silk against his palms. She pushed against him, grinding her pelvis against his seeking fingers. *Wild. Fierce.* He reached for her heat, for wetness, for glory. Just as his fingers found the first outer petals of her intimate flesh, he froze.

Crush Taylor's daughter.

He pulled his hand out of her shorts and released her so she slid to the floor. She would have stumbled if he hadn't held her steady. Eyes huge, mouth moist from his kiss, she stared up at him.

"I shouldn't have done that. I'm sorry." Closing his eyes against the temptation of her, he swiped his arm across his forehead. His face was damp with sweat. Holy fuck. How had a simple kiss gotten him to this state?

"No, it was my fault," she whispered. "I wanted you to. Oh God. I'm sorry. I guess it's . . . I'm so embarrassed." She covered her face with both hands. Her ponytail fell forward and he pushed it gently behind her shoulder.

"Embarrassed?"

"I've been going through a divorce, and it's been awful, and sex became this *loaded* thing, it was never just fun or pleasurable. I guess I forgot what it felt like when . . . I shouldn't have gotten carried away like that, and just so you know, I tend to babble during awkward situations. Can we mutually block this out? Make a pact of denial?"

"Pact of denial," he repeated dumbly. He was still stuck on the divorce part. She looked much too young to be married.

"Yes. This never happened." Her eyes clung to his, color flooding her face.

That didn't sit well with him. He wasn't about to forget something like this. Even now his hands pulsed with the memory of her touch. But if that's how she wanted it . . .

"Do we have to shake on it? Because I'm not sure I can touch you without wanting to throw you down on the floor and—" He broke off as her eyes went the starry violet of a Texas twilight.

"That's okay, we can make it a verbal agreement," she said in a slightly choked voice.

He looked down at the still-hard erection distending the front of his jersey. "I'll have to have a talk with my nonverbal side, straighten a few things out."

She let out a bubble of laughter. "I'll leave that in your hands," she said, then turned scarlet. "I mean . . . I'd . . . uh . . . better get to the owner's box before my father comes looking. Pact of denial?"

"Can we add in a pact of stay the hell away from each other?"

"That might be hard. I'm going to be working here. Mission 'Win the Championship' is now my life."

Just his luck, to share the hottest kiss of his life with a woman he couldn't go near. He ran his hand across the back of his neck. "You'd better go. There's a cold shower calling my name."

She hurried toward the exit. Damn those long legs. How would he ever forget the way they'd felt wrapped around his waist? "One question," he called after her. "Going through a divorce. Does that mean . . . ?"

"It means I'm divorced." Her face was the bright red of a St. Louis Cardinals cap. "I'll see you around, Trevor Stark."

"See you, Paige Mattingly Austin Taylor."

With a fleeting smile, she whisked herself out of the clubhouse.

Chapter 5

IT TOOK PAIGE the entire trip to the owner's box to recover her poise. Good golly, even in the early days with Hudson she hadn't gone up in flames like that. As soon as Trevor touched her, she'd felt electricity sizzle across her skin. That kiss, hot and deep and demanding. *Addictive.* She still felt the aftereffects, her body tingling like the echoes of a bell still rippling through the atmosphere. Trevor Stark was dynamite wrapped in the body of a Viking angel.

Nothing in her sexual history had prepared her for that chemical explosion. On the surface, Trevor wasn't even her type. He was so controlled, so intense, so mysterious. He was the "bad boy" type that had never appealed to her. She was more of a "one of the boys" sort. For her, things usually started casually, with a hike in the hills or a few pizza-and-beer dates with a group of friends.

Of course, her entire dating experience came from college, so maybe she was just uninformed. She and Hudson had lived in the same dorm. She'd gotten to know him over ice cream in the dining hall and working on an anthropology project together. They clicked, the sex was fun, they'd had an easy, drama-free relationship from the start. When he graduated and signed a contract with Virtus Roma, he proposed. They'd gotten married, moved to Italy, and voilà. End of dating experience.

Trevor Stark, on the other hand? Oh my God. The way he'd held her, so she felt the force of his strength, the control of his grip. The way his kiss had absolutely consumed her, lighting her up like a torch. The way her inhibitions had melted away in the face of her primitive, embarrassing lust.

What was wrong with her? Was she just sex-starved, as she'd told Trevor, scrambling to explain her mortifying behavior?

She knew one thing for certain. It wasn't his fallen-angel face. It wasn't his ripped body. It was something else, something deeper. On the surface he was all ice and control, but underneath there was molten magma, intense and fierce. She'd felt it. It had surged from his body into hers, electric and dangerous and irresistible.

What fueled Trevor Stark?

Reaching the door to the owner's box, she slipped in and went to the seat next to her father. Trevor was right, they couldn't do that again. They might burn down the freaking stadium. And cause Crush's head to explode.

Sorry, Paige, she told herself. No hot sex with the ballplayer, no matter how sex-deprived you are.

But maybe there was something else she could do with Trevor Stark. She'd always been curious about people. One of her favorite courses in college had been psychology, even though Crush had mocked her for it. Maybe she could put some of her curiosity to work on the enigmatic ballplayer. Could she figure out what made Trevor tick? Why he was throwing away his talent? Why he was still playing Triple A in Kilby when he ought to be with the Friars?

She stole a glance at her dad, who was firing eye bullets across the stadium. Following his gaze, she saw a gray-haired man in a bolo tie and cowboy hat. Roy Wade. Her father's longtime nemesis.

"Still feuding with the Wades?"

"You don't feud with people like that. You squash them under your boot like gnats. They're trying to steal the team."

"Excuse me?"

"They want to buy the Catfish, and they have the commissioner convinced they'd be better for the league."

All the pieces fell into place. "That's why you vowed to win the championship? Because of the Wades?"

"Everyone loves a winner. If we win under my watch, they'll have a hard time making the argument that I'm an embarrassment to the league." His gaze moved sideways, across the crowd, then settled on a blond woman coming down the aisle. "Well, look who deigned to visit the Catfish."

Paige lifted the binoculars from the counter that ran the length of the owner's box. The woman had the classic Texas big hair and a curvaceous build. She wore blue jeans but didn't look comfortable in them, as if she usually dressed less casually. "I don't recognize her."

"That's the mayor of Kilby, Wendy Trent."

His tone, somewhere between intrigue and suspicion, made her look more closely. "Is that her husband?"

Crush snatched the binoculars away to check out the man following the mayor down the aisle. "Don't know."

Interesting. Something was definitely going on there. Paige sat back and switched her focus to the players on the field. A bunch of young, attractive, physically fit men in tight baseball pants and blue caps. Well, maybe baseball wasn't *so* bad. She could probably put up with it for a few weeks.

"With slugger Trevor Stark on the injured list for the moment, the Catfish are going to have a hard time gaining any ground in the standings. And that's bad news for Crush Taylor and his vow to win the championship." Trevor rarely listened to the local sports radio shows, but right now it was his only baseball fix. He had the morning off from the ballpark, and had finally gotten the tires replaced on his Escalade. He'd duct-taped the mirror into place, and so far it was holding.

"Duke Ellington hasn't said much about the nature of Stark's injury. Bar brawl? Jealous husband? Or something actually baseball-related? With Stark, you never know."

"He is the biggest mystery on the team. All the talent in the world, but he just can't seem to put it together into a cohesive package."

"You're right, Bob, that's about the size of it. Some say he could be the next Barry Bonds or Mark McGwire, without any rumors of steroids, ha ha. He's got power, speed, and smarts. Never seen the guy play stupid. On the field, he's got it together. Off the field, he's definitely not ready for prime time."

"Sometimes it seems like he doesn't want to leave Kilby."

"Well, it is a pretty good place to live." They both chuckled, though every listener knew the absurdity of that theory. Triple A players, by their nature, wanted to move to the big leagues. "We've got a caller on line three. Billy, you're up. What do you think of Crush Taylor's determination to win the Triple A championship?"

Trevor punched the button to shut off the commentators who thought they knew him. He couldn't avoid the Friars forever, he knew that. But the more time passed, the more the danger would subside. His one true talent had always been baseball, but he couldn't fully develop it in juvie. After he'd gotten out, he figured he'd get a job in construction or something equally low profile. But Nina had thrown a fit. "You belong in baseball," she kept saying. "Don't you dare quit playing. Promise me, Trevor." So he'd joined a local independent league team. He'd worked his ass off, listened, learned, built his strength, worked on his power, refined his swing. After a couple years of that, he'd gone to a tryout and caught the eye of a scout for the Mexican Leagues.

More work, more training. He'd set records, then broken those records. Finally, he'd gone to a major league tryout and impressed a famous sports agent. The agent had gotten him into the draft, where he went in the third round. Big contract . . . *bingo*. He'd put a bucketload of money into an account for Nina and arranged for her to move to Tucson. If he was going to have a baseball career, he wanted her somewhere unconnected with their previous life.

The fact that his sister was now far away from Detroit took a huge load off his mind. But the danger was still too great. The Wachowskis had destroyed his father with their drugs and threats. They'd gotten him sent to juvie. No way in hell were they going to touch Nina.

He parked in his usual spot at the Kilby Boys and Girls Club and loped inside, his duffel bag full of signed balls slung over his shoulder.

"Hi Trevor." The counselor on shift waved him in. "They're waiting for you."

He went into the common area, where teenage boys of all races and ethnicities filled every available spot on the sagging hand-me-down couches. He recognized a few from previous visits. Piercings, tattoos, strange eye makeup, all par for the course. Didn't bother him. He'd seen all that and much more during his time in the system.

"For those who don't know me, I'm Trevor Stark from the Kilby Catfish. Anyone here like baseball?"

A general rumble of indifference answered that question. He set down the duffel and pulled out a couple of signed baseballs, displaying them to the kids. "That's all right. You don't have to like baseball. But do you know how much these are worth on eBay?"

Now he'd gotten their attention. They tossed out guesses. "Million dollars? . . . Two million . . . About twenty bucks?"

"They're worth a lot more than that." Trevor scanned the room, meeting every boy's eyes, making sure they knew that when he said things, he meant them. These boys were on the edge. Fall one way, they might end up in juvie like him. The other way, maybe they had a chance. He couldn't tell them his story—couldn't risk it getting out. But he could give them some motivation.

"Who here went to school every day this past week?"

Three boys raised their hands. Only three. Christ, there were probably twenty kids in the room. He beckoned the three forward and deposited a ball in each boy's hand. "Well done, kids. Want to know who signed these balls? Barry Bonds, Cal Ripken Jr., and Ozzie Smith."

The boys grinned—those were pretty famous names, after all. Trevor had been collecting balls like these for years, every spring training.

"What do you think these balls represent?"

One wiry Hispanic boy took a stab. "Bank?"

"That is true, they're worth money because they're signed by those particular players. Do you think those players woke up one morning with a million dollar swing and a big contract?"

They shook their heads.

"Damn right they didn't. So what do those balls represent?"

"Hard work," one boy called out.

"Mad skills," said another.

"Yes and yes. Anything else?"

"Um . . ." The boys exchanged shrugs and confused glances. "Testicles?"

Everyone cracked up, the room filling with laughter. Trevor didn't mind. Now the ice was broken and they could get down to real conversing.

"How about this." He paced across the length of the room, tossing the ball in the air, rolling it on the back of his hand, flipping it behind his back. Kids had short attention spans, and it was important to keep them from drifting. "How about persistence? Know what that means? Means you keep on doing something even when it gets hard. Even if you don't want to go to school, you go. Have a bad day? You shake it off and try again the next day. It means you don't give up." He spun the ball in the air, the red stitches forming a mesmerizing blurred pattern. "These balls were signed by people with persistence, and now they're yours, because you guys went to school every day last week. That's persistence."

"Nah, man, my teacher, she's hot." A black kid with barrettes in his braids grinned, showing off a mouthful of braces. "I hate to miss a day."

They all hooted, and Trevor winked at him. "Ladies' man, eh?"

"Just like you, playa."

He winced at the realization that his reputation had extended even to the Boys and Girls Club. "Gotta have respect, though. Respect is everything. Respect your-self. Respect the ladies. Respect the game. You know?"

"Respect, man, respect." The boys murmured agree-ment with that concept. Trevor had found that particu-lar word to be very powerful for kids.

"You want respect, you gotta give respect. I respect you guys for going to school even when it's tough. Those of you who didn't manage to get to school every day, keep on trying. Make it, and I'll have a ball for you next time."

The black kid raised his hand. "Mr. Trevor Stark, how'd you get so many balls? Did you steal 'em?"

He laughed along with everyone else.

"'Course he didn't. He ain't no criminal," another kid scolded the first. "He ain't like us."

Trevor busied himself with zipping up the duffel. "No, I didn't steal the balls," he said tightly. If these kids only knew *how much* he was like them—except he was even worse. These boys hadn't been sentenced to juvenile detention. "Those players gave those balls to me, to give to you. Those Hall of Fame players are out there rooting for you. Wanting you to do well. You remember that every time you think about quitting, or getting on a bad path. Got me?"

"Yes sir, Mr. Trevor Stark. Yes sir."

He went around the room sharing low-fives and fist bumps. The kids might not all be rabid baseball fans, but every young boy he knew admired physical strength.

When he'd connected with every kid in the room—making sure no one was left out—he shouldered his gym bag and headed for his Escalade. A white Chevy Cavalier was just leaving the parking lot. As it turned on the road, the right front tire skimmed the curb. A white car, sketchy driving . . . He squinted at the brown-haired girl at the wheel. Nah, it couldn't be her.

Why would Paige Taylor be at the Boys and Girls Club? She was probably home pampering her one-eyed cat or working with Crush on new plans to torture him.

He smiled, thinking of those incredibly hot moments in the clubhouse. Why he and Paige had such intense chemistry, he had no idea. They had nothing in common. She was the daughter of a sports legend, while his father was a drug addict. She was protected, sheltered. People, including her famous dad, cared about her. He, on the other hand, was on his own and had been for years. No one had his back, and he didn't need anyone to. Paige was warm and alive, while he was nothing but ice inside.

He unlocked his Escalade and tossed the duffel in back. His phone buzzed as he slid into the stifling heat of his vehicle, which had been sitting in direct sun for the past hour. As always, he checked the number before he answered. When it came through as "unknown," he stiffened. He'd changed his last name when he got out of juvie, and there should theoretically be no trace of his former self out there. But you never knew.

"Yeah," he answered brusquely.

"Trevor?" The light female voice on the other end was so muffled he didn't recognize it. But he relaxed. Why did he always have to imagine the worst possible scenario? This wasn't a call from Detroit. It was a girl who'd managed to find his number. Maybe—maybe it was Paige.

A grin split his face, and his spirits lifted. A sparring session with Paige Taylor was just what he needed. "I just saw your rental car," he said. "Are you stalking me?"

"Trevor, it's me, Nina. Do you really have girls stalking you?"

"*Nina?*" Panicked, he looked around, as if one of the

Wachowski gang might be eavesdropping. He slammed the door shut and jabbed the button that closed the window he'd left partially open. "Is something wrong?"

"No, nothing's wrong. This is a disposable phone, so relax."

"*Relax?* You promised to call only for emergencies. Do you need money?"

"Trevor, that's insulting. I don't need your money. I want to come see you, that's all. I miss you."

"You can't come here. It's too risky. We'll do our usual visit after the season's over." Every year, they met somewhere different, someplace nowhere near Detroit, Tucson, or wherever he was living.

"No." His sister's voice thickened. "I'm sorry, but that's months away. There's something I want to talk to you about. I'm going to come see you."

"*No!*" He punched his fist against the steering wheel. "Nina, listen to me. Don't do anything crazy. Just stay where you are. Can't we talk about it over the phone?"

"You said the phone's only for emergencies."

"Okay, then, can't it wait until after September?"

"I don't want to wait. Are you mad? You sound mad."

Terrified was more like it. "I'm not mad. I promise. But we should hang up now. What if someone heard you?"

"You're so paranoid, Trevor."

If Nina knew what had happened three years ago, she wouldn't say that. A Wachowski underling had spotted him at a nightclub in Syracuse. That's when he'd acquired the scar on his cheek, along with two broken ribs. The bright side was that those injuries had kept him off the field for a week, and he was traded to the Friars after that. He didn't think the Wachowskis had yet realized that Trevor Stark, baseball player, was

Trevor Leonov from Detroit. But he didn't want to take any chances.

"Better safe than sorry, that's my motto. At least when it comes to you."

"What about lonely. Where does lonely fit in?"

"You have Mrs. Shimon." The woman he paid as a bodyguard slash housekeeper.

"She's not you," Nina said simply. "She won't hit fungoes with me."

He couldn't help laughing at the image of the stern Israeli, a former paratrooper, goofing around with a ball and glove. "There are more important things than baseball."

"I want to see you play. Please."

The determination in her voice gave him chills. If she came to see him play, and let something slip, and it got back to the wrong people, they'd both be in danger. He didn't care about himself, but Nina was *not* going to get hurt.

But what if she took things into her own hands, the way it sounded like she might?

"I'll think about it," he finally said. "We'll figure something out."

"Are you happy I called?"

"I'm furious, and I'd fire Mrs. Shimon if she didn't have so much special weapons training."

"You can't blame her. She's a very good prison warden." The bitterness in Nina's voice made him feel like a total shit. He hated that it had to be this way. Even the wistful sound of her voice made him ache with missing her. She was the only family he had left.

"Yes, Nina, of course I'm happy you called. Just be careful, okay?"

"I will. And you start making plans for that game. Please?"

"I'll try, sweetheart."

He hung up before she could press him further. Plans? No. Not happening. If only Nina was right, and the Wachowskis had filed him under Ancient History.

But they hadn't. At least they hadn't three years ago, and what would have changed since then? An attack on a member of the top echelon had to be avenged. *Would* be avenged. A three-year stint in juvie wasn't enough. The scars on his back and the one on his cheek were a constant reminder. The Wachowskis would demand more if they found him. And if they learned the whole truth . . . if they learned about Nina . . . He shuddered.

Now *that* was never going to fucking happen.

Chapter 6

CRUSH TOLD PAIGE to start her "internship" in the marketing and promotions department, since his battle against the Wades required extra ammunition.

"We need to get the town on our side. Part one will be to win the championship," he told her as they headed through the management wing to Marcia Burke's office. "But we need more than that. We need to recreate ourselves. Perception is everything."

"Are you saying we need to put the Catfish on the map?"

"I wish it was that simple. The Catfish are already on the map, but not in the way we want. They have a reputation. A bunch of wild and rowdy partiers who like to have a little too much fun."

"Hm. I wonder who that reminds me of?" Paige scrunched up her face, squinting into the distance as if searching her memory. "I'm sure it'll come back to me, along with every time I got sent off the ranch for All-Star weekend."

"Funny." He chucked her under the chin, a gesture left over from her childhood. "You know those parties were no place for a child."

"I wouldn't know. I never got to attend one. Maybe now that I'm grown up I'll finally get a chance."

Crush snarled like some sort of bossy lion. "Absolutely not. I don't want you hanging out with the players."

"Dad, that's ridiculous. How am I supposed to help market the team without hanging out with the players?"

He scratched at his chin. "Good point. Okay, maybe a few ground rules, then. Don't smile at them. Don't bring them food. Feed them and they'll be like puppies following you everywhere you go. Never, ever, buy them a beer."

"No food, beer, or smiles. You drive a hard bargain. Any wiggle room on the smiles? Because I didn't smile for the last three months I was with Hudson."

Sympathy flashed in her father's hazel eyes as he held the door to the marketing department open for her. "Smiles, but no laughs. Don't get a big head, but your laugh is irresistible."

"Aw, Daddy. That's such a nice thing to say." She beamed at him, and he groaned.

"Damn it, I might have to change my mind about the smiling."

"Don't be ridiculous, Crush. Have you seen the girls who hang around the ballplayers? I think they can withstand an ancient, jaded old divorcée."

Marcia Burke, who headed the Catfish marketing and promotions department, had retired from a high-powered New York advertising job but still wore nothing but black. She wore square black eyeglasses and kept her silver hair in a bob that bisected her ears.

She rose to her feet and put her hands on her hips, scanning Paige from head to toe. Literally, she was about half Paige's height. "So. You ready to work hard?" Her raspy voice reminded Paige that she'd come back to Kilby to battle throat cancer.

"Yes ma'am."

"I need ideas, brilliant ones, and I need them yester-
day. We need to make Catfish synonymous with . . ."
She cocked her head at the baseball field. " . . . impact.
Glamour."

Crush muttered something under his breath, something that sounded suspiciously like "bullshit." He told
them, "I'll leave you to it, then," and hauled ass out of
the room.

As soon as he was gone, Marcia plopped back down
at her laptop and started jabbing at the keys. "Impact,"
she muttered. "Glamour. Social media, we need something on social media, something that'll really make
a national splash. Viral, we want viral. Grab a chair,
brainstorm with me."

Paige scanned the office for an extra chair but didn't
see one. There were plenty of Catfish posters and piles
of T-shirts and little key chains and pens, all in bright
Catfish blue. The infamous poster of Trevor Stark hung
next to the window that looked out on the field.

She stared at it. Trevor Stark, man of mystery. The
last person she'd expected to see when she'd stopped
by the Boys and Girls Club to see if they needed any
volunteer assistance from a well-intentioned student
who had yet to finish her degree. They'd assigned her
to a summer tutoring program, but the real revelation
had been the sight of the enigmatic Catfish slugger putting on some kind of presentation for a group of at-risk
youth. They'd been completely enraptured by whatever
he was saying, but she was too far away to make out
any of his words.

But the impact he made still reverberated through
her. He'd worn gray trousers and a simple white shirt
with the sleeves rolled up. The size and power of him
was amplified in comparison to the kids surrounding
him. Every so often he turned his head so she saw his

profile. The fluorescent lights made caves under his cheekbones and turned his hair platinum. He was just so good-looking it was almost scary.

But then there was that scar on his cheek, that thin white line that took him from angel to badass.

In the poster, he had no scar. Pulling her gaze away from it, she looked out at the field, where the game was in full swing.

"Just wondering," she said to Marcia, "if watching the game wouldn't help us get ideas."

"The game? Why?"

"Well, I've never been a fan of the game myself, so maybe we could talk to the real fans, see what they love about the Catfish and baseball. It might help to get some inspiration, that's all."

"You want inspiration? Two words: baseball pants."

Though it was strange to hear that from a seventy-year-old, Paige had to admit that the players on the field wore the uniform well. Particularly Trevor Stark, who stood like a colossus in left field. For the first time, she actually got to see him in baseball pants, since he hadn't worn them in Crush's office. The memory of his long, bulging thigh muscles and light covering of golden hair would stay with her for a long time.

Then again, the addition of baseball pants worked too.

"Um, is that appropriate, really, talking about baseball pants like that? We're supposed to be marketing, not pimping."

"It's a thin line sometimes," Marcia said. "Sex sells, girlie. Always has, always will. Keep that in mind. There's a reason they changed the design of the pants back in 1972. Got me and my girlfriends to the games."

"I see your point." She wrenched her gaze away from left field to the pitcher going into his windup. He delivered a fastball, a little outside. The batter fought it off, sending a high fly ball to right field. The runner on first dashed toward second, the infielders scurried to cover their bases, and the right fielder leisurely tracked the ball. She'd never seen him before, but from her quickie research she knew his name was Shizuko and that he was half Japanese, half Brazilian, and had a worldwide following on his Tumblr page. He caught the ball easily.

With a graceful motion, Shizuko gunned it into first base; the runner had to dive to make it back in time. The center fielder yelled some encouragement and punched his glove. As she focused on the captain of the outfield, Paige's eyes widened. The center fielder was pretty amazing looking as well. African-American, with absolutely chiseled forearms exposed by the warm weather uniform. Radiating charisma, he grinned at the crowd, making the "two out" sign, then prowled back to his position.

From the center fielder—Dwight Conner, she suddenly remembered—her gaze traveled to left field, where Trevor Stark, a blond Viking god, staked out his territory. He said something to Dwight, and they both laughed. Jesus Christ, the amount of sheer good looks in that outfield would make a modeling agency faint. "That's got to be the sexiest outfield in baseball," she murmured.

"Excuse me?"

"Oh nothing. Just appreciating the view from up here."

"No, you said something. Something that caught my radar, but I wasn't listening. Say it again."

Paige tried to reconstruct it. "I think I said that's got to be the sexiest outfield in baseball. But don't listen to me. I just got divorced and I'm not completely myself yet. I've been doing and saying some strange things lately."

Marcia jumped to her feet, sending her rolling desk chair spinning across the room. "That's it. Baseball's Sexiest—no . . . something with Texas—Outfields are Hotter in Texas . . . no . . . Outfields are Hotter than Your Fields."

Paige sidestepped away from the runaway chair. "What the heck are you talking about?"

"The campaign that's going to get everyone talking about the Catfish."

"Baseball's Sexiest Outfield? That's how you want to market the team? I don't think the players would like that."

"You're right. Baseball's *Hottest* Outfield. First, it's Texas and it's always hot. Second, I'd have to check the stats, but off the top of my head, those three combined have a pretty remarkable OBP. Third, look at them."

By now Marcia was next to her, pressing her face against the glass. "Those three are hot, and that's with my seventy-year-old hormones. Not only that, they're multiracial. This is goddamn genius. Your father is going to love me. I gotta write this up, girlie. Take a bathroom break. Cry your little heart out. Sorry about the divorce. Go on now." Marcia gave her a friendly shove toward the door.

Paige resisted the tiny whirlwind. "But I don't need to cry right now. And it was my idea."

"No it wasn't. You didn't even know what I was talking about. All you did was lust after some ballplayers. We'll present this to Crush tomorrow, so I have a lot of work to do. Don't say a word to him before then. Top secret. We have to present it just right. Think visuals. Get inspired. Bye-bye."

The door closed behind her. Paige shrugged. She couldn't bring herself to care very much. Would Baseball's Hottest Outfield really inspire the right kind of media attention? Hudson would have hated a campaign like that. He was actually a shy person, which was something she'd found endearing. He didn't like to promote himself or trash-talk or anything like that. The problem, he'd once told her, was that he'd shot up to his full height so early in life that people were scared of him. A tall black dude, no matter how nice a guy, made people nervous. He'd learned to hide behind a smile and minimize his height.

Paige wasn't even close to shy. She was insatiably curious about people and loved nothing more than to coax their stories out of them. At parties, Hudson used to hang next to her as much as she'd let him, relaxing in her flow of conversation and only speaking when necessary or when he spotted a basketball buddy. Off the court, he always kept a set of large, very obvious headphones handy in case he needed to ward off strangers who might want to converse with him. His roommates at college used to call Hudson and Paige "Big Black and the Chatterbox."

Oh, snap out of it, she commanded herself. It was a screwed-up relationship anyway, as she'd discovered in her counseling sessions. She was Hudson's crutch in so many ways. In return, he'd given her a temporary purpose in life. As Hudson's wife, she was no longer torn between two homes, two entirely different families. She'd acquired a firm place in the universe, even if it was a little strange, since the people around her spoke Italian and pounded up and down a basketball court. She'd latched onto Hudson just as much as he'd latched onto her.

The really pathetic thing was that when he fell in love with Nessa, Paige had wanted to stay friends. Splitting up with Hudson had felt like losing a brother, someone very familiar and safe. But Nessa hadn't been interested in anything like that. No friends, no checking in with the occasional text message, even a passing encounter in the Via del Corso made her hackles rise.

Enough. Hudson was history. Time to live in the here and now. Baseball pants and a hot summer day. Things could be worse.

She texted her father. *Up for some Cracker Jack and cotton candy?*

Is that code for Daddy time or are you starting to enjoy America's pastime?

Actually, I'm just hungry.

We'll hook you. Just wait.

That night, the Catfish made one of their legendary appearances at the Kilby Roadhouse. An eager crowd swelled the club well past its fire-safe capacity. The bass line blasting from the sound system vibrated the sawdust-scattered floor. Bursts of laughter rose like bright balloons toward the raftered ceiling. Trevor watched the action from the safety of a bar stool, his elbow throbbing from his first game since the BB gun incident.

Dwight Conner slid onto the stool next to him and squinted at the dance floor. "What the fuck is Bieberman doing out there?"

Trevor glanced over his shoulder. The shortstop was twitching his way across the dance floor at the head of a chain of girls. Every once in a while he kicked up a leg like a dog taking a leak.

"Having a lot more fun than we are." Trevor snorted. "You should get to it, man. Show 'em how it's done."

"What are you saying, I'm black so I can dance?"

Trevor blinked at him. "You're black? Dude, you're supposed to be my friend. You gotta tell me these things. You can't be keeping secrets like that."

They both laughed. Somehow, mysteriously, he and Dwight had achieved the kind of friendship in which they could say any old shit and neither one minded. "You sure you're okay? You seem a little off."

Trevor took a swallow of his Lone Star by way of answer. The call from Nina had really rattled him. No matter how well he got along with Dwight, he couldn't talk about that.

"Playing it strong and silent," Dwight said, clapping him on the shoulder. "Good call. I'm going in. If you need any help with the hottie on your left, just give me a sign."

Trevor glanced to the side. A gorgeous brunette was sliding him a flirtatious look, elbows propped behind her on the bar, legs crossed, one black stiletto dangling from her toe. She smiled as he caught her eye, and that smile told him everything he needed to know. If he wanted to forget his troubles by burying his cock in a warm, willing body, done and done.

He gave her an apologetic smile and turned back to his beer. Not interested. Her eyes weren't sapphire blue, and she probably didn't say things like "pact of denial." She wasn't the adorable and off-limits Paige Taylor. Apparently he wasn't interested in any girl unless she had a fluffy one-eyed cat and an attitude.

He finished his beer and pushed away from the bar. The smart move right now would be to go home and think about how to distract Nina from her determination to come to Kilby. He signaled the bartender, Todd, for his tab.

Instead, Todd brought him a shot of Grey Goose. "Courtesy of Dean Wade with best wishes for speedy healing."

Across the bar, a towering man in a snap-up shirt and cowboy hat gave him a salute. He had the jawline of an ox and looked just as stubborn. Trevor had heard a lot about the Wade family, all bad. He knew Crush was feuding with them.

Just to prove Crush didn't own him, despite being the team owner, he nodded back to Dean Wade and downed the vodka. The man looked pleased.

The vodka settled into his system, making things warm and blurry. He swiveled around to scan the dance floor, and blinked twice. Was that Paige Taylor, in a slinky black top and purple leggings clinging to those long, long legs?

"Who is that?" The soft, awed voice of Shizuko Ruiz interrupted his lustful thoughts. The right fielder leaned on the bar next to him, watching Paige walk their way.

"*That* is foul ball territory. Owner's daughter."

"Crush is a big fan of mine," Shizuko said smugly. "He wants to party with me in Rio for Carneval."

"Well, stay away from Paige. She's having a hard time. Just got divorced."

"Paige . . ." He mused over the name. "Like Satchel Paige?"

Trevor blanked for a moment, since Paige had reached them and her light scent had gone to his head. Her pretty lips were upturned in a wry, sexy curve.

"Yes, I'm named after Satchel Paige," she answered. "My father's favorite player."

Trevor cocked his head. "He always says Don Mattingly was his favorite."

Laughter flashed in her eyes. "Don Mattingly was his favorite hitter. Satchel was his favorite pitcher."

Shizuko said, "So your name is . . ."

"Paige Mattingly Austin Taylor."

"Why Austin?" Shizuko leaned in to hear her answer. A little too close, in Trevor's opinion.

"It's where Crush pitched his perfect game, asshole," he explained, irritated.

Paige's gaze swept to meet his, and he caught surprise and a satisfying amount of respect.

"Exactly. Whenever I complain, he tells me to be glad he didn't pitch his perfect game in Pittsburgh. Hi, Trevor. And you must be Shizuko."

The right fielder lifted her hand to his lips and kissed it. Murder filled Trevor's heart. "Drop it," he muttered so fiercely that Shizuko instantly obeyed. Paige shot an annoyed glance at Trevor. She'd added smoky eyeliner or something. Her eyes sparkled and glowed, sexy as hell, and her hair flowed loose over her shoulders. A long purple feather earring dangled from one ear. She shouldn't be in this bar, with that slinky top baring her skin and that name that would make any baseball fan salivate.

"Is Dwight Conner here too?" she asked.

"Sure. Out there somewhere." He beckoned to the dance floor, where Sonny Barnes, the first baseman, was now doing the "worm" across the entire floor.

"Conner," Trevor called into the mob on the dance floor. "Outfield meeting at the bar."

It took a few minutes, but finally Dwight fought his way out of the laughing mob. "What's up?" He spotted Paige and plastered on his "lady boner" grin, as he called it. "Paige Taylor . . . I heard Crush's cute daughter was in town, but I didn't believe it until I saw for myself."

She shook his hand, then pulled out her iPhone. "I was hoping I would find you all here. There's something the Catfish management would like to discuss with you. Would you mind if I took a quick photo of the three of you? Sort of a selfie-style, casual shot?"

Trevor snorted. "Don't trust her, guys. Next thing you know you'll be duct-taping your sideview mirror back on your car."

She made a face at him. "I told you I'd take care of

that. This is perfectly harmless, it'll just be easier to explain things this way."

"Why so mysterious?" He leaned close to her ear, delivering his question through the fragrant waves of her hair. She shivered, almost imperceptibly.

"*You're* calling *me* mysterious? This is perfectly innocent. Just pretend I'm a groupie asking for your autograph. If you want to take your shirt off, be my guest." Her saucy smile was nearly too much for him. He wanted to scoop her into his lap and lose himself in her adorableness.

Maybe that vodka had been a bad idea.

As the three outfielders posed together, arms around each other's shoulders, a wide smile spread across Paige's face. "There's a lot of testosterone in this picture. And some really great DNA. I think Marcia might be on to something after all."

She finished snapping pictures and stuck her phone back in the little leather backpack that hung from one shoulder.

"Don't mean to be rude to the owner's daughter, but what are you talking about?" Dwight asked.

"Are you guys up for saving the Catfish?"

Trevor exchanged confused looks with Dwight and Shizuko. "Again, what are you talking about?"

"Nine o'clock tomorrow morning, marketing department. I'll bring donuts." Throwing up one hand, she added, "But don't fall in love with me just because I'm going to feed you."

She put some cash on the bar and signaled to Todd. "Please bring these guys a round of Lone Stars on me." With a grimace, she turned back to the three of them. "And *don't* fall in love with me just because I'm buying you beer. I've been warned about both of those things, but this is strictly business."

With that, she disappeared into the crowd, nearly getting mowed down by Bieberman's conga line. They all watched her go, and Shizuko let out a long sigh. "Pretty girl."

"Donuts," said Dwight, with his own sigh. "And beer."

Trevor ground his teeth, wondering if he could get rid of the other two guys and cover the entire outfield by himself. Where that possessiveness came from, he didn't even want to know.

Chapter 7

THE MAN IN *the black leather blazer has Pop up against the wall. A fist at his neck. A flash of light on steel. Knife. A line of dark red seeping from the edge. Don't, don't. Threats spilling from the man's maw like bats. Panic, paralysis. What to do? Phone 911. But the numbers don't dial, the 1 keeps disappearing. Jabbing at the keys. Help, help.*

Too late. The phone is gone. The man is on the ground. Someone is shouting. Screaming. Running. But it isn't the man. He's a silent crumpled lump. As if he'll never speak again.

Trevor woke up clawing for air, his heart jackhammering. He threw the hotel sheets off his body. Heaved deep breaths into his lungs. Swinging his legs over the side of the bed, he dropped his head into his hands. The familiar feeling of his own hair, his own skull, grounded him. He was in Kilby, Texas. A baseball player. A grown man. Here. Now. Alone.

When he'd gotten a grip on his heart rate, he got up and double-checked the door of the hotel room. Locked, of course, not only with the standard latch, but an extra dead bolt he'd added himself. He'd had to pay the Days Inn management for the privilege of an extra sense of security, but it was well worth it. The dead bolt didn't keep the nightmares away, but it helped him recover more quickly.

He checked the alarm clock on the bedside table: 5:30 am. Walked to the window and drew aside the drapes. It was just getting light outside, long fingers of pink reaching across the lower horizon. Fuck, he'd never get back to sleep now. He didn't want to, not if it meant reliving that night again.

In the little kitchenette, he poured himself a tall glass of water and downed it, then started the coffeemaker. Watching the drip, drip, he released the horrible aftereffects of the dream, moment by moment.

Dream . . . no, it wasn't just a dream. Those memories were burned into his brain forever. They would never leave him. He just had to live with it. And he'd learned how. Empty his mind. Let all emotion seep out of him. Focus his rage somewhere it couldn't hurt anyone.

Oh, and read. He picked up a novel from the pile on his bedside table. It didn't matter what kind of book it was. Mysteries, thrillers, romance, science fiction . . . anything to send his mind somewhere else. *Song of Ice and Fire* . . . that would do the job. A thousand pages of death and destruction—exactly what he needed.

With his coffee and his book, he lay back on his bed and escaped into a fictional world that seemed only a little over the top to him. The Iron Kingdom had nothing on Detroit.

The next morning at nine-fifteen—he didn't want to seem too curious—Trevor strolled into the promotions department. A tiny woman with aggressively silver hair clapped when he walked in. "This couldn't be more perfect," she exclaimed. "Why did I never think of this before?"

Wary, Trevor scanned the rest of the room, spotting Crush Taylor, Shizuko, Dwight, and, nearly dwarfed by all the big ballplayers, Paige. Her hair was in a high ponytail and she wore cowboy boots and a striped dress that ended somewhere above her knees. She looked fresh and sassy and made his mouth water.

"What's this all about?"

"They wouldn't tell us anything until you got here, dude." Dwight's usual high-voltage smile was missing. "Twenty minutes late, you missed the donuts."

Paige stepped forward and whipped something out from behind her back. A paper towel wrapped around three Krispy Kremes. "I got your back, Stark." She winked at him, while a low growl sounded from Crush's direction.

Trevor propped himself against the wall and, eyes narrowed at Crush, took a slow, deliberate bite of the sugary donut. He knew that Paige was hands off, but he didn't need Crush reminding him of it.

"Now that everyone's here, let's get started." The silver-haired woman whipped out an iPad and punched a button. Every movement seemed to happen in double-time.

"For those who don't know me, I'm the head of the marketing team here. To support Crush's mission to bring fame and fortune to the Kilby Catfish, we came up with a fabulous new campaign that's going to take Kilby by storm. Not just Kilby, but the entire country."

The shot that Paige had taken of the three outfielders at the Roadhouse filled the screen. Trevor, looking stone-faced as always, the Viking warrior badass. Dwight, who'd modeled for a sunglass manufacturer in college. And Shizuko, whose genetic mix of Brazilian and Japanese made him almost freakishly good-looking. Objectively, Trevor had to say, they were breathtaking.

"Paige, you posted this on the team Instagram account, right? Can you tell us what kind of response you got?"

Paige cleared her throat and checked her iPhone. "Two thousand and thirty-two likes so far. Eighty-two comments."

"What do the comments say?"

Amusement flashed into those sparkly blue eyes. "Really? You want me to read them? Okay. Here's one. 'Bring that triple-decker man sandwich over here, baby!' Then there's 'Hot, hotter, and hottest.' And, of course, 'Too many clothes.' Should I go on?"

"We get the point," said Crush dryly. "The ladies are on board."

"On board with what?" Trevor still didn't get it, and he wasn't too crazy about being on Instagram. What if the Detroit guys monitored social media for some reason?

"Viral marketing. It's also global, thanks to Shizuko here. We have a global viral thing happening, and that's gold. You can't buy that. All we're going to do is jump on board and ride it for all its worth."

"Ma'am, you better explain what the hell you're talking about." Dwight leaned forward to rest his elbows on his knees. "I ain't Jay Z, I'm a baseball player. And though I don't like to think of it this way, we're minor league here."

Marcia marched toward him and poked him in the chest. "Oh no, Dwight Conner. You're not just a minor league outfielder. You're part of Baseball's Hottest Outfield, and you're going to be famous."

Dwight's jaw dropped, and Shizuko yanked his earbuds out of his ears. "Could you repeat, please?" He spoke excellent English but sometimes liked to pretend he didn't.

"You heard me. Viral marketing. Sex sells. Hot guys

sell. You're going to become a sensation and it's only going to help your careers. Good for Crush, good for you, good all around."

Cold fear wrapped a fist around Trevor's gut. Publicity wasn't his friend, at least not national publicity. Yeah, he had a different name now. And he'd bulked up by about seventy pounds since the age of fifteen. But he could still be recognized.

"Count me out," he said, making it casual, like he didn't care that much. "I'm not a trained monkey. I'm a ballplayer."

"A ballplayer who's on a thin line right now," Crush said sharply. "A ballplayer who said he'd help me."

Trevor bit back an automatic *Fuck off.* "I said I'd help win the championship. Not go viral."

"This isn't going to work unless you're all on board," said Marcia. "Baseball's Hottest Outfield needs all three positions. It's an opportunity, fellas. Make a name, get some press. If you think all you have to do is go out and play, you're living in the olden times, boys. My era, as a matter of fact. You gotta market yourself. Brand. Platform. Buzz."

As she ticked those items off on her fingers, Shizuko slowly straightened. Marcia was speaking his language right now. During the off-season he toured in a thrash-metal punk band, and all year round he put a lot of time into his social media. "I'll do it."

"I'm in," said Dwight. "I'm the Captain of Hot."

Everyone looked at Trevor. *Oh, hell.* Marcia came close enough for him to catch a whiff of her body lotion. She narrowed sharp brown eyes at him through those intimidating black frames. "You need this more than anyone. Conner's Mr. Popular, Shizuko's a heartthrob in Japan, but you . . . you're the bad boy. You could use some love from the people."

"I don't need love." Each word sounded like an ice cube.

Dwight got up and slung an arm around his shoulders. "You know I love you like a brother, Stark. But sometimes you gotta step up and be there for the team."

Trevor shook off his arm. "I'm not doing it."

Tense silence fell across the room. He set his jaw and stared back at the array of faces. Then Paige stepped forward. "I know what might make a difference. What if we attached some sort of charitable cause to the campaign, like, say the Boys and—"

"Hang on." Trevor raised a hand to stop her. No one with the Catfish knew about his time at the Boys and Girls Club. He'd asked the Club to keep it quiet and they had. He couldn't let the team know; it might mess with his bad boy reputation. "What I *meant* was that I'm not doing it without Paige."

Her jaw fell open, her expression of shock repeated in every other face in the room. "What do you mean, without me?"

"You know your social media, obviously." He gestured to the Instagram photo on Marcia's iPad. "If we're going to do this, you should be part of it."

"No problem at all," said Marcia promptly. "Right, Paige?"

"I have a problem with it," Crush said, prowling across the room toward Trevor. Paige stepped between them.

"Please don't embarrass me, Dad. I'm more than happy to work on this campaign." She shot Trevor a look that implied something more like, *You owe me a new car for doing this.* "I think it would be fun. I get to take pictures of baseball players. Think of all the girls who will wish they were me."

That argument didn't seem to impress Crush much

at all. He glared at his daughter, then at Trevor, then at Dwight, who made a *Who, me?* gesture. Finally he threw up his hands and stomped out of the office.

Marcia spent the next few minutes setting up a schedule with the four of them, and then the meeting broke up.

As they left Marcia's office, Trevor lagged behind until Shizuko and Dwight were out of sight. He snagged Paige's arm and whirled her through a side door, into an empty stairwell. If they were going to work together, they had to get a few things straight. But before he could say a word, she preempted him.

"You don't want anyone to know about the Boys and Girls Club, do you?"

Automatically he looked behind him to make sure no one was listening. "It's no one's business."

"So you don't mind everyone knowing about all the girls you sleep with, but you don't want them to know you work with troubled kids during your down time?"

Yes, that was exactly right. But he didn't know how to explain the reasons for that. "It's personal, and if we're going to work together, you have to promise not to tell anyone."

She gave him a long, level look, the kind that made him uncomfortable because it meant she was actually looking past the surface. He didn't want anyone looking there. "Sure, I'll promise. As long as you give me a good reason."

"The reason is that I don't want people to know."

"That doesn't count. An actual reason why you would want people to think you're more of a jerk than you really are."

The way she was looking at him made him nuts. He felt her gaze like a hand stroking his body. This close to her, he noticed a million little details about her. The scattering of golden freckles across her cheekbones, the purple rim around her true-blue irises, the way her chest rose and fell, the swell of her breasts against her striped dress. The pendant she wore, in the shape of a branching tree. Everything about her was fresh and sparkling as an April morning. He braced one hand on the wall next to her. "Are you so sure I'm not a jerk?"

Instead of being intimidated, she raised her chin. "Yeah, I'm sure. I'm pretty intuitive, and I did happen to see you doing a great job with those kids."

"Kids are one thing, women . . . that's a different story," he drawled. He hovered his face close to hers, letting her know—with only an inch between them—how much she turned him on. The sensory memory of what she'd felt like in his arms flooded him in a wave of lust. Her pupils widened, a flush stained her cheekbones. Her throat moved with a hard swallow, but she didn't shrink away.

"I don't believe you," she said in a low whisper. "That night in the parking lot, it was a dangerous situation. And every step of the way, you kept trying to protect me from the guy with the BB gun." Her voice gained in strength. "You didn't do one single inappropriate thing except take your shirt off. And I kind of goaded you into that. You want everyone to think you're a bad seed. But you're not."

"Your father thinks I am. You should listen to your father."

"Do you always listen to your father?"

The question slammed into him like an arrow. He flinched backward, unable to hide his reaction. "That's different," he choked. "Your father's a legend, mine was a—"

He pushed away from the cement block wall, raking his hands through his hair. She followed him. "What? Your father was a what?"

"Nothing, anymore."

"He's dead?"

Yes, he was dead. If only he'd died ten years earlier, before he'd taken his first hit of heroin, before he mortgaged the house, gotten into debt, and destroyed every single solid thing in his and Nina's life. "He's dead. And before he was dead, he was bad."

That sour, twisted mouth, the deadened eyes. The memory of his father didn't belong in the same stairwell as Paige Taylor.

"So don't be so sure you know me, Paige."

"But I want to know you."

"Not going to happen." He took her chin in his hand, blocking out the feel of her soft skin. He had to make her understand, make her stay away from him. "I'll do your damn campaign, you can take your photos, but that's it. Don't be thinking I'm some kind of good guy. I've done things and been places you have no idea about."

Their eyes locked, his words echoing around them in the dusty stairwell. He formed his features into the stony, intimidating mask that warned most people off. But at the same time . . . he couldn't help feathering his fingers across her fine skin, a light touch like a butterfly landing on a flower.

Her eyelids fluttered, though she continued to hold his gaze. Behind his hard expression, he felt like a fraud, because all he wanted was to pull her against his body and revel in her softness. Beg her to look at him this way—as if he was worth a damn—all day, all night, tomorrow and the next day.

Rattled by that thought, he dropped his hand. Paige was dangerous, so dangerous, with her shining blue eyes and tempting mouth.

She rapped him on the chest, right over his heart.

Surprised, he dropped his hand from her chin. "No, Trevor Stark, I don't just *think* you're a good guy. I'd stake the future of the Catfish on it."

With a saucy nod, as if that settled everything, she dashed back up the staircase toward the marketing department.

Damn it, once again she'd gotten the last word.

Chapter 8

SHE WAS NOT . . . *not* . . . going to let Trevor rattle her. She'd be a disgrace to the family name "Taylor" if she let that happen. She'd grown up around tough, driven, athletic, freewheeling, occasionally profane men. Granted, that was only when she was with her father, which was during school vacations and summer. But she'd learned early on that you couldn't back down from a man like that. You had to hold your own.

She had her own way of doing that. Her tried and true method with Crush was to let him bluster and lecture, then simply go her own way. Sheer persistence could get you far. There was a Ninja kind of Jedi mind trick to it.

Take road trips. As a girl, when Paige stayed with her father during the season, he left her behind with a nanny when he went on the road. For years she'd begged and pleaded to go with him. He wouldn't hear of it—too dangerous, too boring, too logistically challenging, too distracting. Then the summer she turned twelve, she showed up at Crush's apartment with a four-ring binder filled with photos of landmarks from every city he'd be playing in. The St. Louis Arch, the Empire State Building, the Margaret Mitchell house in

Atlanta. School project, she informed him. If she wrote a personal essay for each city, she'd get extra credit.

He'd laughed so hard he cried. Instead of yelling or crying—which would always earn her a lecture about "no crying in baseball"—her sheer doggedness won him over. She'd traveled with him for several weeks that summer and loved every second of it. Her persistence paid off just in time; it turned out to be his last season, since he retired when she was thirteen.

From what Paige had seen of Trevor Stark, he had some similar characteristics, pigheadedness being right at the top of the list. Well, he could act as tough as he wanted, but she'd seen something in him that night outside the stadium. She'd seen how hard he tried to protect her. Even though she'd been annoyed when he tried to grab the wheel, she understood his reasons. And all those lectures about putting herself in danger . . . bottom line, he hadn't wanted her to get hurt.

Trevor might be a badass, but he was a protective one who related well to troubled kids. He wasn't a bad person, no matter how much he tried to convince everyone.

He definitely had Crush fooled.

"I don't like you being involved with this 'selfie' campaign," Crush told her after whisking her off to dinner at an Italian place near Kilby City Hall.

"It's not just selfies. We're going to do billboards too. And I told you, I want to really dig into something. I want to help you keep the team. Go Catfish. Down with the Wades."

"I like that enthusiasm, it's the company I'm worried about."

"Let me guess. Trevor Stark."

"Bingo." Crush shook parmesan over his pasta with a violence that indicated all sorts of strong opinions about the left fielder.

"I don't get it. He's a ballplayer like all the others. What's your problem with him?"

"He's too good-looking."

Paige took a large swallow of her merlot, remembering his powerful shoulders and crystal green gaze pinning her to the wall in the stairwell. And then that gentle, feathery touch on her cheek. What she wouldn't do to feel that again . . . to stand so close to the molten volcano that was Trevor Stark. "That's absurd. They're all good-looking. That's why they're Baseball's Hottest Outfield."

"I've seen the effect he has on women. I don't want you going near him. I've watched him watching you, and it makes me want to tear his head off."

A thrill traveled through her. Did Trevor really watch her? *Good.*

She decided to toy with Crush a little bit, while also prying some more information out of him. "I'm surprised, Dad. You always talk about how much you respect baseball players who have real talent. Is Trevor not actually all that good?"

Crush pushed his plate to the side, clearing a spot for his forearms, bowing forward with his intensity. "Let me tell you something, Paige. Hitting a major league fastball is the hardest thing in sports, I've told you that. I've seen thousands of players, millions of hits. More importantly, I've *heard* the sound of a bat hitting a ball countless times. Only four times in my life have I heard it sound a certain way. Like a fucking trumpet, like a call from God, like this ball is going to be obliterated and turned to dust because bigger forces are at work. One of those times was Bo Jackson. Another was Mark McGwire. Barry Bonds. And one was Trevor fucking Stark. *That's* how good he is."

Chills rippled up and down Paige's spine. When

Crush Taylor displayed his passion for baseball, it was a sight to see. "Okay, so he's very, very good. Why do you hate him?"

"Because he fucks himself over, again and again. He gets distracted by girls, by drinking, by being a big shot. Sometimes I think he'd rather be a big fish in a small pond than actually develop his gift the way it deserves. He's so goddamn smart, it just about kills me. Do you know that the first time I saw Trevor play, he was nineteen or so, playing in an independent league up North. Michigan, somewhere like that. Buck O'Neil, great scout, calls me up and tells me I have to see this kid. I fly up there and rent a car, drive out to the town park. It's one of those ramshackle teams of misfits, mostly just a chance to drink beer after the game. There's a guy mowing the outfield during the first inning. Anyway, I see this blond kid out there, big, muscular, standing in left field, *reading a book*."

"During the game? He was reading a book?"

"Yup. When a fly ball came his way, he'd put the book on the grass and chase the ball down. Then go right back to his book. I nearly got up and left right then. Disrespect for the game, I thought. Buck says, 'Just wait, you gotta see him hit.' Inning ends, he comes up to bat. Crouches over the plate like a junkyard dog on steroids. And there it is, that sound. Incredible bat speed, tremendous power, horrible form. I knew if he kept that up, he'd blow out his shoulder. I don't know where he got his coaching, but if he was that good without any decent coaching, well . . ." Crush whistled.

"I called up an agent I trust and told him to keep an eye on this guy. Get him somewhere with a good hitting coach and a good manager. Then call me when he's ready for prime time."

Paige put down her forkful of spaghetti. "That was what, five or six years ago?"

"Something like that."

"You've been following him all that time?" She felt a pang of jealousy, since nothing she'd ever done in her life had inspired that sort of interest from her father.

"In between other things, yes." Crush shrugged. "That's me, honey. Baseball is . . . I wouldn't say 'everything,' but close to it. When I see a player who could be great, I take notice. But in the end, it's up to the player. Trevor Stark has taken every opportunity and spit in its face. He's been traded three times, and every time he gets on a major league roster he fucks it up. He should be anchoring the Friars lineup by now, but instead he's here seducing local girls and getting chased by jealous husbands with BB guns. *That's* why I don't like him."

Paige looked down at her plate, uncomfortable at the mention of the night she'd met Trevor. Someone had certainly been chasing him. But did anyone really know the full story? And what about the things he'd said in the stairwell? *I've done things and been places you have no idea about.* She stabbed at a black olive with her fork. "What if there's more to the story, something we don't know?"

Crush reached over and gripped both her wrists. "Oh no, you don't. None of that counseling crap. Don't go thinking you can fix Trevor's problems because you took one class in college."

"Excuse me?" She tugged against his grip, but he didn't let her go.

"Whenever you start spouting therapy crap, I know we're in trouble. I usually zone out and let you go on. But if it starts leading you in directions I don't like—"

Paige finally got her hands free. "Directions *you* don't like? Do you even hear yourself?"

Crush set his jaw, muscles jumping. "You know what I mean. I didn't like Hudson, but you wouldn't listen to me."

She slammed both hands on the table and glared back at her father. "You didn't 'know' Hudson. I'm glad I married him. If he was here right now, I'd marry him again. *Double*."

"Double? What the hell does that mean?"

Paige wasn't exactly sure. All she knew was that her father was pulling his usual King of the Mound act. And that she needed to make a statement, right here and now, if she was ever going to get along with Crush. "It means, Dad, that marrying Hudson wasn't a mistake, no matter what you think. We had three really fun years. I ate some great veal Milanese. I learned a lot about life."

Crush's forehead creased. "Veal Milanese?"

"Yeah, it's got this delicious breading, we used to order it in every city he played in. The point is, I don't regret marrying Hudson." Even though she'd just this moment realized that fact, it felt true. She'd taken a chance with Hudson, and it hadn't gone the way she'd dreamed. But she'd make the same choice again. "I also don't regret meeting Trevor. You have no right to interfere in my love life."

"*Love life*? You're using the word 'love'? That makes me nervous. Are you in love with Stark? Has it gone that far? I'd take ten Hudsons over Trevor Stark. I'll bench him. I'll trade him. I'll—"

She jumped to her feet. "Stop it, Crush. You'll leave him alone and let him do his job. Same applies to me."

With the way Crush glared at her, there ought to have been sixty feet and six inches between them instead of the width of a tabletop. But Paige knew the drill. If she gave in, she'd get trampled. She held her ground, giving thanks that Crush couldn't nail her with a 95-mile-per-hour brushback.

A cool voice interrupted. "Do you know how long I've been waiting for someone to talk to Crush Taylor that way?"

Paige spun around to see a blond woman pausing next to their table. Her hair was sprayed to Texas-big perfection and she wore a tailored black suit and a thin chain that disappeared under a thin pink shell.

"Mayor Trent," Crush said, rising to his feet like the gentleman he occasionally bothered to be. "Must be my lucky day, I get berated by my daughter and scolded by my mayor all at the same time."

"Your daughter?" The mayor turned to Paige with a curious smile. "I'm Wendy Trent, it's good to meet you."

"I'm Paige." They shook hands. All of Paige's life, even during the times Crush had been married, women had pursued him, and she knew the signs well. One of them was the way women looked at her—assessingly, as if to figure out if she was friend or foe.

Wendy Trent didn't look at her like that, but there was something there . . . curiosity, surprise. "Crush must be very protective of his family, since I had no idea he had a daughter."

Paige smiled winningly. "To be honest, I've been locked in the basement for the past twenty-four years."

The mayor laughed, and winked. "Probably safer, knowing the type of people Crush hangs out with."

"Those people are called ballplayers." Crush looked back and forth between the two of them. Nervous? Alert? Something. Paige found the undercurrents fascinating.

"Indeed." The mayor's smile took the edge off her cool tone. "Well, Paige, welcome to Kilby, and if I can do anything to make you feel at home here, you make sure to let me know."

Some instinct told Paige to jump at this opportunity. "Actually, I'm looking for ways to volunteer while I'm here in town. Maybe you could point me in the right direction."

"Well, sure. We love volunteers around here. How do you feel about slugs?"

Crush coughed into his hand as if hiding a laugh.

"Excuse me?" Bewildered, Paige looked from one to the other. They seemed to be in on a shared private joke. *Interesting.* "Actually, I'm more interested in working with troubled kids."

"I see." Wendy directed a sweet smile at Crush. "Have you exhausted the possibilities right where you are? The troubled kids with the catfish on their caps, putting Kilby in the news every time I turn around?"

"If that's a dig at my players," Crush said, "no go, Mayor Trent. The only thing they're at risk for is gaining multimillion-dollar contracts. And the stray bullet now and then."

Paige found it downright fascinating, watching their interaction. She'd never seen Crush outmatched by any woman before. Not even her mother.

Another man appeared at the mayor's shoulder. Eagerly, he shook hands all around, ending with Crush. "It's an honor to meet you. I happened to catch your perfect game in Austin. Unforgettable night, truly fantastic. Great day for the state of Texas all around."

"It was a long time ago," Crush said stiffly. Paige stared in amazement. He usually loved talking about his perfect game, or any game, for that matter. Apparently he didn't want to chat with the mayor's date. More and more interesting.

Crush seemed deep in thought as they drove back

to Bullpen Ranch. Paige wondered if he was thinking about Mayor Trent or about his wayward daughter. Or maybe he was thinking about his most troublesome player. Was it true what Crush said, that Trevor kept screwing up his own chances of making it to the Friars? And why was Trevor so worried about people learning about his work at the Boys and Girls Club? Why did he keep everyone away with his "don't tread on me" attitude? The man was a mystery. One Paige intended to solve, no matter what Crush said.

The next morning, she waltzed into Catfish Stadium bright and early, excited for the first shoot. Not many people knew what ballparks were like first thing in the morning. At that hour, the stadium belonged to the groundskeepers, to the vendors and the cleaning crews, to the management staff and the trainers. It had the same atmosphere as a theater hours before the curtain rises, or a college campus while the students are on spring break. Giant beer delivery trucks backed up to the unloading ramp. The souvenir shops unpacked boxes of Catfish caps and bright blue T-shirts.

When she was little, she'd been awed by the big, smiling baseball players who paraded through her life like friendly giants. Then, at a certain age, she'd seen baseball as the enemy, the thief of her father's time. Now it felt different. For the first time in her life she was *working* in baseball. Working with her father. Baseball wasn't the enemy, it was like a sexy, fascinating new friend she was just getting to know.

She hurried down to the dugout. As she reached the door, she heard raised voices, but didn't pay much attention. Ballplayers—probably arguing about who got the highest score in Grand Theft Auto or something. The smell of wet grass greeted her as she stepped inside

the weather-beaten structure. Sprinklers were gener-
ating misty clouds of condensation in the outfield. A
low wooden bench stretched the length of the dugout,
whose walls were painted a baby blue, like a kitchen
appliance from the sixties.

Some kind of quarrel was unfolding in front of her.
Dwight sat on the bench, bent over a magazine, shielding it from view with his elbows. Shizuko was peering
over his shoulder, his black hair flopping over his forehead. Trevor was trying to snatch the magazine away
from Dwight.

"It's none of our fucking business who she was married to," he snarled at the other two. "Hand that shit
over before I kick your ass."

"Two against one, T," teased Dwight. "You know
I'm a Nessa fan, so step off."

"Everything's easy with Nessa Brindisi." Shizuko
sang the show's theme song, adding his own twist.

"Our Paige is a nice-looking chick, but just look at
that rack." Dwight whistled, holding the tabloid farther
away from his face, as if to view the entire landscape of
Nessa's chest.

"Say one more word . . ." Trevor growled, ice and
murder in his voice.

"Relax, T. We're not the ones who cheated on her in
front of a whole foreign country."

Shizuko was trying to read the article. "Hudson got
signed by the Golden State Warriors. Nice. The upgrade
must have helped his career."

Trevor made an inarticulate sound and ripped the
tabloid out of Dwight's grip.

Paige couldn't take another second, couldn't stand
to see Trevor looking at pictures of her ex-husband and
Nessa Brindisi. Just when she'd stopped picking at the
scab of her divorce, the ballplayers' words ripped it off

all over again. She tiptoed backward, stomach clenching, humiliation washing over her. No matter how far away from Italy she went, she'd never escape this story. The entire world, forevermore, would be talking about the cooking show star and the basketball player.

In her confusion, she didn't notice the rack of bats in the corner until she bumped into it. It teetered precariously; she put a hand out to steady it, but then one bat rolled free and bonked her on the forearm. She snatched her hand back as a cascade of falling timber crashed around her like thunder. Crouching down, she shielded her head with her arms, tears flowing into her fingers.

And then she was being whisked up and away by a force so strong it felt like a tornado.

Chapter 9

TREVOR WAS CARRYING her out of the dugout, through the corridors of the stadium. His scent filled her awareness. Leather and spice, spiked with grass and something else, like the nose-prickling ozone smell that indicates an oncoming rainstorm. He was hauling her through the tunnel like a sack of potatoes. He kicked open the door of a room filled with exercise balls and other medical items and set her on an exam table covered with a white cloth. He kept both hands on her, his warmth penetrating through her clothes. For a player known for his icy control, he sure put out a lot of body heat.

"Do you hurt anywhere? Did any of those bats hit you?"

She tried to answer no, but it came out as a hiccup. Great, now she was making weird sounds on top of everything else. Mortified, she covered her face with both hands. Of all moments to revert to her awkward, gangly worst.

"You have nothing to be embarrassed about," murmured Trevor. "Those guys would be flipping out if they were in a magazine. They have no fucking feelings, that's their problem. Now do you have any bruises? If you don't answer, I'm going to have to put my hands all over you, and I know how you feel about the 'pact of denial.'"

"Give me a minute," she finally managed. The "putting my hands all over you" part sounded pretty appealing, but that would be big trouble, and they both knew it. Trevor stepped back, allowing her a little space. When he returned to her field of vision, he stuck a box of Kleenex under her nose. Gratefully, she took a handful of tissues and blotted the tears off her cheeks. "I'm fine."

"Take a few breaths. You're in the head trainer's room, in case you're wondering. I can go find Terry, if you want. She's a little scary, but she might be nice to you since your father signs her paycheck."

"No, don't leave. I'm okay. I don't think the bats hit me, they just surprised me." She didn't want to talk about the rest of it. The Nessa part.

"I apologize for those guys. I tried to get that tabloid trash away, but Dwight was being a dick. He's probably going to want to buy you a Mercedes or something to make up for it."

She sighed. So much for not talking about the article.

"Dwight didn't do anything wrong. It's a magazine, it's meant to be read. Obviously Nessa and Hudson posed for it. They want people to see it." Her gaze dropped to the tabloid stuffed haphazardly into the front pocket of his jeans. "Let me look at it."

"No." Trevor stepped back, but she snagged it right out of his pocket before he got too far. "Why do you want to look at that crap? It made you cry."

"Everyone else is going to see it. Why not me?" She spread it open on her knees, smoothing out the wrinkles. Nessa, with her voluptuous dark beauty, and Hudson, with his height and sculpted muscles, looked stunning together posed at the TV show's fake counter-top. Hudson held a cupcake in one giant palm, while Nessa put a cherry on top, Betty Boop style, ass sticking out, one hand covering her mouth. She was looking at the camera, while Hudson gazed only at her. *Love is easy with Nessa Brindisi,* read the caption.

"Hudson doesn't even like cherries," she said wistfully. "Cherry anything. He's really hard to buy cough medicine for, but I guess I don't have to worry about that anymore."

Trevor shifted uncomfortably. "I had no idea you were married to an NBA player."

"I wasn't. I married a shy guy from college who got signed by an Italian league." She scanned the article, even though it felt like needles stabbing into her eyes. It included a quote from the owner of the Golden State Warriors, saying how happy he was that Hudson Notswego was going to be anchoring their defense. Nessa Brindisi, his fiancée, planned to move to California with him to explore her options in the entertainment industry.

Resentment washed over her. Everything was working out perfectly for Hudson and Nessa. No one seemed bothered by the fact that Hudson had a wife when he met Nessa.

"It looks like that 'upgrade' worked out well for him."

"Shizuko didn't mean that. He's an ass. He doesn't even speak English all that well."

"Save it, Stark. It's okay. She's a celebrity cooking show host, and I'm a college dropout."

"So? I'd take a thousand Paige Taylors over one ego-maniacal Nessa Brindisi."

Her breath caught. Crazy thoughts cartwheeled through her head. That maybe Trevor liked her. Wanted her. Appreciated her. Afraid to show him how much his statement affected her, she kept her gaze on the tabloid. "You don't have to try to make me feel better."

"I told you, I'm not that nice a guy. I mean it. Nessa is all about Nessa, it's written all over her face."

The garish photo spread blurred. "You were actually looking at her *face*? Dwight and Shizuko were pretty focused on other parts."

"Paige, listen to me." Trevor cupped her chin in his hand and forced her gaze away from the tabloid. "I've been with . . . let's just say, I've seen many women in my time. Bodies are bodies. I'm not knocking them, I appreciate a beautiful woman. Nessa's beautiful. You're beautiful. But you have something else, something she doesn't have."

He'd called her beautiful. Her blood sang in her ears. Trevor Stark thought she was beautiful. Then he ruined everything with the next word out of his mouth.

"Kindness."

Kindness. The word might as well have been a wrecking ball demolishing her confidence like a house of cards. "That's my selling point? Kindness? No wonder he wanted Nessa instead."

"Yeah? Well, he's got his head up his ass. If I had the choice, I'd rather have a girl who'd drive to the rescue of a total stranger, who cares about people, who wants to help people. Why were you at the Boys and Girls Club?"

She didn't answer. *Kindness.* That's what Trevor saw in her. Kindness wasn't sexy. Kindness wasn't fascinating. Kindness could never compare to Nessa's allure.

Trevor was still talking. "You were there to help out, right? To volunteer, see how you could contribute?"

She jumped off the massage table, making him take a step back in surprise.

"You're so full of shit, Trevor. When you see a hot girl at the bar, do you ask her about her volunteer work? No, you check out her boobs or her ass or how willing she is to sleep with you. All those . . . groupies who want your number. Do you make sure they're 'kind' before you screw them?"

"No, but that's just sex. I'm talking about—"

"What, Trevor? Talking about what?"

She must have stumped him, because he just stared at her with a confused frown.

"*Since* you brought up sex, Hudson and I never had a problem in that area until the last year. We had plenty of sex, and it seemed okay to me. But maybe I was wrong and there's a lot more to it, and Nessa has some magic sex formula I just can't compete with, and if she does, I really think as a public service she should share it on her show. Like a recipe. Nessa's recipe for outstanding sex that will keep your man from ever leaving you. She could make millions from that. I'd buy it. But I wouldn't waste it on Hudson, because screw him anyway. We were friends before we got married, and you don't treat a . . . a friend like—" The words stuck in her throat like a chicken bone. She tried, but nothing came out, just a sob. Then another one.

Was it just last night that she'd announced to Crush that she'd marry Hudson again, *double*? She was an idiot, clueless, naïve. She shouldn't be allowed near men. Crush *should* have locked her in the basement for the past twenty-four years.

Trevor's arms came around her, surrounding her with his rock solid weight. "Shh," he murmured. "It's okay."

"No. I . . . I thought I was okay . . . but I just realized . . ." Trembling, she pushed the words out between sobs. "I lost my friend. We . . . we . . . probably should have stayed friends instead of getting married. Now we'll never be friends again. Sorry, my emotions are just all over the place, I guess."

Her grief engulfed her like a tidal wave, and there was nothing she could do to stop it. Anchored to Trevor's strong frame, she let it flow over her, around her, through her. With one big hand gently cradling her head and the other stroking her back, he murmured an occasional "It's okay," or "Go ahead and cry," but other than that said nothing.

As her tears slowed, and the emotion passed, a new feeling came over her. It felt as if the core of her body had been replaced with a well of fresh honey. Warmth and sweetness spread through her veins, until her entire body felt boneless.

"I want you," she whispered to Trevor.

His arms tightened around her. "Don't say that. You're upset. You just had a shock. We agreed. Pact of denial."

"I know all that. It doesn't change anything. I want you. You said you think I'm beautiful." She lifted her head from his chest and tilted it to meet his gaze. His was blazing with heat.

"You are."

"You said you'd take a thousand Paige Taylors. Well, there's one standing right next to you."

"You're not playing fair. I don't want to hurt you."

"Because I'm 'kind'?"

His eyes narrowed, glittering at the scorn in her voice.

"Just a kiss, that's all. Short. Brief. Right here." She pointed to her lips, and watched his gaze follow her finger, then stall. Oh, the way he looked at her, like he wanted to plunge inside her and turn her inside out.

"You're killing me," he whispered. Her lower belly clenched, hard, with an electric jolt of lust.

He leaned down, those crystal eyes pure green flame. His lips brushed hers, just the barest, slightest touch, but enough to make everything stop.

Then, with his body tense as steel, his lips moved against hers. "You are a very dangerous girl, you know that?" It was more of a growl than a question.

"Why?" A breath more than a word.

"Because you make me forget things I shouldn't forget."

Tension arced between them. Everything vanished but this strong, enigmatic man meeting her lips so tenderly, so gently, as if she was something to treasure. As if he wanted her to *know* she was something to treasure. In that moment, she felt as if she saw into his soul, to the wounded, beautiful, caring man within.

With a visible effort, he straightened and snapped the connection. The loss made her shiver. She hugged her arms to her body, searching for her composure.

"Do you mean our pact of denial?" she asked.

"Among other things." She could practically see him retreat from the intimate space they'd just shared. "Are you going to be okay?"

Was she going to be okay? She did a quick survey, inside and out. Physically, she noticed only one twinge in her elbow, where a falling bat must have bruised her. Emotionally . . . actually, she felt pretty good. As if a new part of her had been brought to life. She looked back at the photo spread, still open on the massage table. "It looks so staged, doesn't it? Kind of embarrassing, really."

"Absolutely. Just imagine the shit the Warriors are going to give him. Bet they'll smear cupcake frosting all over his locker or something."

"That shouldn't make me feel better, but it kind of does." She laughed up at him. His gaze dropped to her lips. Desire surged between them again, hot and volatile.

"What the hell is going on in here?" The deep voice of her father made her spin around. Great, just what she needed, her father misunderstanding the situation and taking it out on Trevor.

"Nothing. Trevor was comforting me because of this." She grabbed the tabloid off the table and waved it at him. "Did you know about it?"

Crush transferred his angry glare to Trevor. "Yes, and I was trying to keep you from ever having to see it."

Trevor did his best Greek statue imitation, face like marble, arms crossed over his chest.

"It wasn't Trevor's fault. He didn't write the article, he didn't pose for those photos, and he didn't cheat with Nessa. And actually, I'm glad I saw it. It makes it easier for me to move on."

Crush still held Trevor in his sights. "She's been crying. What'd you do?"

"Don't blame Trevor for that, Dad. And I'm right here. Look at me." She waited until he'd unlocked his gaze from Trevor's. She kept it simple, stating each sentence with careful enunciation. "Trevor was being *nice*. Thanks to him, I feel better. He was comforting me. We now have to do this photo shoot. Okay?"

A muscle in Crush's jaw jumped. "Fine. Just . . . take it easy with the 'nice' shit."

No more touching Paige, anywhere, anytime. It wasn't just that she was sexy and appealing and someone he could look at all day long and not get bored. It wasn't just that he wanted her in his bed. The problem was that when she looked at him, something happened. He felt . . . seen. Appreciated for something other than good looks or baseball.

What she saw, he had no idea. But he couldn't get enough of being with her, talking to her.

And that was bad, bad, very bad news. Could *not* happen again. Not because of Crush Taylor, of course. He couldn't care less what Crush thought of him. Actually, he appreciated how protective the baseball legend was of his daughter. Someone had to be, after what Notswego had done.

After Paige left the room, he ripped the tabloid into little shreds and buried it in the trash. When he reached the dugout, Marcia had arrived and was arranging Dwight and Shizuko for the shot. The marketing head was in her element, though it was funny watching such a tiny woman prodding two big baseball players where she wanted them.

As the center fielder, Dwight took the middle spot, posing with both hands resting on a bat. Shizuko casually rested one arm on Dwight's shoulder and held his glove to his heart. Marcia pointed Trevor to Dwight's other side.

"Turn your body sideways, toward Dwight," she directed. "Fold your arms across your chest and look at the camera."

Just to get this crap over with so he could go murder some baseballs, Trevor did as he was told. He was in no mood to smile for the camera. He kept thinking about the article in the tabloid. The only mention of Paige had come when the reporter referred to Hudson's first wife, the "daughter of sports legend Crush Taylor." It didn't even say her name. As if she'd been whitewashed out of the storybook basketball romance.

The problem was, Hudson didn't know what it felt to be alone in the world. If he did, he wouldn't toss away a wonderful girl like Paige. He would worship the ground she walked on, he'd shower her with love, give her anything she needed. That's what he would—

No. Trevor stopped that thought before it could fully form. The best thing he could do for Paige was keep away from her. If the Detroit guys came for him, if they knew Paige existed, that he'd held her, kissed her . . .

No. No more Paige.

"Uh, Trevor Stark, do you think you could give us more of a smile?" Marcia was saying. "You're going to scare off the little kids."

He spread his mouth wide in a mirthless grimace.

"Maybe we're better off staying in his comfort zone," Paige said to Marcia. "The stare of death."

"The ladies love it," Dwight agreed. "Doesn't have to say a word, just lets his cheekbones do the talking."

Trevor ignored their teasing. "Smile or no smile? I'm here to please."

"How about some sunglasses?" Marcia suggested. "That way it won't matter so much."

Trevor grabbed onto that idea like a lifeline. If he wore sunglasses in the photo, he'd be less recognizable. He'd changed a lot since Detroit, but his eyes were the same. The ballplayers relaxed their pose while he dug in his pocket for the sepia brown shades he often wore against the Texas sun. Once he had them on, he was able to relax.

His new look had the added benefit of allowing him to watch Paige without Crush or anyone else noticing. He wanted to keep an eye on her. After all, she'd been crying her heart out half an hour ago. Now she was back at work, trying to act normal. She might fool everyone else, but he could see how shaky she still was.

Right now she was saying something to Shizuko that made the right fielder smile. Trevor tightened his hands into fists. That Brazilian bastard didn't deserve her kindness. He'd hurt Paige. Trevor muttered something to that effect under his breath.

"Get a grip, man," Dwight said, just as low. "You know you shouldn't be messing with her."

"Keep out of it." Did every damn guy within a thirty mile radius have to be involved in this thing?

"Thought I was your friend."

"Shut up and smile."

They all gathered together for the pose one more time. Dwight grinned, Shizuko looked soulful, and Trevor did the badass thing he did so well. *Click.*

Paige and Marcia high-fived each other, and the ball-players were set free. Crush gave them all a curt nod as they filed onto the field. "Nice work, guys. Prepare to be viral."

Out on the field, Dwight did a few hamstring stretches, while Trevor launched into the light jog that always kicked off his workouts. They each did their own thing for a few moments, then Dwight said, "I was out of line, bro. Paige is a sweet girl and I shouldn't have been looking at those photos. I apologized to her too. She's a cool chick."

Trevor shrugged as if it made no difference to him. "That's between you and her."

"Yeah, and you don't give a shit, do you? No, because you're ice man Trevor Stark and feelings are for pussies."

Trevor shot him an annoyed look but didn't rise to the bait.

"You know, I met Hudson once." Dwight dropped that little nugget of info, then stopped, waiting for Trevor to react. *Don't fall for it. Don't do it.*

But Trevor couldn't help it. "Yeah? What's the ass-hole like?"

"You do like her!" Dwight moved into a lunge, raising his arms over his head in a gesture of triumph. "The mighty Trevor Stark has a crush."

A *crush*? Trevor scrambled to cover his tracks, to bring back the badass Trevor Stark no one would ever accuse of having a crush. "What are you, in third grade? I'm curious about the guy who's fucking Nessa Brindisi, that's all. I want the 411. What I want to know, is cocksucking easy with Nessa Brindisi?"

Dwight didn't laugh, and that's because it wasn't funny, not even a little. Trevor flashed on the memory of Paige staring at that cupcake photo, tears swimming in her big blue eyes. He felt like a total piece of shit in that moment.

"You know something, T? You're a liar. And a coward. I've seen how Paige looks at you. You should go for it. Ask her out. Act like a human being for once. It's not like your life could get any emptier than it is right now. And you know something else?"

Trevor kept jogging in place, letting Dwight's words bounce off him as if they were hitting a wall of ice.

"Stop saying you're my friend if you're going to act like a stranger."

Chapter 10

PAIGE POSTED THE first series of "Baseball's Hottest Outfield" photos on the team's Facebook page the next day. A few hours later a thousand people had clicked *Like*. Not only that, but the viewership of the page soared. It was shared all over the Internet, on Pinterest, on Twitter, on Instagram. It wasn't just that the three men were criminally gorgeous. A big part of the appeal came from their racial mix and the blend of personalities. Trevor the stone-cold badass, Dwight the dynamic charmer, and Shizuko, the soulful rock star.

Paige knew it was all a crock, of course. Trevor wasn't stone cold, Dwight wasn't playful all the time, and Shizuko could outcrude most of the clubhouse, and that was saying something. But once those identities became set, people loved them. They were like cartoon characters instead of real people.

At the next game, the crowd roared when the outfielders took their positions on the field. Fans held up even more signs than they normally did. From the owner's box, Paige scanned the crowd with her binoculars and read the signs out loud to Crush.

"'Kilby Hearts Baseball's Hottest Outfield.' Thank you very much, we heart you too! 'We make 'em hot in

Kilby, Texas.' That might be taking a little too much credit. None of them are from here."

"Details." Crush waved it off. Unlike Paige, he was focused on the game. The Catfish were second in the standings behind the Albuquerque Isotopes, and if they won this game they'd crawl a whole game closer. Unfortunately, the Isotopes were having a great year. The best hope for the Catfish was for a whole bunch of Isotopes to get called up to the Colorado Rockies.

"'Eenie meenie miney moe, catch a Catfish by the toe.' Okaaaaay," Paige said. "Oh, here's a copy of the photo in poster form. That's a great idea, maybe we should sell prints."

"Do it. Make the players sign the prints. If these guys are going to be famous, they need to work on their people skills."

Paige aimed her binoculars at her father. "What do we have here? A Hall of Famer jealous of a bunch of sprouts?"

"Not just any sprouts," he muttered. "But I could still get them out. Every single one."

"Now that would be a good promotion. Let's do it, Dad! Imagine the publicity that would get."

"No way in hell. I don't want to humiliate them."

"Yeah, yeah. All hat, no cattle." She trained the binoculars back on the crowd, having spotted the name Trevor out of the corner of her eye. Yup, there it was. *Trevor Stark*, with the *Stark* crossed out and replaced with *Sucks*. Well, you can't win them all, she thought. Crush probably wasn't the only jealous one out there. Then she looked closer at the man holding the sign. His body shape looked familiar. The last time she saw him, he was aiming a weapon at Trevor.

Chills chased up her spine. "Dad, did they ever arrest the man who attacked Trevor in the parking lot?"

"No, he was gone when the police got there. They never identified him."

"Call Security. I think he's in the crowd." She handed him the binoculars. "The one with the sign."

"Sure looks like the guy on the security tape. And Trevor did mention seeing some threatening signs during the game." He pulled out his cell phone and called the head of Security. When he finished the call, he gave her an odd look. "When did you see that tape?"

"I . . . uh . . . just caught a glimpse of it. Do you think he's dangerous?"

"I'm sure he doesn't have a weapon on him, because we tightened the security checks. But clearly he has it in for Trevor Stark. Yes, baby!"

Paige jumped, having forgotten for a moment that there was a game going on. Jim Leiberman had just hit a single and was bouncing up and down at first plate, yelling something to the Catfish dugout.

Trevor stepped from the on-deck circle—more like strutted, actually. He looked neither at the catcher nor the umpire. The catcher said something to him with a grin, but he ignored it and focused his concentration on the mound.

"See how he's playing mind games with the pitcher?" Crush said. "He's looking through him like he doesn't even exist."

"Really?" Paige aimed the binocs at Trevor. Under his batting helmet, his profile stood out, clear and proud, firm chin, slashing cheekbones. But she couldn't see his eyes or his expression. "How can you tell?"

"I've seen him do it. For most batters, it's a duel between pitcher and batter. For Trevor, it's 'throw me that fucking ball so I can smash it into a million pieces.' He sees the pitcher as more of a delivery boy, and pitchers pick up on that. Rattles them. They always want to start him off with their best pitch just to show him they exist. Watch."

The Isotope pitcher slung a beautiful fastball over the plate. Trevor almost lazily swatted it off into foul territory.

"Strike one, right?"

"Yes, but that pitch is Gordon's best, and Trevor didn't even break a sweat. It's disheartening for a pitcher to have your best stuff shrugged off. That's Stark getting inside his head. Watch, next pitch will be a little wild."

Ball one, which Trevor watched pass by, his posture expressing disdain for the offering. The atmosphere at the plate was pure tension.

"They don't like him, do they, the other team?"

"No opposing player likes Trevor. But they respect the hell out of him. He challenges a pitcher to be his best. If you beat Trevor Stark, that's something to be proud of. He's a pure talent, and you can't deny it. The Catfish didn't like him at first either, because of his reputation. But they do now. Beats me why."

It didn't seem strange to her. Not at all.

Crush's phone beeped with a text. He scanned it, then told her, "Guy with the sign checks out clean. Just an avid Isotope fan, not a stalker."

"Darn. I wish they'd catch that guy."

"I doubt he'll be back, and he definitely won't get a weapon through the gates."

He was interrupted by a *crack* from the field that made them both jump to their feet. The ball flew into the air as if it had rocket boosters. It soared so high Paige nearly lost sight of it.

"It's gonna hit that bird," someone yelled through the cacophony of cheers and stomps.

"Gonna hit the scoreboard!"

But no, it went *over* the scoreboard. "Hot damn," said Crush, clapping his hands together. "That's a frickin' thing of beauty. All right, Stark!" he shouted at the field. Trevor was jogging around the bases on the heels of Leiberman, who bounced along the base paths like an overexcited nine-year old.

"You like him now?" Paige teased her father.

Just then Trevor looked right at the owner's box. Right into Paige's eyes. And smiled. A genuine, heartbreaking, happy smile that just about melted her knees to jelly.

Crush stopped clapping and growled. "Motherfucker."

No one realized just how successful the Baseball's Hottest Outfield campaign had become until the Catfish's first road trip. As the team bus pulled into the El Paso Marriott Courtyards, where the team was staying, a surreal sight greeted them. A throng of teenage girls screamed as the bus arrived. It looked as if the entire high school girl population of El Paso had skipped class to be there.

"Holy freaking shit," said Ramirez. "Some kind of celebrity in town?" He assessed the makeup of the crowd. "Maybe Taylor Swift?"

Then they spotted the giant blow up of the Baseball's Hottest Outfield poster being held aloft in the sea of girls. "Oh boy." Shizuko clambered over the seats and aimed his camera phone out the window. "This is crazier than Kilby."

"Looks like we're big in El Paso," quipped Dwight, though he looked as unnerved as Trevor felt. He stood, even though the bus was still moving, trying to inch into the parking lot without running anyone over.

"Trevor! Trevor!" Girls called his name, held up their iPhones, snapped photos.

"It's the Shiz," another girl yelled.

"The 'Shiz,' you hear that, Shizuko? You got yourself a lame-ass new nickname." Sonny Barnes collapsed into laughter.

"No one out there for me?" Dwight peered out the window. A young girl saw him and started screaming his name. "Dwight, Dwight, I love you, baby! I love you!"

"Geez Louise, is it safe to go out there?" Leiberman crawled over Ramirez to get a closer look. "Do we need bodyguards or something?"

Ramirez pushed him off his lap and stood up, flexing his muscles. "Sonny and me, we got this." The two biggest guys on the team exchanged high fives. "'Course, if any of those girls slips me some cash in exchange for a phone number, it's on."

"I'm the bodyguard here." Duke puffed up his chest. "If anyone's used to dealing with hormonal young people, it's a minor league manager."

"That's cold, Duke," complained Manny Becker, the new catcher.

The bus jerked to a halt and the girls swarmed around the door. Trevor jammed on his shades. "Are you guys seriously afraid of a bunch of fans? I'm going out there, and I'm gonna smile and act nice. Who's with me?"

After working his way through the crowd, he thought facing the Detroit gang might have been easier. Everyone wanted to touch him, talk to him, stare at him. It was insane and it made him very uncomfortable. *I'm just a loser from Detroit*, he wanted to scream. *I spent three years in juvie. I grew up in a shithole with a druggie father and I'll have a target on my back if certain people ever figure out who I am.*

The words were so loud inside his head that he couldn't believe no one heard them. But people saw what they wanted to see, and in his case they saw a good-looking ballplayer with a big contract. If *that* Trevor Stark had a worry, it would be about the next ball game, or which girl he'd take out that night. So he signed scraps of paper, notebooks, wrists, shoulders, whatever the girls offered. Luckily, no one felt inspired to present a boob in the parking lot of the Marriott Courtyards.

"How many dates you line up for tonight?" Dwight asked as they finally broke free from the crowd and made it through the glass doors.

Normally he would take someone out for an expensive steak—a different girl every night, of course. He had to keep the "legend of Trevor Stark" alive. Tonight he wasn't in the mood for any of that.

"Zero. Just me and my pillow."

"Any particular reason why?" Dwight shot him a narrow-eyed look.

Yes, because there was only one woman he wanted to talk to, and he wouldn't see her until she met them at the Children's Hospital the next morning. But he didn't say that.

"Because I don't like checking a girl's ID before I take her out."

"I hear that."

Dwight's usual easy smile was a little tight. As they approached the concierge desk, Trevor racked his brain for a way to get things back to normal. "What about you? Got a hottie on the line?"

Dwight signed his name on the registration slip the clerk passed to him.

"I was thinking I might see what Paige is up to. I owe her for the other day. Since me and Hudson met once, I figure she might want to pour her heart out to me. I'm a good listener. Everyone knows that about me."

Trevor's entire body went rigid. "Paige isn't here yet. She's meeting us tomorrow."

"I heard she's staying in town tonight, just like the rest of us. Might even be here at this hotel. Ain't going to let details stand in my way if I can be of assistance to the lovely Paige Taylor."

Without a word, Trevor scrawled his name on the registration form and headed for the bank of elevators. Either Dwight was messing with him or he was trying to goad him. Fuck him either way.

In his hotel room, he slung his overnight bag on top of the rack, then paced around the room a few times. He splashed cold water on his face, hoping to clear his head. But all he could see was Paige's wide smile and sparkling blue eyes, her tumbling hair and golden spray of freckles. What would her intimate skin be like, the skin not revealed to the public, to the sun? More freckles, or would she be all cream and sugar?

He slammed off the faucet and stood up, head dripping. After dragging a towel across his face, he snatched up his phone.

Got mobbed at the hotel. Campaign is working.

After a few minutes of agonizing delay, she answered. *I heard. Ur a superstar.*

Feel more like a super idiot.

Price of fame, hotshot.

Then he put it out there. *Want to talk?*

Talk? What do you mean?

Pour your heart out. About your ex and all. Wasn't that how Dwight had put it?

No way. I'll talk about anything EXCEPT Hudson.

Was that a yes? He couldn't tell exactly. *Gotcha.*

Filled with a surge of energy, he flipped through a restaurant app on his phone and found a good steakhouse. *Pick you up at 7?*

You mean, like for a date?
Yah. Does that break the pact of denial?

Long pause with no communication. Then, *See you at 7. Room 243. No steakhouse, plz. I've heard stories about you and steakhouses.*

Oh Lord. Sometimes his reputation was a chain around his neck. Quickly, he deleted the steakhouse and did a search for sushi. Sushi would make him look sophisticated, right?

A grin spread across his face. Paige had agreed to go out with him. He was going to have dinner with her. He was going to experience an entire evening in her presence, soaking in her smiles, her expressive blue eyes, her soft skin.

No touching, though. He'd have to stick to the "no touching" rule or he'd be doomed from the first appetizer.

But before he could even get to that appetizer, everything changed. A knock sounded at his door.

"I'm not here," he called. There was only one person he wanted to talk to, and he was going to see her at seven.

"It's me," answered a soft, female voice. Young-sounding. One of the girls from outside?

"Sorry, sweetheart, this isn't happening unless you have a note from your parents."

A short silence, then a wry response. "That would be difficult. Dad wasn't much for writing notes, even when he was alive."

The realization hit him in a wave of pure shock. He bounded off the bed and raced to the door. When he swung it open, his heart nearly stopped. There in front of him stood Nina.

Chapter 11

AFTER A QUICK scan of the hallway, Trevor dragged his sister into his room. "What the hell are you doing here? Sorry." He raked a hand through his hair. "Are they feeding you? You look so skinny."

She laughed. "Trevor, I'm twenty-one years old. No one's feeding me, that's my job now."

"Right, right." He ran his hands up and down her arms. "Are you okay? Did someone find you? What are you doing here?"

Her lower lip quivered. "Don't I get a hug from my big brother?"

"Oh God. Of course you do." He snatched her into his arms, his gut churning with emotion. Topmost among them, fear. He dragged her over to edge of the bed and sat her down. Scanning her from head to toe, he noticed heavy bags under her eyes, strain on her achingly lovely face. His sister had always been pretty, even as a twelve-year-old. The twenty-one-year-old version was no tomboy leaping over broken glass. Eyes the shade of melted caramel, cropped blond hair, strong winged eyebrows like punctuation marks, all added to her fairylike appearance.

If the Detroit guys got ahold of her . . . the thought made him literally sick, bile seeping into his throat.

"Why'd you come here?"

"I told you I wanted to come to one of your games."

"I said I'd think about it."

"Well, I thought about it, and I decided one of your away games would be much safer. You're here to play the Chihuahuas." She giggled at the name.

"Don't laugh, the Chihuahuas are a tough team."

"I'm not surprised. Chihuahuas are much tougher than you might think. You try clipping their toenails and see what happens."

Trevor had a sudden vision of clipping the El Paso Chihuahuas' toenails and let out a bark of laughter. "So you're still working at the dog groomers?"

"Yes. I got a promotion and a raise. And a few days off. So I checked the Catfish schedule online and I saw that you were playing here in El Paso. It's only a few hours away from Tucson."

"How did you get here? Did you take a bus?"

She tilted her head back. "You're looming. Do you have to loom?"

He realized he had his arms crossed over his chest as if he were a bouncer. "Sorry." He dropped his arms but couldn't bring himself to sit still. "Did anyone see you?"

"Yes, but it's okay because I used that cool memory deactivator from *Men in Black*."

"This isn't funny, Nina. It's life or death. I'm not going to allow anything to happen to you."

She dropped her head, staring at the backs of her hands. "I know that," she said in a small voice. "That's the problem."

"*What?*" He didn't like the sound of that one bit. He resumed looming over her. If he had to use his size to prod some common sense into her, he would.

"It doesn't feel right making you suffer for the rest of

your life. It was one thing when I was twelve and couldn't make my own decisions. But I'm grown up now."

"You're barely twenty-one. And you're . . . my little sister."

At that, she swung her head up, eyes flaring. "You were only fifteen when you went to juvie. You had to grow up in a hurry."

A big hurry, but he didn't want to talk about the past. "Yeah, and . . . it's done. I did my time, and I don't regret a second. End of story."

"But it isn't the end of *my* story. What do you think it's like for me, knowing how much it cost you?" Face twisted with passion, she surged to her feet. "I can't live with this, Trevor. We're both living in fear all the time. It's like those guys are in our head, controlling everything we do. You have a different name, we hardly ever see each other. They destroyed our lives once, but now we're doing it to ourselves! And I hate it."

"Nina, Nina . . ." He caught her against him, making shushing noises. She was overwrought, that was all. If he could just get her through this crisis, everything would go back to normal. Or what passed for normal since that one brutal night.

"I know what you're doing," Nina murmured against his shirt. "You're trying to pacify me. It's not going to work. We deserve better, Trevor. We deserve to have regular lives. Get married, have families. None of this is our fault."

Her words found their way to a part of him he'd tried to kill off. The part that believed there was more to him than the baseball intimidator or the off-hours lady-killer. He couldn't go there, couldn't let that wound get ripped open again. But he also didn't want to get her more upset.

"It's not our fault, but it got dumped on us and we have to deal with it. We can't just pretend it's not real."

"I'm not! I know it's real, I can't ever forget it." Those words seemed to rip right of her heart. "And every time I pick up the phone to call you and my heart races because I know it's a risk, I remember all over again. Every time I see a baseball game on TV, or even a baseball cap, I think about you and how I should be there for you, rooting you on. It's not right, Trevor. It's not right and I hate it."

"Shhh, shhh. You have to calm yourself, sweetheart." He soothed slow circles across her back. "Whatever we do, we have to do it carefully. We can't be reckless. You understand?"

Slowly, she nodded. "I'm sorry for rocking the boat, Trevor. But it's been eating at me. It's like I can't move on with anything until I make this right."

"Honey, you did nothing wrong. Now let's talk about something else. We have a lot to catch up on. Are you hungry?"

At her eager nod, he remembered that he had a "date" with Paige. Picking up his phone, he saw that it was already after seven. Crap. Standing up Paige Taylor was the last thing he wanted to do. "Let me just text someone quickly."

"I'm interrupting something."

"No . . . I mean, I had plans, but nothing that can't be changed."

He was composing a text to Paige when a knock on the door made him startle. Nina's eyes went huge. "I wasn't followed, I swear," she whispered.

Trevor's mind raced. It could be Dwight, Duke, any of the guys . . . it didn't have to be something menacing. "Go in the bathroom while I see who it is," he said tensely.

"Be careful," she hissed, and scampered into the bathroom. He had a flash of ten-year-old Nina and how she used to play hopscotch on the front walk, hopping between irregular boxes drawn in blue chalk. Despite his fear, it was good to have her with him. It meant he didn't have to worry about what was happening in her life. She was a few feet away, and that made something inside him relax.

The hotel door had no peephole, so he called through it, "Who's there?"

"Your seven o'clock date, reporting for duty," came the answer.

Paige.

Shit, what should he do about Paige? He didn't want to blow her off; what if she took it personally and never spoke to him again? "I . . . uh . . ." He coughed. "Think I'm coming down with something. Can I take a rain check?"

A short silence. "Sure, Stark. We can reschedule for some time when you don't have a baseball groupie in your hotel room."

A *what*? "That's not it, I promise." He coughed again, making a bigger production out of it, adding a gasp for air at the end.

"That is the fakest cough I ever heard." Paige called. "You sound like Jerome with a hair ball." She made a god-awful sound in her throat, sounding just like a cat hacking up a dust bunny. "You don't need to lie to cancel a date, you know. And believe me, I know when a man is lying. I've had on-the-job training."

Trevor cringed, leaning his forehead against the door. He hated deceiving Paige. But he couldn't tell her the full truth either. "I don't have a groupie in here. I wouldn't do that to you."

"You do whatever you want, Trevor. See you at the shoot tomorrow."

He heard soft footfalls receding down the hallway carpet. He swore under his breath. She'd probably never want anything to do with him again.

"Move," said Nina from behind him, shoving him out of the way. "I'm not going to be responsible for messing up your love life too." She flung open the door.

"Nina," he hissed, but it was too late, she was already flying down the hallway.

"Paige?" Paige turned to see a pretty blond girl running down the hall toward her. "Please come back. Trevor handled that very badly, but he really does want to have dinner with you. I can stay in the hotel room while you guys are gone, that's fine with me."

Paige blinked a few times. Baseball groupies were apparently very open-minded, despite being so young and innocent-looking. "I don't want to get in the way," she said stiffly.

"As if!" The girl smiled and took her by the wrist to guide her back to Trevor's room. "I can tell by the way Trevor was talking to you that he really likes you."

Paige glanced up the hallway. Trevor was planted in front of his room, a stormy expression on his face. "Good to know," she said dryly.

The girl lowered her voice. "He's going to be mad that I told you this, but I'm Trevor's sister, Nina. He's very sorry he faked the hair ball, but he was doing it to protect me. Will you come back?"

Trevor's sister? Oh now, that wasn't fair. Not only did she feel like an idiot, she felt like a *clichéd* idiot. Now that she looked more closely, the girl's resemblance to Trevor was hard to miss. Same hair color, same cheekbones, same angelic good looks. Of course, Trevor's were in the form of a hard-bodied ballplayer, so they were hardly identical.

"I didn't know Trevor had a sister," she said. "Nice to meet you, Nina. I'm Paige."

Nina took her hand and tugged. "Please come back, pretty please. I surprised Trevor by showing up out of the blue, but I don't want to mess up his social life."

"No no, it's not like that," Paige protested. Nina ignored her, dragging her back to the living storm cloud that was Trevor Stark. When they reached the door, Nina skipped past him, but Paige stopped short, unwilling to go inside. While she was relieved that Trevor hadn't been stashing a groupie in his room, he'd still lied to her. He'd faked a cough so she wouldn't meet his sister.

Levelly, she met his eyes, glittering chips of Caribbean ice, a contradiction if ever there was one. "Well?"

He held her gaze for a long moment, then, as if he couldn't help himself, gave her a quick head-to-toe assessment. She'd dressed for her "date" with him. Could anyone blame a girl for wanting to look her best for Baseball's Hottest Outfield? She'd dug up a Pucci dress she picked up at a flea market in Naples. It clung happily to her body in psychedelic swirls of green and hot pink. It ended halfway down her thighs, with lots of leg exposed between the hem and her favorite cowboy boots.

"Damn," he breathed. "You really know how to make a guy regret a coughing fit."

The heat in his eyes scrambled her brain. "Yeah, well . . ." was all she could manage. Electric energy pulsed between them.

"I'm sorry," he finally said. "I didn't know Nina was coming. I . . . was rattled."

"Big Bad Trevor Stark, rattled? Don't tell the other teams, they might try to hire her."

He didn't seem to think that was funny, since he

scowled. His hand tightened on the edge of the door. "Well, Paige Taylor . . . are you finally going to take me up on my invitation to my hotel room? I've been waiting since that first night we met."

"Poor baby. All sad and lonely, no doubt."

He raised an eyebrow. "Yes, as a matter of fact."

Well . . . now she was rattled. Trevor Stark, lonely? She walked in, telling herself not to make a big deal out of it. According to the rumors, girls frequently shared his hotel rooms. Was he saying that wasn't true?

Inside the room, Nina was crouched in front of the minifridge. "There's nothing in here except a bottle of water."

"I have some protein bars in my overnight bag," Trevor told her. "If I'd known you were coming, I'd have packed some animal crackers."

She straightened up, her entire face beaming as if it had been replaced by the sun. "You remembered."

"Of course I remembered." Voice gruff, Trevor shoved his hands in his front pockets. "We don't see each other very often," he explained to Paige in a mutter.

"Last time we lived together was when I was twelve and he was fifteen. I just turned twenty-one." Nina uncapped the bottle of water and drank about half of it in one long swallow.

"Nina," Trevor warned in a low voice. Clearly, there was a story here, a story Trevor didn't want to tell. Paige was torn between wanting to grill Nina for every bit of information she could and respecting Trevor's privacy. She decided on the latter.

"I only have half brothers and sisters. One of each. I don't see them much either."

Trevor shot her a grateful look, but Nina paid no attention to their attempt at shifting the subject. "I came to see Trevor so he can take me to one of his baseball games. Can you believe I've never seen one in a real ballpark? You probably have, right?"

Paige laughed. "You could say that. My father was a baseball player. A pitcher. His name is Crush Taylor."

Nina plopped down on the bed and stared at her. "Oh my gosh. You're Crush Taylor's daughter? The owner of the team?"

"How do you know about Crush?" Trevor asked her sharply.

"I have Internet, you know. I follow your teams. So far I like the Catfish best. You know who I like? Jim Leiberman. His official team photo is so adorable. Do you think I could get his autograph?"

Her wistful tone made Paige's heart melt. Despite her love-hate relationship with baseball, she couldn't imagine never seeing a game, never breathing in the heady scent of a ballpark, witnessing the thrill of a home run or a perfect double play. "What are you doing tomorrow afternoon?" she asked impulsively.

"She's going to be on a Greyhound bus," said Trevor. "Nonstop, express."

Nina bounded across the room and clasped Paige's hands in hers. "Tomorrow's the game against the Chihuahuas, right?"

"It is. I have field level seats, since I'm a member of the Catfish organization. If you come with me, you can watch your brother from only a few yards away."

"Really?" Nina's ecstatic expression was a shocking contrast to Trevor's grim one. "Oh, Trevor, can I? Please?"

"No," he said in a quelling voice. "That's not a good idea."

"I don't see why not." Paige looked from one to the

other, completely confused by the undercurrents passing between them. Nina's face fell, but she didn't offer any protest. "Nina, can you give us a minute?"

The girl swiveled her head to check with Trevor. For Pete's sake, couldn't she make any decisions on her own? At Trevor's quick nod, she skipped back into the hallway. "I'm going to find the Coke machine and stock up. Any requests?"

Paige and Trevor both shook their heads. As soon as the door had closed behind her, Paige whirled on Trevor. "Why on earth can't Nina come to a game?"

"She hasn't been to one so far, why start now?"

That made absolutely no sense. "Is it a superstition or something?" Most ballplayers were prone to superstitions. Crush used to eat exactly twenty-five sunflower seeds before each start. "You think Nina would bring you bad luck?"

"I don't believe in luck. I don't believe in superstition. I just don't want Nina at the game."

"But *why*? Give me one reason that makes any kind of sense."

He ran his hand across the back of his neck. "Maybe I'll get distracted."

"You won't. I've seen you out there. Your focus is phenomenal. But even if you got distracted, so what? One game isn't going to make or break you."

"I have a responsibility to the team to play my best."

"But what if you play even better with your sister in the stands? Did you ever consider that?"

An odd expression flashed across his hard face, and she could just imagine his inner scoffing at the idea of playing "even better."

"Your sister just came to see you all the way from . . . where does she live?"

Trevor didn't answer.

"From wherever she lives, and you're refusing to let her watch you play? That seems pretty cold, Trevor."

"I'm a cold man." Since his face resembled a frozen mask, it was hard to argue with that. Except she saw the rapid pulse in his neck, the dilated pupils that turned his eyes dark.

"You're not." She shook her head vigorously. "I know you're not. Something else is going on. And I'm going to find out what it is."

Quick as lightning, he wrapped his big hands around her upper arms and dragged her against his chest. The sudden contact sent tremors through her. "Damn it, Paige. I'm a prick and everyone knows it. Why can't you just leave it at that?" He spoke low, fierce and passionate. In his eyes she read hunger, fear, desperation, and blazing, blazing heat. It was like being trapped in the force field of a two-hundred-pound magnet—she couldn't have looked away if she'd wanted to. It would have been physically impossible to break the connection between them.

His gaze shifted, became more personal, scanning her face, her mouth, consuming her, warming her. Her lips throbbed—literally throbbed—and parted. He lowered his head and a soft gasp escaped her. She could feel the kiss building in the air between them, like a flame before it's lit. A chemical combustion stirred, ready to burst into life.

A soft tap on the door made Trevor jerk upright. She took a step back, freeing herself from his grip as his hands fell away.

"Oh no, Trevor Stark," she croaked, her voice hoarse. "You are *not* cold."

Chapter 12

IN THE SHORT time that Trevor had known Paige, he'd learned that telling her what to do didn't usually turn out that well. Maybe he should have begged her to bring Nina to a game. Begged to let her come to the shoot at the Children's Hospital. But Paige wasn't easily manipulated in any direction, which was why Nina spent the next day hanging around Baseball's Hottest Outfield.

At the hospital, Trevor grudgingly introduced Nina to the other players. Dwight bowed over her hand, then directed a glare at Trevor.

"I told you all about my baby brother, but I was thinking you were hatched in a lab or something. This is what I'm talking about, dude. This kind of thing. Secrets."

"My sister and I haven't seen each other in a while," he muttered, feeling like an ass, once again.

"Don't be mad at him," Nina begged. "If you knew the whole story, you wouldn't be mad."

"*Nina.*"

"Sorry."

The way Nina was spilling things, he was shocked she'd managed to keep their secret this long. He had to get her back to Tucson before she made any fatal mistakes.

"Just so you know," Paige whispered as they walked into the Children's Wing of the El Paso Memorial Hospital, "I arranged this shoot. It's a PSA asking for donations to the children's programs. I thought that might make you happy."

"It would make me happy if Nina went home."

"Are you worried about all the ballplayers who might fall in love with her?"

Trevor gave a double-take. With all his other concerns, that one had never come up. "She's just a kid."

"Isn't she twenty-one? Just three years younger than me. How old is Manny Becker?"

Manny Becker didn't even own a razor yet. "Oh shit." Panic seized him. "We have to get her out of here."

"Would you stop? You're worse than my dad. She seems like a sweet girl who deserves to have a little fun."

Marcia joined them at that point, and bustled Trevor toward the play area where a large Catfish banner had been set up as a backdrop. Five or six kids were grouped in front of it, two with shaved heads, one in a wheelchair. Shizuko and Dwight were already in position, chatting with the kids and signing baseballs.

Trevor took his usual "left field" positioning. Too bad he hadn't brought his baseball collection. But that would lead to too many questions anyway. He slipped on his shades and assumed his usual badass pose. Nina stood next to Paige, watching with her hands clasped under her chin, looking as thrilled as if it were a real movie set.

Maybe this wasn't such a bad idea after all, Trevor reflected. Since Nina was here, why not show her what her big brother's life was all about? As he posed, he stole a glance at Paige and his sister. Nina was whispering something to Paige as if the two had known each other forever. Warmth blossomed in his chest. It felt so good to be near Nina again. And Paige . . . always so warm, so welcoming, so . . . kind . . .

A smile must have snuck onto his face. "Stay in character, Trevor," Marcia warned as she took another shot. "Don't mess with perfection."

Right. People wanted nasty Trevor, and that's what they should get. He erased all trace of that smile off his face.

After the shoot, the kids, all wearing huge grins, were escorted back to their rooms.

"Don't go anywhere yet," Marcia told the players in her rat-a-tat voice. "There's one more shot I want to get. We're aiming for viral, and a big piece of that is inter-activity. We asked fans for ideas on the team Facebook page. The biggest request was that we do a shot without those shirts. What do you say we give them what they want?"

Trevor went cold as a walk-in freezer. Taking off his shirt in the clubhouse was one thing. The guys were more focused on their showers than anything else, and no one noticed how quickly he showered, how he spent the minimum amount of time getting dressed. But strip-ping down, right here, right now, with this audience of hospital workers, not to mention Paige and Nina? No.

"Sorry, I have a nudity clause in my contract," he joked.

But Dwight had already ripped off his shirt and was showing off his chiseled form. "Anything for the fans. They want us to lose the pants too? Just say the word."

Nina giggled. In Trevor's opinion, she was doing en-tirely too much of that around the Catfish.

Shizuko slowly removed his shirt, revealing a golden expanse of hard chest muscles, with some inked letters. "Make sure you get my tattoo in the shot. It's a Japa-nese love poem from the twelfth century."

"Mine's a quote from Jackie Robinson." Dwight rolled his shoulder forward to demonstrate. "T, you got a bird or something, right?"

Marcia clapped her hands. "Brilliant, guys! We'll do one frontal shot, then another in which we can see all your tattoos."

"You don't want to see all of mine," Dwight winked. "Gotta keep this R rated."

Laughter from the audience. Even Paige was smiling, while Nina had gone bright pink. Trevor stood frozen. His hawk tattoo, which covered nearly his entire back, had been carefully designed to hide the scars he'd acquired in juvie. He refused to let Nina see them. How could he get out of this?

"I'll do the shirtless thing, but not the ink," he said, pulling his shirt over his head. "That's private. And make it quick, my sister's here and I want to show her around."

Making sure his back was to the banner, he flexed his arm muscles and glared at the camera—not hard to do, since he was pissed as hell. Dwight and Shizuko struck their poses, and Marcia clicked the camera. Trevor refused to look in Paige and Nina's direction. *Just get this over with, quick quick quick.*

As soon as Marcia stopped taking photos, Trevor bent to retrieve his shirt. But Dwight was doing the same thing at the exact same time, and they collided halfway down. He nearly fell forward, catching himself with one hand on the floor. In the process, his back rotated forward, just for a moment.

He straightened up and yanked his shirt back on. Finally daring to glance in Nina's direction, he saw that her face had gone completely white. *How?* she mouthed.

He went with the Face of Stone. No explanations, no discussions. "Can we get back to playing ball now?"

For just a second he caught Paige's eye. Damn, that girl was sharp. Her arms were folded across her chest and she was looking from the still-shaken Nina to him. He was going to have to be a lot more careful around her.

Although he tried like hell to avoid her, Nina managed to maneuver him into the men's bathroom on their way out of the hospital. "That's the Wachowski emblem, isn't it? The same one Dad had on his shoulder."

"I don't want to talk about it."

"I know you didn't have it before you went to juvie. They did it to you, didn't they? You never would have done that to yourself. You hate those guys. They found you and they did that to you."

"It's over, Nina. It happened, now it's over."

She shoved at his chest. "You got branded when you were in juvie. You didn't even tell me. How am I supposed to live with that?"

"You just have to." He made every word count, as if each one was final. "Do you want to make it up to me? Just keep your mouth shut about anything to do with us. I'm begging you."

Tears swam in her eyes. "It doesn't feel right, Trevor. It just doesn't."

"I'm sorry. Now come on, sweetheart." He hustled her out of the bathroom before she could have a meltdown. "Just stick with Paige, enjoy the ball game, and we'll have dinner tonight. Then you're going home. That's all I want. Promise to give me what I want?"

Sniffling, she wiped away tears with the heel of her hand. "I don't know, Trevor."

"Making your sister cry, Trevor?" Paige emerged from the women's bathroom next door, suspicion drawing her face into a frown. "Why am I not shocked?"

Before Trevor could lob a comeback, Nina erupted. "Why does everyone think everything has to be Trevor's fault? My brother is a *good person*. Better than that! He's a great person. It's not his fault that I'm crying, I mean, I'm crying *because* of him but not because he said or did anything, just because it's wrong that people automatically blame him no matter what, it's just wrong."

Trevor gritted his teeth through her entire outburst, just waiting for Nina to spill the words that would alert Paige. But Nina was used to hiding the truth. They'd both been doing it for so long, it was second nature. Nothing she said would point Paige toward Detroit or the past.

When Nina was done, Trevor attempted a smile at Paige. "We were reliving some childhood shit and it got a little heavy. Right, Nina?"

His sister nodded, still looking seriously unhappy. But he had an idea of what would cheer her up.

"Paige, is that offer of front row seats still good?"

"Of course." Speculation shimmered in Paige's wide blue eyes, but she left it at that.

"Great. Go with Paige, little sis." He kissed Nina on the top of her head. "All I ask is that you don't draw too much attention to yourself and that you don't look at any of the players."

"*What?* How am I supposed to do that?"

Paige shook her head and took Nina's hand. "Come on. I'm going to teach you every trick I know about dealing with bossy, interfering family members."

In the field level box, Paige introduced Nina to Crush. Like everyone else, he did a surprised double-take at the news that Trevor had a sister.

"Why do the players seem so shocked that your

brother has a family?" she asked Nina as they took their seats. "Everyone acts like he's a marble statue come to life or something."

"He definitely has a family," said Nina. "But not exactly a normal one." She snapped her mouth shut and clamped her hand over it.

"Well, don't worry, girl," Crush said. "You and Paige ought to have a lot in common, then. No normal families around here." He winked, and Paige experienced a rush of affection for her cynical father. He had many, many faults, but at least he never put on a false front.

Unlike Trevor, whose front was more like a glacier.

She scanned the crowd, spotting signs for Baseball's Hottest Outfield even here in enemy territory. She also noticed a "Baseball's Horniest Outfield" and a "Baseball's Sluttiest Outfield" sign. Well, that sort of thing was to be expected—all part of the viral nature of the campaign.

They all stood for the National Anthem. Paige watched Trevor, noticing how his eyes kept wandering to their section, and how his face would lighten at the sight of Nina. This slim blond girl must know all sorts of secrets about the man of mystery who had fascinated her. Was there a way to pry them out of her without alarming her?

They sat down as the Catfish pitcher—Dan Farrio, according to the announcer—began warming up. She decided to do the same. Start with some simple warm-up pitches.

"So," Paige began casually, "how long do you think you'll be staying?"

"I don't know. It depends on Trevor."

"I hope you can come to Kilby too. You can visit us at Bullpen Ranch." Keeping with the pitching analogy, Paige thought of this as a setup pitch, something to lull and misdirect the batter. Maybe some of her father's baseball talk was rubbing off on her.

"That would be awesome!" Nina's face dimmed. "But I'll probably just go back after this."

"If it's a long trip home, you should probably wait until tomorrow." Slider, inside. A sneaky question disguised as a kind statement.

"It's not too long," Nina said warily.

Paige decided to change tactics. "You know, the first time I heard Trevor's last name, I thought 'Iron Man.' Where does the name Stark from?"

Nina giggled. "He chose it because of the movie, how'd you guess?" She clapped her hand over her mouth again. "I mean, it's just a coincidence, and I guess it's Russian or something, because—" She clapped her other hand on top of the first, her eyes wide with distress above them.

So . . . Stark wasn't Trevor's real last name, and they came from a Russian background, which made sense given their blond, Northern European good looks. Paige filed the information away, but felt so awful about upsetting Nina that she decided to ask no more questions.

She put her arm around the girl. "Nina, listen to me. Trevor's a Catfish, and that makes him a member of the family. You're among friends here. You have nothing to worry about."

But Nina was looking into left field, where Trevor patrolled the grass like a six-foot-three panther. "He's a really good player, isn't he?"

Crush leaned over. "He is. You should be real proud of your brother."

"Does he always look so mean?"

"That's his game. He plays to win. If you could get your brother to behave himself off the field, he'd be starting for the Friars before you know it."

"Oh, that's not going to happen," said Nina wistfully. "Not for a long time, anyway."

Paige exchanged a confused look with her father. Why on earth would Trevor not make it to the Friars? Wasn't that the entire purpose of a baseball career? "Why not, Nina?" Paige asked gently, breaking the promise she'd just made. "He's got the skills, even I can see that."

Nina looked like she wanted to cry. "Nothing. I just mean, it seems like it's taking forever, that's all, and I shouldn't have come here."

"No, sweetie, it's all good." Paige squeezed her shoulder in comfort, but a roar from the crowd interrupted her. The Chihuahuas batter had fouled off a pitch. The ball was plummeting toward their section. A kaleidoscope of players moved after it, with Leiberman, the shortstop, closest to it, motoring across the infield lines. The third baseman and Trevor were also running toward the action. Trevor yelled something, and Leiberman yelled back, "I got this!"

He closed in on the stands, his eyes riveted to the ball. Paige looked up and saw that it was dropping more or less toward their heads. Acting on instinct, she plastered her body over Nina's. More shouts from the field, gasps from the crowd, and then—with a loud thump, Jim Leiberman tripped on the barrier between the field and the stands and flew across the top of the seats. The occupants had already scurried out of the way, leaving the seats clear for him to land across the seat backs, belly down, like a young whale beached on rocks.

He stared at them, his face only a few inches away.

"Hey, Bieberman." Shakily, Paige peeled herself away from Nina. "Nice play." Emerging from behind Paige, Nina blinked in complete confusion at the scene around her.

"What just happened? Who are you?"

Leiberman blushed. "I'm . . . uh . . . Jim Leiberman and I'm the shortstop for the Catfish. Hi Crush, hi Paige. I was . . . uh . . . looking for the ball."

To their left, Crush burst out laughing. "Did you check your glove, boy genius?"

"Oh." Leiberman seemed to have trouble pulling his gaze away from Nina's flushed face. Finally he opened his glove. The ball nestled inside like a pearl. "I got it!" he yelled behind him.

"Head's up, Bieberman," Trevor called. He and the third baseman grabbed him by the legs and lifted him away from the stands. The shortstop held the ball triumphantly into the air, to wild applause and some boos from the El Paso fans.

As the Catfish players set Leiberman's feet on the ground, he took one peek back at Nina, who sent him an adorable little wave. Trevor gave Leiberman a cuff on the shoulder. On his way back to the outfield, he shot a look at Paige, one scorching glance that seemed to sink right into her soul.

On someone's handheld radio, the announcers were going nuts. "Take that, Baseball's Hottest Outfield. An infielder makes the play of the game. It's not a guy who gets a lot of attention, usually. Jim Leiberman is one of those low-profile players who doesn't necessarily grab the headlines, but holy Catfish. That was some play. Looked like he was body-surfing out there."

"Sure did. If he was trying to get Crush Taylor to notice him, he picked an interesting way to do it. Just crash into the seats right in front of him. Was it my imagination, or was he making a little light conversation with some ladies out there?"

"Well, we are talking about the Catfish, after all. You never know with these guys. They've always been on the quirky side, but that could change if Crush is forced to give up the team."

"True that. So far, the Catfish seem to be rallying to the cause. Since Crush made his famous vow, they've been steadily inching up in the standings. Should be an interesting summer down in Kilby. Up next, we have El Paso third baseman . . ."

Nina had been listening closely. "Why did you call him Bieberman?"

"Oh, that's just a nickname. The team thinks he looks like Justin Bieber. You know ballplayers, they love nicknames."

Nina sighed. "Justin Bieber? Oh, he *so* looks like him. Except better. More muscles, you know?"

Paige bit her lip to keep from laughing. How could this innocent-seeming girl, with her wide eyes and habit of blurting things out, possibly be related to tough, icy Trevor Stark? Except that as it turned out, "Stark" wasn't his real last name, and he wasn't icy at all. Every layer she peeled away revealed something more fascinating.

"Does Trevor have a nickname?" Nina asked.

Paige thought hard but couldn't remember hearing the guys call Trevor anything other than T, occasionally. She turned to Crush. "Dad? Does Trevor have a nickname?"

"Absolutely. I just can't say any of 'em in mixed company." He winked at Nina to take the sting from his words. The girl giggled, then stole another glance in the direction of the shortstop.

Settling back in her seat, Paige decided she'd played CIA interrogator long enough. Nina was too innocent, too appealing, too vulnerable. She refused to use her as a way to gain information about Trevor. She'd just have to use more old-fashioned methods. The Internet. Conversation. Luring him into bed.

Sweet Lord, where had that thought come from? Her face burned as if she'd said it out loud. Of course she wouldn't do anything so underhanded. If she went to bed with Trevor Stark, it would be because . . . oh God, because she wanted to. She couldn't stop thinking about it. Trevor made her feel sexy and wanted. When he touched her, she forgot everything else. She forgot about common sense, caution, their pact of denial. She forgot that he kept secrets from her. That getting involved with another professional athlete was a terrible idea. That he was trying very hard to keep distance between them.

She heaved a sigh. Trevor had amazing powers of control. But she had unbelievable powers of persistence. Just ask the baseball legend on her left.

Chapter 13

TREVOR TOOK NINA to the sushi restaurant he'd chosen for his missed date with Paige and they spent a wonderful evening catching up on the last few months. She'd been working as a dog groomer recently, the latest in a series of no-pressure jobs. Before that she'd been an art school model, a Merry Maids cleaning lady, and a movie theater clerk.

Her life since that terrible night had been so different from his. After he'd been sentenced to juvenile detention, she'd gone to live with a distant cousin on their mother's side of the family. She'd had a relatively normal high school experience but no interest in college. After graduation she'd drifted from one short-term job to the next.

He saw the pattern. She was existing, not living. He thought about Paige and the temptation she represented. Maybe he was doing the same thing. If he was really free, he'd throw her down like a fucking caveman and claim her the way he wanted. Explore every inch of her, body and soul, and pleasure her until she screamed his name and knew nothing but him.

But getting close to Paige might put her in danger. Seeing Nina too often could put *her* in danger. Before

Nina left, he extracted a firm promise that she wouldn't show up again without consulting him first.

"I promise. Also, don't be mad but I told Paige that Stark wasn't our real last name," she confessed anxiously. "I also might have implied that you won't be heading to the majors anytime soon. But don't worry, she's really nice and I trust her. She won't do anything to hurt you. She said you're a friend."

His heart squeezed in his chest. If he could trust anyone with the story, maybe it would be Paige. But he couldn't. The more people who knew, the greater the chance it would leak out, like bilge from a broken sewer pipe.

"I'll handle Paige, sweetheart. I know it's tough, but don't say anything else to anyone."

"Normally I don't, because no one knows you anyway. It just seemed to spill out of me. It's like my secret-keeping ability is all used up. I don't want to do this anymore, Trevor."

"I know, I know. We just have to wait for the right time and place." Somewhere and sometime very far from now. "Be strong, Nina. We've been through much worse than this."

"I know. Okay, Trevor, I'll keep going as we have been." She bit her lip, then looked up at him from under her lashes. "I was wondering . . ." She hesitated. "If Bieberman asks about me . . ."

"I'll explain that you live in a different state."

"Trevor! He seems really nice and I think he's—"

"He's a ballplayer. He's on the road a lot, obsessed with baseball. You don't want that."

"Maybe I do! You can't make all the decisions, forever and ever."

"That's true," he admitted, though it pained him.

"So you'll tell me if—"

"If I change my mind, sure."

She swatted him on the arm while he grinned at her. Damn, it felt good to have his little sister around.

After Nina left, it was as if Paige had never experienced that glimpse into Trevor's personal life. He barely glanced her way during the next shoot, which took place at a pet shelter, though how he managed to ignore the tension simmering between them, she had no idea. Every time he left the ballpark, girls would flock to him, and he made a show of surrounding himself with them, one on each arm, a few trailing behind, as if he were some kind of pimp in a music video.

Maybe the attraction was all on her side. Maybe he didn't feel it—or didn't want to feel it.

Fine.

She needed to focus on other things—anything other than men. Investigating colleges didn't take up enough of her after-hours time, so she spent all her extra energy on the summer tutoring program the Boys and Girls had set up. It was designed to help kids whose home lives had gotten in the way of their schooling. They'd fallen behind and had no chance of catching up without some extra help. She loved the work because it went beyond tutoring; the kids *talked* to her. She asked them about their lives, their families. She listened to the sad stories they told. Sometimes a sympathetic listener was all they needed, other times she referred them to trained counselors or support groups. In return she told them about her experiences growing up around baseball and traveling with Hudson's basketball team in Italy. They loved hearing about her weird life, which made her appreciate it more.

The Catfish turned out to be a great resource in her work with the kids. She devised a reward system using tickets to Catfish games and other paraphernalia from the stadium. The players were great role models, especially the more she got to know them as individuals. When she found out that one of her students was mourning the death of his brother, she brought Dwight to a session. Ramirez, who had been born in Mexico, offered to help the Spanish-speaking kids as often as he could. If only she could rope Trevor into her project—but he was determined to keep his work with kids completely private.

Fine.

It felt wonderful to do something that helped other people—not just one self-centered basketball player. It all helped her move forward from the divorce. Not forget, but at least move forward. Every day that passed, she felt stronger. She didn't need Hudson. She didn't want Trevor. She was . . . *fine.*

Then one day, while she was posting her daily Baseball's Hottest Outfield social media updates, she got a text from Terry that she was needed in the PT room. The thought was so novel that she dropped everything and rushed downstairs. Why would anyone on the team actually *need* her? Instagram posts didn't rank anywhere in the hierarchy of human needs.

As she rounded the corner past the clubhouse, she ran smack into a hard wall of muscle. Her body told her immediately who it was, as if a light switch had turned on inside her. Trevor locked his hands on her hips to steady her, and all her good intentions scattered like dandelion fluff.

Yes, she still wanted Trevor Stark.

"Are you okay?"

She nodded, not trusting her voice. He looked her up and down, checking for injuries. His attention felt like a physical weight, as if he was stroking her instead of studying her. Her nipples tingled, rising hard against her bra.

He noticed. She saw the very moment when it registered. His eyes darkened, a little muscle in his jaw flickered. Something volcanic lurked behind that implacable, fallen-angel face. It called to her like wild wind tugging at a kite. Her body started to sway toward him, but she fought against the urge.

A bright voice shattered the moment.

"Why, Trevor Stark, you bad thing, are you tormenting the owner's daughter?" Donna McIntyre, the promotions girl, skipped past them. She was engaged to Mike Solo, the Friar reserve catcher who'd just been bumped up from the Catfish. She was carrying an armload of rolled-up posters. One tumbled off the pile, but she nabbed it in midair and used it to bonk Trevor lightly on the head.

"Ow." His injured look made Paige smile. She liked Donna, but then everybody did, with her bright smiles and quick comebacks.

"It's okay, I can handle Trevor," she told Donna.

The redhead readjusted her load, using one knee to keep the posters together. "Don't let him fool you. He comes off like the big bad wolf, but I happen to know he's not *entirely* dangerous. Not entirely harmless either, mind you."

"Don't you have some sort of wacky promotion to plan?" Trevor asked her.

"Indeed I do. See these posters here? I have three hundred of 'em earmarked for our awesome paying guests tonight, and every single one needs your signature. Baseball's Most Annoying Outfield, you know." Donna winked at Paige.

"No. No way. I don't have time for that," Trevor

said. "Batting practice is about to start. Get an intern to do it."

"Excuse me?"

Paige rose on tiptoe and murmured in Trevor's ear. "Sign them or I'll give Jim Leiberman Nina's e-mail address." As she pulled away, her lips brushed against his earlobe. The feel of his flesh made her mouth tingle madly—how crazy was that? It was an earlobe, nothing but skin and cartilage. She must have lost her mind.

Trevor gave her a slit-eyed glare, then turned back to Donna. "I have an hour before batting practice. An hour, no more."

"I'll take it." Donna sketched an elaborate bow in Paige's direction. "Wow, you're good, Paige. You're either magic or you have some dirt on our favorite bad boy. Maybe both. Here, have a poster. You've earned it."

She handed Paige one of the rolled up tubes and dashed off. Paige stuck it in her tote bag. "Wow, a signed T-shirt, now this. Must be my lucky day." She tried to duck around him, but he blocked her way.

"I've been meaning to ask you something."

Her breath hitched. Was he going to cash in that rain check? Finally take her on that infamous date that never happened?

"I know that Nina told you some stuff about us. I'm going to ask you to forget it."

Anger and disappointment left a sour taste. *This* was why she needed to avoid men. She gave him a little push; he moved about as much as a brick wall. "Trevor, did it ever occur to you that you can trust me? That maybe we could be friends?"

He went still, staring at her. Enveloping her in his attention. His all-encompassing scrutiny seemed to last forever. Someone opened the door to the clubhouse, releasing a burst of chatter and laughter into the tunnel. So softly that she almost missed it, he muttered under his breath. "Not with the thoughts going through my head right now."

He brushed past her, leaving her positively throbbing with curiosity. If only she could tap into those thoughts and see if they were remotely like hers. If they were, the two of them would be burning up the sheets in no time.

Whew. She fanned herself. Bad idea. Great idea. Who knew anymore?

She hurried on, toward the head trainer's realm.

In the therapy room an odd sight greeted her. Terry, the no-nonsense, nearly six-foot-tall trainer, hovered anxiously next to the even-more-gigantic Sonny Barnes, whose forehead was pressed against the wall, one fist resting loosely overhead, the other gripping something against his chest. He was emitting some very strange, hoarse, moaning sounds that Paige finally recognized as sobs.

"What's wrong?"

Terry answered in quiet tones, as if Sonny couldn't possibly hear her from two feet away. "He came in for some elbow work and as soon as I touched him, he started making that noise. Freaked me the hell out. Then tears started coming out, and I didn't know what to do."

"Did you ask him what was wrong?"

"No, I called you. I heard you're a psychologist. I have no expertise in this shit. Give me an ACL sprain or a postsurgical elbow rehab any day. This," she shuddered, "is why I work in sports, not at a clinic."

"Athletes have emotions too, you know."

"Yeah, well, they can keep them to themselves. You got this?" She started backing away. "The players talk to you. They like you."

"Wait, I'm no expert. I haven't even finished my college degree yet. I'm just a part-time volunteer . . ." She trailed off, since she was now talking to Terry's exhaust fumes.

She eyed Sonny. He wore his sliders and a T-shirt that said *Redneck Delight* on the back. She searched her mind for details about him. First baseman, from a ranch somewhere in the South . . . married, right?

Stepping closer, she put a comforting hand on his back. "You seem a little upset, Sonny. Is there anything you want to talk about?"

More harsh sobs, then he heaved himself around to face her. His face was sloppy with tears.

"Oh Sonny, what's wrong?"

In answer, he thrust his hand toward her. It held a thermos decorated with a collage of photos under its hard plastic casing. The photo showed Sonny and a pretty, beaming girl, their faces squished together.

"She made this for me when we got engaged. Now it's over, and I have to see her every time I drink my coffee."

"Oh no, I'm so sorry. Believe me, I know what that feels like." If there was ever a life crisis she could relate to, it was this one. "What happened?"

"She dumped me. Says I'm never home and the guy at the savings and loan started bringing her daisies. She loves daisies. It's her second favorite flower after dandelions. Ever had dandelion wine? We always said we'd serve it up at our wedding." He swiped a big hand across his face. "Sorry. Didn't mean to get soppy."

"You go right ahead and get soppy, Sonny. I'd be the last one to tell you not to cry. You should have seen me when my husband left."

Suddenly, six feet four inches of first baseman was draped across her shoulder, soaking her T-shirt with tears. She staggered, bracing herself against his weight.

"You cry as long as you want, Sonny." Gingerly, she patted his back. He might be huge, but he was probably about her age, away from his family and friends, traveling the Southwest trying to scratch a living out of his love for baseball. He probably just needed some simple human comfort.

Tears dripped onto her shoulder, sobs racked his huge frame. She murmured comforting things and patted his back. After a few minutes she adjusted her position, worried that she might start to go numb. After another couple minutes, his phone buzzed. He didn't seem to hear through his sobs.

Paige thought about all the international phone calls she'd made to her friends after Hudson had dumped her, and how patient they'd been. She could do the same for Sonny, even if she was getting a crick in her neck.

His phone buzzed again. "Do you want me to get that?"

"No," he wailed. "Not her ring tone."

"Okay. Okay." She patted some more, wondering how much of this her lower back could take. Should she call for help?

"Hey, Sonny!" an impatient male voice called from the corridor.

The door swung open. Trevor stopped short, taking in the spectacle before him with icy eyes. He strode forward and plucked Sonny away from her. Paige nearly collapsed, rubbing her lower back in relief.

"Dude. What are you doing? You were crushing Paige."

Sonny swiped his eyes again. "S . . . sorry, T."

"He wasn't crushing me," Paige said quickly. "He was just upset."

Trevor gave Sonny a bracing slap on the cheek. "Get it together, Barnes. Aren't you supposed to be fielding grounders right about now?"

Sonny nodded, sniffing, stared down at his thermos, then thrust it at Paige. "You can have this. I don't want to see it anymore."

"You sure you're okay?"

"I'll be all right." He hesitated, as if about to say more, but Trevor elbowed him in the ribs.

"Grounders," he said sternly.

Sonny nodded and dragged himself in the direction of the dugout. Paige rounded on Trevor.

"What's wrong with you? The man's grieving and all you can say is 'grounders.'"

"He's a ballplayer. That's what we do." He righted her tote bag, which had tumbled to the floor when Sonny collapsed on her. "Why did he go crying to you?"

"He needed someone to talk to. Terry called me in."

"Paging Dr. Paige?"

She bristled, propping her butt against the massage table. "I told her I'm not a therapist or anything, but I think I handled the situation okay. Sometimes a sympathetic ear is enough."

"Looked like more than an ear. Kind of a full-body sympathy thing going on. And he gave you his thermos? He never lets that thermos out of his sight."

She bit back a smile. Was Big Bad Trevor Stark actually jealous? "Sonny's going to need a lot of support over the next few days. Maybe you could try to be there for him."

"Oh, I'll definitely be there for him. Especially if he mauls you like that again."

"He wasn't mauling me. You sound like a dog guarding a bone." She tried to frown—she shouldn't like that possessive tone so much. It was so macho, so old-school. But the part of her that had been devastated by Hudson soaked it up like rain after a drought.

"Shizuko said you helped him out with a personal problem the other day," he said.

"So?"

He reached for her as if he couldn't help it, touched her shoulder, then let his hand drop away. "So, what was it?"

"Aren't you supposed to be signing posters or something? Why are you here interrogating me?"

"Why won't you answer?"

Her skin was responding to his attention with the usual prickles of cold and heat.

"Because it's Shizuko's business, not yours. I consider any communication like that confidential." Maybe that would make him understand that he could trust her.

"Did he ask you out?"

"What? Of course not." Shizuko had been debating whether his music career was holding back his baseball career, or vice versa.

"And T.J. Gates? When he talked your ear off in the bullpen the other day?"

"Again, none of your business." T.J. was worried that family pressure was interfering with his performance on the field. His parents were both surgeons and claustrophobically passionate baseball fans.

"How about Leiberman?"

Especially not his business. Leiberman had told her about his instant crush on Nina and his insane fear of Trevor's reaction. She'd promised to do what she could, but now was definitely not the time. "It's not a crime to show emotion, Trevor Stark. Even for a tough ballplayer."

For a long, inscrutable moment, he looked her up and down. "I think you've seen me show emotion. In this very room."

Heat flashed across her nerve endings. The last time she'd been in this room, they kissed. She'd tried so hard to forget her attraction to Trevor, but now she couldn't help reliving the exact sensation of his lips on hers.

"So all the players are pestering you to listen to their problems like you're, what, some kind of team psychologist?"

Her patience snapped. She pushed past him, toward the closed door. "Does that seem so strange to you? I'm a good listener, and I like helping people. And some guys actually enjoy sharing their thoughts and feelings instead of pushing people away with a big concrete wall. If you ever want to give it a try, call me."

He snagged her arm and whirled her back against him. Heat steamed from his body, or maybe from the combustion the two of them generated. "I like talking to you. Too fucking much."

"You do?" She could barely breathe. "What else do you like?"

He nuzzled her neck, his warm breath filtering through her hair. "I like how you smell. Like apple blossoms."

Her heart raced so much she was afraid it would jump out her throat. "What else?"

"Your voice, your smile, those little freckles on your nose, your laugh, the way you toss everything aside to go help someone, the way you feel against my cock . . ." He pulled her groin against the big bulge in the front of his baseball pants. "You make me so fucking hard I can barely stand. You don't have to do anything, just look at me with those big blue eyes of yours. Shit." He thrust her away from him, keeping his hands on her shoulders. To maintain distance or because he didn't want to stop touching her? "I have batting practice. I gotta go."

Go? After revving her up like that, he was just going to waltz onto the field and hit baseballs? He couldn't destroy her peace of mind like that.

"We have to talk, Trevor," she said firmly. "We can't just keep tiptoeing around this attraction of ours. It's not going away. It's doing the opposite."

He spun away from her, raking a hand through his light hair. "I'll keep a lid on it. I'm sorry. I can control myself."

She snagged his forearm, feeling each taut muscle flex. "What if I don't want you to control yourself?"

He threw her a tortured look, while she let him see every bit of her lust for him. She didn't hide anything, not the desire making her eyes heavy, the flush sweeping across her cheeks, the rapid rise of her pulse. It felt like stripping naked in front of him. If she did that, he'd see her aroused nipples and the shocking wetness between her legs. She tried to communicate all that without a word.

Then he was gone, out the door, while she nearly collapsed against the massage table.

She went to the sink in the corner of the room and splashed water on her hot face, then blotted it with a paper towel. Filling her lungs with deep breaths of air, she slowly evened out her heartbeat.

Trevor Stark was practically lethal. He should come with a prescription—take only in small doses. Guaranteed to drive you wild.

On the other hand, the way he looked at her, the things he said . . . she actually felt sexy and desirable again, not a shoved aside, second-best reject. Whatever happened with Trevor, she'd always be grateful for that.

Chapter 14

THE CATFISH'S NEXT road trip came at the perfect time, in Trevor's opinion, because he didn't know how much longer he could keep his hands off Paige. "Baseball's Hottest Outfield" was scheduled for an appearance at a fundraising event for breast cancer research, but Paige wasn't coming. Crush had switched her to the accounting department.

He ought to thank the man. His control was hanging by a damn thread.

During the swing through Las Vegas, Fresno, and Reno, he tried his damnedest to resume "life before Paige." In Vegas, he hit the craps table, lost track of time, and barely made it to the game the next evening. Operating on no sleep, he struck out twice, but hit his fifteenth homer of the season, so didn't get too much heat from Duke. In Reno, he took three sorority sisters out for a steak dinner. In Fresno, he punched out a guy who called Dwight the N-word and nearly got arrested.

But he didn't take any girl back to his hotel room, and the fight didn't even earn a suspension from Duke. The manager slipped the cop some Dodgers box seat tickets that he kept on hand for special occasions like this.

Face it—adding to the legend of Trevor Stark had lost its allure. Who would ever have thought that instead of the play-hard lifestyle, he'd prefer to hang out with Paige? Maybe cuddle up on a couch with a DVD. Feed popcorn to the one-eyed cat. Who knew? Normal stuff. The sort of normal he'd never had, and hadn't known he wanted.

Of course he also wanted her physically. If she knew how much, she'd probably run for cover.

But Paige didn't seem scared. She kept texting him goofy text messages before the games. One of his favorites included a selfie of herself with a printout of a spreadsheet and a panicked, crazy-eyes face. It made him smile every time he thought of it, even at home plate, which completely confused the opposing pitchers. She also sent a picture of her cat Jerome spread-eagled across her belly, looking like the king of the castle.

He actually felt jealous of that cat.

Every text, every photo, felt like a firefly in a cave, lighting up the dark emptiness he'd lived with for so long.

One night, while channel-surfing in his Fresno hotel room, he caught a glimpse of Nessa Brindisi's show. He watched for a while, clinically admiring her curvaceous, alluring on-air personality. She was a knockout, no doubt about it. The Sophia Loren of the cooking world. But he'd take Paige's long-legged grace and freshness any day, not to mention her mesmerizing smile and caring nature.

At the end of the show an ad appeared. "Join us for a very special event! Getting Married is Easy with Nessa Brindisi! Join Nessa and Hudson as they prepare for the biggest wedding the Food Network has ever known. From centerpieces to catering companies, from hair stylists to veils, be part of Nessa and Hudson's special day in an all-day program, right here, August twenti-eth."

August twentieth . . . that was the day they were scheduled to return to Kilby.

Oh hell, did Paige know about this? Should he tell her? What sort of asshole was Hudson Notswego? Didn't he realize how much pain he was causing Paige, his ex-wife and former friend? He clicked off the TV and lay back, hands linked under his head. His primitive side longed to rip Hudson a new one, but he knew that wasn't in the works. He'd probably never cross paths with the guy. The most important thing right now was Paige, and what she needed. Maybe he could take her out that night. Distract her with some hot flirtation and anything-but-steak.

It would be hell on his willpower, since he was still determined to keep his hands off her. He'd just have to suffer. Paige was more important.

He shot her a text.

Will you go out with me on August 20?

August 20? That's very specific.

He winced. Smooth, Trevor, very smooth. *That's the night we get back to Kilby. Are you free?*

You're not supposed to ask if a woman is free. You're supposed to just ask her out.

I thought I did. Did you miss that part, Ms. Emily Post?

I didn't miss it. Just trying to get over my shock. Besides, the last time you asked me out, you stood me up.

Extenuating circumstances.

How am I supposed to trust you now?

What's the point of being Baseball's Hottest Outfield if I can't even get a girl to go out with me?

I'm sure you haven't had any trouble in that area.

Oh crap, had she seen photos from Reno? Of course

she had. One of them had surfaced on the team Facebook page.

You're the only one I want to go out with. That was definitely true. He'd yawned his way through dinner with the sorority girls. *Please? I want to see you. I have something important to discuss. Kind of personal/emotional.*

If that didn't get her, he had no chance.

You're so full of shit.

Grinning, he tapped back. *Don't turn me down. Rejection's hell on my batting average, and the Catfish need me to get into the playoffs.*

You're shameless. Fine. Where do you want to meet?

My rig is parked at the stadium. We're getting in around 7. I'LL DRIVE.

Really, with no sideview mirror? Is that safe?

Very cute. You're going to pay for that, sassy.

For the first night in a long while, he didn't dream of knives and violence, or his other recurring nightmare, the time the Detroit gang had broken him out of juvie and inflicted their own punishment with a branding iron on his back.

Instead, he went to sleep dreaming of all the ways he could make Paige pay for her sauciness. They all involved both of them naked in bed.

With Jerome draped over her neck like a scarf and a pitcher of root beer in one hand, Paige tracked down her father at the swimming pool behind the ranch. The pool area, which featured a full bar and barbecue grill, along with glossy orange trees blooming in planters, had been the site of many legendary all-star parties, none of which she'd attended. This year's had taken place just before she'd fled Italy with her tail between her legs. If she'd gone to that party, would she have met

Trevor? Would he have been in party mode, and would she have disliked him on sight?

Crush was swimming slow laps, gliding through shimmering blue water. She perched on the edge of a chaise lounge and settled the purring Jerome in her lap. With a splash, he broke the surface of the pool, water gushing off him. "Hi honey."

"Thirsty?"

"You want something."

Trust Crush to make the most cynical assumption—and to be right in this case. "I'd like to throw one of your famous fund-raisers here. To benefit the tutoring program I've been working with. I've already lined up some of the Catfish, and the kids are willing to act as wait staff. I think it could be really great. You don't have to do a thing, I'll take care of it all."

Crush pulled himself onto the edge of the pool and snagged a towel. "Sounds good. I think it's a great idea. I'll do you one better. I'll cover the catering costs if I can pick the date."

Paige grinned at him. "You're such a softie at heart, aren't you? Sure, it's a deal. What date do you have in mind?"

The answer was nearly buried in terry cloth as Crush dried his hair. "August twentieth would work well."

"Excuse me?" It couldn't be a coincidence. Impossible. She jumped to her feet, sending Jerome thudding onto the terra-cotta tiles. He meowed in protest. "Have you been spying on my texts?"

"What?" He dropped the towel and narrowed bright hazel eyes at her. "Why would I do that? *How* would I even do that? I can barely operate my own phone."

"Why'd you choose that date in particular?" He tried hiding in the towel again, but she plucked it away from him. "Is it because I'm going out with Trevor that night?"

"With Trevor?" An odd expression crossed his face. Not anger or unhappiness, as she would have expected. It seemed more like relief. And definitely surprise.

"So you didn't know about that. But you picked August twentieth out of all possible dates. What's going on? Why is August twentieth suddenly so important to everyone?"

"Trevor didn't say anything?"

"Dad, if you don't tell me right now I'll . . . I'll sic Jerome on you." Since Jerome was currently in a one-eyed staring match with a fallen orange next to a planter, it wasn't much of a threat. But it worked nonetheless.

"It's the date of the wedding," Crush said reluctantly.

A chill flashed through her. "What wedding?"

"On the Food Network." He got to his feet and wrapped himself in his robe. "A special edition of Nessa's show. I was kind of hoping we could ignore the whole thing."

"They're getting married on the show?" A sort of numb sensation stole over her. Would the embarrassment never end? She shivered in the hundred degree heat.

"Their publicist is some kind of sadist, I think. I'm sorry, Paige."

She fixed her gaze on Jerome, who stretched out a wary paw to bat the orange. It rolled an inch to the right, which was clearly a call to battle for her cat. He crouched down and stared at it balefully. Had she ever really *known* Hudson? The nice guy she'd befriended in college wouldn't get married on a TV show. Or maybe he would, if it benefited his basketball career. That had always been the most important thing to him. She'd made it into the most important thing in her life too.

She lifted her chin. "It's all right, Dad. I'm a big girl. I can handle it. Why does everyone think I can't?"

"Ah, kiddo. If you need to cry, go ahead and cry. Forget that 'no crying in baseball' thing."

"I *don't* need to cry." And if she did, it wouldn't be around Crush. He didn't handle tears well at all. "Hudson is welcome to get married whenever and wherever he wants. But we can't schedule the party for that night. I have plans." She headed for Jerome, who was still locked into his mind-meld with the stray orange.

"With Trevor Stark."

"Yes, with Trevor." Trevor must have heard about the wedding, that's why he'd asked her out on that date. She didn't know if that was irritating or . . . sweet. Maybe both, with an edge to "sweet."

"What do you really know about Trevor?" Crush called after her. "Doesn't talk much about his past, does he? Most of these guys, you get to know them. Trevor Stark? I have no idea."

Paige bent down to collect Jerome. She couldn't leave him alone outside. Coyotes frequently wandered across the ranch searching for prey or water. "Stay out of it, Dad."

"I know he's got women after him all the time. Is he the kind of man you can trust, after Hudson?"

She picked up Jerome, who instantly went floppy like the ragdoll he was. Everything her father said made sense. But Crush hadn't seen Trevor's protectiveness over Nina. Or the way he'd been with the kids at the Boys and Girls Club. Or the look in his eyes after he kissed her, like a starving man glimpsing heaven.

Foolish or not, she was drawn to Trevor like the moon to earth, and nothing her father said would change that.

"Why don't you worry about your own social life, Dad? Mayor Trent, for instance. There's something between you, I saw it. You should invite her over to dinner."

"Don't talk about that woman to me." Muttering under his breath, he headed toward the pool house. Paige grinned to herself. Distraction accomplished.

Before he got there, he paused. "There's one more thing. I think your boy Trevor might have a record."

"*What?*"

"Just a suspicion, and if he does, it's as a juvenile. Nothing adult. But he's got no stats from any high school. As far as baseball goes, he appeared out of no-where in that independent league. That's very unusual. Most guys were stars in high school, then maybe college. Trevor's about to become a San Diego Friar, and I don't even know who taught him the basics."

When Paige displayed no reaction to that information, he disappeared into the pool house.

Thoughts racing, she buried her face in Jerome's warm, orange-scented fur. Should she tell her father that Stark wasn't Trevor's real last name? That was probably the reason for the gap in his baseball history. Simple as that.

But what if he did have a record? Would he tell her about it? Should she ask him? Or would that lock down all his walls for good?

At 7:00 P.M. on the night of August 20, Paige got a text from Trevor. She was wrapping up some last-minute payroll details in the accounting offices—once again confirming her conviction that the numbers side of the business was not for her.

Dropping some stuff in my locker, be right out. Escalade is unlocked, AC on. Do you like sushi?

Sushi? She made a face. Give her a good Texas steak over sushi any day of the week—but she couldn't tell him that, not after she'd made fun of his steakhouse escapades.

She sent him a quick text back. *Be right there.* Then she shut down the computer and grabbed her backpack. A quick double-check in the bathroom—her carefully chosen "not trying too hard" outfit still worked. Cowboy boots, flirty red dress with lime-green polka dots, and a denim jacket over it. She dabbed on more lip gloss, tried to tame her hair but quickly gave up and left it tousled, then hurried down the staircase that led to the parking lot.

A few vehicles were still filtering out of the lot, but otherwise it was emptying out fast. She spotted Trevor's blue Escalade, parked close to the players' exit, its lights on, as if waiting for her. He must still be in the clubhouse, since there was no sign of him.

Slipping into the passenger seat, she welcomed the cool air, relief from the oppressive heat still lingering outside. She settled back in the leather seat and noticed a Post-It on the glove compartment.

Paige—Look inside—T.

As she gingerly opened the latch, a heavenly smell filtered into the Escalade. A tangle of branches covered with sweet-smelling pink flowers filled the glove box. *Apple blossoms.* He'd told her she smelled like apple blossoms. She smiled, inhaling the heavenly scent, and lost herself for a moment in the evocative images it inspired. Spring nights filled with fireflies, climbing a tree with her journal, dreams, possibilities, crushes . . .

Someone settled into the driver's seat.

"Trevor," she exclaimed, still blissed out from the scent. "Where on earth did you find these this time of year?"

"Shut the fuck up, chick."

The door slammed shut as she whirled around. *The stalker with the BB gun.* She'd recognize him anywhere. He jammed the key in the ignition—how did he have the key?—and started the engine. She tried to open the passenger door but he pressed the All Lock key.

"Let me out," she cried. "Take the car, I don't care. Just let me out."

"Stark took my girl, I'm taking his." He slammed his foot on the accelerator and the Escalade sprung forward.

Oh, shit. "I'm not his girl."

"You're in his car, that's good enough for me."

"This is kidnapping! You'll go to jail."

He was careening across the lot as if he was crazy or on some kind of drug. She didn't know which possibility was scarier. *Talk him down.* "Listen, I'm sorry Trevor did that to you."

He grunted.

"But I had nothing to do with that. Hurting me isn't going to hurt Trevor. It's just going to get you into trouble."

"Shut up, bitch."

Oh my God. What had happened to all the security Crush had set up? The video cameras and fence reinforcement? What was this man planning? Did he even have a plan? Her cell phone was in her purse, and he'd surely notice if she went after it. Her best bet—keep talking.

"Do you ever watch the Food Network?"

"Huh?"

"You know that show, *Cooking Is Easy* with Nessa Brindisi?"

He frowned, pulling the wheel tight to the right to avoid a lamppost. "Yeah, so?"

"Right at this very moment, on TV, she's getting married. To *my* husband. Well my ex-husband. But he was married to me when he met her, so the point is that I know what it feels like to have someone hurt you."

His throat worked, the Adam's apple moving up and down his thick-fleshed neck. "She hates me now."

"I'm so sorry. I'm sure you don't deserve to be treated like that." Or maybe he did. But this wasn't the moment for honesty. *Keep him talking.*

"I love her so much." He gave a ragged, gasping sound.

"I know you do. You seem like a man who . . . uh . . . loves deeply. What's her name?"

"Louann. She's my baby. But I can't even talk to her anymore."

Restraining order? "Why don't you pull over and we'll go get a cup of coffee and you can tell me all about it." While she figured out a way to call 911. "Sometimes it helps just to talk about something. You can tell me how you met, everything."

At first she thought her tactic worked, because the Escalade slowed. But then he punched the steering wheel, making her heart jump into her throat. "I said *shut up*!"

She shut up, as the Escalade zoomed full-tilt toward the exit. Her mind raced, Plans B, C, D, and E forming. For a split second she'd reached him, she knew it. She just had to try again, with a different tactic, maybe in a few minutes when he'd calmed down. Her heart pounded, adrenaline thumping in her veins.

Just as it reached the exit, the Escalade slowed, as if it had lost power. "What the fuck?" the man screamed. He stomped on the accelerator again and again. But it kept slowing, and then the door was being wrenched open and two muscled arms reached inside. As if the beefy man at the wheel was nothing more than a rag doll, he was yanked out of the SUV and thrown to the ground.

Trevor stood over him, fury vibrating in every line of his face and body.

"Watcha gonna do, pretty-boy?" the man taunted.

Trevor pressed his foot to his neck. "It's already done. Cops are on the way."

Paige's hands were shaking so hard she couldn't get the passenger door open. "I think he might be on something, Trevor," she called through the open driver's side door. "Don't aggravate him."

She watched him struggle to control himself.

"Get off me, Stark," the man shouted, his voice made into a squeak by the weight of Trevor's foot. "Let me go or I'll tell the cops everything I know about you. About Wayne County."

Trevor's foot didn't move, even though the man clawed at it.

Sirens sounded, red and blue lights flashing through the parking lot entrance. Armed police officers jumped from the car. Trevor didn't release the man until the cops had reached them. They rolled him over and cuffed him.

Thoroughly shaken, Paige tumbled from the Escalade. Trevor ran to help her, gathering her into his arms. "I'm so sorry," he mumbled into her hair. "I'm so, so sorry."

She clung to him, every one of his hard muscles a kind of reassurance. "Another date ruined," she whispered. "This is getting ridiculous."

Chapter 15

TREVOR KEPT PAIGE tucked under his arm while she gave her statement to the police. He couldn't believe how cool she'd stayed under pressure, trying to calm down the asshole, relate to him on a personal level. Then again, maybe he shouldn't be surprised after the way she'd come to his rescue last time.

He gave a statement too, confirming that the carjacker was the same man who had attacked him in the parking lot last month. He explained that he'd come out of the stadium to see his Escalade driving crazy across the lot, and that he'd at first assumed Paige was playing a joke on him.

Then he'd seen that two people were in the SUV. He'd run after it, cut the power with his spare remote key, and dragged the man out before he could harm Paige.

He didn't mention what the man had said about Wayne County, even though it kept clanging through his mind like warning bells. Maybe he knew something, maybe he didn't. The only thing that mattered—the only thing Trevor cared about—was keeping Paige safe and getting this man off the streets. Going after him, that was one thing. Mess with Paige . . . fuck no.

The only bright side was that he'd just had a giant wake-up call. *Stay away from Paige.* He should tattoo it on his forehead.

Finally, all the official business was over and he was alone with Paige. She still looked pale, but not quite as shaken. "I'll drive you home," he told her.

She crossed her arms stubbornly over her chest. "Have you forgotten we're on a date, Trevor Stark?"

"Have you forgotten what just happened? You got kidnapped because of me."

"I got kidnapped for about two minutes, if that. By a moron who didn't even think you might have an override key. And you rescued me. Nope, sorry, none of that lets you off the hook. You asked me out, and you're taking me out."

"Paige . . ."

God, he had to make her understand what a mistake it would be to get involved with him. He cupped her elbow and turned her to face him. "There are things you don't know about me," he made himself tell her. Once she knew those things, she'd run screaming.

"I know you put apple blossoms in your glove compartment. I know you called the cops even though you hate cops. I know you never would have let that man hurt me. I know you want me the same way I want you." Her eyes were huge in the lamplight, sapphire-dark and urgent.

Desire for her thrummed in his blood like a drug. "Yeah, all that is true. And more. But I'm nothing but trouble for you. What am I supposed to do, put you in danger because I want you?"

"Maybe you should let me have a say," she whispered. "Tell me why I shouldn't be with you. Why you're so bad for me. What's so terrible about Trevor Stark?" She lifted a hand to interrupt him. "And Nina told me that's not your real last name, so you can start there."

He stared at her for a long, long moment, hiding all his turmoil behind the glacier of his face. It felt as if the ground was crumbling from under his feet, as if he stood on a lonely cliff face about to be washed away by the sea. No solid footing, no way to hide. Paige had just been kidnapped because of him, and that man had mentioned Wayne County. He needed to tell her. Even if he lost her.

And he would. He had no illusions about that.

Finally, his voice like a rusty hinge, he said, "Not here."

"Take me to your hotel room."

"Okay, but we're not—"

"Just take me."

She'd nearly ended up in his hotel room the very first night she met him. Then, it would have been a one-night stand type of thing, a shallow encounter between two strangers. Now, it was perhaps the opposite. It was Trevor dragging his hand through his hair, pacing the room, looking scraped raw. It was Trevor tugging his shirt off his back, showing the burn scars in the shape of a W—the gang emblem of the group that had drawn his father into their criminal web.

Now, it formed the skeleton of a hawk that had been tattooed in meticulous detail around the scar.

"That's to remind me never to stop watching my back," he told her, while she stared, speechless, at the work of muscled, inked beauty that was his back. Wide shoulders, tapering to a taut waist, with endless ripples and ridges of sinew in between. Hovering over it all, the harsh image of the hawk, wings spread open.

"That's . . . beautiful."

He gave her an odd look over his shoulder, then pulled his shirt back down and leaned against the wall while she sat cross-legged on the bed. "I don't know where to start with this fucking story. My dad was a pharmacist. Normal, middle-class guy. Taught me baseball, soccer, everything. Then my mom died, and he went to pieces. Started using drugs from the pharmacy. Then he got into harder stuff, using the pharmaceuticals as payment to the dealers. It got worse and worse, but I didn't know most of it. I was always playing baseball. Nina would come to me sometimes and ask what was wrong with Dad, but I had no clue. She was at home more and she knew something wasn't right."

He passed a hand over his forehead, as if even talking about this hurt. "Then I think my dad tried to get out, but they sent some thug over to muscle him into line. That's when . . . well, the guy was no match for a baseball bat. I went into juvenile detention for the rest of high school."

Horror flickered through her. "Did he die?"

"No. Brain damage."

She frowned, sorting through the story. It didn't seem to completely add up. "If you attacked the man who was hurting your father, wouldn't that be considered self-defense?"

He was quiet for a long time. "It didn't play out that way. And I can't say any more about it. Just that my father worked it out with them so the gang wasn't suspected of anything. He was going to take the blame, but I was only fifteen. If he'd been sent to prison, Nina and I would have been on our own. I wanted her to be safe, so I confessed and got sent to juvie. I think my dad thought I'd be safer that way. I probably was, mostly."

"Mostly?"

"A couple months after I went in, they bribed a guard. He knocked me out and I woke up on a folding table next to a smelting oven. That's when I got the scar on my back. They wanted me to know that my time in juvie wasn't payment enough. That they owned me. They said there was more to come after I got out."

She touched the scar on his cheek. "This?"

"That's the first line of a W, but that happened three years ago, and I wasn't unconscious. He didn't get far."

A chill shot through her.

Trevor's jaw worked, his eyes a turbulent green. "Soon as I graduated, I changed my name and got the hell out of town. I had to change my name once more after that, after a Detroit cop put it together. He was working for them. After I signed my major league contract, I sent for Nina. I got her set up somewhere safe in another city. I don't know if they're looking for me anymore, but I know they'd still love to find me. And that's why you should have nothing to do with me."

The flat finality of his voice shook her up even more than his words. And the truth was, she could see exactly what he meant. Anyone would say he was a dangerous person to be around; her father sure would. But was it his fault that his father had gotten involved with drugs? His fault that some gang enforcer had attacked his father? His fault for rushing to his father's defense?

She got up and walked slowly to his side. He tensed. She could practically see the electric barrier rising between them. "Where's your father now?"

"He died of an overdose while I was in juvie. I only saw him a few times after that night."

The stark sadness of that statement horrified her. God, none of this was fair. "I'm so sorry, Trevor."

She took his hand, rubbing her thumb across his big knuckles. After the way he'd manhandled that carjacker, she could imagine what he'd done with his father in danger. With a baseball bat or bare hands, Trevor was a warrior. He defended those he cared for. She'd seen it over and over.

Lifting his hand to her lips, she kissed it. "Is the Trevor part real?"

"Yes."

He tried to pull his hand away but she didn't allow it.

"Paige, listen. I'd like to think all of that is dead and gone forever, but the truth is, it could come back to bite me anytime. I've changed a lot since fifteen, but they'd still recognize me if they saw me. Hopefully, they never will. But I can't guarantee that. And you don't want anything to do with those guys. They're evil."

His eyes darkened, and he shifted his back muscles in an unconscious gesture. She thought about Trevor, a fifteen-year-old baseball prodigy, thrown onto a folding table and branded with a hot iron.

"It's not fair," she burst out. "How long are you supposed to live in fear of them? Forever?"

"I don't know. If it was just me, I'd say to hell with it. But I have Nina to think about. She's what matters most."

"Nina?" Paige frowned. Would they go after her as a way to find Trevor? It seemed like a stretch, but what did she know about this kind of thing? Absolutely nothing. And then something else clicked. "You don't want to play in the majors, do you?"

His head shot up, his startled reaction telling her she was onto something.

"You think it's too risky. You might have to play in Detroit. Someone could spot you and put two and two together. It's safer here in Kilby. Who ever goes to Triple A except the locals? That's why you keep sabotaging your career."

He yanked his hand away from her and strode to the window. "I don't sabotage my career. Have you seen my stats?"

"Yes, I've seen your stats. I'm working in the accounting office right now, and it's like Moneyball back there. I've seen your personnel records too. You keep screwing things up right when you're about to get the call. Drives my dad nuts."

"That's not my problem." Ice cold, as always. But now she knew what was behind that uncaring mask. She wasn't falling for his act anymore.

"They're not going to keep you in Triple A forever. You have a monster contract. What then?"

He turned away from her, rubbing the back of his neck, the flex of muscle in his forearm reminding her of the panorama on his back. "The more time that passes, the better. People die off in that world. Eventually they'll forget about me and my family."

God, it all made so much sense. Trevor's past, his fear, his protectiveness, the behavior that drove Crush nuts. He wasn't disrespecting baseball—he was trying to shield his family. "Just tell Crush, Trevor. Tell him what's really going on."

He was across the room before she could say another word, strong hands gripping her upper arms. "No, Paige. You have to promise. I told you all this in strict confidence. You're the only one I've ever told. Literally, ever. You can't tell. It's not safe for Nina. You gotta promise me."

"But Trevor, you shouldn't have to carry this alone. It's not fair. What about you, your baseball career, your life?"

He spoke in a low, tight growl. "Fuck all of that. *This* is my life. It's the way it has to be. I'd do anything for Nina. I would have quit baseball because of the risk, but she wouldn't let me. Would you do any different if you were in my shoes?"

She swallowed hard around the tightness in her throat. What would she do if she had to face such a terrifying situation? Again she remembered the harsh scars on his back, the way he'd made that brand into his own. The scar on his cheek. "Maybe not," she whispered. A tear spilled from her eye; she felt its soft tickle on her cheek. Then another. She didn't try to hide them, not that she could, the way he was holding her.

He watched her cry for him, everything about him softening with each tear. His grip loosened, his tense posture eased, the lines of his face relaxed into something like awe. After a few long moments he lifted one hand and used his thumb to wipe a tear off her cheekbone. She grabbed his wrist, keeping it right where it was, next to her face. He extended his fingers to cradle her jaw, his hold as tender as it was firm.

"You're so beautiful," he whispered. "I can hardly stand it."

She smiled through the tears that kept falling. "Says Baseball's Hottest Outfield."

"None of that now. I'm talking about you." His thumb brushed over the skin of her cheekbone, his gaze traveled across her features as if noting every freckle and eyelash. "The way your eyes dance when you smile. The way you catch the light, wherever it is. You're always shining. Even now, in this crappy hotel room, tears on your face, all the light in the room is on you. Everything else might as well not be here."

Her breath snagged in her chest. Never in her life would she have expected such poetic words from stone-faced Trevor Stark.

"Trevor," she whispered. "I—"

"Don't say anything. Just let me . . ." He trailed off, words disappearing into breath, breath disappearing into the press of his lips against hers. It felt like the softest kiss in the world, like an inevitability, two paths crossing right where they were supposed to. They kissed long and deep, every barrier between them evaporating like mist under the morning sun. His touch turned her body into a river of fluid sensation, everything in her wanting to soften, to welcome, to surrender.

"We shouldn't—" He began.

"Don't." With a fierce kiss, she plucked the words from the air between them, swallowed them before they could shatter their fragile new connection. "You're not alone in this, Trevor. Not anymore."

She tilted her hips forward, seeking his erection. Under the denim of his jeans, it pressed against her thigh, hot and demanding. Sensation hot in her belly, she swayed toward him. She wanted him hard against her, surrounding her, cradling her the way he had after the carjacking. She wanted him inside her, his strength and power pouring into her. She wanted him in her mouth, in her hands, against her tongue. She wanted him now, all night, again and again.

But he was still fighting with his conscience; she felt his silent struggle for control. Hot desire battling against the urge to protect her.

"Please," she whispered. "Stay with me, Trevor." She closed her eyes, put his hand on her breast, over her heart, praying that her aroused nipple and catapulting heartbeat would do her talking for her.

In the darkness behind her eyelids, she saw a vision of the first time she'd laid eyes on Trevor, striding across the parking lot, powerful but so terribly alone, until that other dark figure had approached him.

You couldn't escape fate, whether in the form of a man with a BB gun or a troubled slugger.

She felt the exact moment when he gave in, when he surrendered to the desire vibrating between them. He swept her flat against him so there was no room for breath, no room for doubt. "If we do this, you gotta know a few things," he muttered in her ear. "I can't make any promises. I don't lie, and I don't say things I can't stand behind. I've never felt the way I do with you, but I don't want to hurt you, and—"

To shut him up, she plastered her mouth against his, throwing her body against him with so much force that anyone with less sheer strength would have stumbled backward. But he received her weight as if she were a tumbleweed, cradling her against his hard chest, those powerful hands gripping the flesh of her rear.

He spun her around so the back of her legs touched the side of the bed, then she was airborne, suddenly weightless, an armful of cotton fluff secured in the muscular circle of his embrace.

Next thing she knew, she was on her back on the bed, a Trevor she'd never seen braced over her. This Trevor was wild, with fever-bright eyes that promised unimaginable things. The heat from his body seared everywhere he touched, even through her clothing. She twisted her body against him, laughing out loud because it felt so amazing, so beyond anything normal.

"Laugh it up, Paige. You'll be screaming before you know it." With a growl, he nuzzled his face against her neck. He nudged her legs apart with one knee, and she nearly came just from that. Her dress rode up to her thighs. He drew a possessive hand up the inside of her leg, the roughness of his palm lighting up her skin like fireworks. If he reached her mound, he'd find her already wet and open. But he didn't get that far, only to the edge of her panties.

He looked down. She knew what he saw: red silk. Selected to state her intentions loud and clear.

"Damn," he swore softly. With that one word, dripping with lust and awe, all the feminine pride Hudson had stolen from her came rushing back. Doubled, tripled, because this was Trevor Stark. And Trevor had a hold on her heart and imagination no one had ever had.

From the restraint that vibrated in his forearms, she knew what he intended. Some kind of slow seduction, taking his time arousing her with his mouth and touch. That's not what *she* had in mind. Oh no.

She wrapped her legs around his hips and thrust her pelvis against his. His erection was hard as a club behind his jeans. Sensation beat hot and fast in the place between her legs—the current center of her world. Wildfire flooded her system, need thundering like a timpani. She rubbed against him, the throbbing in her clit now an electric feverish craving.

"What are you doing?" He groaned painfully, a man in the throes of battling temptation. "I can't last if you do that. You're going to make me—"

"I want you to fuck me." Her rawness shocked her. That wasn't how nice-girl Paige talked. She didn't say things like that. At least not until now. "I don't want slow. I want fast and hard. Come on, Trevor. Do it. You want it just like I do. Touch me."

She snaked a hand between them, working her way past his pants to take hold of his hard penis. It filled her hand with its thick urgency. God, how she wanted him.

With a groan, he pulled her hand away from his cock. He joined both her hands together over her head, pinning them to the bedspread.

She peeked up at him. Had she ever thought he was icy and distant? Not this man, with his fierce electric gaze and hot mouth. Words were pouring out of him now, just as dirty as hers had been. "I want you hot and wild for me, baby. I want your sweet little body spread out naked and begging. Keep your hands up there and open your legs for me, baby."

She spread her legs apart, gasping at how it made her

feel to do that—exposing herself, surrendering, giving in to him. He sat back on his heels and ran one big palm up one thigh, across her crotch, then down the inner thigh. The silk against her sex turned the caress into a maddening tease. She sobbed and pushed wordlessly toward his hand again. *More,* she wanted to say. *I need more.*

But he knew what she meant. Right now, in this moment, he owned her and he knew it.

Slowly, torturously, he dragged his hand back between her legs, taking his time as he reached her clit. He used one knuckle to circle that nest of nerves, to pull a deep moan from the very pit of her stomach. She panted, lungs heaving, about to burst.

He pushed her dress up as far as it would go, then dragged her panties down to her knees. The look on his face, all-consuming and feral, nearly sent her over the edge again.

"God, you're fucking gorgeous."

"Please, Trevor. Touch me." She lifted her hips, need vibrating in every nerve ending.

"You're such a hot thing," he murmured. He ran his hands from the undersides of her breasts down her torso to her hips. She writhed under his touch. So rough and tender. So knowing.

His touch was everything.

When he reached between her legs to the wetness crying out for him, she released a whimper. "Oh please . . ."

"Don't worry, sweetheart. I got you." His deep, lust-roughened voice worked on her like another hand, like another set of fingers playing havoc with her nerves. He cupped her mound—oh God, she wanted to cry from the piercing pleasure. The inside of his wrist pushed against her clit, his fingers tangled in her soft curls. He tugged lightly. Lightning sizzled through her system. But the edge of everything was still out there . . . out of reach . . . taunting . . .

"Oh fuck," she moaned, hips thrashing. "I can't . . . I can't . . ."

"I told you not to worry," he reminded her, his tone drenched in stern command. A rush of pure emotion made her body relax.

"I won't," she whispered. "Just . . . just . . ."

"Just what? This?" He stroked a thumb across her clit. "I feel you swelling for me. Plumping up nice and full. Let it go, sweetheart . . . let it go . . ." He pressed and circled, creating delirious friction between his callused thumb and her own hot juices. "Come for me, Paige. I want to see you come. Don't hold back. Come on."

With his palm still hot against her clit, he inserted two big fingers inside her, the extra pressure releasing a deep flood of heat. It carried her up, up, higher and higher, a wave transporting her into a wide starry sky and hurling her to the wind. And then it broke into a cascade of shuddering release. She lost track of where she was and what she was doing, barely seeing Trevor's head bent intently over her, his hand holding her firm, anchoring her to the bed.

When she was still pulsing from that climax, trying to catch her breath and retrieve her sanity, he snatched a condom from his bedside table and worked it over his rock-hard erection. "How can you be so fucking hot when you look so innocent?"

"I don't know what you mean." She heaved in a lungful of air, but there was no getting her pulse back to normal. It kept skipping and jumping all over the place. Trevor poised his body over hers. The lamplight caught the little golden hairs peppering his thighs. Fascinated, she stroked the front of his thighs, amazed at their honed, sculpted hardness. They seemed to have more muscles than other men's thighs, even though she knew that couldn't be anatomically true. His muscles were just more obvious, more defined. Like iron turned to warm flesh.

Between his thighs reared his penis, straight and true and wanting her. She touched it too, feeling the heat burning through the clear latex. "I got tested after I found out about Nessa," she said. "I'm fine."

"I always use a condom. I won't put you at risk. I can at least promise you that."

For a moment the magical connection she felt to him wavered. That word "always" made her think of all the other women he'd done this with. Was she just another woman to him, was this just another situation requiring a condom?

But when he pushed his erection into the soft opening between her legs, none of that mattered anymore. The only thing that mattered was the way he swelled inside her, the way he filled her, inch by glorious inch, until there was absolutely no extra room for anything resembling a doubt or a second thought or any sensation other than pleasure.

"Paige" he whispered as he moved with aching control within her. "Beautiful Paige." He flexed his hips, going deeper inside her. Flutters danced along her inner channel, along her spine, down to her fingertips. She closed her eyes because the sight of him was just too overwhelming. She could look or she could feel, but not both. And right now she wanted feeling. She wanted him driving deep. She wanted his shudders, his restraint. His abandon. And then a wild, intoxicating explosion. This orgasm was different from the first. Deeper. It was a thorough surrender of her being to the powerful man who shook in her arms.

The man who was claiming her heart, bit by bit.

Chapter 16

WHAT HAD HE *just done?* He'd had sex with Paige Taylor, after vowing to stay away from her. *What was wrong with him?* Sex with the owner's daughter, the girl who knew things about him no one else did. Worse, it had been even better than he'd imagined—wild and uninhibited and electrifying. Fucking terrifying.

Trevor didn't want to face any of those facts, so he lay on his back on his impersonal bed in his rented motel room and pretended to sleep. He manufactured a slight snore, which masked the rapid beating of his heart. Did any of it fool Paige? He didn't know, but he didn't want her to stop twining her finger through the hair on his chest. So he didn't move, like a coward.

Eventually Paige's breathing evened out. Then he lay still as a statue, every muscle screaming at him to get up. To get away from the clean apple fragrance of her hair as it draped over his arm, the soft feather weight of her hand still on his chest.

He couldn't do this. This wasn't him. He didn't know *how* to do this. Whatever *it* was. And now she was asleep and what the hell was he supposed to do next?

When Paige woke up, he'd tell her this had been a

major mistake and the smartest thing would be to move on as if it had never happened.

He always offered women exactly the same deal. His intense sexuality in exchange for absolutely no emotion. That's who he was. Made of ice, except when he let his sexual drive off the leash. He'd let himself detonate in the body of a consenting woman, someone who wanted it hard and furious and didn't mind walking away when it was over. Because that's all there was to Trevor Stark. Ice or fire. Nothing in between.

But now Paige was draped over him like a blanket of living silk, and the wires in his brain were cross-firing and sparking like crazy. What was this? Who was he? What now? How could he get the hell out without hurting the kindest, hottest, smartest, wildest girl he'd ever laid hands on?

With his thoughts still churning, he fell asleep. When he woke up, the lamp was on, his cock was in her mouth and pleasure was flooding his veins. "What are you—"

She lifted her head, all pink moist lips and sleepy sapphire eyes. "I couldn't find any more condoms, so I had to improvise. I didn't think you'd mind, but I can stop."

He groaned deeply and spread his arms wide to the sides. "If you stop I might explode."

"I like it when you explode." She smiled wickedly and ducked her head back to his cock. Her tongue passed across the tip, slow and thorough, as if she was experiencing each pulse of pleasure right along with him. As if she could see inside him and feel exactly what he felt.

He fumbled for the train of thought he'd been following when he fell asleep. Something about this being a mistake and . . . "I think . . . uh . . ."

She sucked him deeper into her mouth and his words dried up to dust.

"Don't think." His cock had slid from her mouth as she raised her head to speak. He wanted to cry. "Isn't that what you do at the plate? Swing the bat, don't think?"

"I think. Up until I can't think anymore because there's a fastball coming at my head. Then I let it all go." Yeah, thinking was way overrated. "Come on, baby. Put me back in your mouth."

All his resolutions forgotten, he drew her head back to his cock. He kept his grip loose around her head, suggesting a rhythm with his hips and hands. She picked it up immediately, her thick hair tumbling over his thighs as her head bobbed up and down, her warm mouth a moving velvet sheath around his cock.

"Oh fuck, honey. That feels so goddamn mother—" More swear words clamored to get out, but he clamped his jaws shut, his body tensing like an archer's bow.

Pressure built in the base of his spine, in his balls, release screaming toward him like a bullet train, and it was either going to happen in her mouth or in her sweet, tight channel, and he had to be back inside her . . . had to be . . .

He flipped her over in a motion so quick she squeaked. With his hard-on jutting in front of him like some sort of flagpole, he fumbled for his last condom, which, he remembered now, had fallen behind the nightstand.

"Hang tight," he told her, scooting past her to grab it. He brushed against the wire of the lamp, which was plugged into an outlet on the back wall. The lamp teetered.

"Watch out!" Paige scrambled out from under him and reached up to stop the lamp from falling on his head. Except that in the meantime he had twisted to look at it and his chin intercepted the path of her hand. She knocked him in the jaw at the same moment that the lamp bonked him on the head.

"Ow."

"Oops," she said simultaneously. "Are you okay?"

He tried to wrestle the lamp off his head, but the shade had gotten lodged there, somehow, and the cord was getting in the way, and . . . he burst out laughing. It was just too ridiculous, and now Paige was laughing too, on her heels trying to juggle with the lamp. It crashed to the floor, the cord yanked from the outlet. Out went the light, and there they were, giggling like two kids in the dark.

"These things always happen to me, haven't you noticed that yet?" Her laughing voice warmed the darkness.

Trevor wrapped his arms around her and curled her body against his chest. God, she felt so good and smelled so sweet. "Um . . . where were we?"

"You were trying to find a condom, remember?"

"Right. Fuck."

"Forget that. Stay right where you are, big boy."

Her soft form slid down his front and her wet mouth claimed him again. It took no time, a few deep suckles and he was coming. He bucked his hips and yelled something at the ceiling. No light in the room, but as she pulled the orgasm from him, the whole world flashed bright.

Magic Paige, source of light.

For a few precious days nothing happened. Well, things happened, of course. He played baseball, made his weekly visit to the Boys and Girls Club, even signed up to help with Paige's fund-raiser. Normal things. Precious, normal, wonderful things. But he knew it couldn't last.

In his experience, disaster liked to sandbag you out of nowhere. While you weren't looking, your dad could get hooked on meth. Then one day everything could blow and you'd be sentenced to Wayne County Juvenile Detention, your entire future a question mark.

But this time disaster had sounded a warning bell. He couldn't forget what the stalker—Tom MacPhail, he learned—had yelled. *Get off me or I'll tell the cops everything I know about you. About Wayne County.*

Was there a way MacPhail could have learned about his sealed juvenile records? Did he mean something more innocent, that he knew Trevor's place of birth? That his last name was Leonov, not Stark? Each day that passed with no public bombshell, Trevor relaxed a little more, back to his normal, unheightened state of alertness.

Which freed him to plunge fully into his affair with Paige Mattingly Austin Taylor. They couldn't keep their hands off each other. At the stadium, they ignored each other completely, because if they didn't, they'd be on each other like animals. But after hours, in his hotel room, the leash was off.

Sometimes they didn't even make it to his room. He'd taken her in the hotel stairwell, late one night, when they couldn't wait a second longer. Just opened his jeans, pushed up her skirt, and made her bury a scream in his shoulder. During one epic morning before batting practice, he tongued her up one side and down the other. He bent her over the bed, piled pillows under her ass, and stimulated her with hands and mouth until the sheets were drenched and her throat raw with her moans.

When she couldn't bear another second, she'd rolled over and punched him. "Make me come or you die! I'm serious."

Laughing, he wrapped her legs around his waist and walked her into the shower. Made her hang onto the shower head while he soaped her, nipples to toes, her moans lost in the cascading water. When she finally came into his hand, and he felt her liquid heat against his palm, he was so turned on he had only to grip his own cock and he came all over the shower tiles.

The amount of sexual chemistry they generated was off the charts. He'd fucked her on the carpet, the desk, the kitchenette counter, the bathroom floor, and, very nearly, the hallway floor just outside his room.

After a few days of this they were completely in tune with each other. Once, at the ballpark, he ran into her in an empty hallway. One look from under her lashes and he craved her. His cock went hard as stone, and when he brushed past her, he slid a hand across her mound, and by the way her breath caught, he knew she was just as wet as he was hard.

Then his hand fell away and they continued in their opposite directions. Already he hungered for the next time he'd have her in his bed.

When he was with her, nothing else in the world mattered. Not the past, not her future. All that mattered was the way she looked at him and the light in her eyes.

It wasn't just sex either. Paige had a way of breaking down his barriers and making him talk. She asked a million questions about his experiences in juvenile hall. He told her about Grizz, the old baseball coach who volunteered there. Grizz had believed in him from the first. He'd taken Trevor under his wing and kept him on track. He talked about how baseball was the only thing he'd ever wanted to do but that he'd decided it wasn't safe, until Nina had insisted he go for it. He hadn't had the money for college, so instead he read constantly—a passion Paige shared. That's how she'd passed the time in all those Italian hotel rooms.

Paige had plenty to share too. She told him how she'd adopted Jerome in Milan to help her deal with the loneliness of living in a foreign country. She talked about her split childhood and her ambitious parents. How she'd never felt that she measured up, because she didn't have their drive. What she had instead was a deep desire to help people, to be of use to people. Hudson had benefited from that, and his betrayal decimated her self-confidence.

He had to wonder how Hudson could walk away from someone like Paige. The only clue she dropped was when she told him that they'd hung out in college and had more of a "pal" relationship before they got romantic. Maybe they just didn't have the sizzle he and Paige shared.

It was the same on his end. None of his involvements—he wouldn't call them relationships—had come close to this thing with Paige.

They didn't discuss what sort of "thing" it was. The intensity of their connection blocked out everything else. All he knew was that he wanted her all the time, in every possible way. Sexually and otherwise. But the parameters of his life hadn't changed. At any moment he might have to drop out of sight. At any moment he might get dragged back to Detroit to face more retribution. At any moment he might have to come to Nina's rescue in some way. How could he ask another person—especially one who meant as much as Paige—to share that with him?

No. He'd give her what he could for now. Lots of hot sex. The return of her feminine confidence. The knowledge that he found her to be the most beautiful and desirable woman he'd ever known. More than that? Not possible.

And then the hammer dropped.

* * *

Crush stormed into Paige's cubicle in the accounting department, where she was trying to work on spreadsheets but was actually doodling dreamy patterns on pieces of scrap paper. He held a copy of the *Kilby Press-Herald* in one fist. "Have you seen this article about Stark?"

She jumped up and snatched the paper from him. It was open to the sports section, and the headline read: CATFISH STAR REVEALED TO BE JUVENILE DELINQUENT.

"Juvenile delinquent? Do people even say that anymore?" Wasn't it like calling someone retarded? It sounded so insulting and wrong.

"He did time in Wayne County Juvenile Detention. Seems pretty accurate to me."

As she scanned the article, her stomach cratered. *Assault and battery . . . third degree felony . . . fifteen years old . . .*

Trevor had warned her this might be coming, but a week of nonstop, heavenly lovemaking had lulled her into complacency. Even though he'd described the incident, seeing it in black and white was shocking.

Crush was still raging, stamping back and forth across her cubicle. "And he dares to go near my daughter. He probably didn't even tell you—that kind of person never does. They just take what they want."

"Dad," she said sharply. "I knew. He told me."

"You *knew*?"

"Yes. He wanted me to know before we . . . did anything."

A slow wave of red inched up Crush's neck. "I'll bury him."

"Would you cut it out? You don't know the whole story. He was protecting his father. A gang member was trying to kill his father and he defended him."

Crush shook his head. "I'm not buying it. That's self-defense and wouldn't have gotten him incarcerated. You can't believe what he tells you. He can't be trusted. He's a juvenile delinquent."

She shoved the newspaper back into his hands. "You should talk to him yourself. It's his story to tell. But you have to give him a chance, Dad. Keep an open mind and listen to him."

"If he wants to come to me and explain, he's welcome to."

Would Trevor do that? He'd refused to talk to Crush earlier. But now the secret was out, and maybe he'd feel differently. "If he does, will you promise to keep an open mind?"

"Oh, I'll keep an open mind." He grimaced. "Right next to my cocked and loaded rifle."

"Dad! Why do you automatically think the worst of him? You should really get to know him before you make all these judgments."

"I know all I need to." He shook the sports page, now crumpled in his fist. "And so do you. Are you going to end it, or do you want me to do the dirty work? It'll be my pleasure."

"I'm not ending it." She crossed her arms over her chest. "And it's not your business."

"The hell it isn't." He shook the newspaper again, as if wishing it was Trevor himself. "How can this not be my business? You're my daughter and he's on my team. For now, anyway."

Her chest tightened. "What does that mean?"

"It means Major League Baseball teams want players the kids can look up to."

"They're . . . the Friars are . . . they won't release him, will they?" Paige flinched as she said it. Even though

Trevor claimed he didn't want a call-up, she knew that wasn't really true. He knew, she knew, everyone who saw him play knew, that he belonged in the major leagues. He was incredibly gifted and had a passion for the game. If the Friars released him, he'd be back in the independent leagues, or the Mexican leagues, somewhere where he'd never get to show the world how great he was. It would be a tragedy.

"Who the hell knows?" Crush dug in his back pocket for his silver flask and took a long pull from it. "Don't worry, it's root beer," he growled when he was done. "I don't know what the fallout will be. A lot depends on public reaction, media, all that bullshit. I don't care about any of that, Paige. I care about you. Are you going to keep seeing him?"

She rubbed her hands up and down her arms and tried to imagine not seeing Trevor anymore. Or seeing him only on the ball field, or maybe not even there, if he ended up in a cactus-studded outfield in Mexico. "Why should he be punished again? It happened when he was barely a teenager. He's already done his time. And with all this publicity, he's going to need support."

"*Support?*"

"Yes," she said stubbornly. "I'm not going to just walk away when he needs me. Would you walk off the mound just because batters are starting to hit your curveball?"

He stared at her hard for several long moments. Was this going to be a repeat of the scenes they'd had over Hudson? she wondered. When he'd threatened to cut her off—then *had* cut her off?

But no. "It's your decision," Crush said. "But I'll be watching him like a hawk."

She startled, thinking of Trevor's hawk tattoo.

Watchfulness was a way of life for Trevor. What was he going through right now, knowing that his past was public information? She needed to call him right away.

On his way out of her cubicle, Crush tossed a wry smile at her. "And honey, I can't believe you used a baseball analogy on me. We're winning you over, aren't we?"

Chapter 17

SEEING HIS NAME in the paper next to the damning words "assault" and "incarceration" was a special kind of hell for Trevor. He called Nina right away and warned her to be extra alert and cautious. But the danger to her right now was probably minimal. If the gang knew where he was, they'd have no interest in Nina.

He thought long and hard about disappearing before word spread to Detroit. But small town Kilby was a different world. The Wachowskis might never see the obscure sports news item about a minor league player. This time, he had too much to lose, so he decided to wait and see what developed.

In some ways, walking into the clubhouse after the article came out required more guts than it took to face the Wachowskis. Knowing that the guys on his team would look at him differently—as a criminal—cut right to his core.

Brazening it out, he strode in as if nothing was different. As he walked through the clubhouse, the back of his neck prickled with heat and a buzzing sound rang in his ears. Were people looking his way? Fuck, some badass he was. What was he, in third grade? What did he care what the team thought?

So what if he'd come to care about his fellow Cat-fish? A guy like him couldn't afford that crap.

As he opened his locker, the ordinary sounds of the clubhouse, the joking and the taunting, the cleat-tying and towel-snapping, quieted. He looked neither right nor left, but kept his focus on his gear. This was a job, nothing more. He was here to play baseball. Hit home runs. Win a championship for Crush Taylor.

He felt an eager presence at his elbow and shot a glance sideways. "Bieberman."

"What was it like? Juvie? Did you call it juvie? Or is that outdated? I looked it up in Urban Dictionary and it says 'juvie' is also a haircut. Or a fictional character who appears when you experience misfortune."

"What are you talking about?"

Ramirez strolled over and put a hand on Leiberman's shoulder. "Easy, boy. You ought to know not to mess around with a guy who did hard time." He winked at Trevor.

Trevor snorted. Judging by Ramirez's tattoos, he had an interesting past as well.

"Were you on a chain gang? Did you have to pick up trash by the side of the road? Make license plates?" Bieberman's ridiculous questions kept on flowing. "What about baseball?"

Now there was a question he could answer. "We had a team. A pretty good coach too. Grizz, an old Negro League player, he was about eighty. I think he had one stint on the Tigers before his career ended."

"Grizz Walker?" T.J. Gates, who was half African-American, had done extensive research into the Negro Leagues. "Great player. Nearly got elected to the Hall of Fame."

"Yeah, he got robbed." Trevor shut his locker door. "He was a great scout too, and he volunteered with our team up until his arthritis got too bad. Taught me how to work the count. I owe my whole career to him."

A couple more players had gathered around. Dan Farrio, Manny Becker, Sonny Barnes. He nodded to them. "What's up?"

"Just want you to know we got your back," said Sonny, the gentle giant of the team.

"Also, if you want to scare the living fuck out of the Express, we got some ideas." Dan Farrio grinned. "Especially their pitcher, Jon Golden. Get inside his head, rattle him up good. I could use a victory, man."

Trevor snorted. "What do you want me to do, wear a jumpsuit?"

"Orange is the new black," Leiberman pointed out.

"We were thinking we'd all wear orange, mix things up." Ramirez gestured toward his locker. "I got a box full of orange jerseys. Goes great with Catfish blue."

"You fucking guys. You're not serious."

"Nah, Crush would have our asses. But maybe during BP?" Ramirez looked around the group hopefully. "The Express would get the message."

"What message?" Trevor still wasn't quite getting it.

"Intimidation, dude. We have Trevor Stark on our team, and we ain't messing around. It's about assault with a deadly weapon, *on the field only,* baby." He high-fived T.J. Gates. "Make 'em think. Make 'em afraid every time one of us comes up to bat. Except Leiberman."

"Stealing's a crime," he piped up. "I'm the top base-stealer on this team."

"True that, my man."

Trevor was laughing by now. "I'd like to see Duke's face if we all walked out wearing orange. Might be worth it just for that."

"Right?"

With his back to his locker, he stripped off his shirt so he could put his jersey on. Then he hesitated. He never showed his back if he could help it. None of the guys had seen his scars in detail. But maybe the time for secrecy was done.

Deliberately, he turned his back and thrust his arms through the sleeves of his jersey. A short silence fell over his team members. The fluorescent lights of the clubhouse probably made the hard ridges of scar tissue even uglier. Good—maybe they'd start taking this shit more seriously.

"That brand don't look like something you chose." Ramirez, who was almost entirely tattooed, would know.

"No. But the tat is." He let his jersey drop over his back like a curtain.

"Nice ink." Fist bump from Ramirez, another from T.J., then he sat on the bench to put on his cleats. His heart was pumping harder than it did when he was at the plate. It felt good not to hide his scars . . . or juvie . . . or Grizz. He'd loved that man. Grizz had probably saved his life. He used to give him extra time, solo batting practice. He told stories from the old days barnstorming with the Homestead Grays. Playing on dusty old fields at the end of country roads, when the games would take place on Sunday after church, so the crowds wore their best hats and the scent of barbecue filled the air. When barely a teenager, Grizz had played with Satchel Paige, Josh Gibson, all the great black players.

And Grizz would tell him over and over how much potential he had in baseball. He drilled it into his head that self-pity would get him nowhere. Even when he'd been dumped back at the juvenile hall, half dead, his back on fire, infection setting in to his burn wounds, Grizz hadn't let up. As soon as his fever was under control, he'd gotten Trevor back on the field. Even though every swing tore at his healing skin, Grizz insisted on practice.

"Gotta keep the skin stretched out. Don't let it affect your swing. This is how you'll get your revenge, boy. On a baseball field, under the lights, with everyone screaming your name. That's how we do it. That's pride, that's respect. That's the game of baseball."

A pair of cleats entered Trevor's field of vision, interrupting the memory. He looked up to see Dwight looming over him. His gut tightened all over again. He couldn't read Dwight's expression at all. "My brother died in a DUI," he said.

"I know." That information had come out last year, when Dwight organized an impromptu tribute to catcher Mike Solo's brother.

"I know you know. Because I told you."

So that's what this was about. Trevor finished tying his cleats and stood up. "I couldn't tell anyone." And that was all the explanation he intended to give. It was just too fucking complicated.

"That's all you're gonna say?"

"No." He took a moment to work out exactly what he wanted to say. For so long, he'd basically kept everything personal to himself. But being with Paige, who talked so easily and asked so many goddamn questions . . . well, maybe it had changed him. "You're my friend. So I hope you trust me that I couldn't tell. I had my reasons. Still do. And I hope you're still my friend."

There. That was about all he could say, and it was more than he'd ever said before. Dwight narrowed his eyes, assessing, as if testing each word for truth. Then he reached out and squeezed Trevor's shoulder. "You need anything, I'm here."

Trevor gave a short nod and turned away to grab his

gear bag. Even for him, so used to hiding behind "the badass," it was hard to keep from showing the emotion inspired by Dwight's statement. He didn't deserve a friend like Dwight. He didn't deserve a girl like Paige. But for some unfathomable reason, there they were. And he was going to do everything in his power not to let them down.

The crowd at the game had a field day with the news about Trevor's juvenile record. Several busloads of Express fans made a special trip to Kilby, armed with banners that said things like *Baseball's Most Wanted Outfield* and *Three Strikes, Go Back to Jail* and *The Kilby Jailbirds*.

Kind of funny, Trevor had to admit. But if they were trying to rattle him, it wouldn't work. As always, hecklers fueled his drive to win. When he stood in left field, he held his glove behind his back, his other hand nestled in the webbing, and every time he heard a taunt, he flashed a subtle middle finger. Anything too obvious would get him busted.

He got his true revenge, as Grizz had always promised, at the plate. He absolutely dominated the Express pitcher. He worked every count as deep as he could, then hit for the cycle. A single, a double, a triple, a home run. In that order. *Fuck y'all.*

The Kilby fans ate it up. Not to be outdone in the signage department, they held banners that said things like *We Heart our Deadly Weapon* with a picture of Trevor's face. Or *Don't Mess with Kilby, Texas.*

He didn't respond to the show of support explicitly, letting his play at the plate do his talking for him. That's where it counted. On the field. He allowed himself one single moment of expression. When he ran the bases after his home run, he pointed at the crowd and put a fist to his heart. They roared in response.

The other Catfish took their cue from him, lighting up poor Jon Golden like a pinball machine. By the fifth inning the score was 10-2, and the Catfish had a swagger like the New York Yankees.

Crush sat in the owner's box alone, Armani shades firmly in place, either watching the game or talking on his phone. Why wasn't Paige with him? Between innings, Trevor paced the dugout, checking and rechecking the owner's box. She must have seen the article; everyone had. She'd left a couple of messages on his voice mail, but he'd been too busy dealing with his agent and Nina to call her back. Would things change between them? Would she want nothing to do with him now that his sordid past was public knowledge?

He wouldn't blame her. In fact, he'd probably encourage her to dump his ass. He would do it himself, except that he'd noticed a tiny item in the entertainment section of the same edition that revealed his juvenile record. Newlyweds Nessa Brindisi and Hudson Notswego had signed a contract to star in a reality show about Hudson's first season in the NBA. There was no way he would add to Paige's pain with another breakup.

Nine innings later there was still no sign of Paige. That fact bothered him more than any banner or harassing comment. Something was wrong. As soon as he made it to the clubhouse, he called and texted her, but got no answer. He quickly showered and got dressed.

The clubhouse was euphoric over the team's victory. "The Express guys are going to the Roadhouse." Ramirez grinned, looking gleeful. "Wouldn't mind rubbing a little salt in the wounds, with a chaser of tequila."

"Don't do it," Trevor warned. "That's asking for trouble."

"Hey, the Roadhouse is our spot and everyone knows it. If the Express are going there, you know they're looking for trouble. Just trying to oblige our guests." Ramirez looked a little too excited about the prospect of a showdown.

Dwight zipped up his tracksuit jacket. "That's right. Gotta be a good host."

Leiberman was looking from one to the other. "Can't we just send them a fruit basket?"

Everyone burst out laughing, and Sonny Barnes clapped him on the shoulder. "Good one. Maybe some oranges."

The clubhouse filled with high-fives, hoots, and hollers.

"Count me out," Trevor said, hoisting his gym bag to his shoulder. "I have to take care of something."

"That something have a name?"

He ignored that. "Mañana, y'all. Good game tonight."

On his way out, he passed the long buffet table the team set up after the games but didn't stop. He'd eat later, once he knew where Paige was.

Taking the stairs three at a time, he hurried to Crush's office, which was still lit up. Crush stood with his back to the door, a cell phone to his ear, nodding. He caught sight of Trevor's reflection in the plate glass and signaled for him to wait.

"We're on the same page, then," Crush said. He ended the call and flung the phone across the room. Trevor jumped. "The amount of trouble you cause me is roughly triple that of any other player."

Trevor bristled. "Did you say triple? Yeah, I hit one of those tonight. And a double and a homer. I hit for the cycle." A little reminder that he might be worth the trouble.

Crush let out a long breath. "Always the smartass. That was the Friars on the phone. You're still in for now, but they're watching very, very, very closely. One wrong move and you're done. How's it going to look for a team with the name of Friars to have a former criminal on their roster? Someone convicted of *assault*?"

Crush's contemptuous tone was like sandpaper on an open wound. He longed to lash out at the man. But he was Paige's father, and for her sake he wouldn't. He cleared his throat. "I . . . uh . . . won't cause any trouble. Any . . . more trouble."

A steely glare raked him up and down. "You and I both know that's impossible as long as you're seeing my daughter."

Trevor set his jaw. Maybe Crush had sent Paige somewhere just to keep him away from her. Maybe he'd locked her in the pool house and confiscated her cell phone. "I'm not going to hurt Paige."

"I've seen how you operate. Fuck, I *was* you for most of my twenties. Maybe part of my thirties. Then again in my forties, come to think of it. You're not talking to a rookie here."

"Look, Crush, I'd probably see it the same way from your shoes. But Paige means a lot to me. I'd never want to hurt her."

"Then leave her alone. You're no good for her."

Trevor clenched his fists, every muscle of his body tight. The memory of that asshole driving away in his Escalade with Paige in the passenger seat flashed across his vision. Who was he kidding? He'd already brought danger into her life. He couldn't disagree with Crush, so he said nothing.

"If you had any integrity, you would walk away from Paige so she can meet the right guy. Not some juvenile offender who disrespects the game of baseball."

Crush's scorn was amplified by a sort of Greek chorus of baseball legends lined up on the walls of his office. The row of photos seemed to grin mockingly down at Trevor. A jersey behind a glass frame, a plaque, a ceremonial letter from the city of Austin . . . all the accouterments of a long and respected career. Trevor had never felt more worthless.

"I don't disrespect baseball. I love baseball. And I—" He caught himself. Fuck this. He wasn't going to defend himself to Crush Taylor. The man would never understand. And anyway, this wasn't about him—it was about Paige. He straightened to his full height and braced his legs apart. "You can sling insults at me all you want. I'm not walking away from Paige. Not after what Notswego did to her. If she wants it over, it's over. But I won't be the one to leave her, and there's nothing you can say that will make me."

Crush tilted his head back, looking at him down his long nose, showing no expression. His phone buzzed but he ignored it. "What'd you come up here for?"

"I . . ." He swallowed. "Paige didn't come to the game. I saw the bit in the paper about Nessa and Hudson's reality show. I was worried she might be upset."

"Trying to make me think you're a sensitive guy? Ice man Trevor Stark?"

Trevor fought to keep a grip on his temper. Fought to push all emotion inside where no one would see it. "Paige is the sensitive one. She might be hurting."

"And you think she wants you?" Crush raised a scornful eyebrow.

Trevor clung to his stony silence by the skin of his teeth. It sounded ridiculous, now that Crush put it that way. If Paige had wanted his help, she would have called him. He should never have come up here and subjected himself to her father's derision.

Crush picked up his flask and fiddled with the top. "She's at the ranch looking for that damn cat. He's missing and she's afraid a coyote might have gotten him. She asked me to tell you after the game. Didn't want to distract you."

"You could have told me right away." Trevor turned on his heel. With Jerome missing, Paige must be a wreck. Damn Crush for making him wait.

"Fuck that. I wasn't going to tell you at all, but you surprised me by coming up here. You've got balls, I'll give you that."

But Trevor was already out the door.

Chapter 18

Aᴛ Bᴜʟʟᴘᴇɴ Rᴀɴᴄʜ, Trevor found Paige in the barn, an airy, newish structure sided with planks of gray pine. His heart clenched at the sight of her huddled on the floor, her back against a hay bale. She held tight to the white ball of fur in her arms. Her sobs echoed through the barn. The earthy aroma of manure and hay wafted around them, and her hair streamed down her back in tangled waves.

He dropped next to her. "Is Jerome okay?"

"He . . . he's fine," she managed, the words skipping between hiccups. "I found him curled up in an orange tree planter. It's . . . it's . . ." Moisture dropped onto Jerome's fur, but the cat didn't seem to notice.

"Hudson?"

"Sort of . . ." Shaking her head, she scrubbed away the tears. "It's me. My mother called to tell me about their new reality show. It's the first time I've really talked to her about everything. I felt like such a loser. I shouldn't have married him, I should have stayed in college, I should learn from her example. Etcetera etcetera. She wants me to come to Philadelphia so she can fix my life."

He went cold despite the stuffy heat of the barn.

It hadn't occurred to him that Paige might leave, but this wasn't even her home. It was a temporary stopover between her life in Italy and whatever came next. He cleared his throat. "Are you going to?"

She glanced up, her big blue eyes sheened with tears. He fought hard to keep the need out of his expression. Logically, it would be best for her to leave. Crush didn't want Paige hanging out with him. And with the article exposing his past, things in his life might get intense. He didn't want her to get caught up in the mess. But still . . . God, he didn't want her to go anywhere. It would feel like ripping out his insides, to say good-bye to her now.

"No," she said softly. "I'm not going anywhere." She dug her fingers into Jerome's fur, rubbing the skin on the back of his neck until his purr sounded like a Harley. "I have that fund-raiser coming up, and . . . there are other reasons."

He tried not to let his relief show. "Maybe it would be good to see your mother."

"No. My mother is . . . she's very busy. If I went to Philly, she'd have me booked up with cocktail parties and job interviews and class schedules and . . ." She shook her head. "I came here because I knew Crush would give me some space. And because I needed . . . I wanted . . . I knew he wouldn't make me feel like a failure. He's screwed up so much himself, you know. Nothing surprises him."

He reached out and touched her hair, both to soothe her and indulge himself in the feel of its vibrant silkiness. It slid across his palm, and right away he wanted more. "Your mother's never screwed up?"

"I wouldn't say never. She's dated a few jerks. But as soon as she realizes they're jerks, she cuts them off. Me, on the other hand . . . she thinks I'm too soft. She compared me to Jerome!"

The indignation in her voice made Trevor give a snort of laughter. Jerome lifted his head from her lap, then laid it back down on Paige's knee.

"Sorry," Trevor said, tucking a strand of hair behind her ears. "Why Jerome?"

"I told you he's a Ragdoll. They're bred for their affectionate nature, and look what happens when you pick them up." She stood, holding Jerome under his middle. His head drooped to one side of her hand, his rear end to the other. It looked as if all his bones had gone on strike. "They turn into floppy little rag dolls. And my mother thinks that's me! She thinks because I care about people I'm a floppy rag doll. Am I a floppy rag doll, Trevor? Is that what you think of me?" She gestured with the hand that held Jerome; he swayed back and forth, his blue eye blinking sleepily.

Right now she looked like a pissed-off spitfire, not a rag doll. He rose to his feet. "I've been to bed with you, Paige Taylor. I don't think you're a floppy rag doll."

The last time they'd made love, she'd straddled him with her long-legged body, milking his cock while he filled his hands with nipples the color of cinnamon candy. Paige was no rag doll. She was passionate. Maybe a little impulsive. Reckless with her heart. Soft, yes. In the most rare and precious way.

She gave a sob. Jerome leaped from her arms and landed with a thump on the dusty hay-strewn floorboards. Trevor took one of her hands in his, feeling its slight tremble.

"Paige, let me tell you something. It's not braver or smarter to shut people out. Just ask Crush. Or me, for fuck's sake. It takes courage to care about people the way you do. Kind is not the same thing as soft."

"Kind, again." She tried to tug her hand from his, but he wouldn't let her.

"Yeah, kind. And sometimes you might get burned for that. You might get hurt. But it's a beautiful thing to be the way you are. If it was up to me, you'd never change." With his other hand, he twined a shank of her hair around his wrist and tugged lightly. "You're only twenty-four, you're gorgeous, smart. You could do anything you want. Go anywhere. Get your degree, don't get your degree, it doesn't matter to me. Just be Paige, and that's enough. It's more than enough. It's a fucking miracle."

She stared at him, her lips parted in wonder. "Oh, Trevor . . ."

Oh hell. He'd said too much. Revealed how much she meant to him. He felt stupidly weak all of a sudden, as if power was leaking out of him like air from a balloon. He stood there cursing himself for a sappy-ass fool.

But he couldn't turn away. Even with tears marking her face, she lit up the dusty barn like firelight.

She lowered her eyes, wiped a tear off her cheek with the heel of her hand, then shot him a look from under her lashes. "Did you know there's a room with a lock in this place?"

"What?" She knew what that come-hither look did to him. And suddenly the barn felt very private, very quiet, as if the still air was just waiting for something to stir it up.

"I'll show you." She took his hand and pulled him toward the back of the barn. He went, excitement tightening his chest and prodding at his cock. "It's a tack room, and it has thousands of dollars' worth of hand-tooled leather riding gear. I made my father put a lock on it because you never know with the people he brings out here. But I . . ." She dug in her pocket. ". . . have the key."

Glancing over her shoulder, her eyes danced in the

golden, dusty light. He couldn't have resisted even if he'd wanted to. She pulled him into an overcrowded room that smelled like linseed oil and leather. A heavy anticipation pulsed through his veins. He wanted to see her fresh, freckled skin against all that dark leather. He wanted to see the line of her throat, naked, the rich fall of her hair. He wanted to see the pink lips of her sex wet and begging.

From the quickness of her breath, the flush in her cheeks, she was right there with him.

She turned the key in the lock, closing them inside. Then she spread her hands apart, as if to cede the moment to him.

"Get naked," he ordered. Her eyes flared, then narrowed.

"I'm not a rag doll, to just do what you say."

"No. You're not." He advanced on her, wanting her so badly he could barely walk. "You're a passionate, sensual, sexy woman with a will of your own. Now get naked."

She put a hand on his chest, stopping him a foot away from her. "After you."

"As you wish." He tore his clothes off so quickly, he hit his elbow on the wall. His cock was already hard. He gripped it at the base, watched her tongue run across her lips. "Your turn."

She wore a thin-ribbed tank top with a picture of cowboy boots on the front. Underneath, her nipples were already hard. "I changed my mind," he said, staring at them, stroking himself. "Leave your shirt on and play with your nipples. Pinch them."

Her pupils expanded to a deep midnight blue. Her chest rose and fell, quick breaths stirring the dust motes in the air. His excitement was nearly unbearable as he watched her bring her thumb and index fingers to the tips of her breasts and gently pinch.

"More," he ordered. "Harder."

She squeezed harder, rolling her nipples slightly. Her eyes fell halfway shut, and she tilted her chest toward him, as if chasing the sensation.

"Is that material rough, sweetheart? Does it feel good?"

She nodded, as if afraid to spoil the mood by speaking.

"Show me. Lift your top. Show me your nipples."

Face flaming, she did as he asked, revealing nipples so aroused they'd turned a deep, brick red. They trembled slightly as her breasts moved with her rapid breaths. Her torso was slim and long, breasts proud and perfect. Arousal swelled his cock. "You're so beautiful, Paige. Take off your shirt. The rest of your clothes too."

She made a show out of it, undulating her upper body and wiggling her hips until he wanted to throw her down, the tease. *Not yet.* First he wanted to bring her to an orgasm she'd never forget.

When she was completely naked, he said, "Lean back against that saddle. I want to see your skin against it."

"Like this?" She posed provocatively against the dark leather with its whipped seams. She was a vision, her skin smooth as milk, her light sprinkling of freckles glowing like gold flakes, her erect nipples so dark they looked bronzed. She spread her legs hip width apart, just enough so he saw the pout of moisture deep in her soft brown curls.

His mouth watered, his tongue moving in hungry anticipation. He gripped his cock again, felt it pulse against his palm. *Not your turn yet.* He gave it a hard pull, a promise of what was to come, then approached the naked woman posed before him.

"Well?" She asked, a little cheeky, a little nervous. "Are you going to ride me, big boy?"

In answer, he dragged two fingers along the seam of her sex, feeling her delicious plump clit warm under his touch. Her head fell back against the saddle. The perfect arch from chin to clavicle was exactly as he'd imagined. He traced it with his tongue while he gathered her soft nether curls in his fist, tugging, claiming. She pushed against his hand, making him aware of how outrageously wet she was.

"You want to come?" He tugged at her mound, finding her clit with his thumb.

"Oh my God, yes."

"Then stay still. Spread your legs farther apart."

He could barely wait to taste that liquid honey, the living essence of her arousal. He dropped to his knees, reaching up to fill his palms with her breasts. Closing his fingers, nipples pressed between them, he pulled a deep spasm from her. She arched her back, pushed her breasts into his hands. When Paige wanted something, she was fierce about it. And she wanted to come, every quiver of her body screamed it.

Bending his head to her mound, he brushed his face against her curls, inhaling the scent of aroused woman.

"You're going to come in my mouth," he told her. "I want to feel your sweet little clit swell up against my tongue."

"Fine. Please. Just do it."

"Close your eyes." He didn't want to shock her with what he was about to do.

When her eyes had drifted shut, he reached for one of the riding crops hanging from pegs on the wall. A slightly curving black pole with a soft swish of suede fringe at the end. Slowly, he drew the hard tip across the seam of her sex, ending with the drag of fringe across her clit. She gasped, her inner thighs trembling. When he withdrew the crop, the end was slick with moisture.

"What was that?" she asked, voice shaking.

"Did it feel good?"

"Yes. A little scary, but good."

"I'm not going to hurt you. I just want to make it good." He stroked his tongue where the crop had gone, placing his own warm flesh where the hard ebony had traveled. He knew the contrast would make her crazy.

"Again," she gasped. "That feels amazing."

He did it again, alternating the hard stroke of the crop with the wet drag of tongue. This time he pushed the thumb of his other hand inside her, and explored the crevice of her ass with his fingers. He wanted her off balance, utterly focused on him and what he was doing to her. The room was completely quiet, the only sound her soft quick breaths and the swish of suede on her skin. The smell of sex hung around them, heavy and arousing.

"Trevor, I can't . . ." She shuddered, her body straining for release. "Please."

"I want you to come into my mouth. Hard. You hear?"

"Yes. Yes, I hear. Please." Her head turned from side to side, frantic, her hair damp with sweat. God, she was sexy.

He stroked her with his hand now, the rough calluses adding even more stimulation. "Do you know what I'm famous for in hitting?"

"*What?*" Her voice rose to that frantic, impatient level when she started ordering him around. He loved it when she got like that. "You're talking about baseball? *Now?*"

"I'm famous . . ." He touched his tongue to her clit, then withdrew. ". . . for working the count as deep as possible. Every time. Drawing it out. Making contact. Making the pitchers work for it."

She released a sob of frustration. "Don't you mean toying with them like a cat with a mouse? Just . . . just . . . hit a grounder or something. I don't care."

He laughed. "Why hit a grounder when you can swing for the stars?" He buried his face between her legs, lapping up the sweet juices, chasing each tremble and swell.

"Does that analogy include a . . . an orgasm?"

He smiled against her sex. Saucy Paige. Her legs were shaking, so he draped them over his shoulders. He settled her ass in his hands, right where he could control her movements. She wanted more friction, but he drew it out as long as he could manage, reveling in the scent and feel of her intimate self. When her gasps came closer and louder, her movements more desperate, he vibrated his tongue hard and fast against her clit, exactly how he knew she craved it. She came hard, her wails rising to the ceiling. She thrashed against the saddle, pressing her heels into his back. Her creamy juices drenched his mouth. Paige orgasming was the hottest thing he'd ever seen, and his cock rose heavy between his legs.

While she was still shaking from that climax, he turned her around, bent her over with her hands on the saddle, and slipped on a condom with clumsy, overexcited hands. He parted her thighs and buried his aching cock into her hot flesh. Her channel was still quivering from her orgasm. Good. She was about to have another one.

He took a moment to calm himself, shaping the globes of her ass, stroking the smooth curves. Then he gripped her harder and levered his hips against her rear while pulling her tight against him. "Come for me again, Paige. Do it." He drove into her with steady, powerful strokes, a hammering rhythm that made her pussy clench tight like a fist. They were perfect together, hot and slippery and wild and . . .

With a cry, she crested, her body strung taut between the saddle and his hips. He followed in a wild explosion of pleasure.

Shaking, Paige straightened, though her legs could barely hold her up. She gripped the saddle horn for support. "Okay, now I really feel like a rag doll," she murmured.

"Well, you're not. Believe me, I wouldn't be feeling this way about a rag doll."

Feeling what way? She waited for him to say more, but he clammed up. An awkward silence fell between them. As if they'd gone so deep neither knew what to say about it.

With fortunate timing, Jerome meowed loudly from the other side of the door. She turned the key and allowed him in. Tail held high, swinging his head to take in the scene with his one eye, he stalked in like some sort of hall monitor come to investigate misbehavior. "Make way for the real Ragdoll," Paige announced, winning a smile from Trevor.

Whew. Jerome had a way of showing up at the perfect moment.

Trevor bent over to pull on his jeans. With sweat gleaming on his rippling stomach, arm muscles flexing as he tugged at the denim, it was almost impossible to look away from him. She reached for her clothes as well. The memory of how quickly she'd shed them made heat stain her cheeks. She stepped into her panties and shorts.

"Listen . . . I'm sorry about the newspaper article. I left you a few messages, then I got distracted looking for Jerome. Are you okay?"

He fastened his jeans, his expression settling back into the usual unreadable mask. "I'm fine. Shit happens."

"Yeah, and unfortunately the Internet makes it spread so much faster."

"Internet?" He swung his head toward her with a look of shock. The hawk on his back rippled with his movements. "I thought the article was just in the local paper."

She bit her lip. "It got picked up by several online sports publications. I'm sorry, I assumed you knew. It wouldn't be getting so much attention if not for the Baseball's Hottest Outfield campaign. And then there's the reputation of the Catfish, all the parties and brawls and pranks and so forth. Marcia's been calling me. She's afraid Crush is going to blame her."

"Crush knows where to put the blame." A muscle ticked in his jaw.

Her heart sank. Trevor and Crush must have already faced off over the article. She put a hand on his forearm. "Is there anything I can do?"

He looked down at the floor, where his bare feet glowed pale against the stained floorboards. His boots lay halfway across the room, and he went to retrieve them. "Would you like to spend the night with me?" he asked her. "Takeout and some DVD's might hit the spot. No sports shows."

Of all the things he could have suggested, that invitation surprised her the most. It sounded so . . . normal. "I'd like that, but I promised to help Crush tonight. He finally took my advice and asked the gorgeous mayor over for dinner. I told him I'd cook. I was in the middle of chopping vegetables when I realized Jerome was missing. Do you want to stay here and help me?"

"Trust me, Crush doesn't want me around right now." He shook his head and bent down to pull on his boots. The sight of his big-knuckled hands on the leather of his Timberlands made her blood hum.

"Where did you learn to do that? With the riding crop?" The question slipped out before she could help it, and she instantly flushed. "I'm sorry. I don't mean . . . you're just . . . I've never . . ." She trailed off, since she couldn't think of any way to fix it.

"It doesn't matter." Trevor pulled his bootlaces tight. "That's all in the past."

She turned away from him. Maybe she didn't want to know anyway. It was bad enough knowing that Hudson was now married to another woman. She didn't need to torture herself over Trevor too. Obviously he was experienced. Expert, even. He'd pulled reactions from her body that she didn't know were possible.

"Hey," Trevor said gently, stopping her hand as she reached for the doorknob. "Don't go there."

"I'm just letting poor Jerome out."

"Not that." The stern, perfect lines of his face had softened, his eyes a tender, warm peridot instead of their usual crystalline shade. "Don't think about the past. As far as I'm concerned, there wasn't anyone before you."

Confusion flashed through her. What was he saying? But then his phone buzzed and the moment passed, leaving her to speculate about every possible interpretation of his words.

Chapter 19

TREVOR TOOK OFF shortly after that phone call. He wouldn't say anything about it, but when she asked if there'd been any repercussions from the direction of Detroit, he reassured her that nothing like that had surfaced.

Paige went back to her dinner preps. She'd even gone to the embarrassing extent of looking up some of Nessa Brindisi's recipes online. Say what you would about the woman, she knew how to cook.

She'd found a good chicken pot pie recipe that looked doable, but now she didn't have time to bake anything. Thank Trevor and his talented hands, mouth, body, etcetera, for that. Every time she thought about their session in the tack room, she went hot and liquid inside. How long had they been in there, lost in that feverish dream world together? She'd completely lost track of time and everything else.

Luckily, she could blame the delay on Jerome's disappearance.

Instead of making pot pie, she fried the chicken, added the vegetables she'd already cut up, and scattered pieces of pie crust on top of the whole thing.

"Chicken cobbler," she told her father and Mayor

Trent when she presented it to them with a flourish. "My own recipe." *Take that, Nessa Brindisi.*

"I've never heard of chicken cobbler." The mayor—who insisted Paige call her Wendy—smiled with only a tiny trace of skepticism.

Paige liked her.

Clearly, Crush did too, since he kept reaching for his root beer as if forgetting that it wasn't alcohol. She knew her father; she'd seen him get married twice, and date dozens and dozens of women. When he actually liked someone, he got very nervous. The lack of liquor probably made it worse.

Before he even took a bite, he managed to knock his fork off the table. Jerome, filled with an unusual amount of energy since his disappearing act, raced after it. Wendy reached down for it and got a handful of fur instead. She shrieked, which frightened Jerome. The cat scrambled away from her and clawed his way to safety, which, in his one-eyed confusion, he thought would be Crush's pants leg.

Crush huffed and shoved away from the table, lifting his leg with Jerome still clinging to it.

"I'm so sorry. I'll take him away." Paige rushed forward to collect her panicked cat. He didn't even do the boneless thing, that's how freaked out he was. "Do you need anything else, Dad?"

"No," he said firmly. "I think we can take it from here."

"Thank you very much, Paige." Wendy smiled at her. She looked different without her usual helmet of hair. She'd left it soft and loose around her shoulders and looked about ten years younger. Her deep green tunic top and black slacks gave her a relaxed, sexy look. Crush appreciated the change, judging by the way he sent the silverware flying. "It's really nice of you to make such a lovely meal for us. Isn't it strange that a man can reach retirement age and not know how to cook?"

"Now wait one chicken-frying second," Crush said. "Just because I retired from baseball doesn't mean I'm 'retirement age.' I'm still young and impressively vigorous."

Wendy raised an eyebrow, as if daring him to prove it.

"Ahem." Paige cleared her throat while backing out of the room. "I'm still here. Please don't use words like vigorous."

Neither one of them looked at her. Maybe Crush had chosen his vocabulary well. Energy crackled between him and Wendy.

"I'm leaving now. I'll be upstairs if you need anything."

Still no reaction from the two.

"I think you broke the ice," Paige whispered in Jerome's twitching ear. "Nice job."

Back in her room, she settled Jerome into his cat bed, then checked her computer. She'd been monitoring the news reports all day, checking for updates on the article about Trevor. Marcia had called her first thing in the morning, asking her to do whatever damage control needed to be done on the club's social media accounts.

Even though it had torn her away from her fundraiser organizing, she'd spent the day answering comments and e-mails, repeating the same basic statements. *Trevor Stark's record as a juvenile has no bearing on his performance on the baseball field today . . . The Friars organization stands behind Trevor Stark . . . No, this isn't a reflection on Crush Taylor's fitness to be a minor league team owner . . . No, we have not seen the newest "Can the Catfish" petition . . . The Catfish are focused on winning the Triple A National Baseball*

Championship for the wonderful Kilby fans who have stuck with the team through the years.

Earlier, she'd sent an e-mail to the legal department asking why his juvenile record had been made public. Finally an answer arrived.

Looks like his records were hacked. The police department has notified us that MacPhail has some computer experience but hasn't admitted any involvement. They don't know how he knew to hack Wayne County, since Stark uses a different name now. But it wouldn't be too difficult to find out, since he went through a legal name change and those records are all public.

She worried at her thumbnail, wondering how she should pursue this further without setting off any alarm bells. Was Tom MacPhail working with someone, or for someone? Had he made contact with anyone else, say, from Detroit? Was this an isolated action by a jealous boyfriend or something more sinister?

Out of curiosity, she Googled "Detroit gangs" and looked for something with a W, since that was the emblem burned onto Trevor's back. One recent article surfaced about a shipment of pharmaceuticals that had been carjacked and stolen. The Wachowski syndicate was suspected, but no solid evidence had been uncovered. Alarms were being sounded about the security of deliveries of pharmaceuticals. A task force was being formed and a crackdown was under way.

A search for the name Wachowski found many, many references to the creators of the Matrix movies. Narrowing it down to Detroit, she found several mentions of the growing menace of this particular gang. One news story from seven years earlier mentioned that a high-ranking member of the Wachowski family, Dinar, was found in a local pharmacy with his head bashed in. He was in critical condition but expected to survive. Although there were no witnesses, a minor had confessed to the attack. Drug involvement was suspected.

Seeing it there on her computer screen in black and white gave her chills. The news article matched what Trevor had said. She could picture the scene, the man lying on the floor of the pharmacy, blood seeping from his head. Trevor standing over him with a baseball bat. What had happened to Dinar Wachowski? Was he still alive? How bad was his brain damage?

She did another quick search for "Dinar Wachowski," but found no more mentions after that particular one. Did that mean he'd left the gang? Died? Lost all brain function?

Didn't matter. He deserved whatever bad thing happened to him. She just wished there was a way to relieve Trevor of his worry about retribution.

Then again, maybe he had good reason to worry. What did she know about this sort of thing?

She put her computer to sleep and went downstairs to make herself a cup of tea. The staircase led to the living room, which she would normally walk through to reach the kitchen, but Crush and Wendy were eating at the small dining area by the hearth. Instead, she circled around the long way, past the downstairs bathroom and the lower level bedrooms to reach the kitchen by the back entrance.

No use . . . she could still hear their murmuring voices when she reached the kitchen. Humming to herself in order to tune them out, she put the teakettle on a burner and turned on the flame.

Just as the water was coming to a boil, the name "Stark," spoken in Crush's rough tones, caught her attention. She turned off the flame and tiptoed toward the living room. As she'd explained to Crush when she was twelve, she didn't believe in eavesdropping except when it was very important. In that case, she'd listened in on a phone conversation between her parents about the big baseball road trip.

This was even more important.

"I'm between a rock and a hard place," Crush was saying. "The Friars are ready to wash their hands of Stark. But I need him if I want to keep the team."

"Why don't the Friars just leave him here in Kilby, then? This championship talk is getting the town all revved up. It's good for the local economy. As mayor, I approve of that. Would it help if I wrote a letter to the Friars?"

Crush laughed at that. "That would be a first. 'Dear Friars, would you consider leaving your obscenely over-paid left fielder here in Kilby so we can improve the local economy? Oh, and please continue paying his ridiculous salary while you're at it.' Good thought, and I do appreciate it. But I don't think it would do much more than entertain the front office for a few minutes."

"Right." Wendy didn't sound offended. Paige got the feeling she was used to Crush's caustic style. "Are you sure you need Trevor to win?"

"Yes. We aren't guaranteed to win with him, but we're guaranteed to lose without him."

A pause, a clink of glassware against a plate. Paige winced, hoping her father wasn't about to knock something else off the table.

"What are you going to do?" the mayor finally asked.

"It's not really up to me. If they call him up, they call him up. Bye-bye championship. But with this revelation about his juvenile record, they're getting antsy. They want me to give them my recommendation. Duke has already said that Trevor's ready and they should take their chances with a call-up. Now they want me to weigh in."

"So if you agree with Duke, you lose Trevor, the championship, and the team."

"Correct."

"And if you don't agree, what happens? Will they drop Trevor Stark?"

"Probably. He has a morals clause in his contract. It won't be hard to find a reason to dump him. They probably could have already if they wanted to. But he can hit like an all-star, so they keep hoping he'll straighten out."

Don't drop him, Paige wanted to scream. *He deserves better. He's screwing up on purpose, just for his sister.* She fought with her conscience for a long moment, standing there in the kitchen, with the teakettle starting to whistle.

Crush was in an impossible situation. So was Trevor. And so was she. If she told Crush what was really going on, Trevor would be furious.

"What do you think, personally?" Wendy asked. "You must have an opinion on the most controversial Catfish of all."

"You came to a game the other day. You saw him hit. What do you think?"

The mayor got a teasing note in her voice. "Well, he's a baseball player, so . . ."

"So he's superior in every way," Crush said, finishing her sentence.

"Arrogant and cocky, was more where I was going."

"All a matter of perspective. If you can back it up, it ain't arrogant. So who was that man you were with at the Italian place?"

Paige took that as her cue to get out before the pair interrupted their flirting long enough to notice someone was in the kitchen making tea. She tiptoed out the back door, snagged her flip-flops, and ran to the Range Rover her father had told her to use during her stay.

The least she could do was warn Trevor about what the Friars were considering.

Stomach growling with hunger, Trevor swung by the Smoke Pit BBQ on his way back to his hotel. During his time in Texas, the local obsession with charred and sauce-drenched meat had grown on him. As a city kid, when he first arrived in Kilby he'd seen nothing more than a slowpoke town with a shortage of tall buildings. But now he actually cared about the place. The people were friendly—at least the ones not chasing him with a BB gun. Or the ones writing petitions to send the Catfish to another town.

He loved the way people brought signs to the games, the way they really got into the ridiculous promotions. Kilby was a fun town where people watched out for each other. And best of all, he'd met Paige Taylor here.

How she'd managed to sneak under his extremely well-constructed defenses, he had no idea. Somehow, she was just there, as inevitable and glorious as the sun. What was he going to do about Paige? She'd changed things inside him, and he no longer knew what end was up. For so long, his guiding purpose had been to keep Nina safe. That need still existed, but others clamored for attention too.

Especially the one with wild hair, endless legs, and dazzling blue eyes.

At the Smoke Pit, he talked a little baseball with the owner, Bud, and ordered baby back ribs, a side of corn bread, and a bottle of Snapple to go. With his white to-go bag in hand, he headed for the exit.

A hand on his arm made him pause just outside the door. "You gotta minute?" The low voice with a Texas drawl didn't make it sound like a question. Three big beefy men in cowboy hats muscled him behind the

Smoke Pit, where a Dumpster squatted against the back wall. The stench of meat and smoke and grease hung heavy in the air.

He didn't struggle, figuring three huge men in a dark alley probably had the advantage over him, but every muscle in his body went on full alert. He clung to the fact that these guys were wearing cowboy hats and worn jeans. They weren't from Detroit.

"What do you want?" he asked, pulling his arm from the man's grasp.

"Let him go." Someone stepped from behind the Dumpster, avoiding the hazy light cast by the rear window of the Smoke Pit. His build, stocky and imposing, with the stance of someone who'd spent plenty of time in a saddle, looked familiar. The last time he saw the man, he'd gotten a shot of vodka out of the deal.

"Dean Wade?"

"That's right." Wade came forward to shake his hand. Trevor had no desire to make friends with the guy, but considering the three huge men still hovering around them, he decided to comply.

"How y'all doin', Trevor Stark?"

"Well, aside from the fact my barbecue's getting cold and I'm hanging out next to a Dumpster, not too bad."

Dean Wade chuckled. With his bolo tie and black leather jacket, he didn't look like a power-hungry millionaire, but Trevor knew that's what he was. He'd seen the kind of clout the Wades wielded in Kilby. But what did the most powerful family in town want with him? "Sorry about that. I saw the opportunity and seized it. You're not the easiest guy to reach."

That's because he wasn't listed anywhere and didn't give out his e-mail address. "You must have a real good reason to come between a man and his baby back ribs."

"Got a proposal for you. I've been watching you, and I see someone I can work with."

A cold snake of suspicion slithered into his gut. "How do you mean?"

"You're all business on the baseball field. Cold as ice, they say. You're all about domination. Intimidation. I look at you and I see . . . myself with a helluva lot faster swing." He chuckled, as did his entourage of beefcake.

Trevor didn't smile. He put his game face on, the one that revealed absolutely nothing of his thoughts. "You want my spot on the Catfish?"

"Nah, I'm a bull-riding fan. Don't care much for baseball."

"I thought you all wanted to buy the Catfish from Crush Taylor."

Wade pushed his cowboy hat back on his head. "We do. That's where you come in. Crush made that stupid-ass vow to win the championship or sell the team. I sent him an entire side of prime Grade A Wade beef when he did that. Made it easy on us. The Catfish ain't had a playoff season in twenty years."

"We're at the top of the standings right now."

Wade made a signal with his index finger, and suddenly Trevor's right arm—his power arm—was yanked behind his back. Pain lanced through his shoulder.

"Don't remind me." Wade smiled grimly. "Y'all started to win, thanks to 'top prospect' and slugging sensation Trevor Stark. Even that wasn't so bad, because you were gonna get called up before long, and then the Catfish would go back to losin'. Then your juvenile crimes came to light and the way I hear it from my inside sources, you ain't goin' anywhere unless Crush gives the okay. I don't like him holding all the cards."

Trevor was sweating from the pain. "What are you going to do, break my arm?"

"That's always an option. But my brother, he pulled the reins on that one. He says he's a fan." Dean sounded disgusted by that. "But he agreed to do things my way if you don't line up."

Trevor could feel the tendons in his shoulder straining. A few more moments and the arm-breaking would be a done deal. He stomped on the arm-twister's instep and swung around, plowing an elbow into his throat. The other two closed in on him, but he slammed his bag of barbecue against the edge of the Dumpster and smashed his Snapple bottle. He brandished the bag at the guys. A jagged edge of glass jutted through a mess of barbecue sauce.

"If you have a simple business proposition, why'd you bring these guys along?" Crouching, he pointed the broken bottle at the closest thug. "Is that how you do business in Kilby?"

Dean stuck his thumbs in his front pockets, a laugh shaking his stocky form. "I shoulda known you could scrap, growin' up as you did. Fair point, though. Back off, boys."

Trevor kept his weaponized Snapple bottle aimed at the men even as they backed away. "What do you want from me, Wade? Spit it out."

"I want you to throw the championship. Or make sure the Catfish don't even get that far. I want Crush to hand me the team on a silver platter."

Throw a baseball game? Trevor scowled. The infamous Black Sox had been paid to throw games, but that was back in 1919. And it had taken a few players, not just one. "I'm just the left fielder. Baseball has nine guys on that field."

"You're worth all nine put together, according to Roy," said Dean. "And that part ain't my problem. How you do it, it's up to you. Hell, break your own arm for all I care. Just make sure the Catfish lose. Should be easy. They always lost in the past."

"That's unethic—" He stopped before he could finish the word, since there was no way Dean cared about ethics in baseball.

"This is the minor leagues, Trevor Stark. No one cares what goes on down here. From what I hear, you sure don't. It's a paycheck, ain't that right? Well, think of this as the price you gotta pay."

"Pay for what? What's in this for me? You said it was a business proposition. Right now, it's a little one-sided."

"Well, interesting question, that. We got ourselves a carrot and we got a stick. Carrot is, once you do your part and we own the team, we'll get you some kinda bonus."

From the vague nature of the "carrot," Trevor guessed the true enticement was in the stick. "And if I don't go along with this?"

"Then we get hold of those Wachowskis and tell them who we found here in Kilby, walkin' around like he didn't nearly kill one of their top guys."

It had been so long since Trevor had heard that name spoken aloud. The hand holding the broken Snapple started to shake; he clamped down on it with all the accumulated experience of hiding his emotions behind a mask. "They're not exactly easy to contact."

"We already have a phone number. Handy to have, in case any other business interests line up."

Trevor flinched. He could imagine many things the Wachowskis and the Wades could collaborate on, once they got past their cultural differences.

"Is that a 'yes' I see?" Wade asked, the smugness in his tone making Trevor want to hurl the bottle at his face. "I thought so."

A gruff voice called from within the Smoke Pit. "Takin' a smoke break. Be back in five." Footsteps sounded, coming toward the door, and Dean Wade gave a signal to the guys. They stepped into the shadows.

Dean kept talking, adopting the friendly, casual tone of an old buddy. "Nice running into you again. You know we're rootin' for you guys. I got a steak dinner riding on tomorrow's game, so don't let me down."

Trevor took that warning literally, since it was clearly meant that way. "We'll do our best, Mr. Wade. A real treat running into you." He backed out of the alley, keeping his broken glass at the ready. But no one bothered to follow him. The message had been delivered.

Delivered and understood. The ball was now firmly in his court, his choices crystal clear. Sabotage the Catfish or get outed to the Wachowskis. Some fucking choice.

Chapter 20

AFTER FAILING TO find Trevor at his hotel room the night before, Paige swung by again the next morning. The team was scheduled to leave on a road trip as soon as the afternoon game was over, so her best chance of catching him was early on.

Outside the Days Inn, the sprinklers cast lazy swirls of water over the lawn, creating a mist above the tidy hedges that lined the exterior. A delivery truck was parked at the entrance while two men with dollies unloaded boxes of packaged coffee.

A busy day lay ahead, with a coffee date with Shizuko kicking things off. The international heartthrob had asked Paige to meet him at the stadium. A record label was interested in signing his band, and he really needed to decide which career path appealed to him most. Everyone in his life—family, friends, agent—had very strong opinions on the matter. According to him, only Paige was able to listen without inserting her own bias. He'd begged her to meet him first thing, and how could she turn down that sweet smile and soulful eyes?

But first she had to talk to Trevor.

He answered the door in drawstring cotton sweatpants that rode low on his hips. Even with sleepy eyes and mussed hair, he exuded coiled power and strength. He reached for her hand and tugged her through the door so she collapsed against his warm chest.

"I'm not here for sex," she said quickly.

"Are you at least willing to keep an open mind?" He nuzzled kisses into the crease of her neck. She squirmed from the tickling sensation, already feeling her resolve melt. How much could she want this man? There seemed to be no limit.

She wriggled out of his grasp before they ended up in bed and she missed her session with Shizuko. "I have to talk to you. It's serious."

"Am I late for BP? What time is it?" He was adorable, so sleepy and confused. A new growth of bronze stubble covered his jaw and gave his handsomeness a rougher edge.

"No, you're fine. It's still early. I have a packed day and wanted to make sure I caught you."

He rubbed a hand across his face. "All right, then. Shoot. What's up?"

She braced herself for the news she had to deliver. "I happened to overhear something I thought you should know. And you can skip the lecture on eavesdropping. Extenuating circumstances."

"I'm not in the habit of lecturing anyone except troubled kids trying to stay in school." Fully alert now, he scratched his stomach. "Should I put on a shirt for this?"

"Please don't." She offered him a shadow of a smile, just to lighten things up. "I heard Crush talking about the Friars. Apparently they're trying to decide whether or not to invoke a morals clause in order to release you. They don't want to keep paying your salary if you're never going to get to the majors."

He nodded once, twice, showing no other expression—classic, impassive Trevor Stark. "That's understandable."

"No, it's not. It's not fair. Juvenile records are supposed to be sealed."

A muscle in his jaw tensed, but other than that he didn't react. "That's just the last straw for the Friars. I've been riding that bubble for a while. It's all right. I made enough money to sock away and get Nina set up. That's all I wanted." As nonchalant as if he was talking about what movie to watch, he shrugged and crossed to the kitchenette, where he grabbed two bottles of water. He offered her one, but she shook her head.

He shrugged, as if nothing she said or did mattered to him, and unscrewed the top. "Suit yourself."

As he tilted the bottle to his lips, she thought back to her college psychology course, which had touched on body language. The tightness of his shoulders, the way he turned away from her, as if to shield himself, the way he wouldn't entirely meet her eyes . . . he might pretend to be unaffected, but his body told a different story.

"So . . . you're okay just walking away from the Friars."

He let a stream of liquid slide down his throat. He looked like an ad for special vitamin-loaded water. It was unfair that he looked so good while acting like such an ass. "Won't have much choice if they release me."

"But that's just it. It's not decided yet. You should talk to Crush. Tell him everything. If he advocates for you, they might change their minds."

"No."

"Why not? What's the harm? Your juvenile record already came out in the newspaper. What's wrong with explaining to Crush what really happened? He needs to know that you're still in potential danger from those people in Detroit."

Something flashed in his eyes, something fierce and vengeful, but also despairing. As if it didn't matter who knew or who did what. As if Trevor knew his fate was sealed.

"I'm not going to go crying to your father about my hard-luck life. No fucking way."

"My *father*? The fact that he's my father is totally irrelevant. He's the owner of the Catfish. The Friars listen to him."

"When they're not trying to get rid of him."

"That's a low blow. They respect his baseball knowledge. He's on the phone with the GM all the time. They play golf together. If you want to stay in the Friars organization, Crush can help you. But you need to tell him why he should. It won't mean anything unless it comes from you personally."

He put down the bottle of water and paced toward her, danger riding on his every step. "You didn't say anything, did you?"

"Of course I didn't. That's why I'm here. *You* have to tell him. And you have to tell him now, before it's too late and they drop you."

"And if I don't tell him? What then, since you seem to know so much about it?" He was less than a step away from her, an overwhelming presence. But she was Paige Mattingly Austin Taylor; she knew how to stand up to dominating men. She matched him stare for stare, jutting her chin up and daring him to take one more step.

"If you don't tell him, you lose everything. No more baseball contract, no more salary, no more Triple A, no more anything related to Major League Baseball. Is that what you want?"

His flinty composure didn't falter. "That's what I want."

"Liar. You're a baseball player. How can you say you don't want to play?"

He turned his back on her, so she faced his inked hawk with its talons and hooked beak. "I'll find a way to play. I'll even get paid for it. I don't need MLB. Don't need the Friars."

"You don't need anyone, is that it?"

Back muscles flexing, he disappeared into the bathroom. Paige took a few deep breaths for calm. What was she missing here? Why wasn't Trevor more upset at the idea of getting dropped? It was almost as if he *wanted* to get released. But that made no sense. The worst had happened, his past had been unearthed. What benefit was there in leaving the Catfish now?

She heard running water, some splashing, and when he came out, drops of water clung to his hair and a small rivulet traveled down the hard planes of his chest. He gave her an almost insolent look. "If you're waiting around to tell me what an ass I'm being, save yourself the time."

"I could tell Crush myself," she burst out.

"Wouldn't do any good." He snagged a towel and swiped it over his hair. "For all you know, everything I told you was a lie. It's secondhand information. It won't mean a damn thing to anyone."

"There's proof. I looked it up online. There was an article about Dinar Wachowski and how a minor was suspected in the attack." She trailed off, remembering all the details the story left out. The fact that he'd been protecting his father, that it was self-defense. None of those mitigating circumstances had made it into the article.

"Spying on me?" The ice in his voice made her shiver. So this was the side of Trevor that intimidated pitchers so much they lost five miles off their fastball. "Or were you checking up to see if I told you the truth? Maybe I didn't. Who knows? You'll never be sure."

Paige took a tiny step back, her conviction faltering.

She didn't know this cold, hard man who looked like Trevor Stark. It was impossible to believe that only a few hours ago he'd been licking her naked body in a tack room. "I wasn't spying, I was trying to find out what that man is up to now. Maybe he's dead and you don't have to worry anymore."

"Playing girl detective? That's adorable. Did you crack the case yet?"

"Don't be like this, Trevor," she whispered. "Why are you so angry?"

"Do I seem angry?" He shrugged, tossing aside the towel, then prowled toward his clothes drawers. "Maybe I should call up Hudson Notswego and see if I can get him to divorce Nessa Brindisi. That would solve all your problems, right?"

She recoiled, feeling as if he'd slapped her in the face. "What's your point? Why bring Hudson into this?" She couldn't understand what was going on. Her mind was moving so sluggishly. It felt as if she was missing big chunks of the situation, as if Trevor was operating at light speed while she chugged along in a dune buggy. She couldn't take her eyes off him as he roamed the room in search of clothes. Maybe this was how mice felt while a cat batted them around.

Maybe this was what Trevor did to pitchers—he drove them mad, in slow, deliberate steps.

"The point is, don't you have your own life to fix? Maybe you should stop messing around in mine. What does it matter to you if I play baseball or don't play baseball?" He snapped his fingers, as if it all made sense now. "I got it. You're here working for Crush. He wants me to stick around so I can help win that fucking championship. And you . . . you're in Kilby because you want a pat on the back from your daddy. It's all falling into place like a chain of dominoes."

The blood rushed from her face. "I'm not here working for Crush. I'm here because I—" She was about to say something crazy. Something about what she felt for him. That she . . . God, that she loved him. Yes, that ache in her heart, the magic she felt only with him, that was love.

Where was the Trevor who'd captured her heart? Was he still in there somewhere, buried under this horrible icy behavior?

She needed to reach him, desperately needed to get back the Trevor she loved.

"I'm here," she said with all the dignity she could muster, "because I love you and I want you to be happy. I don't believe you'll be happy if you torpedo your baseball career. You never will be."

"I'll be happy if Nina is safe." His voice rasped like a dry razor over stubble. Had he even heard what she'd said? The part about loving him? He showed no reaction to it.

Walk away, Paige. He doesn't want you here. He doesn't care about your feelings. He doesn't love you, or he wouldn't talk to you this way.

But her foolish, reckless heart wouldn't let her walk away. "I don't think so. And what about Nina? What does she want? Does she want to stay hidden forever?"

His icy facade finally broke. He closed the distance between them in one long step. "Nina is none of your business. You don't talk to Nina, you don't try to find Nina, you stay away from Nina. You hear me?"

Fury flooded her in a hot rush that made her ears ring. How dare he treat her like this? She was trying to *help* him. She'd just told him she *loved* him.

He loomed over her, all heat and bare chest and impossible good looks. "My life is not your worry. Don't turn me into another Hudson Notswego."

All on its own, her hand flew up and whipped a slap across his cheek.

"*Now* you're being an ass," she choked out. "But I guess you like it that way."

Showing no expression—of course—he brought a hand to his left cheek, where the white scar slashed below his cheekbone. It stood out against the surrounding skin, now pink from the blood she'd brought to the surface.

"I shouldn't have done that, I'm sorry." She cradled her hand against her chest. The palm tingled, as if her body was just as shocked as she was.

He stared at her stonily, as if he couldn't care less what she did. As if he didn't even understand why she was still there. All her fury came flooding back—double.

"I'm on to you, Big Bad Trevor Stark. I know what you're doing right now. You're trying to drive me away so I won't rock the boat for you."

Awareness flashed across his face like heat lightning on a muggy day, gone before you knew it was there.

She shouldered her little backpack, which had slipped to the floor, and marched toward the door. He watched her go, white-faced save for the rosy hand print darkening his cheek.

"I stand by my slap," she told him as she walked out the door. "And I stand by everything else I said too."

Batting practice in Sacramento. Trevor at home plate. About fifty feet away, Lou the batting coach swung his arm in circles to prepare. A few hundred miles to the south, the Friars were debating Trevor's future. Another few hundred miles to the southeast, Crush Taylor was going to, any minute, pick up his phone and make his recommendation. They'd either drop him or keep him in Kilby, but a call-up was out of the question now.

Trevor felt like a fucking chess piece. His life was officially out of his control. Up until now, he'd been torn between the risks of a call-up and staying low-profile in Kilby. Fuck it, he should have let himself get called up and taken his chances with the exposure. That option was gone now. If the Friars kept him on the payroll, he had two choices. He could play normally and let the Wades rat him out to the Wachowskis, in which case there wouldn't be a *chance* of exposure; it would be 100% *guaranteed*. Or he could sell his soul. Betray baseball. Betray his team. Betray Crush.

Betray Paige.

But that was where he slammed the door on his thoughts. He couldn't bear to think about Paige. Even the sight of a fluffy white cat outside a gas station off the I-5 felt like a flaming arrow straight to his heart.

Trevor told himself it was for the best. One way or another he was going down, and he didn't want to take Paige with him. He was either going to get booted out of baseball or hunted down by the Wachowskis. Neither option offered much of a future for a bright, kind, beautiful girl like Paige. She deserved so much better in every possible way.

A low strike came at him. Following his usual routine, he sent the ball into left field. Every guy did something different during batting practice. Some liked to hit home runs, but not Trevor. He liked to hit everything to the opposite field and save the homers for the game. He hit ten pitches, max, then let the next guy go.

Once, he'd watched Don Mattingly hit one hundred pitches in the cage.

Mattingly. Crush's favorite hitter. Paige's namesake.

He was doing Paige another big favor by forgetting the words she'd spoken in his hotel room. *I'm doing this because I love you.*

He watched pitch number two come in right over the plate, saw the numbers on the ball. Slammed it into left.

Because he loved *her,* he was going to pretend she'd never said that.

Besides, she didn't really love him. It was a rebound infatuation at best, or the natural result of their fricking fantastic sexual chemistry. *Love* love . . . no.

Pitch number three. Against the wall in left field. Solid.

He could count the people he'd loved on the fingers of one hand. His mother, who'd died before he even understood the concept of love. His father, who'd warped into someone he didn't recognize, then sent him to juvie. And his sister Nina. Of those three, only Nina was still alive, and still held a place in his heart. He'd never loved a woman. He'd lusted, he'd desired, he'd crushed, he'd fantasized. But loved?

No one had ever made him feel the way Paige did.

He slapped a hard line drive just over Lou's head, forcing him to duck. "Hey!" the batting coach yelled.

"Sorry." God, when was the last time he'd misdirected a ball in batting practice?

"You changing things up, T?"

"Nah, my foot slipped."

Lou wound up and delivered a nice fastball on the outside corner, which Trevor took deep.

Grizz. He loved Grizz too. How could he leave Grizz off that list? In so many ways, Grizz had stepped into the gaping hole left by his father's addiction. He'd been a steady, rock solid presence who understood what he was going through in those years.

Grizz had slapped him once too, he suddenly remembered. The Wade County JD baseball team was playing a showcase game against the high school he'd attended before he got arrested. The idea of seeing his former

teammates churned up so much rage and embarrassment that he'd been acting like an asshole the entire
bus ride across town. He'd led the team in a chain-gang
song. He'd solicited bets on how many hits he was going
to get. He'd said insulting things about the cheerleaders,
even giving out a few of their names.

When they reached the high school, Grizz hauled
him into the locker room and shut the door on the rest
of the team. Then he'd delivered a short, sharp slap to
his face, as if he was trying to wake him up from some
kind of trance.

"I know it's tough," the old man had said, his jaw
quivering. "Comin' back here might be one of the hardest things you gotta do. But what do you do about that?
What I been teaching you? What I keep sayin', over and
over again?"

"Get your revenge on the field."

"S'right. Just like Jackie Robinson did. You don't go
out there feelin' shame, like you ain't good enough. You
go out there and swing that bat and show them. *Show*
them. It ain't about spoutin' baloney on a bus. You know
that ain't right. What's the right thing? Say it again."

"Keep it on the field," he mumbled.

"Hold yer head up. The Lord is testing you, but He
sent us Jackie to show the way."

"Sure, Grizz. I'm sorry." Trevor didn't always buy
into Grizz's religious take on things, but at the core, the
man was right, one hundred percent. *Get your revenge
on the field.*

Now, power flowed through his core, his arms, his
hands, through his second best bat, the one he used
for batting practice. He whacked a vicious line drive
through the gap into left. Unhittable. Fucking satisfying. Swinging the bat cleared his head. Made everything fall into place.

Paige. Knowing Paige was the best thing that had ever happened in his life. Even if it was selfish, he couldn't let her go. *Wouldn't*. Had he screwed things up too much already? If he could just get through this mess, he'd beg her to forgive him. He'd have to figure out a way to protect her from all his disasters. Once he was sure she wasn't at risk, he'd throw himself at her feet.

No way was he going to let Paige go. That was final.

"That's it, Trevor," called the batting coach. "Leiberman, get your butt in here."

Trevor made way for Leiberman, whose shoulders sagged as he made his way to the plate. No one liked following Trevor in batting practice, he knew that. Leiberman must have drawn the short straw. He smiled at the guy with real affection as he passed. "Keep your bat speed up. Watch the ball. Plant your back foot like it's a fucking oak tree and swing from the hips. Got all that?"

Leiberman gave a few rapid blinks and stood up a bit straighter. "Since when do you hand out batting tips?"

Trevor shrugged and strode toward the dugout. Since when did he hand out batting tips? Since he realized that his time with this team was probably almost over. Since he realized that he loved his teammates. Not the way he loved Paige, but nonetheless.

A few kids were waiting at the railing by the dugout, waving baseballs for him to sign. He pulled off his batting gloves and offered them a big grin as he came over. "You guys play at all?"

Thrilled, the kids launched into a rapid-fire description of the Little League team they played on.

One boy looked familiar; he recognized him from the few times he'd stopped in at the Sacramento Boys and Girls Club. "They said you ain't coming back to the Boys and Girls anymore. Is that true?"

"Well . . ." He'd thought long and hard before he made that phone call to the club. "I want you kids to have good role models in life. Not . . ." The kids, un-comprehending, waited for him to finish that sentence. God, didn't they read the newspaper? Didn't they know what he was? Didn't they see why he had no business lecturing anyone?

Head down, he signed the last ball. "Want some advice?"

They nodded, a row of eager little bobbleheads.

"Enjoy every moment you get on the baseball field. Win or lose. The important thing is being on that field. It's a privilege, and you thank your lucky stars every time."

He'd never meant any piece of advice more.

Chapter 21

CATFISH STADIUM WAS a very different place during away games. Without the presence of the players and the daily rhythm of ball games, things got quiet and casual. Without the anticipation of throngs of ticket-holders or promotions to conduct, people went around in shorts and flip-flops, took long breaks, sunbathed in the stands. All the vendor stands were closed, so the stadium even smelled different. The cleaning crew took the opportunity to give all the aisles an extra wash-down, so the smell of bleach drove out the familiar peanut-mustard, burnt-cotton-candy scent.

Paige met with her father over coffee in the break room to go over the expense spreadsheets she'd worked up.

"I can't believe baseballs cost ninety dollars a dozen. Do we really need this many baseballs?"

"Well, we do get hand-me-downs from the Friars, but yes, it's hard to play the game without those little suckers."

"I'm surprised no one has ever lobbied for balls that don't use cowhide," she grumbled. "Isn't there a vegan baseball out there?"

Crush pushed his sunglasses onto his head. "You'd

better keep that thought under wraps, missy. The cowhide baseball is like a . . . a sacred cow. You don't mess with it. Especially in Texas. Especially to a Texas rancher."

"Bullpen Ranch is hardly a real ranch. You don't even have any cows." Paige knew she was acting like a brat, but she couldn't stop herself. Damn Trevor Stark.

No. Trevor was Trevor. She couldn't blame him for that. Better put the blame where it belonged—on *her*. She was a certifiable idiot for falling for him. She should have let him get shot up by that guy with the BB gun.

"Paige? Honey?" Her father waved his hand in front of her face.

She started. "What?"

"Take the day off. You've been working hard. It's going to take me a while to go through these spreadsheets. We'll get to them tomorrow, how's that?"

"Am I done with the accounting department?"

"Yes. I have to figure out your next assignment. I might take you with me to some meetings in San Diego so you can see the schmooze fest in action."

"Okay." She shrugged listlessly. "Whatever you like. Anything's better than accounting." Pushing the spreadsheets across the table, she dragged herself to her feet.

Crush watched her with narrowed eyes. "I thought you'd be a little happier about going to San Diego. We might take my plane."

"Sure. Should be fun." She couldn't muster any enthusiasm for the idea. Since her fight with Trevor—if that's what it was—she couldn't get excited about much at all. More than anything else, she felt stupid. As if everyone had seen the truth except her. She'd been too infatuated to notice that he was a coldhearted bastard. "I'll see you tomorrow, then. Oh . . ." She paused on her way out of the break room. "Any decision on Trevor Stark yet?"

"No."

She nodded, as if it didn't really matter one way or the other. And maybe it didn't. Either way, he was no longer hers. Not that he ever had been.

Stopping at her desk to grab her backpack, she found a little envelope with her name on it, just delivered by the mail room. Heart racing, she ripped it open. But it wasn't from Trevor. It was from Shizuko, a thank-you note featuring a sparkling Hello Kitty with a zombie superimposed over it.

Well, at least someone appreciated her interference.

Day off. *Day off.* What was she supposed to do with a day off? Being at loose ends was dangerous. She might do something crazy like Google Nessa Brindisi recipes or try to find a live-stream of the Catfish–River Cats game. She might call her mother and set off all sorts of alarms. Maybe she should go home and snuggle with Jerome. Decide which college she'd choose. Stream *Gossip Girl* episodes until her brain cried out for help.

Call Deanna in New York? No. Her best friend would never understand why she'd gotten involved with another pro athlete in the first place. This was her problem and she'd just have to claw her way through it on her own.

After all, wasn't that what Trevor had meant when he said, *Don't turn me into another Hudson Notswego?*

But then there was also the time he'd said, *Be Paige. That's more than enough. It's a freaking miracle.*

Gah! How was she supposed to make any sense of that?

Cruising down the concourse, she almost didn't hear the voice calling her name. "Paige. Paige, wait up!"

She swung around to see Donna MacIntyre waving at her. She was with a tall, slim, dark-haired woman.

"Paige, this is my friend Sadie Merritt-Hart. We grew up together, and she recently got married to Caleb Hart, who used to be a Catfish. Sadie, this is Paige Taylor, Crush's daughter."

Paige forced a smile and shook hands with Sadie. "It's nice to meet you. My father still talks about Caleb. Says he's one of the best he's ever seen."

"And he doesn't know the half of it." Sadie gave the merest ghost of a wink. Donna burst out laughing.

"Sadie, I'm so proud. That sounds like something I'd say. About Mike, of course," she added hastily.

"Well, your naughty ways had to rub off on me eventually."

Donna clutched at her coppery head as if it might explode. "Rub . . . naughty . . . so many ways to go with this one. Paige, help me out here."

Instead, Paige burst into tears.

Immediately, the two girls surrounded her, patting her on the back, pulling her into an empty cotton candy stand saturated with the scent of burnt sugar. "What's the matter? Are you okay?" Donna materialized a Kleenex from somewhere and Sadie found her a bottle of Coke. "What happened?"

"N-Nothing, it's just . . ." It was just *stupid*, that's what it was. "I'm just sad."

"Hudson?" Donna asked sympathetically.

For a long, stunned moment, Paige drew a complete blank on the name. "Oh. Um, yeah, something like that."

Donna's face lit up as if she'd swallowed a firecracker. "It's Trevor, isn't it? You and Trevor have something going on. I knew it when I saw him crack a smile on the ball field a couple weeks ago. He never smiles. He was looking right at you, Paige. I'm telling you, the mighty Trevor has struck out."

"Trevor Stark?" Sadie pulled a worried face. "That's pretty radical. This might call for margaritas."

"Well, duh." Donna dabbed at Paige's face with the Kleenex. "It's a good thing you ran into us. You can't go getting involved with a ballplayer without a solid blueprint and some Grade A advice from the experts. You in?" She clasped her hand around Paige's wrist and led her out of the cotton candy stand, Sadie following close behind.

"It isn't even noon yet, is it?" A margarita sounded pretty good, to be honest. But day drinking could be trouble. She might make a phone call she'd regret.

"Nope, it's not noon," Donna said, "but normal laws of time and space don't apply when you're dating a ballplayer. That's rule number one."

"Oh. How many rules are there? And honestly, I wouldn't say that we're dating." In fact, every time they tried to "date," something had interrupted them. Maybe that should have been her first warning sign.

"Screwing?"

"Donna," scolded Sadie, while Paige turned guilty-as-charged red.

"If Paige is sleeping with Trevor Stark, that might call for more than margaritas," said Donna ominously. "That might call for whiskey and a six-gauge rifle."

Only one place in town served alcohol at eleven-thirty in the morning, and that was the Kilby Roadhouse. All the bartenders kept watching Donna suspiciously, as if she might spontaneously pick a fight while they restocked the Chex Mix. Paige had heard about a few of the crazy incidents that had taken place at the Kilby Roadhouse over the years, many of them involving the Catfish, and an especially famous one involving Donna and Sadie.

The three girls settled into the most tucked away table in the bar, nearly invisible behind the jukebox. Donna ordered margaritas and guacamole, waited until everything had been delivered, then pounced.

"If we're going to be of any help, you should go ahead and tell us everything."

She couldn't tell them "everything." Trevor's secrets weren't hers to share, and no way was she going to describe all the insanely hot sex. But there were some things she wouldn't mind getting off her chest.

"You both probably think I'm crazy, right? Crush does. I know my friends would. What sane woman gets dumped by a future NBA player and immediately starts dating a future MLB player? Do I have some kind of sports star death wish?"

Sadie shook her head, her sleek dark hair swinging in its high ponytail. "I wouldn't look at it like that. They're two different people. I don't know your ex, but I know Trevor a little. He's kind of like . . . an iceberg."

Paige groaned and dropped her head into her hands. "Exactly. Shows no emotion, made of ice, blah blah blah. That's what everyone says, but that's not how he is when . . . never mind. I guess I got fooled."

"No, no, that's not what I meant when I said 'iceberg.'" Sadie plucked a piece of pineapple from the tiny red plastic sword that came with her margarita. "I meant that there's a lot more underneath than you see on the surface. At first he seems like a play-the-field type, arrogant, full of himself. When Caleb and I first got together, Trevor was a total dick and nearly ruined things for us. But he actually apologized later and they made peace. They're buddies now. Know what else Caleb told me? Most of the kids who walk up and down the aisles selling peanuts and so forth, they got their jobs because of Trevor. He's got a side he doesn't show to most people."

Paige gave an even deeper groan. "I suppose you're trying to make me feel better, but that's not helping."

Donna licked the rim of her watermelon margarita. "You want us to trash him? Sorry, I'd like to help, but I can't lie. He helped me last year when I was trying to get custody of Zack."

"Really, what did he do?"

"Well, he flirted with Bonita, my ex's ex. She kind of lost her head over him. Maybe it doesn't sound like a good deed, but it did the job. Also, he kicked some major Wade ass during that . . . incident here at the Roadhouse. He stepped in and took some punches aimed at Mike. Mike says Trevor probably saved the rest of his season. So I can't hate Trevor Stark either. He's a badass in the best way."

Paige loaded up a tortilla chip with guacamole. "I have to tell you, you two are completely useless," she said gloomily.

"Sorry." They shared an embarrassed look.

"If it helps, everyone says they've never seen Trevor like this," Donna added. "I'm around the ballpark a lot, and I hear everything. The players think he's crazy about you. Since you came along, he hasn't even looked at any of the baseball groupies flinging themselves at him after every game. The players keep mentioning your name to see what happens. They say his ears turn pink. It's like a game to them. Then again, they're idiots."

Paige felt her eyes fill with tears again. "This guacamole is so spicy," she murmured, hoping to hide the fact that she was embarrassing herself with all these tears. "I don't know, guys. I thought Trevor and I had something pretty amazing going on, but then he froze me out. He acted like he didn't care if I lived or died. It was like talking to a . . . a . . . giant icicle."

"He has that badass thing down," Donna said sympathetically. "Especially on the field. It might be his comfort zone off the field too."

Paige took a sip of her margarita, the sting of tequila barely registering. "I think he was trying to get rid of me. Honestly, it's working."

Sadie smiled at her gently. "Listen, Paige, the life of a ballplayer is pretty intense. They're on the road a lot. They're under a lot of pressure. The most important thing is that you have to trust each other. If you're not on the same page with your relationship, it'll be a disaster."

"Oh, I think we're on the same page. It's the one that says 'The End.'"

Laughing, Donna lifted her glass in a toast. "She made a joke. Things can't be too bad if she's making jokes."

Paige smiled along with the other two women, but was it a joke? Maybe a dark one, based on the sad fact that things with Trevor were as dead as one of Jerome's squeaky toys. "Let's talk about something else. Something completely unrelated to baseball players or men of any kind."

"I'll drink to that!" Donna clinked her glass against Paige's. "But first, I have to say one thing, and I'm finally buzzed enough to do it." She put down her glass, planted her elbows on the table and leaned toward Paige. "Nessa Brindisi's recipes are crap. I've been trying to learn to make better meals for my kid, so I made a few things from her show. Zack wouldn't eat a single one. I've been wanting to tell you that for ages, but the moment never felt right until now."

Paige caught her bottom lip between her teeth, laughter bubbling up. "That's . . . uh . . . thanks?"

"I'm just saying." Donna sat back, as if she'd finally fulfilled some kind of mission. "We can go on now. I got that off my chest."

"Thank you for sharing, Donna." Sadie exchanged a mirth-filled look with Paige. "On a completely different topic, do you all remember that we've actually hung out together once before?"

"What?" Paige pushed her hair behind her ears. "When? I don't remember that."

"You were probably about thirteen. You were riding your bike near Lake McGee. Donna and I were swimming out there. You offered us some of your marshmallow fluff and peanut butter sandwich. It was the best thing I'd ever tasted in my life."

The memory flashed back. Paige sat bolt upright. "I remember that day! That was so much fun, I lost track of time and got in huge trouble with my dad's housekeeper. It was one of my last summers here. After that, my mother started sending me to camp."

"We thought you were great, and not at all stuck up the way we thought you'd be."

Paige frowned. "Stuck up?"

"You were gorgeous and tall," Donna said, "you had that long wavy hair, you looked like a movie star to us. And you were Crush Taylor's daughter—like a rich celebrity kid." She winked. "We were totally jealous, except that you were so nice and fun."

The waitress appeared, and Paige signaled for another round of margaritas. "That's crazy. I was the most awkward kid alive. I think that was the time I rode my bike into a tree, as a matter of fact. I was actually jealous of you two, because you were such good friends. I was lonely all the time when I was growing up. My mom kept moving from one TV market to another. Every time I made a friend, she'd get a new job.

And I went back and forth between my parents, but they were both really busy. I remember riding back to the ranch, thinking, 'If only I had friends like them.'"

"And look!" Donna spread her hands wide. "Now you do. As long as you keep those marshmallow fluff sandwiches coming."

Paige grinned. "Done. I bet Zack would love them too."

The next round of margaritas arrived, and Donna launched into a hilarious story about the first time Zach tasted peanut butter. Sadie told them about the crazy competitive stunts the students at her law school pulled. Paige talked about plans for the fund-raiser for the tutoring program. Sadie offered to locate prizes for the silent auction, and Donna asked if she could emcee the event. As they launched into party brainstorming, Paige sipped her margarita and tried to put her finger on what was missing.

No one was comparing stats. No one was talking about free throw conversions or after-game parties or who signed what contract with which team.

And that's when the truth behind Trevor's statement dawned on her, clear as day. For three years she'd poured her heart and soul into Hudson's career. *Hudson's* career. And then—she'd started to do the same thing with Trevor! But Trevor was different from Hudson. He was a grown man, not a shy kid, and he didn't want that from her. Not only that, but he was right, the jerk. She didn't want to lose herself again. Couldn't . . . *wouldn't* . . . lose herself again.

Chapter 22

BY THE TIME they wrapped things up, Paige was thoroughly buzzed. It was still only mid-afternoon and she didn't feel safe to drive, so she walked around town for a while, enjoying the breeze that had kicked up. It rustled the tops of the cottonwoods and made the traffic lights sway back and forth.

When her phone rang, the idea that it might be Trevor sent her scrambling for her little backpack. But a different voice spoke, one she hadn't heard since she'd left Italy.

"Hey girl."

"Don't you 'Hey girl' me," she snapped.

"Chill it, Paige. You don't need to be jumping all over me."

She gritted her teeth to keep all possibly inappropriate responses to herself. "What's up, Hudson? I'm very, very busy, so get on with it." Busy walking off her buzz, but no need to share details.

"You sound different." His tone reeked of disappointment.

"Well, yeah, I am different. For one thing, I'm not married to you anymore. Does Nessa know you're calling me?"

"Doesn't matter. She knows it's not like that."

"Like what?" She still had no idea what this was about, but her head was spinning so she propped herself against the outer wall of the old Kilby Fort, her back against the sun-warmed brickwork.

"Nessa . . . she says I need to relax when we're on TV. I just . . . I don't feel like myself with all the cameras. I'm used to it during games, but not hanging out at home. It's easy for her, but I just can't get comfortable."

That didn't surprise her, since she knew how shy Hudson was. During interviews, he'd often wanted her nearby just so he could look at a friendly face. The misery in his voice made her soften. "I'm sorry, Hudson. But what do you want me to do about it? I'm in Texas. And I'm your ex. Your ex in Texas." She giggled, still feeling those margaritas.

"You making fun of me?"

"No, no—"

"I call you up hoping for a kind word and this is how you act?"

"Oh, good grief, Hudson, I'm not laughing at you. Grow up." She snapped the words before she could even think.

An offended silence followed. "What'd you say?"

She took a deep breath and said, bluntly, "What I meant was, you're going to have to work it out for yourself."

"You *are* different." He sounded thoroughly disgruntled.

"You're right, I am. I've been tutoring some high school kids here in Kilby, planning a fund-raiser—" But he disconnected the call before she could finish the thought.

Shocked, she stared at her phone for a second before propelling herself away from the wall. He hadn't even bothered to listen to her news. All he'd wanted was the familiar comfort she could offer. And when he didn't get it—wham.

Still fuming, she stalked back to the sidewalk. Why had she been willing to put up with such a one-way relationship? Come to think of it, she knew exactly why. Because she'd craved connection. She'd loved the feeling of being on a team with someone. That's why she'd been willing to ditch everything and devote her life to Hudson.

Was that longing such a bad thing? People needed connections. Even a frozen iceberg like Trevor needed other people. If he didn't, then she didn't want him.

Sure, she might be a little tipsy, but all this made perfect, crystal clear sense to her. If she could tell off Hudson, why not Trevor too?

She stopped at an intersection and put her phone back to her ear. For an epic moment her sensible side struggled with her tipsy side. *Bad idea. Don't call Trevor. Don't do it.*

It lost.

As soon as Trevor picked up, with his usual, "Stark here," she launched into her speech. "Only some things are good frozen, Trevor. Margaritas for one. Ice cream for another. Maybe peas. Fine, peas are a good frozen thing to have around. Ice packs in general."

Oh sweet Lord, she was even more toasted than she'd realized. Why was she talking about ice packs? *Get back to the main topic.*

"*People* should not be frozen, Trevor. At least not living people. Maybe dead ones, but that's—I don't know, I don't even want to go there."

What the heck . . . now she was talking about frozen dead people? She rubbed her forehead, hoping to force some oxygen into her brain.

"Paige?"

"Yes, it's Paige, and I'm just calling to tell you that if you're going to be an icicle, you can't be in my life. I should say, *back* in my life, since I don't think you're in it right now."

"I'm not?"

She detected an undercurrent of amusement in his voice, which infuriated her. "No, you're not! You can stay alone in your ice cave forever as far as I care."

For a moment, he was quiet. Then, "I don't think I'm okay with that."

"What . . . what do you mean?"

"Ice caves aren't very comfortable. Especially when they don't have you."

She yanked the phone from her ear and glared at it. A woman pushing a stroller down the sidewalk shot her a nervous look. "You're confusing me, Trevor," she said, the phone at her ear again. "Last time I saw you, you gave me the ice face. I don't like the ice face."

"I'll make it up to you." The heat in his voice made the soles of her feet tingle. "Where are you right now?"

"I'm . . . uh . . . at the corner of Pine and Courthouse Way. Waiting for the light to change. Where are you?"

"I'm at the stadium in Sacramento. Game's going to start soon. I've been thinking about you nonstop." Oh crap. Just when she had everything figured out, he had to throw a grenade into the mix.

"Really? That's funny, because I haven't been thinking about you at all. *At all,* you hear me?"

"I'm going to take that as a personal challenge." His voice reverberated through every cell of her body. "I have to tell you something, sweetheart. I can't stop thinking about you or wanting you. I tried, because I know it's best. But every time I close my eyes I see that amazing smile of yours, or your long legs wrapping around my hips. The way your whole body arches when you come."

"Stop that," she said weakly. Slick from her sweat, the phone slipped in her hand.

"I can't. I keep picturing you naked against that saddle. You need to wear more leather."

"I'm not wearing any leather for you." The light changed, and the woman hurried away from her.

"Even if I begged? If I told you what it did to me? How hard I am right now just thinking about your nipples all hard and lickable? When you're turned-on, they're the color of cognac. Or grenadine. I could get drunk sucking them. Sucking all of you."

"Trevor!" She nearly ran into a lamppost as she reached the opposite side of the street. "I'm hanging up now. You're giving me whiplash, and I'm too buzzed for whiplash."

"Don't hang up yet. Not until you take back what you said before."

"What?"

"The part about you not being in my life. You're in my life, Paige Taylor. I'm not letting you out. I just have to figure some things out."

Thrills chased up and down her spine, a reaction that infuriated her. "It's not fair! You can't do this to me. You're so hot and cold. In and out. Up and down."

"Just hot, Paige. Getting hotter every time. Bear with me, okay? Promise you'll bear with me. I'll be back in three days and I want to see you. I want to tell you some things you don't know. Tell you how I feel."

Before he could confuse her any more, she stuffed the phone in her bag as if it were a burning coal. As if the hot feelings he'd conjured could be banished along with her phone. Her body throbbed all the way to her core.

Bear with me.

She didn't know which was more confusing, the iceberg Trevor or the volcano version. She hated him. No, she *should* hate him. Would. Did. Didn't. *Gah!*

Paige was still reeling from that conversation—not to mention the one with Hudson—when she got back to the ranch and received another shock.

Her mother sat in Crush's living room, ivory linen-clad legs crossed, a glass of white wine cupped in one hand. Crush stood behind the bar as if it was a fortress and he was manning the defenses.

Deal with Jenna Jarvey after all those margaritas? *This* was going to be interesting.

"Mom. What are you doing here?" Paige bent to kiss her mother on her cheek—or rather, near her cheek, since in the past she'd ended up with smears of foundation on her lips.

"I came because, clearly, your father is not performing his parental duties." Jenna stood to give Paige a hard hug. Over her mom's shoulder, Paige aimed wide eyes at her father. *What's going on?*

He responded by sticking his finger in his mouth and pretending to pull the trigger.

"Any weight loss? Weight gain? Both can be signs of postdivorce trauma." Jenna inspected her, head to toe. Paige wondered if she had a scale in her lizard-skin briefcase.

"Weight's holding steady, thanks for your concern."

"Weight's just one symptom. How about sleep? Are you sleeping okay?"

"Mom, I'm handling it. Crush has been great. You didn't need to airlift in here."

"I smell alcohol. Have you been drinking? Is the situation driving you to drink? I heard some nasty rumors from our sports intern at the station. What's this about you and some minor league baseball player?"

Her mother's sharp blue eyes, the same color as her own, scanned her face. Paige resembled Jenna in some respects—brown hair, blue eyes, general face shape. But her build came from Crush; she towered over her petite mother. Jenna had a controlled quality that Paige would never achieve. It showed in the way she did her makeup, her precision bob, the tiny diamonds at her earlobes. And when Jenna interrogated her, she always folded like a house of cards. "Do you mean Trevor? What about him?"

Crush intervened before her mother could pounce. "If it's any help, he's the Friars top prospect. Helluva slugger. Reminds me of a cross between McGwire and Bonds."

Jenna shredded him with a quick look. "When we divorced, you got baseball. Let's keep it that way. Minor league, major league, that's not the point. Rebounds are not healthy, Paige. It's too soon. You need to give yourself time to recover from the pain of your divorce."

Paige pulled away from her mother and crossed to the bar. She tapped on the counter. "Hey bartender. You got anything back there for me? Any specialty cocktails for a recovering divorcée?"

Crush tilted his head, a grin touching his lips. "Looks like you're way ahead on that one." He lowered his voice. "Did you know she was coming?"

"No, those margaritas were just a coincidence. Don't worry, I walked most of it off before I drove home."

He nodded and poured her a root beer. "Consolation prize of champions."

Paige took a long sip before turning back to her mother, who stood with her arms crossed over her chest. "I don't need a lecture on who I see and when, Mom. Crush already tried that. Right, Dad?"

"Right. It was a very humbling moment in parenting history."

Jenna tap-tapped toward them, high heels clicking on the slate tiles. "Well, I did a little research on this one, and I really think you must have lost your mind, Paige. I don't believe you're thinking clearly. He has a *police record*. A record! My daughter with a criminal. I'm shocked that you would let this happen, Crush."

"Excuse me?" Paige waved her glass of root beer at her mother. "Crush doesn't have a say in it. Neither do you."

"Someone has to! How many divorces do you want to fit in before you turn twenty-five?"

Paige sucked in a breath. Growing up, she'd hated disappointing her mother more than anything. But it seemed to happen no matter what she did.

"Jenna," Crush said softly. "Take it easy."

"You're going to take her side, then?" her mother said. "We're right back to the old days, when Paige would come here and run wild. No rules, no discipline, no common sense."

Paige was starting to think that margaritas weren't nearly enough for this kind of conversation. She should have ordered bourbon.

"Do you know that Stark isn't even his real last name? It's Leonov. What does that tell you?"

"Jenna, you're out of line," said Crush sharply. "Paige can make her own choices. What exactly do you suggest we do?"

"Fire her."

"*Excuse* me?"

"Stop giving her work with the Catfish. Send her away from here. If she leaves Kilby, she won't even re-member that guy."

She turned to Paige, who gaped at her. *Fire her? Send*

her away? She wasn't thirteen anymore. But those margaritas had slowed her reaction time, and she couldn't find her voice.

"I got you a ticket to Philadelphia. Come home with me. If you must date someone, we'll find you a nice Main Line lawyer or doctor. I know several who would be perfect choices. But I'd really rather you focused on finishing your degree." Jenna adjusted her tailored fawn jacket over her hips, as if everything was settled. "You're not making good decisions right now. It's understandable, after such a public humiliation. Anyone would lose her head. And from the sounds of it, this Trevor person is quite attractive. It all makes perfect sense and I should have seen it coming. But enough is enough. I know Crush feels the same, that this ballplayer is very wrong for you."

They both looked at Crush, who murmured, "Not my first choice."

Paige glared at him. *Thanks a lot, Dad.*

"You've never been a rebellious child, Hudson aside." Jenna put a hand on Paige's forearm, but Paige shook it off. "You've always wanted to make your parents happy and proud. Please think about what you're doing. Take a break from Kilby. Come back to Philly with me." Jenna put all the charisma and power of her on air persona into that speech. She made it sound reasonable and inevitable.

Before the divorce, it would have been. And for a second, it was.

But Paige had margaritas and a smokin' hot phone conversation with Trevor under her belt. She should hate him after the way he'd treated her in his hotel room.

But that's not what she felt, not at all.

Bear with me, he'd said. *I'm not letting you go. I just have to figure out some things.*

Well, so did she.

"Stop it, both of you." She jabbed a finger toward her father. "*You* don't really know Trevor." She swung toward her mother. "And *you've* never even met him. You're both crazy. However, I know I'm lucky to have parents who love me. Trevor had no one, and still he made himself into an amazing person. I'm going to keep seeing him no matter what either of you say or do."

"But Paige, another athlete, after the disaster with Hud—"

"He's Trevor to me, not just an athlete. *Trevor.* The man I . . ." She clenched her teeth to keep the word back, but it slipped out. ". . . love."

"Don't be ridiculous," exclaimed Jenna. "Love? That drama with Nessa Brindisi has scrambled your brain. I should have slipped her a mickey that time I interviewed her."

Paige flung up one hand in a *stop* gesture. "This has nothing to do with Nessa, Hudson, or either of you. This is about me and Trevor. No one else. Maybe it is a mistake. But I'm the only one who gets to decide that. Dad, if you want me to stop working with the Catfish, just say the word."

"I don't." Her father was watching her intently, his hazel eyes narrowed as if she were a batter he was trying to figure out. "I'm getting some pretty good free labor out of you."

"Thank you. I like it there. You know why I like it? Because I like talking to the players on a personal level. I like how they sign baseballs for kids. Some of them are practically kids themselves. I like how they work hard and try to make something of themselves. I like how much they enjoy the game. I actually like . . . baseball."

Crush grinned, as if she'd just handed him a huge victory. But that smile disappeared at her next statement.

"It's made me realize what I really want to do. I'm going to finish college as quickly as I can, then I'm going to work on a degree in social work. I want to be a therapist or a counselor." She turned to her mother. "Maybe you're right and I am soft. So I might as well make the best of it. I want to help people, and this is how I'm going to do it. And if you really think I'm soft, just try to change my mind. Either of you. About any of this."

Chapter 23

TREVOR GOT THE news from Duke right before the team boarded the bus back to Kilby. The San Diego Friars had decided to release him. The official announcement would be made in the morning, but the sports forums were already buzzing with rumors.

"Sorry, Stark." Duke clapped a hand on his shoulder and squeezed. "It kills me to tell you this. Fucking waste of talent. I told them they were making a mistake. They should be building an offense around you, not dumping you. If you could just keep your shit togeth—"

"It's all right, Duke. It's baseball. Shit happens." Trevor felt nothing. Or at least, nothing yet. He'd been anticipating this, dreading it, steeling himself for it. The reality was almost anti-climactic. Three words. *They're releasing you.*

No more baseball. No more Catfish. No more team buses. No more long road trips.

Word must have spread in that mysterious way of baseball teams, because the bus was unnaturally quiet on the way back to Kilby. The team had crushed the River Cats, sweeping the series in their own stadium, in large degree thanks to Trevor's six-for-ten performance. They were on top of the standings, nearly guaranteed to make the Pacific Conference finals.

Even though, on an individual basis, each player would choose a call-up over a minor league championship in a heartbeat, the Catfish had gotten swept up in the excitement of a pennant race. They wanted to win, and without Trevor it would be a thousand times more difficult.

Trevor put on his headphones and stared out the window at the flat countryside slipping by, the metronomic flicker of telephone poles, the intermittent smear of lights when they passed through a town. *Released.* On the bright side, he wouldn't have to betray his soul and throw any games for the fucking Wades. On another bright side, he wouldn't have to worry about the Wachowskis catching sight of him on the news.

Independent league players never made the news.

Maybe he should leave baseball. He could follow his other passion, working with kids. He could work at a juvenile detention center, the way Grizz had. He didn't need money; he'd socked away enough to get by for a while. After he got Nina set up, he'd put his entire signing bonus into an investment fund. He'd be all right, financially. Not as wealthy as he would have been with the Friars. But what did bank accounts matter compared to Nina's safety?

A few seats ahead, Dwight was bobbing his head in time to whatever song was playing on his big Bose headphones. Across the aisle, Leiberman scowled at his iPad, flipping pages on a virtual book. Shizuko tapped his fingers in a complex drum pattern on his leg. T.J. was fast asleep, head cushioned by the cervical neck pillow his surgeon parents insisted he use. The snuffle of snores filled the bus; they had a long ride before they reached Kilby.

Once he got back to Kilby—

It slammed into him, harder than a fastball to the

stomach. Once he got back, he'd have to clean out his locker. Grab his third-favorite bat, which he'd left in the clubhouse, his extra cleats, the spare T-shirts he stashed in his locker. Turn in his Catfish uniform. Someone would come and rip the masking tape off his locker, the one with the handwritten 45-Stark on it. And that would be it. He'd be erased from the Kilby Catfish.

From baseball.

If someone had stabbed a knife in his gut and yanked it upward, through his heart and lungs, it would probably feel like this. Baseball was like the air he breathed, the blood circulating through his body. Baseball had saved him, lifted him up, given him a place to shine. It had allowed him to take care of Nina.

It had brought him to Paige.

And now, baseball would be gone from his life. Independent league baseball . . . who was he kidding? It wasn't the same. He'd be facing 80-mile-an-hour fastballs, not 90. He'd be like a college graduate going back to junior high. He wouldn't be able to test himself against the best, hone his abilities, take his talent as far as it would go. For all practical purposes, it would be the end of baseball for him.

And what about Paige? How could he expect her to be with some minor league reject? She was the daughter of baseball royalty. What would he be by tomorrow? Some asshole who used to be a prospect.

All this time, he'd been operating under the belief that he was in baseball because of Nina, because she'd made him promise. *Bullshit*. Nina was right, he did belong in baseball, and it was going to fucking kill him to leave. He played baseball because he loved it. And now it was being ripped away from him, and it felt like giving up a vital organ.

Around two-thirty in the morning the bus stopped

to fuel up at a rest stop in a random town in Oklahoma. Trevor, who'd been sleeping so lightly that every shift in the bus's speed woke him up, decided to stretch his legs. While the other guys were just starting to stir, he jumped out of the bus and jogged into the convenience store. A sleepy-eyed kid in a Red Bull T-shirt rested his head on one elbow while leafing through a magazine.

Trevor gave him a nod, then went to the cooler and surveyed the soda selection. Maybe a ginseng green tea would give him a lift. The bell tinkled as someone else walked in.

"Morning. Got any hot coffee?" Dwight asked in a sleep-graveled voice.

"Nah."

"I'll take it cold."

"All out."

Trevor glanced over at the coffee setup. The pot was full, probably even warm, or at least tepid. Asshole. Shit like that made him nuts. Maybe the clerk didn't know there was coffee. Maybe he didn't feel like getting up, or even pointing. Maybe it wasn't racist bullshit. In his current mood, none of that mattered.

He grabbed the pot and took it to the clerk. "Ask him how he likes it," he told the kid in a steely voice.

The kid hesitated. Trevor reached over and grabbed the neck of his shirt.

"We have video cameras," the clerk squeaked.

"Good. Someone will finally get to see you give good service. Ask him how he likes his coffee."

"You have no right—"

"Ask him how he likes his coffee." Trevor heard the icy menace in his own voice, saw how much he was scaring the kid, who was probably no more than twenty. It felt as if he was floating over his body somewhere, watching this encounter. Seeing the violence barely con-

tained in the fist wrapped in the kid's shirt. Watching the anger flow through his body.

The clerk swallowed hard. Trevor felt the movement next to his knuckles. "How do you like your coffee?"

"Trevor," said Dwight in a low voice. "Forget it."

But no, Trevor wasn't going to forget it. The injustice of the entire world boiled down to that moment. All the ways people mistreated each other. The lack of respect given to the best people he knew. This was for Grizz, who'd had to eat stale sandwiches on the road because restaurants wouldn't serve the Negro League teams. For Grizz, who'd never gotten his shot at a major league career because of his "beautiful tan," as his friend Buck O'Neil called it. For Grizz, who loved baseball despite those heartbreaks. "You like it black, right, Dwight?"

"Yeah. With a little sugar."

"There you go." He released the kid's shirt and thrust the coffeepot at him. "Pour a cup of coffee for the man. You might want to keep in mind that you're pouring it for the best fucking center fielder I've ever played with and a future San Diego Friar. If you're the kind of idiot that means nothing to, just remember you're pouring it for a stand-up guy who treats everyone with respect. *Everyone*, even punks like you. Pour, you little twerp."

While Trevor loomed over him, watching every movement, the clerk grabbed a foam cup from the counter behind him and filled it with coffee. He added one packet of sugar, then glanced at Dwight. The center fielder flashed him a smile and took the cup. He slid a five dollar bill across the counter.

"Thanks. You can stand down now, T. I got my coffee, I'm good."

Trevor didn't move. Couldn't move. Because he'd just remembered the scene that smashed his life to bits eight years ago. The man with the knife to his father's throat. The menace, the relentless, impersonal viciousness.

Without baseball, that might be him. One man imposing his will on others. Not through a baseball bat, but with his fists, his size, his anger.

Dwight put an arm around his shoulders and guided him out of the store. Outside, the crisp night air bit into him.

"What the hell, T?" Dwight said in a low voice. "Last thing you need is more bad PR. Hope those video cameras were only for show."

"It doesn't matter." Trevor headed for the bus. "If I'm going down, I want to do it right. You deserve better than that crap."

"You know I don't like to get into it over little things like a cup of coffee."

"Yeah, I know. That's you. This one's all me. Listen, Dwight—" The knowledge that in a matter of hours he'd no longer be this man's teammate weighed like a boulder on his chest.

Dwight interrupted him. "Respect, man. Respect. Friends for the long haul, right?" He offered his fist for a bump. Trevor touched his fist to his, then they knocked shoulders. "You need anything, you tell me. And stay out of trouble, mother-effer."

"Yeah right," Trevor muttered, then swung back on board the bus.

He knew he'd been stupid, making a scene over a cup of coffee in a hick town in the middle of some Oklahoma oil field. But it felt good to fight back against one tiny piece of bullshit in this fucked-up world.

The doorbell at Bullpen Ranch rang at five-thirty in the morning. Even without the early timing, this was unusual.

No one casually dropped by the ranch. The bell rang continuously, like church bells tolling some kind of morning service. Jarred awake, Paige lay still for a moment, Jerome a heavy mass of purring fur on her chest.

Was it Jenna, coming back from the Kilby airport for more lecturing? Paige groaned and shoved her wild bed-head tangle of hair away from her face. She slid out from under Jerome, who briefly opened his one blue eye, then buried his head beneath his paws. She threw a Catfish zippered hoodie over her sleep shorts and ran down the stairs to the urgent rhythm of the doorbell.

She nearly crashed into Crush as he emerged from the master bedroom downstairs. He'd thrown on an even stranger outfit—a plaid blazer over basketball shorts. "Are you expecting someone?" she asked him.

"Nope. You?"

"No."

"If it's Trevor Stark, let me handle it," he told her.

She startled, pausing halfway across the foyer. "Why would it be Trevor?"

"The Friars decided to release him last night."

Her stomach plummeted. "Oh no. Is he okay?"

"Haven't talked to him. Duke said he took it well. But still waters run deep with that guy."

Poor Trevor. Why hadn't he called or texted or *something*? She was up late submitting college applications last night, and her phone had been on. In fact, she'd fought the urge to call him for another of those sex-drenched conversations that made her toes curl. He'd told her to bear with him, and she was. But he had to make the next move.

She practically flew across the foyer. It must be Trevor, here to break the news in person. Or maybe he'd come to her for comfort. Finally, maybe she'd gotten through to him and convinced him to trust her.

Flinging the door open, she saw the last person she'd expected to find on Crush's doorstep. "Nina?"

"Hi, Paige. Hi, Mr. Taylor." The poor girl looked exhausted, her eyes ringed with purple, a sleep crease bisecting her right cheek. She wore khaki cutoffs and a dirty red sweatshirt with the slogan *Stay Calm and Eat Bacon*.

"Are you all right?" Paige pulled her across the threshold. "You look like you haven't slept in a week."

"I haven't, much. I took an overnight bus to get here."

"You don't have a car?" Paige swept a glance across the front drive, searching for something to explain Nina's surprise appearance.

"No, I hitched a ride to the front gate and walked from there."

"Hitched a ride? Does Trevor know about this?" Closing the front door behind her, Paige steered Nina to the big couch near the hearth. The girl collapsed into it, forlorn and knock-kneed.

"No, of course not. Trevor would flip if he knew I was here."

Paige slid into the oxblood leather armchair opposite her and rested her elbows on her knees. "Did something happen?"

"I just . . . I just can't do it anymore." Tears welled in her eyes, but she stubbornly blinked them away. "I know I promised Trevor, and he's going to be so angry when he hears that I came here. But I just had to. I couldn't let this go on anymore."

She gave a furtive look at Crush, who hovered half in, half out of the room.

"Dad, why don't you give us some privacy," Paige said, but Nina cut her off.

"No, I want him here. That's why I came."

Crush's eyebrows went nearly to his hairline, but he came closer, dropping one hip onto a stool by the bar. "Is this baseball-related?"

"Not really. But sort of. It's about Trevor."

She gave a few more sniffles, using the sleeve of her sweatshirt to wipe the moisture off her face. Even though she was dying of curiosity, Paige jumped up and fetched a box of Kleenex from the bathroom. With a grateful look, Nina grabbed a few and blotted her face.

"I'm sorry. It's just really hard to talk to strangers about this. But you're not exactly strangers, and you were kind to me, Paige. I know Trevor cares about you just from how he says your name. I hope he doesn't get mad at you because I came here."

"Let's not worry about that right now," Crush said. "Between the three of us, we can probably handle Trevor. Why don't you tell us what's going on?"

The touch of impatience in his voice made Nina sit up straighter. "Okay. Well, I saw on a sports forum that the Friars fired Trevor. And it's probably because of the article that came out, right? The one about how he went to juvie?"

"It's part of the reason. More like the last straw, but yes. It was a big factor."

"Well, shouldn't it matter *why* he went?"

Paige shot a glance at Crush, who was fighting back a yawn. She knew that her father had already written off Trevor. "It should make a difference, Nina," she said, "but it probably doesn't. He did still attack that man, even though it was to protect your father."

"He told you that?"

"Yes, he told me. He made me promise not to tell anyone, though."

"I can see why." Crush laughed cynically. "It makes you look stupid when you try to explain yourself nine years later."

"That's not the reason why!" Nina surged from the couch, fists clenched like a vengeful blond fairy. "And he didn't do a bad thing. That's what I'm trying to tell you."

Crush pushed his stool in a slow half twirl. "I'm sure there's a sad story in there, Nina, but none of it makes a difference now. You're wasting your time here."

"Dad!" Paige jumped to her feet and placed herself between Nina and Crush. "At least let her finish her story."

"He confessed to the attack because of me! For me!"

Paige swung around to face Nina. "What are you talking about? He was trying to keep your father from getting killed."

"No! He was calling 911 when it happened. He didn't hurt that man. It was me."

"*What?*"

Even Crush had gone still and watchful. "Explain."

"Those horrible men kept coming around the pharmacy and the house, and I hated them. Every time they came, Dad would get weird and quiet and refuse to say who they were. I just had a bad feeling, so I started following him. I felt like nothing too bad could happen if I was watching. That night, he went to the pharmacy and so did I. And I brought one of Trevor's baseball bats because it made me feel safer. When I walked in, that man was up against my dad, like he was going to kill him, and I just swung that bat as hard as I could."

Tears flowed down her face in thick smears.

"He dropped down to the floor and I just stood there, still holding the bat. Trevor had been working with me on my swing. We used to play in the vacant lot on the corner . . ."

She trailed off, tucking her chin into her chest. Maybe for some people it felt good to unburden themselves, but that didn't seem to be the case for Nina.

JENNIFER BERNARD

"What happened next?" Crush asked gently.

"Two other Wachowskis were outside in a car, and they came in. Trevor was there too, because my dad had asked Trevor to meet him at the pharmacy for backup. He'd already called 911, so the police were on the way. I was totally freaked out, and so was my dad, but Trevor fixed everything. He told the Wachowskis that he'd hit the man, and that he was going to tell the police it was all his fault. No self-defense because that would have implicated the Wachowskis. Since he was only fifteen, he figured the justice system would go easier on him than on my dad. The only thing he asked my dad to do was send me somewhere safe, out of Detroit. He was afraid I wouldn't be able to keep the secret."

She blotted her eyes with her thumb. "He was right. Obviously. It's hard to live with yourself when you know your big brother is paying for your actions. And now he's lost his contract, and it's all my fault. I just . . . hate it. I don't want to lie anymore. If they come after me, I'll run, I'll hide, I'll do whatever I have to. But I'm not going to ruin Trevor's life any more than I already have."

Chapter 24

IT SEEMED TO Trevor that he'd barely put his head on the pillow when the banging started. Groggy from the long, emotional night, he tried to block out the hammering as long as possible, but finally gave in and rolled out of bed.

"Paige," he mumbled as she stormed past him. She was a blur of blue jeans and a clingy green top that had him rethinking the whole "sleep" thing.

"Trevor," she shot back, whirling on him with her hands on her hips, hair fanning behind her. "You lied to me."

He racked his brain for *which* lie she might be referring to. "I was going to call you about the Friars as soon as I woke up."

"I'm not talking about the Friars."

"Okay." He rubbed a hand across the back of his head. "What's going on?"

"Nina came to see us."

His head snapped up. Paige's angry presence seemed to send wild sparks around the dull hotel room. "My sister Nina?"

"Yes, your sister. The one who *actually* attacked someone with a baseball bat. The one you took the fall for."

He turned away, his mind spinning a mile a minute. Maybe he could still fix it. Say she was being an over-protective younger sister. That she was delusional, that she was too young to really remember what happened. He'd figure something out.

"Trevor, why didn't you tell me?"

"I have to talk to her. Where is she? I don't know what she's thinking, coming here and telling stories."

"*Trevor.*"

He felt a hand on his arm and jerked away. This was wrong, all wrong. Nina thought she could change this situation, but she couldn't. If anything happened to her . . . A sudden rush of air exited his lungs—a sort of gasp, or a wheeze, something that didn't sound like it should be coming from his body. He hunched his shoulders, feeling the muscles of his back pull wide, the hawk spreading its wings.

And then softness came against his skin, arms wrapping around him, hawk and all. He felt Paige's cheek against his back, her hands on his bare chest. "It's going to be okay, Trevor. No one's going to hurt her. You don't have to do this alone. You have me, and Crush, and lots of other people."

Another sound threatened to erupt from his chest. He quaked with the effort of holding it back. It felt as if his rib cage was a dam of bones holding back a wall of water. It built and built until it towered over him. In a blinding rush, it swept him off his feet, and he staggered. Paige held him, murmuring soft words, keeping him anchored against the force of the emotions storming through him.

Maybe he cried, or maybe he didn't. Maybe he just let the lost years wash through him. He didn't really know, all he knew was that he held tight to the window frame and Paige held tight to him, and when his vision cleared, everything looked different.

"I guess she had to tell someone." His voice scraped like razor blades against his throat.

"Yes," Paige agreed. "She's a brave girl."

"She always was. That's why I didn't mind taking the rap. If I'd had the bat, I would have done the same thing, except I probably would have killed the guy."

"Why didn't you just tell the police the truth? They wouldn't have sent a twelve-year-old to jail."

"We weren't afraid of that. We were afraid of the Wachowskis. They don't care about details like age or gender. You mess with one of them, you pay." Trevor touched his stomach, realized he was drenched with sweat. He still couldn't look at Paige; he felt too exposed.

"Then why didn't your father take the blame? He was the one who got you into the situation to begin with."

He shook his head wearily. Why relive the nightmare? It was dead and gone. "Dad was the only security Nina had. I was only fifteen. Nina still needed a home and a father, such as he was. He promised he'd send her someplace safe, get her away from the Wachowskis. It was the best thing all around. For a while I hated him for it. But then Grizz said something to me once."

He swallowed hard, remembering.

"Grizz said that sending me away was probably the hardest thing my father had to do, but that it was the only way he could ensure my safety. Then again, I have a scar on my back that says I wasn't that safe."

"You made the best out of that scar." Her cool fingers traced the outline of his hawk. Her touch sent shivers across his skin. She spread her fingers apart, the thumbs at the inside corners of his shoulder blades, her fingertips feathering his upper arms. Desire stirred, a bird rising from the ashes. "You made the best out of a lot of things. You watched out for your sister. You made a baseball career happen."

He gave a dry laugh. "For a while."

She skipped past that. "You try to help kids who are facing the same sort of problems you did." Those clever, magic fingers stroked down the outside of his arms. Blood sank to his groin, his cock reacting to each soft caress.

"Where are you going with this?" he murmured. Wherever she was going, he'd follow, as long as she kept touching him like that. Biceps, elbows, forearms, each body part coming to life under her palms.

"I wish you saw yourself the way I do. You're not a badass." Her hands flexed to cover the backs of his big slugger's hands. She interwove her fingers with his. "Well, not *just* a badass. You're also a hero."

He jerked back against her. "I'm no fucking hero."

"Oh no? What do you call someone who goes to prison for something they didn't do, just to protect their little sister?"

"You don't get it—" He turned, determined to make her take those words back. But as soon as he met her eyes, filled with all the magic and light that was Paige, he lost his train of thought.

She gave him a little shove with one hand, then let it linger on his chest—as if she knew that her touch was turning everything inside molten. "I get it. Why wouldn't I get it? *You're* the one who doesn't get it. You're stuck in this idea that you're a bad guy. And I hate that because I love you, and I know I'm not in love with a bad person. I'm in love with an amazing, incredible, loyal, strong, protective, phenomenal person."

"No. No." He shook his head over and over. "It's you. You see the good in everyone, that's how you are. Even after I pushed you away, after I acted like an asshole, you still do. Whatever good you see in me, it's because of *you*."

She tossed her hair, planted her hands on her hips, a righteous goddess in denim shorts. "Are you saying I'm delusional? That I can't see what's right in front of me? I mean, maybe you're right, given my history with Hudson. I must be blind, right? That's the only explanation there could possibly be for these crazy off-the-wall things I'm thinking—"

"This has nothing to do with him," he said. The mention of Hudson made him crazy. Something shifted inside, some primal instinct coming to the fore.

"No, this is about you and me. You said to bear with you, and I believed you. I believe *in* you. But now I don't know what you're saying, and—"

Clearly, the only way to make her stop talking was to kiss her. He snatched her against him, one arm wrapped around her waist, bending her over. Her beautiful blue eyes went wide with shock. "My turn. You, Paige Mattingly, are the best, absolute *best* thing to ever happen to me. I love you. I love you like I didn't know a person could love. You're everything light and wonderful and real and perfect. I want you, I want to be whatever you need. I want to make you laugh and smile and moan and drop your clothes the second we're alone. I want those things. I love you. But look at me. I'm an unemployed minor league washout with a juvenile record and a target on my back."

But he didn't get to finish all the reasons she shouldn't be with him because she smiled that wide grin and nearly stopped his heart. "You love me?"

"I love you." He staggered under his armload of sweet, passionate Paige.

"You *love me*?" Her face lit up with so much sheer delight that he couldn't help laughing.

"Is that such a surprise? You're fucking irresistible. You're like catnip or pancakes or a cold longneck on a hot day." He grinned, feeling as light as a long ball hitting the air currents.

She swatted him on the back of his head. "You can't compare me to beer. That's not romantic."

"I'm a guy. You want to know what romance is to me?" Still holding her in place, plastered against him, he walked her back toward the bed. When he got there, he tossed her onto it. Her hair fanned across the beige bedspread in rich waves alive with glints of copper and bronze. "Romance is the way I want to strip you bare. I want to kiss every bit of your skin. Especially the parts that make you squeal. Romance is how I want to fuck you until you forget there ever existed any man but me. You're mine, Paige. Everyone else can go to hell, because it's you and me now. We'll just have to figure out the rest."

Paige's heart felt like it would burst out of her throat and soar to the ceiling. Trevor was looking at her the way she'd always dreamed a man would—with complete and utter want. As if she was the only thing that mattered, or would ever matter, from now to forever. As if she was beautiful and absolutely necessary to his survival.

He kneeled on the bed next to her and wrapped his fist in her hair. His lids went to half-mast. "You know something, Paige? There's no part of you that doesn't feel perfect to me. I don't know how you do it. It's like you're the only woman I can see anymore. The only woman I want to see. You're like the sun blotting out all the other stars."

"You're crazy," she whispered.

"Too bad. You can't back out now. You're with me,

Paige. You're mine, and I'm yours." From the way he looked now, passion and devotion written in every line of his face, it was impossible to believe that anyone ever saw him as ice cold. His eyes weren't crystal clear, the way she'd first seen them. Now they shone like the sun blazing through stained glass.

"Yes," she whispered, knowing the word was just the last piece of the puzzle. She'd been his for some time. It had happened mysteriously, without her knowledge, but irrevocably. "For better or worse."

A shadow fell across his face, and she kicked herself for ruining the mood. "I vow to you, Paige, that I'll do everything in my power to keep my crap from hurting you."

"You don't get it, do you, Trevor? If it hurts you, it hurts me. We're together in this. I want your dreams to be mine, and my dreams to be yours. Equals." She touched his chest, traced her fingertips across the hard ridges that turned her on so much. Her mouth watered, and she lifted her eyes back to his, letting him see all the desire and need he inspired.

After that, he made love to her with single-minded intensity. He didn't let her do a thing. Every time her hands fluttered to touch him, he firmly chained them together with one strong hand. He worked his fingers under her jeans, the tightness of the fabric adding an extra layer of pressure. When he felt her wetness—she'd been aroused since that first "I love you," he made a sound like a snarl of satisfaction. Pulling off her jeans and soaked panties, he spread her open. After staring at her for so long that little prickles of anticipation skittered across her sex, he bent down and buried his face between her legs.

"Oh God," she moaned, twining her legs behind his head. "That feels . . . oh my God, Trevor . . ."

It felt as if every stroke of his tongue, every flick of his teeth, every press of his fingers, was saying the same thing. *I love you. I adore you. I live for your pleasure.*

She came almost right away, unable to hold back the rolling tide of her climax. But that was just the beginning. When that talented tongue went to work on her nipples, maneuvering the fabric of her top across the sensitive tips, she reached a level of frantic she would have found embarrassing if Trevor wasn't urging her on with hot words.

"Tell me how good that feels. Tell me what you want. You want my cock? You want it hard for you?"

"God, yes," she gasped.

"Touch it."

Reaching blindly toward his hips, she felt hot velvet against her fingers. Thick, so incredibly thick, hard and urgent, jumping beneath her feather strokes.

"You want that cock in your mouth?" It drove her wild when he talked dirty like that. In answer, she shifted her position, angling her mouth over his erection. She sucked him into her mouth, her throat, her very being, nearly mad with wanting him. With his big hands on the back of her head, he cradled her, adjusting her pace with his fingers. His panting breaths and murmured curses filled her world, the scent of his skin making her dizzy. She surrendered to the rhythm consuming her body and soul, made herself into a vehicle for his pleasure. She stroked his muscular ass as it flexed, let her fingers drift toward the soft sacs of flesh between his thighs.

So vulnerable, in the end. *You need me, Trevor Stark. And I need you.*

Just before he reached his peak, he pulled his erection from her mouth with a soft pop and spread her back open, flat on her back, legs wide. "I need to be inside you," he muttered. "Now, before I fucking explode."

"Yes," she agreed, since nothing in the world could be better than that. He slipped on a condom and entered her inch by slow inch.

"I'm so hard right now, I don't want to hurt you."

"You won't." Her inner channel clung to him, the friction making her eyes roll back in her head.

"Oh my God," he groaned. "Paige, you have no idea what you do to me."

And the world fell open around them, wide and glorious and free.

Afterward, Trevor fetched a washcloth and carefully tended to both of them. Feeling fresh and deliciously cared for, she brushed a strand of gold hair away from his face.

"Crush wants to make you an offer," she told him.

He frowned, and she felt a moment of regret that she had to bring reality back into things. "If he's thinking I can be a coach or front office, no way. I'll figure something out, I don't need your dad trying to save my ass."

"Honestly, I think he's trying to save his, and you're just a side benefit."

He balled up the washcloth and took it into the bathroom. She drew her knees up to her chest and wrapped her arms around them. She knew Trevor had a prickly pride that didn't allow him to accept help. But he'd just have to suck it up.

When he came back into the bedroom, she hit him with Crush's proposal. "He wants to keep you on the Catfish through the end of the season and pay your salary himself."

"*What?* That's nuts. The Friars won't go for that."

"He already worked it out with them. They don't

have a problem with it, in fact they agreed to wait until the championship is over before releasing you. Crush is taking full responsibility for your performance on the field and off. He thinks that if you really show them something amazing, they'll want you in San Diego for the playoffs."

Trevor said nothing. He pulled on a pair of boxers, the honed muscles of his thighs moving smoothly under his gold-spangled skin. Why wasn't he happier about this?

"If you're worried that I'm tending to your life instead of my own, don't. I just submitted five college applications and I'm already looking around at MSW programs. Masters in Social Work," she explained.

"Social work?"

"Yes, I want to work as a counselor. I think I'd—"

"You'd be incredible. I think that's the best idea I've ever heard." He tumbled her back onto the bed, joy lighting up his face as he braced himself over her. "What can I do to help?"

She laughed up at him. "I'm sure I'll think of something, but in the meantime, shouldn't you worry about your own life, slugger?"

He smiled, nuzzling the soft side of her neck. "I deserve that."

"Listen, if you take Crush up on his offer, you don't have to leave baseball and you have a chance to get called up after all."

Still nestled in the space between her neck and her shoulder, he moved his head in a way that could have been a nod or a shake.

"Is it hard for you to let Crush help you out? Because he really, really wants to win the Triple A championship. And he thinks you're the key to that. He's not doing this from any kind of charitable impulse. I don't think he has those. He's a competitive man who just wants to win. And of course he wants to keep the team."

He straightened and sat back on his heels, his physical presence nearly overpowering in boxers and nothing else. "It's not that. I . . ." He hesitated, swallowed.

"There's something else, isn't there? Something you're not telling me?"

He curved his hand around her jaw, his thumb brushing against her bottom lip, his eyes a limpid, sober green. "Yes. And I still can't tell you. But I love you. With all my heart. Will you trust me?"

Chapter 25

THE TRIPLE A National Championship game was a winner-take-all, one-game showdown between the International League and Pacific League champions. But before the Catfish could reach *that* game, they had to win the Pacific League playoffs. In order to do that, they first had to win the Pacific Conference. In order to reach the conference finals, they had to end the season at the top of the South Division.

No problem.

As of September 1, they were ahead of the Isotopes by five games and had clinched the South Division. The North Division champs were the Sacramento River Cats. That best-of-five series ended after a mere three games. The Kilby Catfish were on fire—the official Pacific Conference champions.

Next up, the Catfish would play the American Conference champions, the Omaha Storm Chasers, in a five-game series to determine the Pacific League champion. If the Catfish beat the Storm Chasers, *then*, and only then, would Crush have a chance at making good on his vow.

Most players saw the minor league playoff season as a showcase for their individual skills. It was scheduled in September so that any high-performing prospects could be called up to the parent major league team before the real show—the World Series—and the play-offs leading up to it. Everyone with any hope of a last-minute call-up wanted to make an impression.

Trevor's head was in a very different place. Crush was paying his salary. But the Wades had a guillotine hanging over his neck.

Before the Catfish set out for Omaha, Dean Wade sent Trevor a command invitation to the Roadhouse. Before he went, he checked in with Nina. She was with Paige at Bullpen Ranch, where she'd been staying since she arrived in Kilby. She was playing squeaky mouse with Jerome, happy as a clam. Paige, she told him, was working on invitations to the fund-raiser.

With the reassurance that the two women he loved so fiercely were safe, he headed for the Roadhouse. He found Dean in a far corner, nursing a scotch and puffing on an electronic cigarette. The Wade patriarch ordered a vodka on the rocks, which was quickly placed before Trevor and promptly ignored. Trevor didn't want this man's liquor. Didn't want anything to do with him.

But he didn't necessarily have a choice.

"So . . . Catfish made the playoffs," Dean started mildly enough.

"Yes. That's to be expected. We had a good season. It might look strange if we crapped out now."

"So you got a strategy going, is that what you're saying?"

"You want it to look authentic, don't you? People might get suspicious if we start losing all of a sudden, with no explanation."

Trevor jiggled the tumbler, making the ice cubes clink together, desperately wishing he could toss the alcohol in Wade's face.

Dean laughed, a wheezing bark that sounded like it was being choked out of a squeaky toy. "You ever want a job outside of baseball, you come find me, okay? We can always use a cool head like you."

A cool head. Well, he supposed it was a compliment, but he was tired of being "cool" or "ice man" or anything on the colder end of the spectrum. When it came to Paige, his sister, or baseball, his feelings didn't run cool at all. "I'll keep that in mind, assuming I make it through the season in one piece. Is that it?"

"Not yet. One more thing. Just wanted to let you know that we've made contact with Stan Wachowski. Just an initial meet-and-greet, you might say. We asked him if he had a photo of Trevor Leonov, in case we ever ran across him. They sent this."

Dean turned his phone and flashed him a photo. With a shock, Trevor saw his thinner, sixteen-year-old self, facedown on a folding table. The blistered, blackened lines of a W were seared across his naked back, his arms dangling limply off the table. The photo had been taken after he passed out from the pain. Only the Wachowskis could have taken it. There was no doubt—the Wades had made contact with the syndicate.

Trevor fought not to show his gut-churning reaction. "You don't know who you're messing around with, Wade. If that photo proves anything, it's that you should keep those people out of Kilby."

"I'm not afraid of a branding iron. I got about ten of 'em back at the ranch. Are you getting the picture, slugger?"

Trevor got it, all right. He was more fucked than ever. "I have the situation handled," he said brusquely. "It's got to look natural, so you have to let things play out."

"You better not be playing *us*, Stark."

Trevor pushed his drink away and stood up. "Just out of curiosity, why do you want to buy the Catfish so bad? You're not a baseball fan. What's in it for you?"

"Ain't your worry. We got plans, and they don't involve steak dinners every time someone hits a homer. The team's a relic. The stadium ain't bad. Could be useful. The land, now . . . that's a sweet piece of property." Wade grimaced, his long nose giving him the look of a gargoyle. "Not saying one way or the other what we'd do with the Catfish. Kilby's our town. We do what we want."

Sickened to his core, Trevor strode away from the man. In the scheme of things, the ownership of the Kilby Catfish didn't rank as high as Nina's safety or his future with Paige. But the idea of the Wades getting their slimy hands on the team revolted him. They might disband the Catfish and turn the stadium into "Wadeland," for all he knew. Why this should bother him, he wasn't sure. But it did. It was baseball, the Catfish were a part of baseball, and baseball was a part of him.

On his way out the door he texted Dwight. *All good. TY for the backup. I'll explain everything later.*

You better. Is he ready for his special delivery?

Give me a minute to get on the road. Wish I could see his face, but better not.

But he knew perfectly well what the rest of the Roadhouse patrons would be seeing. He passed the delivery truck on his way out of the parking lot and chuckled out loud. In a minute, several delivery men bearing coolers would parade to the bar.

"Delivery for Dean Wade," they would announce. "Special gift from Crush Taylor and the Catfish." Then they'd open the coolers and display the fresh-caught catfish on their beds of ice. Then they'd march back outside and place those catfish in carefully arranged letters on the hood of the Wades' mint-condition Chevro-let. F.U., those letters would read.

One of those crazy Catfish pranks. Business as usual for the notoriously fun-loving team.

But none of this was fun for Trevor. The Wades had his balls in a vise. He couldn't see any way out.

Game One of the Pacific League championship, fea-turing the Kilby Catfish versus the Omaha Storm Chas-ers, would take place on September 13 in the beautiful city of Omaha, Nebraska. Even though local fans got excited if their team made the playoffs, the games rarely got much mention on the national news.

This year, with Crush throwing the weight of his leg-endary reputation behind the Catfish's prospects, things were different. People were talking about the series, and not only in Omaha and Kilby. ESPN planned to broad-cast the games—tape-delayed at two in the morning, but still a first. Crush's vow and the team's performance since then, along with Trevor's "scandal," got written up in *Sports Illustrated* and was a hot topic on vari-ous baseball forums. If he weren't Crush Taylor, the "Playboy Pitcher," no one would have cared. But Crush knew how to work the media. He even managed to up the ante at the press conference Mayor Trent held to talk about Kilby's historic moment in the championship spotlight.

The entire team watched the press conference from the visiting clubhouse in Omaha. With the two of them—the blow-dried mayor and the lanky former pitcher—standing before the assembled reporters, Crush threw down the gauntlet.

"If Kilby wins, I'll donate twenty thousand dollars to the Save Our Slugs fund."

"If Kilby loses?" a reporter asked.

"If Kilby loses, which is not going to happen, Mayor

Trent agrees to console me by going out to dinner with me." He sent a wink in her direction.

"As if I needed any more reason to root for Kilby," Mayor Trent shot back. The reporters laughed.

"So you agree to Crush's bet?" someone shouted.

"Absolutely not." A smile played across her face, her perfectly teased hair glinting in the sun.

The assembled reporters laughed and "oooohed."

"But I'll offer up a different bet. If the Catfish win, Crush donates twenty thousand to Save Our Slugs, ten thousand to Paige Taylor's summer tutoring fundraiser, and he can take me out to dinner."

Crush scratched his chin, mulling it over. "And if we lose?"

"You donate twice as much."

"Done. And I'll take you out twice." They were shaking hands before the mayor seemed to realize what was happening. "The bet is on. You're all witnesses."

Trevor turned to Dwight. "Does Crush have the hots for the mayor or is this all for show?"

"Got me." Dwight shrugged. He had his game face on, even though the game didn't start for two more hours. His meticulous pregame ritual demanded it. The rest of his preparation involved drinking a cup of black coffee exactly one hour before game time and crooning "You Send Me" to his bat.

Trevor's routine was much simpler. After batting practice, which he kept light, he spent half an hour with his noise cancellation headphones on and his eyes closed. The other players thought he was jamming to some music, but the headphones were just for show. They blocked out the noise from outside so he could clear his mind and do his visualizations. He focused on the ball, on the letters, the red dot that formed a perfect target. He pictured his own swing, smooth and power-

ful and *right*. He imagined the satisfying sound the bat
would make against the ball. The way it would jump off
his bat in a joyful leap for freedom.

He wasn't just smashing that ball, he was setting it
free.

Yeah, crazy thoughts like that came into his head
during his visualizations. Like Paige, naked in his bed.
For long moments, he lost himself in the bliss of that
image. His Paige, luscious and wild, his sexy woman,
the one who always had his back.

Then another image snuck into his mind. Dean
Wade, with his stupid bolo tie and nasty sneer. Watching him from a field box at the Kilby stadium. Wanting
him to fail. Waiting for him to give less than his best.

Unnerved, Trevor ended his visualization early. He
skimped on the rest of his routine, barely remembering
to mutter a little prayer to the photo of Jackie Robinson
stuck to the back of his locker. He wasn't a particularly religious man, but he didn't mind asking for a little
assist from the greats.

The Catfish were at bat first, and before Trevor even
got to the plate, they'd scored two runs. The Omaha
pitcher was shaky, and Leiberman singled, stole a base,
then cruised home on a homer from Ramirez.

Thank you, Catfish. Trevor relaxed. If the Catfish
were going to play like that, even if he sat out the game
he wouldn't cost them anything. The smart thing to do,
with the Wades watching so closely, would be to make
an out. Everyone would be focused on the fact that the
Catfish were winning 2-0. No one would notice if he
didn't contribute much.

His gaze strayed to the section of the stands set aside
for the management from the visiting team. Paige sat in
the front row, chatting with Marcia Burke. She wore
a creamy summer dress with a lacy top and shoulder

straps made out of ribbons. A bright blue cowboy hat—Kilby colors—kept the sun off her face and brought out the gorgeous blue of her eyes. He imagined her wearing cowboy boots and no underwear.

Before the game, inspired by Crush's bet with the mayor, he'd dared Paige to do exactly that.

"Fine, but I want to make sure I'm getting something out of this. If you've gotten two hits by the seventh inning, I'll take my panties off during the seventh inning stretch," she'd told him with a saucy toss of her head. "And if you win, you can have your way with me."

"Using sex as bribery?"

"Is that against the Baseball Code of Conduct?"

"Pretty sure the rules and regs don't mention your undies."

At any rate, her bribery must have worked, because without thinking twice, he slammed the first pitch into the center field bleachers. The ball flew so fast and far that they probably had to slow-mo it on TV just to see where it went.

As Trevor jogged around the bases he alternated between triumph and dread. A solo home run only counted as one run, after all. Would the Wades see this as a giant middle finger or would they give him the benefit of the doubt? Assume it was part of his strategy?

All thoughts of the Wades fled as he rounded third base and arrowed in on Paige, who was on her feet, her glorious hair loose under her cowboy hat, clapping and practically bouncing in her joy. He raised one finger as he passed her, then pumped his fist against his heart.

She twitched her skirts, the little tease.

If the Wades knew what they were up against—the temptation of Paige—they might pack their bags and go home.

To the right of Paige, Crush also wore a huge grin. Beyond him, Nina was also bouncing up and down, yelling something to him between her cupped hands. For the first time in his professional baseball career, he had a cheering section—a real one, not barely dressed groupies, but people who cared about him. What a new and amazing experience. And when he trotted into the dugout, his teammates' butt pats and low fives added another layer of satisfaction.

He caught the play-by-play from someone's radio: "Trevor Stark is famous for working the count and never swinging at the first pitch. But that's why he's so dangerous, because he keeps pitchers on their toes. You can't predict what a great hitter will do, and Stark has all the makings of a great."

Grinning, Trevor slapped hands with T.J. Gates and yelled, "Let's keep it going" to Dwight, who was stepping into the batter's box. He paused for a moment, soaking in the cheers, the fellowship, the presence of Paige. *This moment has been brought to you by the game of baseball,* he thought. That was the way it worked. Long periods of slogging through the season, punctuated by moments of transcendence.

As he sank into his accustomed spot in the dugout, he caught sight of a black cowboy hat across the stadium. *Aw fuck.* It was Dean Wade, right there in Werner Park, Omaha, Nebraska. He was staring grimly at the field.

All of Trevor's joy evaporated. Ice surrounded him like a shield. The Wades were here to keep an eye on him. To fuck with him, control him. They held all the cards and they knew it.

Be smart, he told himself. *The Wades plus the Wachowskis, you don't want that combination. Keep your head down. Lay low, the way you have been. You're used to it.*

But no, he wasn't used to holding himself back on the field. That was different. That was disrespecting the game of baseball. Could he do it?

His inner struggle lasted until his next at bat. The Storm Chasers were a feisty team and by then had squeezed in a few runs, though the Catfish were still up by one. If Trevor struck out, he'd still be batting .500 for the game. He'd get the Wades off his back with no cost to him.

Work the count this time, he told himself. *Be smart. Don't do anything crazy.*

When the count was 2-2 and the pitcher was shaking off signs from the catcher, his glance strayed to the box where Paige sat. She perched on the edge of her chair, hands clasped under her chin, as if sending waves of encouragement in his direction.

He tore his gaze away and planted it back where it belonged, on the pitcher. A moment later the ball was hurtling through the air in a tight, perfect spin, the blur of seams coalescing into a clear red dot.

He swung. Made contact with a sound like the ringing of a bell, so clear and pure it echoed through the stadium. The ball ripped off his bat in a straight line toward the farthest reaches of left field. He put his head down and ran for first base, caught the signal from the coach to keep going, and charged toward second. The third base coach was giving him the stop signal, so he cruised into second with a stand-up double. Exhilarated, panting, electricity pouring through him.

He was a baseball player to his core. For a moment, nothing else mattered.

Baseball had saved him in every possible way. How in the hell could he lay off a sinking fastball that forgot to sink? He was Trevor Stark, baseball player.

He looked over at Paige, grinned and held up two

fingers. Brimming with laughter, she covered her face with her hands. Damn, he was looking forward to that seventh inning stretch.

In the meantime, back to business. The base runner on second, with his vantage point behind the pitcher's mound, had the job of trying to steal signs that the catcher flashed to the pitcher, which happened to be one of Trevor's specialties. When you were on second, you were essentially behind enemy battle lines. Your job was to gather intel that would help your team. On top of that, you had the opportunity to disrupt, to distract. Trevor saw it as his job to mess with the pitcher's concentration, make him wonder what the big slugger was up to behind his back. Even a tiny lapse in the pitcher's focus could give an edge to Dwight, who was at the plate now.

And then there was his other job. With dread, he looked over at the section where Dean Wade had been sitting. This time, he saw no black cowboy hat. Had Dean left to place that phone call to the Wachowskis? Or would Dean remember what he'd said about letting things play out? This was only the first game. Next game, he'd do what needed to be done.

Suddenly, alone on second base, Trevor felt more exposed than he ever had before.

Chapter 26

THE CATFISH WON Game One with the emphatic score of 10-5. Although Trevor wasn't the only standout, Paige couldn't tear her eyes away from him. After the game, he took her to dinner to celebrate. They took a cab on an oddly roundabout route to a quiet, upscale part of town, where they walked along streets steaming from a late evening rain shower. Charcoal clouds paraded overhead, a half-moon playing peekaboo behind them. Trevor seemed lost in thought as he held her hand in his, big and warm as a bear's paw.

When they passed a darkened side street, he tugged her into it, found a spot sheltered by a parked SUV, and backed her against the outer wall of an antique store. Shielding her with his body, he inched her dress up her thighs. The silky fabric combined with the rough surface of his fingers sent shivers along her nerve endings.

"I was thinking about your bare pussy the entire last two innings," he murmured against her neck. "Distracted the hell out of me. Did you see me hit into that double play? Good thing the game was already in the bag."

She spread her hands across the hard muscles of his back. "Hmm, I think that Omaha shortstop robbed you. If that's your version of distracted, maybe I should never wear underwear to a game again."

"Now you're just torturing me." He bit the tendon of her shoulder lightly. Her nipples hardened into hot little pebbles. His hand reached the crease between her thighs and he dragged a finger along her sex.

She moaned. "Are you trying to return the favor?"

"I just can't keep my hands off you." He touched her tenderly, reverently. "Sometimes I step back and think this is all like some kind of dream. Meeting you. Being able to fondle you whenever I want."

"It must be a dream we're both having. I never thought I'd feel like this, like I'd die if you didn't want me."

"I want you. Never, *ever* doubt that." He claimed her entire mound with a firm, possessive grip. Her insides went liquid, heat radiating from each point of contact. "I want to make you come right here in my hand. Right here against this wall."

Oblivious to anything except how he made her feel, she wrapped one leg around the back of his thigh and pressed her groin against his hand. "Can we?" she whispered. "Could we do that? Because I've been turned on ever since you hit that first home run."

He glanced over his shoulder and adjusted his position. "Watch the street, okay?"

"Okay." She was already breathless, already close to the edge from the gentle friction he'd been applying in slow, steady strokes. Now he intensified things. A fast, hard rhythm struck sparks that arced through her system. One of his long, knowing fingers went inside and searched out a spot she hadn't known existed. He pressed against it. Spots danced before her eyes. She kept her gaze fastened on the end of the little side street.

Trevor enveloped her with his heat and his strength,

from inside and out. She pushed back, wanting more friction, more contact, more pressure. With a growl, he gave her what she wanted and more, taking command of her body and its myriad sensations.

A car drove past, music blasting. A cat jumped onto the hood of a nearby Honda and began cleaning its paws.

Paige gasped and panted. "I don't know if I . . ." *can come,* she was going to say. Too public, too risky. But then Trevor curled his index finger deep inside her, bore down on her clit with his wrist and she was gone.

Sobbing, she climaxed against his hand, the end of the street nothing but a vague blur seen through a haze of ecstasy. She chased that orgasm with something like greed, her mound and his hand in a kind of grinding, push-and-pull dance. Maybe Trevor was driving that orgasm, or maybe she was. It was hard to tell.

With Hudson, she'd always been a little embarrassed by her sexual side—maybe because they'd begun as friends and he was so shy. She never felt that way with Trevor. With him, she could be as nasty as she wanted. She could come all over his hand in a random side street in Omaha and he'd grin and say, *Now that was hot.*

"What about you?" She asked, still trying to catch her breath, holding tight to his shoulders while he put her dress back to rights.

"Obviously, you owe me." His wolfish grin made her stomach tighten. "And you will pay up. At the time and place of my choosing. And you won't be able to say no because you owe me. Deal?"

Oh yes, that was a deal she could definitely sign on for. "Nothing that would ruin my good-girl reputation, right?"

"Honey, if you're going to be with me, you might have to let that reputation go."

"Oh no, I don't. Everyone knows you're the bad boy and I'm the do-gooder." She flashed him a mischievous grin. "No one needs to know the truth, do they?"

"What's the truth?" He adjusted his pants over his erection.

"That you're a good guy, and I'm a lot naughtier than I look."

"Yeah you are." He gave her a little spank on the ass, and even that felt good, his big hand burning through her thin dress. God, was there anything she wouldn't enjoy with this man? Could she possibly be any happier than right at this moment, hand in hand with this intense and magnificent ballplayer?

He drew her close to his side as they strolled back onto the main street. He scanned both directions thoroughly before guiding her to the right. The way he held her felt more than possessive; it felt protective, as if he was shielding her from some danger.

"What's wrong?"

"Nothing. Actually, there is something. Paige, I want you to be careful. With all this media attention, I'm a little nervous. I—" He broke off. "Just be careful. And please keep an eye on Nina. It means a lot to see you both in the stands when we're playing. I know you're safe when I can look over and see for myself."

She swung his hand between them. "You're so silly. Where else would we be? Of course we'll be at the games. I'll be staring at you the entire time, and Nina . . . well, she might be looking Leiberman's way now and then."

A cloud gathered on the finely molded planes of his face, moonlight glittering in his narrowed eyes. *"Bieberman."*

"Oh stop. She's been pretty lonely. And she's afraid you're still angry with her."

"I'm not angry. I understand why she came to you and Crush. I even understand why she didn't warn me first."

"She knew you'd stop her."

"I'm starting to think there's no way to stop her from anything. Leiberman better watch out." A wry smile twisted one corner of his mouth. "I won't get in her way, though. She's a big girl. When I was her age, I was playing in Mexico, living on rice and beans. I knew two words of Spanish, 'safe' and 'out.' Nina deserves to have more of a life than she's had so far. I won't hold her back anymore. It might be even harder than going to juvie, but I'll support her, whatever she chooses."

She lifted their clasped hands to her lips and kissed his middle knuckle. Trevor was such a strong, caring person. And no one else had any clue about his true nature— except Nina. And maybe Crush, now that Nina had revealed the truth. A lot of Kilby kids knew too. Everyone else bought into the legend of Trevor Stark.

Well, she wasn't going to tell anyone. She'd tuck it into her heart and savor her secret knowledge.

She gave his knuckle a gentle nibble. "By the way, I have a surprise for you."

"You got rid of all your underwear, for good?" His hopeful tone made her burst out laughing.

"You want all of it to go? Even my red lace teddy?"

"Are you trying to give me a heart attack?"

"No, you need to stay alive until tomorrow's game. That's when you'll get your surprise." She refused to say anything more, no matter how much he nuzzled her neck and whispered hot threats about bending her over his knee.

Game Two was advertised as a pitcher's duel, with the two best ERAs from each team facing off. Trevor got dressed for the game without a fixed plan, but in the back of his mind a ticker tape of warnings ran on repeat. *Be smart. Remember what's most important. We're only up one game, it would be reasonable for them to win the next one. Let's do this thing. It's not too late.*

But then came time for the ceremonial first pitch, something Trevor rarely paid attention to.

"Here to throw out the first pitch of Game Two of the Pacific League championships, please welcome the legendary Grizz Walker!"

Trevor's head shot up, and there was Grizz, making his way onto the field with the assistance of a cane.

The announcer went on. "Former catcher in the Negro Leagues, one of the great scouts of all time, and longtime volunteer baseball coach, he's one of the legends of the sport. Give him a big hand!"

A full-bodied roar followed, as if every person in Werner Park recognized true greatness even in the form of a frail eighty-nine-year-old man with grizzled white hair.

Trevor walked to the edge of the dugout and applauded along with the rest of the players. He hadn't talked to Grizz in about a year. It had never occurred to him to invite his favorite coach to Omaha. This was Paige's doing—the big surprise. He looked over at the visiting owner's box, where Paige waved, grinning from ear to ear. And then he got another surprise. She was wearing an enormous T-shirt that hung off her body and had something scrawled on the front in black Sharpie. Squinting, he realized it was the Catfish T-shirt he'd given to her the first night they met, in her rental car.

He burst out laughing and blew her a kiss, though it was the barest fraction of the love churning in his heart.

Grizz. Nina. Paige. Could he ask for anything more?

He managed to intercept Grizz for a gentle hug before the man climbed into his prime front-row seat. As he strode to the plate, it occurred to him that he'd rather gouge out his eyes than play anything less than his best with Grizz Walker in attendance.

But his nerves got the best of him. In his first at-bat, he hit into a double play. In his second, he popped up to the pitcher. In his third, after banging his head against the back of the dugout wall for about ten minutes, he finally managed to rip a triple. Grizz cheered as if he were Mickey Mantle.

He'd played his worst game in weeks, but it hadn't been on purpose. In fact, that one taste of near-failure was enough to drive home the truth. He couldn't—wouldn't—throw a game. But maybe the Wades would think that he had.

Unfortunately, the Catfish did just fine without him at his best. They won by one run.

The Catfish went back to Kilby two games up, needing only one to reach the final championship game. Trevor wondered if he should return himself to incarceration. Because unless he was behind bars or incapacitated, how was he going to bring himself to do what the Wades wanted?

He lectured himself during the long bus ride through America's heartland to Kilby. No more showing off. This wasn't about him and his pride. He'd just have to find a way to torpedo the team. Crush's team. *Paige's father's team*. How could he do that and still live with himself? His thoughts were still going in sleepless circles when he trudged down the hall to his room at the Days Inn and saw that someone had beaten him there.

A giant red W marked his door. Bloodred, the color the Wachowskis always chose.

He spun around, half expecting to see a group of en-
forcers converging on him. But the hallway was empty.
He was alone with his ominous thoughts. No way was
he going inside his hotel room. Who knew what awaited
him there? He should go out to Bullpen Ranch, grab
Nina, and the two of them could disappear to Mexico
or something.

But then he'd never see Paige again. Or Dwight. Or
anyone else in the baseball world. He'd be running and
hiding forever. Most importantly, Paige would think
he'd run off on her, that he didn't love her.

But what else could he do?

There was only one choice, really. Quickly he turned
and headed for the exit. Twenty minutes and he'd be at
the ranch.

Paige couldn't believe she'd ever thought baseball wasn't
exciting. The anticipation before Game Three had the
entire town of Kilby on the edge of celebration. *Sweep,
sweep,* was the rallying cry.

Then came the shocking news. Trevor Stark was
out of the lineup for Game Three. He wasn't even in
the stadium, which was extremely strange. No one explained why. Crush refused to answer when Paige asked
him. He disappeared halfway through Game Three and
spent the rest of it talking to someone in his office. Even
the players seemed confused. On the field, they looked
lost.

The Storm Chasers took advantage and rampaged to
a 7-2 win. The series was now 2-1, the Catfish with the
edge. An atmosphere of nervous stress swept through
Kilby. No one talked about a sweep anymore. They talked
about "hanging on" and "fending off the Chasers."

But Paige's biggest concern was Trevor. Where was
he? He didn't answer any of her messages. He'd checked

out of the Days Inn. Dwight didn't know where he was. *Nina* didn't even know. When she asked Crush, he told her not to worry about Trevor. He also said that security was being doubled throughout the stadium, and to be alert for anything unusual.

The whole thing was unusual.

Then, mysteriously, came word that Trevor would be batting fourth in Game Four. The news electrified Kilby. With Trevor back, the talk changed to "clinching in four" and "resting before the championship game."

Paige had no idea what was going on, but whatever it was, she was going to strangle Trevor the next time she saw him. Even if she had to run onto the field to do it.

On the evening of Game Four, Paige and Nina reached the stadium about half an hour before game time. Paige dropped Nina off at the staff entrance, then parked Crush's Range Rover in the owner's parking area. It was going to be a beautiful night for baseball. Streaks of gaudy persimmon glowed on the horizon. In a sky the color of lilacs, the first pinprick star flickered into view. The scent of sun-heated asphalt pricked her nose. The stadium was sold out. Long lines of vehicles snaked all the way out to the road, their metal catching the sunset like mirrors. Paige had to shield her eyes from the flashes of light.

Inside the stadium, the organist played a rising set of chords, the sound wafting into the parking lot. *Duh-duh-duh-duh, duh-duh-duh-duh.* Paige could picture the happy fans searching for their seats, stocking up on hot dogs, peanuts, beer, and the Kilby specialty, Catfish jerky. She hoped the special playoff season T-shirts she'd ordered were selling well, and that the Baseball's Hottest Outfield posters would be considered collector's items rather than a reminder of yet another embarrassing moment in Catfish history.

After locking the Range Rover, she hurried toward the staff entrance, her favorite cowboy boots thudding on the still-warm pavement.

Nina must have already gone inside, because she saw no sign of her. She pulled open the door and stepped inside. The staff entrance opened onto a small foyer with an elevator on one side and a staircase on the other. It was a small space, something cobbled together during a stadium renovation from the 1970s. There wasn't much place to hide, so a soft squeal seemed completely out of place.

"Hello?" she called. "Nina, is that you?"

She stepped into the foyer, jumping when the front door crashed shut behind her.

She took a few deep breaths to calm herself. What was wrong with her? This was a busy baseball stadium, not some haunted house.

Shaking off the feeling that something was wrong, she went to the bottom of the staircase. "Nina!" She called. "Where'd you go?"

Stupid question. There was only one place to go. Up. She started up the stairs. Nina must have dashed ahead for some reason. Maybe she'd seen Leiberman. Maybe she had to pee. Maybe Nina was tired of being shadowed by her.

Halfway up the stairs, a scuffling sound drifted from the direction of the elevator. Now that definitely wasn't right. Nina would never have taken the elevator. Nina had told her that she'd once been trapped in a mall elevator and since then always took the stairs or an escalator.

Paige launched herself down the stairs. At the elevator, she punched the button. The door opened an inch, then closed, opened again, then closed. Was it malfunctioning or something else? She looked around

for something to jam between the doors, but the foyer
had nothing in terms of decorations. The next time the
doors opened, she stuck her right cowboy boot between
them. Not wanting to risk any broken bones, she quickly
she pulled her foot out of the boot. With a steel inset
in the toe, the boot worked like a charm, preventing
the doors from closing. Able to peer inside through the
narrow opening, she saw a terrified Nina in the grasp of
a tall, wiry man in a black leather blazer. His hand was
clamped over her mouth, her face turning red.

Paige pulled out her cell phone to dial 911. *No reception.* She turned and ran toward the front door as the
elevator doors whooshed open behind her.

"Give me that phone," the man ordered in a nasal
voice that definitely did not come from Texas. She kept
running. If she could just get outside, she could get a
signal and call for help. But just as she reached the door,
the man, dragging Nina along with him, managed to
catch up and grab her. He knocked the phone from her
grip and smashed it under his heel.

She backed away. "Who are you? What do you want
with Nina?"

Nina's right cheekbone looked swollen. She seemed
to be in shock, barely aware that Paige was there. The
man had *hit* her. The bastard.

"You stay out of it." He pulled a pair of handcuffs
from his jacket, yanked her forward and locked one
cuff around her wrist. Viciously, he jerked her toward
the stair railing. *Crap.* He was going to imprison her
in the foyer with no cell phone while he did God knew
what to Nina. No one would come this way until after
the game. No one would be able to hear her scream or
yell for help.

The other cuff was a few inches from the stair railing, ready to close her in, when Paige lunged for Nina.

She grabbed the girl's nearest arm and hauled her forward, thrusting her wrist into the cuff. It clicked shut, and there they were, handcuffed together.

Whatever happened next, at least Nina wouldn't be on her own. He probably had the key, but if he looked for it, Paige thought she could try to grab the gun she'd spotted under his jacket. Maybe.

"You crazy bitch." The man in black leather scowled. Paige realized he was younger than he'd seemed at first, probably around thirty, with a wispy beard. "Getting kinky on me. Fine, I'll take two for the price of one. Come on, both of you." He yanked them back to the elevator. Paige didn't struggle. Not only did he have the hidden sidearm, but he also wore a Leatherman attached to his belt. He never would have made it through the metal detectors at the front gates. Pretty smart of him to use the staff entrance. She made a note to inform her father of this gap in security—assuming she made it out alive.

She motioned to Nina to stay quiet, stay calm.

The girl nodded. Though still pale, she wiggled her fingers to touch Paige's and shot her a relieved smile. The kidnapper kicked Paige's cowboy boot across the foyer and pushed the two of them into the elevator. He punched the Up button. "Now where in this building can I find good cell reception?"

Chapter 27

"**W**HO ARE YOU, mister? Can you explain what this is all about? I'm sure we can work it out, whatever it is." Paige tried to stay calm as the elevator ascended through the levels of the stadium.

"We can skip the chitchat, doll. Right now I want a good signal. Fucking technology."

"I can help with that. The best cell phone reception is on the field or in the stands. A few corners here and there aren't bad, but mostly the stadium's pretty bad for cell phones. We use landlines a lot." It seemed ridiculous, talking about cell phone reception with a kidnapper. Or whatever he was. "What's, um, going on? What are you after?"

"Don't ask me questions, 'cause they don't fucking tell me anything," he grumbled. "I'm one step away from a babysitter. Can't believe they sent me down here on *Fight Night*."

"Kilby's actually a really nice place," Nina piped up. "Sure it's small, but the people are friendly."

The kidnapper shot her an incredulous look. "I'm not looking to relocate."

"Are you from Detroit, then?" Paige asked. "Do you work for the Wachowskis?"

He clammed up as the elevator reached the top floor, which was used for storage. An open, low-ceilinged space, it was filled with piles of boxes, some neatly labeled, others simply shoved haphazardly into corners. Pushing Paige and Nina in front of him, the kidnapper prowled fretfully through the space, looking at his phone. Finally he stopped short.

"Two bars."

Paige met Nina's eyes, trying not to laugh. "Do you have Verizon? You should try AT&T."

"Thanks for the tip." The kidnapper hit a number on the phone, then walked a few steps away to conduct his conversation.

"Is he after Trevor?" Nina whispered to Paige. "What's going on?"

"I have no idea. Just don't say a word until we figure out what he wants." Overall, he didn't seem very menacing. If he was with the Wachowskis, he must be more of an underling. Not that he couldn't still hurt them if he chose. He might be on the wiry side, but he was strong.

The kidnapper spoke into his phone; she craned her neck to listen. In the low rumble of conversation, all she caught was the word "sister" and the word "deliver." So this *was* about Trevor.

Flipping his phone shut, the jittery man came back and dragged the two girls to an old couch shoved up against the wall. "Sit down."

Awkwardly, Paige and Nina coordinated the action of lowering themselves down to a sitting position. The handcuffs made it uncomfortable and difficult, and Paige nearly yanked Nina off her feet when she stumbled. He took a zip tie from his pocket and attached Nina's ankle to the leg of the couch. Paige sniffed. It smelled of cigar smoke and locker room. A castoff from Duke's office?

The kidnapper took her backpack away and dug through it for her wallet. He checked her ID. "Paige . . . Notswego?"

"That's right." Paige put on her most innocent expression. She hadn't gotten around to changing her driver's license back, and now she was thankful. It probably wouldn't help this situation if he knew she was Crush's daughter.

"What is that, African?"

"Yes."

"Reminds me of that basketball player just got signed by Golden State, what's his name . . . Hudson Notswego."

"My husband. *Ex*-husband," she added quickly, in case he was thinking in terms of ransom money.

"Yeah?" The man seemed genuinely impressed. "Got a killer jumpshot. Wait . . . isn't he with that talk show lady? The one with the boobs?"

Paige stared at him stonily. One more black mark against Hudson, that she'd have to deal with questions about him and Nessa *while being held hostage*. "Can we change the subject, maybe? Like, why you're keeping us up here in a storage room? It seems a little stupid because there's no way out. When they come for you, you'll be trapped."

But the man seemed unworried about that possibility. "Hudson Notswego. That's some contract he signed. Did he cheat on you? Heard that most of those NBA players get a lot of pussy. You're probably better off without him."

Next to Paige, Nina gave a soft giggle. "You're definitely better off," she whispered in Paige's ear. "Trevor would never cheat on you. He really, really loves you. You love him too, right? You're not going to break my brother's heart?"

"What? Why do you say that?"

"Hey!" The man snapped his fingers. "No whispering."

Paige barely looked over at him. The kidnapper didn't seem bent on hurting them, so she no longer feared him. Actually, he seemed nervous more than anything else, as if he was afraid of screwing up. "What are you talking about?" she asked Nina.

"Trevor thinks you're like a baseball princess, and he's more of a peasant. I'm pretty sure he wants to ask you to marry him but thinks he doesn't deserve you. He didn't say that, because he doesn't talk about this stuff. It's just my theory."

"Doesn't deserve me? Why would he think that?" In dismay, Paige rattled the handcuffs, making Nina flinch. "Sorry."

"Because of his . . . you know . . . our past. His record. All the bad stuff from before."

The man loomed over them like a telephone pole in black leather. "I said, no fucking whispering. Talk out loud, so I can hear."

"That's fine." Nina cleared her throat. "Actually, I want to talk out loud, because I have something to say to the Wachowskis."

"*What?* No!" Paige tried to put her hand over Nina's mouth but couldn't manage it with the clanking iron bracelet. "Don't you dare, Nina."

Nina shoved her hand away. "You can't stop me. This is my life, and my brother, and I want him to get all the good things he deserves."

Paige rolled on top of her. Maybe she could squish the breath out of her, make it impossible for her to talk. Nina kicked Paige in the shin, then wriggled her head free.

"Girl fight." Smirking, the kidnapper held up his

phone to take a picture. "This job just got more fun. Makes up for missing *Fight Night*. I'm gonna have to put my money on Notswego's ex on this one."

"I'm Trevor Leonov's sister," squeaked Nina.

"True that, but you don't got his upper body strength, and the other girl's taller, so—"

"I'm not talking about your stupid girl fight, moron! My brother didn't hurt Dinar Wachowski! I did!"

The traditional singing of the Star-Spangled Banner had barely ended when Trevor and the rest of the Catfish ran onto the field. Game Four. If they won this game, they'd be on their way to the Triple A championship game. If they lost, the series would be tied.

Most importantly, he was supposed to play ball as if everything was normal. That's what the FBI had requested of him and Crush.

At first, when he revealed the whole story to Crush, burn scars, threats, hotel door graffiti, and all, Crush had yanked him from Game Three. "Your life is more important than the damn championship," he'd growled. But then he'd called a buddy in the FBI. The Feds wanted to see if they could trip up the Wachowskis, who they'd been monitoring for some time. Based on their surveillance, nothing big was in the works, they told Trevor. They were just hoping for a slip of the tongue caught on wiretap. He had nothing to worry about, they assured him. They took his cell phone, put him in a secure hotel, and told him to act normal.

Yeah right. Tell that to the anxiety tightening his gut. He hadn't even dared to talk to Paige or Nina; best to keep them out of it for now.

Out in left field, Trevor caught the ball Dwight whipped toward him, then hurled it back to Bunner at second in the last "around the horn" before the game started. His shoulder felt nice and loose, his arm strong. Too bad he wouldn't get one more chance to play before Grizz. He'd begged his old friend to come down to Kilby with the team and watch the rest of the series. But Grizz had elected to go home and rest up.

"It's enough that I got to see you play the way I always knew you could," he told Trevor.

"If I get the call-up to San Diego, I'm flying you in."

"Done deal. I'll be there. But make it quick, boy. I can't hang on forever." He winked at Trevor and the other players, who had clustered around to shake his hand and get his autograph. Watching the respect his teammates gave Grizz made Trevor want to shoulder bump every single one of them.

And to think he had Paige to thank for the chance to see Grizz again. Hungry for the sight of her after a day of deprivation, he glanced over at the owner's box. Two empty seats glared back at him.

No Paige. No Nina.

Crush, armed with his Armani shades, sprawled in his seat as if the outcome of the game made no difference to him. Next to him sat Mayor Trent, her posture upright, hair teased to Texas politician poufiness, a Go Kilby smile on her face. Behind them sat Marcia Burke and a few other members of the management staff who Trevor didn't recognize. And there, at the front of the box, the shocking absence of Paige and Nina.

Maybe they were in the ladies' room. Both of them. Maybe they'd gotten stuck in traffic on their way to the stadium. No reason to be alarmed yet.

Trevor spent the top of the first inning lecturing himself not to panic. There was a perfectly reasonable explanation for their absence; he just didn't know it yet. Luckily, no balls made it to left field. Farrio retired the side with only one hit, a harmless single. As

Trevor jogged to the dugout, he tried to catch Crush's eye, hoping to get a read on whether he was worried. But the owner was caught up in a conversation with the mayor and never looked in his direction.

None of the first three Catfish batters got on base, which meant that Trevor only got as far as the on-deck circle before the inning ended. After handing off his bat and helmet to the bat boy, he jogged slowly to left field again, scanning the aisles and seats for a glimpse of tumbling brown locks or Nina's short blond tuft of hair. Maybe they'd decided to sit somewhere else this time. Maybe Crush had asked them to stay out of sight. Maybe he was being paranoid.

Maybe love was making him nuts.

He barely followed the action on the field during the second inning. With one out, two Storm Chasers got on base, and the next batter hit a long fly ball to left. Lost in anxious thoughts about Paige and Nina, he didn't even notice until Dwight screamed his name. With Dwight yelling the entire time, he ran at top speed to chase down the ball. When he caught it, pure muscle memory told him to twist in midair and whip it back to second base.

A 7-4-3 double play. End of inning. No score.

The radio play-by-play drifted into earshot as he ran to the dugout. "As so often happens, the guy who makes a brilliant play to end the inning is the first up to bat. Trevor Stark has been unbelievable this entire series. Watching him is like watching a chess grandmaster playing in a public park or a NASCAR champ in a bumper car. He's always been a player to watch, but now he seems to have hit turbo boost on his game. The Friars have got to be salivating right about now. My guess is, we get through the championship and bye-bye Trevor Stark."

Trevor rolled his eyes as he swung into the dugout. Stupid commentary. He hoped none of the other players took it seriously. If Dwight hadn't gotten his attention out there, he would have missed that play by a mile. Baseball was a team sport, why didn't anyone seem to remember that? Especially the Wades.

At the reminder, a chill shot through him. In that dark little side street in Omaha, he'd made Paige promise to watch all the games, and to make sure Nina came too. Maybe it was selfish, but it relieved him of worry. She'd said, *Where else would we be?*

But she wasn't here.

Batting helmet and gloves on, he grabbed his favorite bat and went to the plate. The next time he checked, the girls would be there. They'd be settling into their seats with drinks or waving bright blue foam catfish.

But the two seats were still empty. Crush was deep in conversation with Mayor Trent, their heads bent together. Cozy as hell. But where were Paige and Nina?

With one foot out of the batter's box, he took a practice swing. Mechanics were good, no pain, he felt nice and loose and warmed up. Powerful, as if home runs would come streaming off his bat. He knew the Storm Chaser pitcher well, knew that his curveball didn't always drop and that he threw more than his share of wild pitches. Already he could see the fear in the hurler's eyes.

If it weren't so early in the game, he'd probably get walked. But the manager wouldn't call for a walk now, especially with no one on base.

Here came the first pitch. Wide and outside. Ball one. Trevor backed out of the box, glanced again at the owner's box. No Paige. *Where else would she be?*

Second pitch. Another ball, so wide the catcher barely managed to save it.

I'll be staring at you the entire time.

Ball three barely cleared his ankles. In the owner's box, Crush laughed at something the mayor was saying. No Paige. No Nina.

Trevor couldn't take it anymore. He stepped out of the batter's box. "I'm out," he told the umpire.

"Huh?"

"I'm out. Tell Duke or whatever you're supposed to do."

He jogged across the infield diamond. All around him, shock waves reverberated. He heard confused murmurs from the audience and a "What the fuck?" from the Storm Chaser third baseman as he cruised past. The play-by-play radio announcer was going nuts. "With three balls and no strikes, Trevor Stark just did something so bizarre, I can't think of a single precedent in all my years in baseball. Instead of completing the at-bat, he is now *running* across the field, straight toward the third base line. Everyone else is backing away, in case they have a lunatic on their hands. If so, that sure would explain a lot about Trevor Stark's erratic history since he signed that big contract with the Friars."

He ignored all of it and ran straight to the padded barrier along the third base line.

"Crush!" he yelled. "Crush Taylor!"

The entire stadium went quiet. People stood on their seats, craned their necks, shushed each other. So much for acting normal.

Crush's head swiveled around and he ripped off his sunglasses. "What the—"

"Where are Paige and Nina?" Trevor asked urgently. If anyone understood how important this was, it would be Crush.

A frown creased Crush's forehead, but Trevor couldn't tell what it meant. Duke appeared at Trevor's elbow, screaming. "You're out. You hear me? I'm taking you out of this game."

Trevor held him off with one hand. "I already took myself out. Crush, have you seen them here today?"

Slowly, Crush rose to his feet. "Haven't seen them."

"Call Paige."

Holding his gaze, Crush dialed Paige's number, then slowly shook his head. Panic flooded Trevor's body, made the blood pound in his ears. "Something's wrong, Crush. Alert security. Please."

"Calling right now." He pushed a button on his phone. "Meet me in the concourse, Trevor." He bent to say something to Wendy Trent. She nodded and got to her feet.

"What's going on? What's happening?" Duke kept jabbering questions at him. The other Catfish poured out of the dugout to join the two of them beneath the owner's box. Trevor needed to go in the opposite direction, toward the dugout, so he could reach the concourse. He tried to muscle through the throng of his teammates, but Dwight blocked his way.

"Tell us what's happening, Trevor."

"I have to get through." He scrambled for his usual icy calm, but it was no use. Images of glinting knives and vicious men kept chasing through his head. His heart raced so fast he could barely draw a breath, let alone speak. His words came out in a stammer. "Paige is missing, and so is Nina. I can't explain it all right now, but it's bad. They could be in danger. I need to get through. Let me through."

But instead of letting him through, they surrounded him and buoyed him toward the dugout. In his terrified state, Trevor barely understood what was happening. All he knew was that his teammates whisked him through the dugout and down the corridor and before he knew it he was on the concourse. Crush strode toward him, trailed by the head of stadium security, who was issuing commands into his headpiece.

The owner paused at the sight of the throng of players. "What the hell? Who's supposed to be batting right now?"

"Me, I guess," said Ramirez. "Duke, you better replace me."

"With who?" The manager rolled onto the concourse, rubbing his belly. "Ain't no one in the dugout *to* replace you."

Crush raised his hand for quiet. "Question for you all, since you're here instead of where you're supposed to be. Who's up for a search party?"

A jumble of voices answered in a chaotic free-for-all. Finally Dwight's deep voice cut through the chaos. "If Paige is in danger, none of us want to be on that field."

"Fair enough. Bob, brief them on what we know so far while I make a call." Crush turned aside to mutter into his phone, out of earshot of the players.

The security chief, a potbellied, nearly bald former cop, addressed the group of players. "According to the guards at the exits, no cars have left the lot in the past hour. Paige was seen entering in Crush's Range Rover about forty-five minutes ago. What that means is that chances are good that she's still somewhere in the stadium."

"And my sister Nina? Small, blond?"

"There was someone in the Range Rover with Paige, but the guard didn't get a good look at her. We're going on the assumption it was her."

Crush ended his call and rejoined them.

"Mr. Taylor, what do you want me to do with the people in the stands?" the security chief asked.

"I'll handle that. You get these guys organized."

"Yes, boss."

"Trevor, come with me." Crush beckoned him off to the side.

As Trevor followed, a TV mounted in the corridor caught his attention. Donna MacIntyre and Mayor Trent were at the pitcher's mound, where a mic had been set up.

"Hello, Kilby Catfish fans, and welcome to our guests here from Omaha. I'm the mayor of Kilby, Wendy Trent, and I have an important announcement for y'all. The Kilby Catfish have decided to forfeit this game."

The audience erupted into boos.

"I know, I know, they're so sorry for the inconvenience to y'all. Unfortunately, we have a potentially dangerous situation happening here in the stadium, and we want all of y'all to be safe. The head of security has asked that you all stay right where you are until further notice. We don't want anyone taking any risks with their safety. As soon as they feel it's safe for you to leave, we'll let you know. In the meantime, Ms. Donna MacIntyre has some games and contests to help keep you entertained. Thank you all so much for your patience and cooperation."

Crush shook his head in admiration. "Hell of a woman, that mayor. Come on, Manning is waiting for us."

Trevor glanced back at the Catfish, who were now being joined by members of the security team to listen to the chief's instructions. Dwight caught his eye and sent him a reassuring wink.

And just like that, he knew. Never again would he shut anyone out. Paige had melted all that ice away from his heart, leaving nothing but love and a desperate need to get her back in his arms and never let her go.

Chapter 28

"**W**HAT ARE YOU talking about?" The kidnapper scowled at Nina as if she'd grown an extra head. His phone rang but he ignored it.

"I'm talking about the crime that my brother confessed to. That he went to juvie for," Nina explained patiently. "He didn't do it. I did."

"When Dinar got his head smashed with a bat?"

Nina winced. "Yes. I didn't mean to hurt him, I just wanted him to get off my father."

"You're telling me a little girl like you did him in?"

Paige rolled off Nina, since there seemed to be no point in getting her to stop talking now.

"Well . . . I'm not a little girl, although I guess I was back then, and I didn't 'do him in.' He's fine, right?"

"He's alive. Never did get his killer instinct back. It's like you messed something up in his brain."

"Sorry," Nina said in a small voice, dropping her head. "I really didn't mean for that to happen. I didn't mean any of it. Not what I did to Dinar, not what happened to Trevor afterward. I'm trying to make up for it."

"How do you make up for a man's brain not working right? Wait a minute." The man used his phone to scratch at his scraggly beard. "Is it you that's been sending him packages? Books and music and so forth?"

Nina gasped. "How did you know about that?"

"It ain't a secret. Wait'll I tell him it was a girl that bashed his head in." He grinned, revealing a flash of silver in his dental work.

Nina blew a wisp of blond hair out of her face. "You shouldn't make fun of him. I always had a strong swing, just like my brother."

The kidnapper just chortled, as if already composing the insults he was going to deliver.

Paige stared in amazement at the girl handcuffed to her. "You've been sending presents to that man? The one who attacked your father?"

Nina turned pink. "Well, yes. I just felt so bad about everything. I just wanted him to get off my dad, I didn't mean to hurt him that much. I found out that he was still having some cognitive issues and I read that more mental stimulation can help repair the nerve synapses. I was just trying to help him get better."

"Wow." Paige rubbed her forehead, trying to get a grip on this crazy development. "Does Trevor know you tracked down the Wachowski gang member that you sent to the hospital?"

"Of course not! And I never put my address on my care packages. I always sent them anonymously. I never visited him in person because Trevor would have lost his mind if I did that. But I had to do something, especially because Trevor was the one who paid for my crime. Anyway . . ." Nina turned back to their kidnapper. "If you could inform the Wachowskis that they have no more reason to go after Trevor Leonov, I'd really appreciate it. I'm taking full responsibility for my actions. I no longer want someone else to pay for what I did. Can you just tell them that, do you think?"

"Leonov's a marked man, little sister. No matter what you say." The man's phone rang again. He rolled his eyes. "Micromanaging dickface," he muttered, then answered it. Then he flinched, all bravado vanishing. "You're fucking kidding me. Not my fault, boss."

Paige and Nina glanced at each other as the kidnapper took in a stream of ugly-sounding words, color leaching from his face.

"I followed instructions. That's all I got to say. I told you we should've— Right. No excuses. Want me to bring the girl? Hostage, like?" A sharp response made him cringe and go slightly green. "Fine. Just get me out of here and no one's the wiser."

He hung up and stuck his phone into the inner jacket of his pocket, muttering to himself. "This ain't my fucking fault. Shit. They pin this on me, I'm back to zero." He looked at the women with a freaked-out expression that actually made Paige feel sorry for him. "I'm out. You girls owe me a pair of handcuffs."

"What do you mean? What's going on?" As nasty as the kidnapper was, getting left in a deserted storage room made Paige even more anxious. No one ever came up here until it was time to discard another couch.

"What's going on is, they took a half-assed approach and now it's backfired. They didn't let me go after Leonov. Said it wasn't the right time. This is just some frickin' favor for someone. Now it's all fucked up and I'm screwed unless—" Something occurred to him. "Unless Notswego still has a soft spot for you."

She shook her head violently. "We're through. Definitely through."

"Tough luck for all of us. I gotta get out of here." He loped toward the far end of the storage room, where a back stairway led to . . . Paige's heart sank as she realized that it led to a delivery bay that wasn't used anymore. It would be easy for him to disappear over the chain-link fence back there. It wasn't guarded or monitored.

"You can't just leave us here!" Paige called after him. "What was the whole point of this, anyway?"

"The point is, it's always the new guy who gets screwed, ever notice that? I'd go grab Leonov myself, but the boss didn't want to hear about that." With a rude gesture, the kidnapper yanked open the door that led to the stairway.

Paige yelled, "If you let us go, we'll say you didn't hurt us."

The door slammed shut with a loud boom.

Paige and Nina looked at each other as quiet settled around them. Dust rose from the couch every time they shifted position. The air felt warm and stifling. "I get the feeling they didn't exactly send their top guy down here."

"Should we be insulted?" Nina let out a long sigh. "Thank you for getting kidnapped with me. If you weren't here, I'd be pretty scared. And you know what? I'm actually not. Well, not terribly, anyway. I'm more scared of what they're going to do to Trevor later on. They definitely know he's here. Do you think that man will pass my message along to the Wachowskis?"

"I don't know. He sure seemed to get a kick out of it." Paige surveyed the couch. "Can we try dragging the couch to the elevator?"

"Do you think it would fit in there?" Nina glanced dubiously at the couch.

"I have no idea, but maybe we can set off the alarm in the elevator or something. On three, let's try standing up."

On the count of three, they both rose to their feet. Nina tried to step forward with the foot that was zip-tied to the leg of the couch but didn't even manage to budge it. "Should we sit on the floor and try to drag it?"

"Sure." But that didn't work either, since Nina had to face away from the couch and Paige was unable to twist around enough to get a grip on it.

"I know," Nina finally said. "I'll kind of hug the end of the couch and you can go all the way to the back. You can push from there, and I'll pull with my leg."

They managed to bump the couch forward a few feet before Nina fell backward on her butt.

"Are you okay?" Paige peered over the top of the couch. Nina curled on her back like a roly-poly bug, her whole body shaking.

"Ye-es," she gasped, and Paige realized she was laughing. "It's just . . . so . . . silly. All these years we've been so afraid of the Wachowskis and what they would do if they found us. Well, ta-da! Here I am. Handcuffed to a . . . a supercomfy couch. And look! I think I see some spare change under the cushions." She laughed even harder, her face turning as pink as bubble gum.

"But . . ." Paige didn't want to get swept into the gale of laughter overcoming Nina. "It's not funny. This could be really bad. What if no one finds us up here? We aren't planning any redecorating this year."

That just made Nina laugh all the more. "Redecorating!" She pounded her free fist on the floor. "Redecorate . . . we got kidnapped and you're talking about redecorating . . ." Tears of laughter flowed down her face.

"Wait! That's it." Paige scrambled to her feet, using her free hand to leverage herself against the back.

"What is? Redecorating?"

"No. Pounding. Let's lift the couch up and drop it. Just a few inches, not enough to hurt your ankle. If we do it over and over, we should get someone's attention."

Nina's face lit up. "You're a genius! What's underneath us?"

"I'm not sure exactly, but some part of the front office. Someone will hear."

"Do you think they're looking for us?"

"Absolutely." She remembered Trevor making her promise to come to the games. "I guarantee that Trevor knows something's wrong and that he notified someone."

Nina rolled herself back into a sitting position and gave a wistful sigh. "What's it like to have someone be so in love with you, like Trevor is? Especially someone as amazing as my big brother?"

Paige bit her lip. "He is pretty amazing, isn't he?"

"Do you think all baseball players are like Trevor?"

"Nina." Paige jerked her wrist to get the younger girl's attention. "Can we address your not-so-secret crush another time? I don't want Trevor or anyone else to worry longer than they have to."

"I wonder if Jim Leiberman knows I'm missing. Do you think he's worried too?"

"Nina!"

"Sorry. Okay, let's try this."

Paige came back to Nina's side of the couch and sat tailor-style next to her. Together, they lifted the couch two inches off the floor and then dropped it. It made a very satisfying thud. They grinned at each other.

"Again."

With the audience confined to their seats and the press box in a frenzy, the Catfish players and security team divided into teams assigned to search different quadrants of the stadium. Even the Storm Chasers volunteered to help, after word reached them that the game had been forfeited and there might be a criminal at large in the ballpark. The Kilby police were already on their way.

As the searchers split up, Trevor followed Crush upstairs to the management wing, now virtually deserted. They hurried down the aisle to Crush's office, where a man in casual business attire tapped at his smartphone. Trevor hadn't met him before, only spoken to him on the phone.

"Special Agent Manning." Crush shut the door behind him. "This is Trevor Stark."

Trevor wanted to clock the man in the jaw but restrained himself. "You said nothing would happen," he growled at the agent.

"No, I didn't. I said they weren't planning anything big. It doesn't look like this is big. We're thinking one guy, two max."

The man had a cool and cynical air about him that rubbed Trevor all wrong. "Screw you. How many does it take?"

Crush gripped his forearm. "We'll find them, Trevor."

"Not standing here, we won't." Trevor turned his back on the two and stalked toward the door.

"Hang on," the agent called after him. "I have a few more questions for you about what Dean Wade said to you."

"*Now?* How can you guys waste time like this when Paige and Nina are in danger?"

"We don't think they're in any real danger," said the agent, much too casually for Trevor's taste. "The Wades are probably using the girls to get to you. Or maybe simply to be disruptive. They won't inflict any harm, there's no margin in it."

Sharp fury coursing through his veins, Trevor stormed back to the agent and went nose-to-nose with him. "Do you know that for sure? Can you guarantee one hundred percent that Nina and Paige aren't experiencing even one millisecond of pain or suffering?"

"Back off, buddy."

A strong arm wrapped around his chest from behind and dragged him away from the agent. "Do you really want to add attacking a federal officer to all the other missteps in your history?" Crush growled in his ear.

"I don't fucking care. I need to find Nina and Paige." A desperate need for action ripped at him. "I can't just stand here and do nothing."

"You already did the most important thing. You told me what was going on. We can nail the bastards."

"You think I care about that?" He rammed his elbow into Crush's gut and felt the man's grip relax. "I care about Paige. That's all that matters now. And if you don't see it that way, you're even more of a fuckhead than I thought. Leave me be, or you can both forget about my testimony." He was out of the office before anyone could even try to stop him.

"Trevor!"

In the hallway, Trevor turned to see Crush burst out of the office. He braced himself for battle, legs apart, poised to respond to whatever came next. "Bring it on, Crush. I don't want to hurt Paige's father, but I'll do whatever it takes."

Crush stopped a few feet away, just out of swinging distance. "Every inch of this stadium is being searched. We'll find them. Answer me this. Do you love Paige?"

The question threw him even more than a punch would have. "That's not your business."

"I'm making it my business. I screwed up last time. I thought I could hardline it, make her back down from her plan to marry that asshole. Instead I drove her away and didn't see her for three years. Then she hooked up with you and I had to learn my lesson all over again. She's a grown woman who knows her own mind. But I'm asking you as a father, just tell me. Do you love her?"

Trevor straightened, his hands falling to his sides. He'd never imagined seeing that much raw vulnerability written across Crush's cynical face. It disarmed him. He could imagine the torment of losing three years of Paige in your life. He didn't want to lose three minutes. "I love her," he said quietly. "And I will never let her down. I'll never hurt her. Her happiness is everything to me."

Crush narrowed his eyes as if he could bore right into Trevor's soul. "You're starting to convince me."

"I'm not aiming to convince you. I love Paige, and I believe she loves me. What we do about it is our business."

Crush nodded thoughtfully. "That might be true. But there's a part of Paige that knows I was right about Hudson. Do you want to make her defy her father all over again?"

"No, I don't want that." Trevor ran his hand across the back of his head, every nerve ending screaming in frustration. Someone was pounding on a door somewhere and it was making him nuts. "I know I'm not what any parent would want for their daughter. I've been to some dark places. But I've tried to do my best. I have plenty of money, and I'll have even more if the Friars call me up."

"What was that book you were reading back in Lansing?"

The question was so far out of left field that it made Trevor dizzy. *"What?"*

"First time I saw you play. You were playing left field and reading a book half the time. Never missed a play, and hit the seams off the ball, but you had a book out there. What was it?"

Everything went still, except for that damn knocking. "You saw me play back then?"

"Grizz Walker called Buck O'Neil, who called me. Said I had to see you, so I went. I sent my report to the Friars and here you are."

"*You're* the one?" He scanned Crush's face for signs he was making this up, but the owner's hazel eyes met his levelly.

"Yeah. I've been watching you since you were a sprout. I always say you can tell everything you need to know about a man from the way he plays."

Trevor swallowed hard. "I play hard. I play to win."

"You play cold."

Rage flashed through him, tightened all his muscles into one long high-tension cable. "Who's the one who let Paige leave for three years? Who's the one standing around *while she's missing*? I'm not cold. You don't know anything about me. I love Paige. I'll take care of her."

Crush gave a sneer as he hooked his thumbs in his front pockets. "You think Paige needs taking care of? Maybe you don't know her all that well."

"That's not how I mean it." Trevor inhaled deep breaths, forcing himself to calm down. "I want to be the one in her corner, the one she always knows she can turn to, the one who'll love her no matter what. She wants to be a counselor, and I think she'd be great. I'll support her all the way, whatever she needs or wants."

The pounding . . . or maybe more of a thumping . . . stopped. Trevor whooshed out a breath of relief.

"You really do love her," Crush said slowly.

"That's what I've been telling you."

"Are you willing to put it all on the line?"

"What do you mean?" The pounding started up again, or maybe it was the blood in his head, the urgency to act, to do something.

"On the baseball field. The way everything ought to be settled."

"*What?*"

Crush's walkie-talkie blared. He listened to the crackling static for a moment.

"They found a woman's cowboy boot in the staff entrance, along with the broken pieces of a cell phone."

Trevor's heart squeezed. "What does the boot look like?"

"Blue, with embroidered flowers."

"That's Paige's boot." He'd know those boots anywhere. Every time he saw them he wanted to strip off the rest of whatever she was wearing. "God. Did they find anything else?"

"No. There were some signs of a struggle, a plant knocked over, the crushed cell phone, but no blood. Bob thinks they got on the elevator."

"Which comes to this wing." Trevor whirled around, ready to search inside every vent duct if need be.

But Crush stalled him with a firm grip. "Manning searched this area already. Every office, every cubicle. They must have moved on to somewhere else."

"Then *let's go.*" Trevor's patience with this conversation was long over, and that irritating *thump-thump* just made it worse and—

He stopped. Grabbed Crush's elbow. "What's that noise?"

"You mean that hammering from . . ." He trailed off, and they both looked up. An especially emphatic *thump* made them both jerk to attention.

"Upstairs," Trevor choked.

As one, they ran down the hall toward the elevator. "I forgot there was an upstairs," Crush said. "There's nothing but junk up there."

"And something banging around."

"Manning!" Crush called to the agent as they passed his office. "We could use some backup."

Trevor reached the elevator door first and jabbed at the button.

"Stand back," said Agent Manning, joining them with his gun raised as the door slid open. The elevator was empty. He ushered the other two men inside. "Same routine when the door opens. You two stand out of the line of fire."

Trevor nodded tightly as the elevator whooshed upward. Adrenaline was racing through his body. What would they find up there? Paige and Nina held hostage by some unknown number of Wachowski gang members? Or a few redneck Wade cowboys? Maybe a combination? Would they be hurt, unconscious, bleeding? It was incredible how many scenarios raced through his mind in the short time it took the elevator to rise from the second to the third floor.

But not even his wildest imagination could have conjured up the sight that greeted him.

Paige and Nina seemed to be wrestling with a broken-down couch. They were sweaty and dusty, and a pair of handcuffs linked them together. Nina slid to the floor at the sight of the men.

"About time!" his sister said accusingly. "Do you have any idea how heavy this couch is?"

But Trevor had already locked gazes with Paige. Everything else faded away. With a smudge on her cheek and that wild bird's nest of hair, her smile shone brighter than a torch in the wilderness.

Chapter 29

PAIGE COULDN'T STOP smiling at the sight of Trevor Stark in his baseball uniform stepping out of that elevator. His eyes were wild, as if he'd walked through a fire to get to them.

He rushed toward them, reaching the couch in a few short strides. Crouching between them, he hugged them both to his chest. "Are you okay? Any injuries?"

"Just another day at the gym," Paige told him. "If by gym you mean lifting heavy furniture over and over again." In fact, her body was throbbing from the exertion of manhandling that stupid couch. "That man went down the back stairway. I don't know his name but he was definitely connected to the Wachowskis."

Crush strode to the rear door and peered down the stairway. "I see footsteps in the dust. Christ, I'd forgotten all this was up here. Gotta send a note to the cleaning crew."

An efficient looking man in a business suit squatted down next to Nina and took out a knife. He sliced through the zip tie as if it was butter.

"Who are we looking for?"

Paige gave him a description of the kidnapper, but she had a feeling it was a waste of time. "I think someone was going to pick him up."

"We'll take you to a sketch artist," the agent said. "We'll find a dummy key for these cuffs too. I'm going to need detailed statements from both of you."

"Of course." Paige leaned to give Nina enough slack so she could scratch her ankle. Trevor had his arms around his sister and one warm, reassuring hand firmly placed on Paige's back. She hoped he never took it off.

"How long have you been cuffed together like this?" Trevor gently slid a finger under the steel circlet around Paige's wrist.

"Paige did that," Nina said proudly. "He was going to cuff her to the stair railing so she couldn't make trouble, but she didn't want to leave me alone with him. She got herself cuffed to me instead."

Crush paused in the midst of striding back to their group. "You're telling me Paige crashed your kidnapping?"

Nina giggled. "I guess so. It was a lot less scary that way. Sometimes it was even fun, like when we started trying to move the couch and kept falling over each other . . ." Paige didn't hear the rest because Trevor fixed his crystal green eyes on her with a look so intense it nearly set the room on fire.

"You put yourself in danger for my sister."

"Well . . ." She hadn't really thought of it that way. "I didn't want her to be alone. And he was going to stick me in the foyer where no one would ever hear me. I figured we'd have a better chance together."

Turbulent expressions chased themselves across his face. Gratitude, fury, amazement . . . love. Had he ever looked icy? Impossible. "I love you," he said in the softest voice imaginable, as if he felt too much emotion to speak more loudly. "You are the most incredible person I've ever known."

"Hey," interrupted Crush. "Family members present."

But Paige and Trevor were already deep in the kind of soul-searing kiss no external words could penetrate. As she closed her eyes and let a sweet, strong river of happiness lift her up and away, she forgot they had an audience that included her father, Trevor's sister, and an FBI agent. None of that mattered. This kiss was a public claiming, an announcement to the world, loud and clear. Paige and Trevor, Trevor and Paige. Just let someone try to pry them apart. It would take much more than a handcuff key to accomplish that.

The Wachowskis and the Wades turned on each other right away. The nervous man who had so briefly kidnapped Paige and Nina was pulled over by the Texas State Troopers just outside Kilby city limits. Special Agent Manning got plenty of opportunity to question him. Manning learned that Dean Wade had contacted the Wachowskis and offered a deal. He told the syndicate where to find Trevor Leonov. In exchange, they sent a bottom-rung operative to Kilby with instructions to use Nina as leverage against Trevor. When the entire team walked off the field, the Wachowskis pulled the plug.

Both the Wades and the Wachowskis offered to testify against each other, but the Wachowskis were a much bigger catch, so the Wades got the deal. Crush was disappointed, but not Trevor. He looked forward to telling the FBI every single thing the Wachowskis had done to him and his family.

But amazingly, it turned out that he and Nina were already safe from the Wachowskis. Nina's confession had changed everything. Once Dinar Wachowski discovered that the person who had injured him was also the kind girl who'd been sending him gifts and cards and drawings over the years, he put his foot down. No more retaliation against either of them. Not Trevor, not Nina, not anyone. It was over. Once and for all.

Trevor was free. Free to love Paige, free to play ball.

Since the Catfish had forfeited Game Four, the series was now tied. Whichever team won the next game would earn the right to compete in the Triple A National Championship. With all the off-field drama, the game garnered national attention. How often was a team owner's daughter kidnapped and a stadium put under lockdown? How often did an entire team spontaneously walk off the field and forfeit a game? A thousand baseball analysts couldn't find any previous instances of such shenanigans.

Paige made Trevor tell her the story over and over again. How he'd watched their empty seats. Abandoned his at-bat. How Dwight and the other Catfish had followed right behind once they knew what was up.

"It was because of you," he told her. "You've helped just about every one of those guys and they care about you. That's fine, as long as they know that you belong to me."

"I think they know," said Paige wryly. "You've barely even let go of my hand since it happened."

"Not until I have to." He lifted their clasped hands to his lips. "For, like, baseball stuff."

Crush, of course, ate up the publicity. Even though the Wades were going to escape charges by testifying against the Wachowskis, there was no way they'd be permitted to buy the team. But Crush wasn't taking any chances. He still wanted to keep his vow and win the championship.

"If you win, it will be thanks to Trevor," Paige told Crush, cornering him on the field before an interview with ESPN. She'd insisted on dragging Trevor along for this confrontation. In every corner of the field, players were stretching, working out, tossing the ball around. The buzz of the upcoming game generated a low simmer of excitement. "He's done so much already. How about helping him out now?"

"I'm already paying his damn salary," Crush grumbled. "What else does he want from me?"

Trevor stiffened. "I don't need your charity, Crush. I can make my way just fine."

Paige gave him a "shush" sign. "Dad, you said if Trevor played well, the Friars might call him up. He's played more than well."

"Yes, well, they probably will, then." The camera operator approached with a body mic, which he attached to Crush's Catfish shirt.

"*Make* them," Paige insisted. "They'll listen to you."

"There's only one person who can make them pay attention." Crush jerked his head toward Trevor. "Him. And the Friars are burnt out on Trevor Stark. He's got to do something spectacular. Something they can't ignore."

"Like what?"

"He's a slugger. He'll figure it out." At a gesture from the cameraman, he tapped the mic with a murmured "Testing, testing." Paige bit her lip, frustration rolling off her in waves. "Tell you what," Crush said when the audio check was done. "Trevor, if you accept my challenge, I promise to do my part with the Friars."

Challenge? Trevor wasn't sure exactly what he was talking about, but he wasn't going to back down from a challenge. He tilted his head in agreement. "I'm in, whatever it is. And whatever it is, you're going to lose."

"I might. I just might. But—are you sure it'll be a loss?" With a cryptic wink, Crush turned to the waiting camera crew. As they began their countdown, Paige tugged Trevor out of camera range.

"What challenge?" she asked, looking perplexed. "Do you know what he's talking about?"

"Nope." He guided her away from the crew. "But I intend to win it."

"Game Five. Give me something spectacular," Crush called after them.

Game Five took place on a muggy, leaden evening under a sky filled with sullen clouds. The flags hung limp on the flagpoles, moisture heavy in the air. Low scoring weather, the commentators agreed. Look for ground balls, as the batters will try to tire out the fielders. And don't expect home runs. With that amount of humidity, the balls just wouldn't get enough lift.

Trevor had never felt so ready for a game. It all came down to this moment. For the first time in his adult life he was able to fully focus on a game without a whisper of worry about the Wachowskis.

Paige was right where she ought to be, in that seat in the owner's box, her brilliant smile scattering sunshine wherever she looked. Crush sat next to her. He realized, as the stirring tones of the National Anthem rolled through the stadium, that he actually wanted to win for Crush. He cared about the man. The revelation that Crush was largely responsible for his baseball career had really thrown him for a loop. All this time he'd thought the owner despised him. But really, Crush just wanted him to be the best he could be.

Which was exactly what Trevor wanted.

The need to prove himself, to show everyone some spectacular play, consumed him. At batting practice, the power flowing through his body had actually unnerved him. He'd held back, focusing on control and precision. During his pregame visualization routine, his usual crystal clear imagery had taken on a different appearance. Intense, rimmed with fire, as if formed from flame instead of ice.

As he walked onto the field for his first at-bat, it seemed surprising that the grass under his feet didn't burst into flames. He nodded to the umpire and the catcher, whose eyes widened at Trevor's intensity. Settling into his stance, he used the dirt of the batter's box to ground himself. Plant his feet. Become aware of his thighs, his body, his connection with the ground. *Focus*.

Too much adrenaline. To work some of it off, he purposely overswung on the first pitch, a fastball. The pitcher's shoulders relaxed as he received the ball back from the catcher. *Good, let him get overconfident.* Trevor made a show of getting down on himself, stepping out of the batter's box, muttering to himself. He didn't look over at Paige, but he felt her presence filling him with light and warmth. *Something spectacular.* He needed something spectacular.

When he stepped back into the box, one word described how he felt. *Invincible*. The next pitch came to him like a message from destiny, a fat, juicy ball drawn inevitably to the middle of plate, where it met a perfect lethal blur of a swing. He crushed that pitch. Obliterated it. Every head whipped around to watch the ball fly. An awed roar lifted him and sent him cruising around the bases. Kids scrambled all the way to the top seat of the bleachers to find the ball. Had anyone ever seen a home run hit that far in Catfish Stadium? He doubted it.

In the dugout, the electrified Catfish surged to their feet, exchanging high fives.

As he rounded third, Trevor stole a glance at Paige. One look into her eyes and he got fired up all over again.

Sure, an extra-long home run was spectacular, but he was just getting started.

In his next at-bat, he hit another home run. Another in his third. Three home runs in four innings. In his fourth at-bat, with a man on second, the Storm Chasers walked him. Despite the pregame predictions, it was a high-scoring game, with several pitchers brought in on both sides. The Omaha team beat up on poor Dan Farrio, who gave up seven runs in one inning. But Trevor kept the Catfish in the game. By the sixth inning he was personally responsible for five runs batted in. And he felt stronger than ever.

In his fifth at-bat, he reached for a curveball that dipped low and outside and muscled it into a long drive that slipped over the right field fence, just over the wildly gyrating Storm Chaser trying to stop it. Home run number four. Number five should have been a foul, but even the winds were blowing in his favor today. At the last second the ball wafted two inches to the right of the left field foul pole.

Then, in the eighth inning, he made minor league history. He hit his *sixth* home run of the game, a floating butterfly of a ball that landed at Brian the peanut vendor's feet. With a huge grin, the kid brandished the ball high in the air, then handed out all the peanuts on his tray for free. The crowd and the radio commentators went absolutely wild. "No one has hit six home runs in a game since 1902, when Jay Clarke hit eight home runs in one game. But that game was played on a temporary field with a right field wall only 210 yards from home plate. That puts an asterisk next to that record, if you will. It's considered unbreakable. No one's come closer than five until today. You're witnessing history, folks. Absolutely phenomenal. Can Trevor Stark keep this going and become the only guy to hit seven?"

In the owner's box, Paige was jumping up and down,

shrieking, but Crush sat back, arms folded, a slight smirk on his arrogant face.

Instead of celebrating with the rest of the Catfish, Trevor set his jaw and kept his focus on the field. The game wasn't over. If Crush wasn't impressed, the Friars wouldn't be.

And now that the brakes were off, Trevor wanted to be on the Friars postseason roster the way he wanted air in his lungs.

In the ninth inning, with the Catfish down two runs, the bottom of the batting order came up to bat. Shizuko, Backman, and T.J. Gates combined for a beautiful rally that tied the game.

In the top of the tenth inning, "Killer" Garrett, the new reliever just called up from the Double A team, put a lid on the Storm Chasers except for one slip, a wild pitch that allowed in one run.

The Catfish went to the bottom of the tenth inning down one, with Trevor scheduled to bat second. Leiberman struck out. Trevor strode to the plate, glared at Crush Taylor, and slammed the first pitch so hard it knocked a light out of the scoreboard, sending a spray of sparks into the velvety night air.

Home run number seven. Tie game.

The crowd sat in awed silence for a long moment, suspended in disbelief at what they were witnessing. Trevor jogged around the bases, not cracking a smile. Even the Storm Chasers offered tips of the cap as he passed. At third base, he held up, just for a moment, to look at Paige. Tears streamed down her face.

Crush had finally come to his feet, clapping slowly while the rest of the crowd exploded into an ovation.

Trevor put his hand to his heart, held Paige's misty blue gaze, then dove into the dugout.

"The display of power and consistency we've seen tonight is unlike anything I've seen in this game," the play-by-play guy raved from a radio within Trevor's hearing. "We always knew Trevor Stark possessed the sheer strength and ability to hit homers. But what we have here isn't about strength. It's about focus and will and consistency. If the Friars don't call him up to San Diego, stat, they'll have a fan rebellion on their hands." Someone's radio was turned to maximum volume. In baseball, when something historic happened, everyone gathered around their radios or TVs or streaming feeds, whatever they had available. It was a shared experience, and it humbled Trevor to have inspired this moment.

He put his elbows on his knees, leaned forward and stared at the dugout floor, which was littered with sunflower seeds and infield dirt from people's cleats. The weight of what he'd done pressed onto him. He'd just grabbed a piece of history. Forevermore, he'd be in the baseball annals. Never again would he be able to hide.

He looked right and caught the eye of Benny, the equipment assistant who traveled with the team. He'd gotten to know Benny at the Boys and Girls Club, and got him the job with the team. Even though Benny had slow speech from being abused as a kid, he was the most dedicated equipment assistant the Catfish ever had. Right now, he was staring in awe at Trevor, blinking back tears, as if he was witnessing an angel.

Trevor tried to smile back but his face felt frozen. It was too much. That wasn't him, that guy Benny looked up to. He turned his head away and caught Dwight's eye. Dwight winked and made a "shaka" sign—*hang loose, dude. It's all good*.

When the Catfish took the field for the top of the eleventh, Trevor had found his calm again. With a strong inning, the Storm Chasers could put things out of reach. Trevor might get more at-bats, or he might not. That was baseball. You took what it gave you and gave it everything you had.

A two-run homer put the Storm Chasers in the lead, but "Killer" Garrett shut them down for the rest of the inning; 13-11, Storm Chasers.

The home team Catfish came to bat in the bottom half of the eleventh, which turned into a grind-it-out battle for every out, every base. Trevor watched with his heart in his mouth, just like everyone else in the stands. With every particle of his being, he rooted for his teammates, every swing and miss feeling like it was his. He screamed encouragement until his throat was raw. Three times the Catfish were one strike from losing, but each time they fended off defeat. They got one run back when Ramirez hit a home run. T.J. hit a pop fly for out number two. Leiberman beat out a dribbler to first. Dwight walked, sending Leiberman to second. The Catfish now had two men on base with one out left.

And then it was Trevor's turn. If he made an out, Omaha would win. If he hit a single, Leiberman would score, tying the game. Anything more than a single would score both Leiberman and Dwight and win the series for the Catfish.

Trevor's hands shook as he stepped into the batter's box. He looked over his shoulder at Paige. She deserved to be with the best. She deserved a major leaguer. She deserved whatever he could lay at her feet. She'd put herself on the line for him, and then again for his sister. Paige was all heart and light and she deserved something spectacular.

Barely aware of what the pitch was, he put his entire heart into his swing. The ball rose off his bat and traced an arc as graceful as a rainbow, a towering parabola. Was it too high? Would it come down short of the outfield wall? The whole stadium went quiet as the ball reached the height of its rainbow arch and headed toward its pot of gold. Amid a breathless hush, it touched down just past the right center wall.

Home run number eight.

As Trevor rounded the bases, he heard people crying in the stands—and not just Paige, who was sobbing openly.

Record-tying number eight—a walk-off homer—wasn't a home run so much as a love letter.

His yelling, exuberant teammates poured onto the field. As they gathered him in a mass embrace, he felt tears soaking his face. Where had so much unleashed power and drive come from? It felt almost mystical, as if it came from someplace beyond him. From love, perhaps. Who knew? All he knew was that whoever said there was no crying in baseball would have to eat their words.

Chapter 30

Two days later Trevor took a break from the deluge of interview requests for something even more important. While Paige chatted with the director of the Boys and Girls Club about the fund-raiser, set to take place right after the championship game, he faced the group of teenagers gathered in the common room. It was a bigger than normal group, which made him a little nervous because of what he had to say.

"I owe you guys an apology," he told them. The kids stopped messing with their cell phones and fixed their eyes on him in fascination. "I've been coming in here talking to you like some kind of big shot, but I haven't been telling you the truth. The truth is, I spent the last three years of high school in juvenile detention. I was scared shitless most of the time. I got into trouble, I fought, I learned some bad habits. You guys know the kind of thing I mean."

"Did you do drugs?" one kid asked.

"No." Keep it real, no matter what. "My father was a drug addict. I know what that's like, and I hated it. Besides, I had baseball and I had a coach who would have kicked my ass."

Snickers and eye-rolls all down the line.

"What's it like in juvie?"

"Sometimes it's boring. Sometimes it's scary. You have no freedom. You don't know who to trust. I kept to myself a lot. The food sucks."

The kids laughed, but they were hanging on every word.

"I was ashamed, and I started feeling real bad about myself. Like I'd never be or do anything good." He scanned the room, meeting each teen's gaze. This was the key point, for him. The one thing he wanted to get across.

"That might have been what happened, if it weren't for my coach. He didn't let me get too far down. He'd always bring me back and make me work even harder. So that's what I'm here for. Even if you don't play baseball, I want to be your coach. If you start feeling down, or like you aren't worth anything, I want you to call me. I'm going to give all of you my phone number."

A goth kid wearing black lipstick snickered. "You're getting out of this hell pit, unlike us. They said on the Internet you're going to California. What do you care about us?"

Trevor hooked his thumbs in his jean pockets. "Yeah, you're right, I am going to San Diego. I finally got the call. But phones work in San Diego, don't they? That's why I'm giving you my number, so you can call me wherever I am. You think I don't care? Do you get a lot of major league baseball players in here giving out their cell numbers?"

The kids, even the goth skeptic, shook their heads and laughed.

"Besides, I fell in love with a Kilby girl. I'll be back."

That statement really broke the ice, and Trevor spent the next hour talking with the kids, answering questions and handing out signed baseballs.

On their way out of the Boys and Girls Club, Trevor pulled Paige right up against his side so he could bury his nose in her hair.

"Why do you always smell so good?" he murmured. "Like apples and raspberries. Drives me wild."

"You know what drives me wild?"

"I have a few ideas." He let his hand dangle perilously close to her breast.

She swatted it lightly. "You're impossible."

"Impossible is my middle name. I did just tie the unbreakable record." He grinned, still amazed by how everything in his life had changed. "Okay, tell me, what is it that drives you wild?"

"When you play, you're so stoic. I know people say you're ice cold on the baseball field, but I don't see it that way. I always knew that all sorts of stuff was going on inside you. So when you look over at me during a game, and just for a flash I see the real Trevor, the one I know, the one you are with me, it makes me want to run onto the field and jump your bones. Drives me absolutely wild."

He smiled with the softness only Paige could bring out in him. "I hope you don't mind if we keep that Trevor your private, personal secret. No one in baseball needs to know about him."

"It might be too late for that. Your teammates have your number. So do all the batboys and vendors and the kids here. I just wish Crush would get on board. Do you know what he admitted? After I had all those margaritas and announced to him and my mother that I loved you, *he* was the one who told the Friars they should release you. How dare he interfere like that?"

He steered her toward his Escalade. "Don't worry about Crush."

"What do you mean?"

"I've got Crush handled." He and Crush had worked out all the details of the "challenge" and agreed to keep it quiet until the right time came. He clicked the remote key, and the rig answered with a beep. He still hadn't replaced the sideview mirror. It had sentimental value at this point.

"How? When? What do you mean?"

"Championship game, seventh inning stretch. All will be revealed."

The Triple A National Championship game took place in a different city every year; this time it was El Paso's turn. Southwest University Park was jam-packed with fans of the Catfish and their opponents, the Durham Bulls. Even Caleb Hart and Mike Solo had flown in from San Diego for the event. They came by to shake hands with Crush and meet Paige. She was happy to find out that Trevor was going to have such cool—not to mention good-looking—teammates.

Riding the high of Trevor's incredible performance, the Catfish took command early. By the seventh inning, with the score 10-3, there was little doubt about who would win. Paige celebrated for her father, who would get to keep the team. But mostly she wanted to know why he disappeared at the start of the seventh inning, and what the heck he and Trevor had up their sleeves.

After the stadium had sung the traditional, seventh-inning stretch, "Take Me Out to the Ballgame," Donna McIntyre skipped onto the warning track near the visitor's dugout. She had a cordless microphone with her.

"We have a special treat for you today, ladies and gentlemen! As you know, the Kilby Catfish are owned by baseball legend Crush Taylor, but it's been ten years since anyone got to see him pitch. That's about to change."

A gasp went through the crowd.

"That's right, Crush Taylor has been lured out of retirement in order to pitch to *one batter only*. He's been challenged by one of the Catfish players, or maybe he issued the challenge, I'm not completely sure about how that came about. Do one of you guys want to explain it?"

Trevor and Crush stepped forward to join Donna at the mic. In the stands, her heart racing, Paige clenched her fists so hard she dug crescents into her palms. Crush bent toward the mic. "Apparently this young man here, Trevor Stark, isn't satisfied with making history and hitting eight home runs in one game. He has his eye on something else."

He paused for a dramatic moment of silence.

"My daughter."

The crowd roared and stomped their feet. Trevor grinned and turned toward Paige to blow her a kiss. Crimson with embarrassment, she covered her face with her hands.

Crush continued. "Now, my daughter Paige is a strong, smart, kind young woman who can certainly make up her own mind about who she dates. But for my own peace of mind, I wanted to make sure Trevor knows what a prize he's after. So here's the challenge. I pitch to him for one at-bat. If I strike him out, he spends another year proving he's worthy."

The crowd roared again. Trevor took the mic from Crush. "And if I get a hit, Crush will stay out of it."

Laughter rippled through the stands. Paige peered over the tips of her fingers as Donna claimed the mic again. "What if you hit a home run, Trevor? Chances are pretty good, right?"

More cheers from the crowd. Crush answered that one. "If Trevor hits a home run off me, I'll throw them the biggest wedding Texas has ever seen. As long as he can close the deal and get Paige to say yes." He squeezed Trevor's shoulder, then left his hand there while camera flashes rained down. Paige drew in a breath. That one gesture, that companionable hand around Trevor's shoulder, told her that Crush had accepted the man she loved. The sweetness of that moment, after three years of estrangement, nearly melted her heart.

Trevor jogged to home plate, while Crush took his place on the mound. Two baseball greats, one barely at the start of his career, one past the end, facing each other on the field of battle—what a moment.

Yeah . . . baseball was a great game. She could no longer deny it.

Wendy Trent, Crush's date, whispered in Paige's ear. "I think your man is blushing. I thought Trevor was known for his icy manner on the field, but he must be a little rattled."

"I'm going to murder them. Both of them." She sank down in her seat, hoping that everyone was watching the field and not her.

"I think it's extremely romantic. You know this is going to make all the papers. You're going to be the talk of the sports world. Two baseball legends clashing on the field, all for the love of Paige Mattingly Taylor."

Well, when you looked at it that way, maybe it was pretty cool. It was certainly better than being known as an NBA player's rejected wife. But then something else occurred to her. "How do you know my middle name?"

Now it was Wendy's turn to color. "I . . . might have done a little research."

Paige swallowed her smile as she watched Crush go into his windup. Maybe Crush had an ulterior motive for this stunt. Maybe he wanted to show Wendy something of the old Crush Taylor, the one who had dominated the American League for so many years.

Trevor took the first pitch for a strike. Paige knew he could have annihilated that pitch. But he didn't. The next pitch was a ball, which he also let fly past him. He got a piece of the next pitch, fouling it off into the stands. Same for the next two, leading Paige to wonder if he was doing it on purpose. Three fans now held souvenirs from this once-in-a-lifetime event.

The next pitch was just low. Two and two. Paige's heart fluttered in her throat. If Trevor struck out, he'd feel honor bound to give things another year. But she didn't want another year. She wanted him now. And tomorrow. And next week.

The next pitch from Crush cruised down the middle of the plate right where Trevor liked to feast on fastballs. The slugger didn't hesitate. He smashed it long and hard, an emphatic, unquestionable statement of intent. The ball flew like a rocket smack into the middle of the right field stands. Paige let out a wild cheer, then held her breath in shock as Trevor jogged to the section where Paige was sitting about three rows back. Under her astonished gaze, he lowered one knee to the field and spread his arms wide.

"We have the best diamond in the world, right here." He grinned, his heart shining in his eyes. "Paige, I love you. Will you marry me?"

A din of noise rose up around her. On one side, Nina uttered a little scream of excitement, while on her other side, Wendy put a supportive arm around her. Strangers assisted her over the rows, transported her to the edge of the railing. She leaned over, feeling like Juliet addressing Romeo, hoping she didn't tumble right over. Breathless, head spinning, she searched for the right words. "Nice hit," she finally said. "Took your time getting it, though."

"You know I like to work the count. Besides, your

father's no pushover." He was so beautiful, kneeling on the field, that she wanted to climb down and fling herself into his arms. In his expression she saw all the contradictions that made Trevor Stark so fascinating. Confidence warring with vulnerability, brashness with caring, ice with fire.

But more than anything else, she saw love, hard won and unshakable. "Yes," she said simply. "I'll marry you." Leaning forward, she lowered her voice to a whisper. "Do you think maybe we could finish this conversation in private?"

His eyes darkened in that way that drove her absolutely wild. "Count on it."

No one who saw the look on Trevor's face at that moment—which included a lot of people, since several hundred smartphones were recording it—ever again used the word "icy" to describe him.

From the first moment Trevor Stark set foot in Friars Stadium, he was known for his intensity and drive on the field. In his very first season in the major leagues, he set records, and he continued to do so as the years passed. Paige Mattingly Austin Taylor Stark, MSW, Ph.D., also set a record—for the highest graduation rate among the teenagers she worked with. No one knew about that record, but that didn't make it any less satisfying. A few people knew about Trevor's contributions to the Boys and Girls Club, and plenty knew what a devoted father he was to their three sons.

But no one else knew that her husband's passion on the field paled compared to his passion off the field.

She kept that secret all to herself.

*Keep reading for an excerpt from the first book in
USA Today bestselling author
Jennifer Bernard's Love Between the Bases series,*

ALL OF ME

Playing for the Kilby Catfish is hotshot pitcher
Caleb Hart's last chance to salvage his career
after a major league meltdown. But the day of his
opener with the minor league team, Caleb strikes
out with the gorgeous woman who is delivering
a petition to run the unruly Catfish out of town.
Now, to stay in the lineup, Caleb will need to
score big with the feisty brunette he can't keep
out of his thoughts.

After the nasty lies Sadie Merritt's rich ex-
boyfriend spread about her all over town, she's
lucky to have a job at all. She can't afford to screw
it up by falling for the player who is supposed to
be helping her change the image of the fun-loving
Catfish. But that's easier said than done when
Caleb's voice alone is enough to make her pulse
race. And when he surprises her with a mind-
blowing kiss, she knows there's no turning back.

IN CALEB HART'S first start as a Kilby Catfish, he set a minor league record—and not the good kind. By the top of the fourth inning he'd given up seven runs, five homers, three walks, and nearly taken El Paso Chihuahua Steve Hunter's nose off with a wayward fastball. Sweat was running down his back in rivulets of failure, and under his brand-new cap, with its cartoonish blue catfish logo, his head felt as if it might spontaneously ignite.

He stepped off the mound and swiped his arm across his forehead. Mike Solo, the catcher, called for time, the pitching coach jogged onto the field, and suddenly his new infielders surrounded him. Apparently they thought he needed some support. What he really needed was . . . well, he hadn't quite figured that out yet.

"You can take this guy," said the tattooed first baseman, Sonny Barnes. "He can't hit the changeup for shit."

Caleb didn't bother mentioning that he couldn't *throw* the changeup for shit.

"Just keep 'em down," said Mitch, the pitching coach, clearly some kind of baseball genius. "And get 'em over the plate."

"That's right, you're overthinking it," said the fast-talking shortstop, who looked about twelve. "I saw you pitch with the Twins. Over three games you had an ERA of 2.78, average of five strikeouts per game. 'Course, then you had that crazy fourth game. Whatever you do, don't think about *that game*. Do what you did during the first three. Forget the fourth. Easy peasy."

Caleb stared at the smaller player, trying to remember the last time he'd heard a baseball player say "easy peasy." Never, that's when. And why'd he have to bring up the worst game of his entire life?

Solo, the only guy on the team Caleb had played with before, gave a wolfish grin and a wink. "Yeah, easy peasy, big guy. The natives are getting restless. And since it's Texas, they're probably armed."

Caleb looked at the half-full stands, where the crowd of maybe three thousand diehards was starting to shout catcalls. For a painful moment he remembered the noise level at Target Field in Minneapolis. It was like comparing a 747 jet to a mosquito. But the Twins had traded him to the San Diego Friars, and the Friars had sent him down to their Triple A team in Kilby, and here he was. Blowing it.

The pitching coach headed back to the dugout, with an air of having done all he could. Caleb glared at the remaining players. "What is this, a damn committee meeting?"

The baby shortstop looked offended. "Excuse me for trying to help you resurrect the correct firing of your synapses."

Caleb looked incredulously at the other Catfish. "Is this kid for real?"

"He was studying brains before he signed on," explained Mike Solo.

"Not brains. Neurophysiology," piped up the shortstop as everyone scattered, jogging back to their positions.

Christ. He'd heard the Catfish were a little . . . odd. So far that seemed to be an understatement.

Caleb settled himself back on the mound, inhaling a deep breath of humid, grass-scented air. *It's just a baseball game. Pretend you're back home, when base-*

ball was the only fun thing in life. When you ruled the diamond, any diamond.

Solo called for the fastball, low and away. Good call, since an inside pitch might hurt someone, the way he was pitching, and his changeup wasn't doing shit today. He went into his windup, lined the seams up just right in his hand, and let fly.

Boom. Home run number six cracked off the bat with a sound like a detonation. Maybe it was his career blowing up, come to think of it.

Just to torture himself, Caleb swiveled to watch the ball soar high overhead, winging toward the right field bleachers like a bird on speed. Lowering his gaze, he caught the shortstop's reproachful stare. The Chihuahua batter cruised around the bases. The guy ought to send him a thank-you note, the way he'd served up that pitch with extra biscuits and gravy.

Someone cleared his throat behind him. He turned to find Duke, the Catfish manager, facing him, hand outstretched. He wanted the ball. Wanted him out of the game. But as much as Caleb hated giving up home runs, he hated giving up the ball more. How could he turn things around if he got yanked from the game?

"I'm just trying to get my rhythm going, Duke," Caleb said in a low voice.

"And how's that working out for you?"

Sarcasm. Ouch. "My last pitch had to have been in the upper nineties."

"Yup. It sure went over the fence fast." Duke, a barrel-chested former catcher, didn't sugarcoat things. "I'm taking you out before your ERA looks like a Texas heat wave. Let's talk after the game."

A sickening sensation made Caleb's gut clench. In the minor leagues, being called into the manager's office was either good news—you were being called up to the

major league team—or bad news of a variety of kinds.
Caleb was a hundred percent sure he wasn't being
called up.

"Nothing bad," Duke assured him. "Just want to talk."

Caleb nodded, and handed him the ball. It felt like
handing over a piece of his heart. He needed the ball,
needed to pitch. Because the only chance he had in life
was when he had that ball in his hands.

Walking toward the dugout, he caught a "shake it
off" from the third baseman, along with a rumble of
boos from the stands. His replacement, Dan Farrio, ran
onto the field from the bullpen. Farrio was, theoretically, his rival for one of the spots on the Friars pitching
staff. But after today that rivalry might be history.

From someone's radio, he heard the color announcer
saying, "We're checking the history books, but one-
time blue-chip prospect Caleb Hart just had possibly
the worst first start ever on a Triple A team. He should
have been pulled after the second inning, but the Catfish bullpen's about as ragged as my kid's blankie. If the
Caleb Hart trade was supposed to add some juice to the
Friars pitching staff, maybe they should have gone with
a shot of the cactus instead. How much you want to bet
Crush Taylor's squeezing the limes already?"

At the mention of the owner of the Catfish, Caleb
groaned. No one cared what most minor league owners
thought, since the major league front office called all
the shots. But Crush Taylor was a legend, a Hall of
Fame pitcher who had purchased the Catfish shortly
after his retirement. Not to mention that he was Caleb's
childhood idol.

He'd just had a record-setting horrendous start for
the team owned by his childhood idol. And he'd been
lectured by a shortstop barely out of high school. Could
things get any worse?

He reached the dugout and grabbed a drink of water at the cooler. Man, it was hot today. All he wanted to do was hit the showers and get the hell out of this stadium. But since it was his first game, he ought to stick around and support the team. Before he could sink onto the bench, Duke caught his eye and gave him a jerk of the head, releasing him to retire to the clubhouse.

First break he'd gotten all day. He seized the opportunity and stalked out of the dugout. He'd get to know his fellow Catfish sometime when he didn't want to knock someone's head off.

As soon as he entered the rabbit's warren of back corridors that wound through the stadium, his tightly maintained control disappeared. He ripped off his sweat-soaked uniform shirt as if he could ditch the sense of failure along with it.

"Fuck," he bit out, slamming a fist against the wall. "Get it together, Hart." He usually kept his emotions under tight wrap, but . . . *damn it*. If he screwed this up, he'd be letting down his sister and brothers, and they'd all been through enough. His entire family was depending on him, and he'd just given up six home runs in about five minutes. His frustration boiled over.

"What the fuck is wrong with you? You can't afford another fucking fuckup." Veering around the corner toward the home clubhouse, he nearly tripped over someone standing at the double doors that guarded the entrance.

The someone pushed an elbow into his stomach, making the breath whoosh out of him. It wasn't a hard blow, probably accidental, but still, not what he normally encountered on his way to the shower.

Struggling to get his breath back—and his composure—he steadied his attacker. A woman, a young one. Though he still hadn't gotten a good look at her, she felt soft and shapely under his hands.

"Geez, you should watch where you're going." Her voice had a drawling, husky cadence; a local girl. She stepped out of his grasp and spun to face him. He received a quick impression of brilliant but wary dark eyes, quicksilver slimness, and a haphazard ponytail. He was six feet five inches, but he didn't tower over her as much as he did most girls. He guessed she was at least five-ten, with a lanky, slim build, all arms and legs. She held a manila folder filled with papers about to spill out. "You must be one of those crazy Catfish players."

"What clued you in? The uniform or the overuse of profanity?" He gave her a rueful smile, remembering his exuberant cursing. He should have waited until he was *inside* the clubhouse, but he hadn't expected to run into anyone. Let alone someone like her.

Something sparked in her eyes, and her lips quirked. "Well, I guess it must be the profanity, since I don't see much in the way of a uniform." She glanced down his torso. He remembered he was bare-chested, having ditched his shirt.

"Yeah, well . . . had to let off a little steam."

"So that was you cussing up a storm? I thought I was about to get trampled like a barrel of grapes."

"No trampling, I promise." From the gleam in her eye, she was probably teasing, but just in case, he took a step back. Again her gaze flicked down his chest, as if she couldn't help it. "I'm not coming on to you either. Too sweaty. But if you want to hang around until after my shower . . ."

He said that mostly to get a rise out of her, since something told him she'd be fun to get all riled up.

But her face changed, the playful sparkle vanishing. She took a big step back and narrowed her eyes at him. "No, I do not. I want to deliver this message and get

on with my day. Can you tell me where to find Mr. Ellington?"

Ellington—that was Duke's last name. Most baseball
guys had a nickname, though not many were named
after jazz greats. What did this girl want with Duke?

"He's busy bossing around baseball players. I guarantee he wouldn't want to be interrupted." He folded
his arms over his chest. Excellent. Now those lively
dark eyes were taking in his forearms as well as his
torso. Usually, at this point, a girl would do something
to signal her willingness to spend intimate time with
the hotshot pitcher who'd gotten half a million dollars
for signing with the Twins.

Not this girl. "I can see you want to be difficult,
which is exactly what I would expect, given the con-
tents of this document." She tapped the folder. "Fine. In
the interests of moving on with our lives—you to your
shower and probably a six-pack and a groupie—why
don't you give me a hint about where Mr. Ellington's
office might be? I'll wait for him there."

Holy RBI. This girl could certainly talk. Her face
moved as she spoke, her eyes danced; every bit of her
seemed alive and in motion. She looked to be in her
early twenties and had a sort of student-gypsy vibe
about her. Her lips curved in a way that suggested she
liked to laugh . . . and talk, and tease. She wore a tight
white T-shirt molded to high, pretty breasts, and a
flowery skirt that ended just above her knees. And red
cowboy boots. Damn. How could he resist red cowboy
boots? Those things ought to be banned.

He plucked the folder from her hand. "Got a pen?
You seem like the kind of girl who would have a pen."

"What's that supposed to mean? And yes. But no.
Why?"

"Want to clarify any of that?" He raised an eyebrow

at her, while trying to get a surreptitious peek at the typing on the document inside the folder. *Whereas we, the residents of Kilby County,* it began.

She snatched the folder back. "Yes, I have a pen. No, you can't write on the petition. And why do you want to?"

He put on a wounded expression. "I was going to draw you a map. These passageways can be superconfusing. It's completely understandable that you got lost and found yourself at the place where the guys get undressed." He winked, watching the flush rise in her cheeks. Yes, she was definitely fun to get riled up.

Then her words sank in. "Petition? What petition?" He tried to take the folder back, but she whisked it out of his reach. He barely missed grabbing her breast instead.

Before he could apologize, she stepped back with an exaggerated gasp of outrage. "There you go again. You Catfish really are a menace to decent society. Just like the petition says."

"What?"

"That's right." She waved the folder. "They say you're completely out of control."

Caleb had heard the talk about the Catfish too. They liked to party a little too much, and they indulged in the occasional bar-clearing brawl, but then, they were fun-loving young baseball players, so what could you expect? Anyway, it wasn't his problem. He intended to put Kilby in his rearview mirror as soon as possible. "I wouldn't know. Can't say that I care either."

"So the stories are true? Did you guys really fill the community pool with rubber catfish? I heard the senior exercise group had quite a scare and had to call the paramedics."

He snorted.

She shook her head sadly. "Things sure have changed since I came to games as a kid. And to think I thought it was safe here for a nice, civilized girl like me. Next time I'll make sure to bring a bodyguard."

A *bodyguard*? Now that was taking it a little too . . . He caught the gleam of mischief she hid under the sweep of her eyelashes. Damn. He'd been right before. She *was* teasing him.

Whether it was the incredible frustration of the last two hours, on top of the preceding frustration of being sent down, then traded—throw in the never-ending worry about his family—whatever the cause, all his emotions boiled over in that moment. In two quick steps he crowded her against the wall—no contact, just heat and sweat and closeness.

He growled in her ear, his lips almost brushing the delicate skin there. "There's only one way to find out if the stories are true. But you have to want it. Bad. You have to be so hot for it, you come chasing after me and beg for it. Then you have to prove you can handle it. Put that in your petition."

She stared up at him, her pupils dilated so far her eyes looked black, with a rim of glowing amber. The little pulse in her neck beat like a drum.

All of a sudden his cock was so hard his vision blurred. *Damn*. Where had that come from? She wasn't even his type. In fact, she was on the irritating end of the female spectrum.

He let her go as if she was a grenade about to explode. "Duke's office is down the hall to your right."

Pushing open the clubhouse door, he headed directly for the shower. It was going to have to be a cold one.

Love comes out of left field in the second novel in
USA Today *bestselling author*
Jennifer Bernard's *sexy baseball-themed series,*

CAUGHT BY YOU

Months of alternately flirting and bickering with
Kilby Catfish catcher Mike Solo just turned into
the hottest kiss of Donna MacIntyre's life—and
that's a major league complication. Any hint of
scandal could keep her from getting her son back
from her well-connected ex. Then Mike comes up
with a game-changing idea: a marriage proposal
that could help win her case—even as it jeopar-
dizes her heart . . .

Mike hasn't been able to get the gorgeous,
gutsy redhead out of his fantasies. The least he
can do is fix the mess he helped create. Yet their
engagement is quickly becoming about a lot more
than doing the right thing. Because after swear-
ing he'd never risk love again, Mike has found a
passion that puts all his emotions in play, and a
woman he'll go to bat for again and again . . .

IF DONNA MACINTYRE made a list of people she'd never expect to see at the Kilby Community Library, Mike Solo would be right at the top. He was the popular catcher for the Kilby Catfish, after all, with a grin promising every kind of fun, and the sort of physique built from squatting behind the plate, not carrying a pile of heavy-looking hardback books to the checkout desk.

"Need a hand, Solo?" She slid next to him, propping one hip against the desk. "In case, you know, you're wondering what all these big, thick things are good for." She flicked one of the books; it looked like a serious biography.

Mike, as always, didn't miss a beat. With a flash of his devil-green eyes, he murmured, "I know exactly what big, thick things are good for, but you can demonstrate if you want."

Frank the librarian, nearly dwarfed by Mike's tower of books, choked a little.

Mike raised an eyebrow at Donna. "Look at that, you've gone and upset the librarian, Red. That's bad etiquette."

"I didn't—you—" *He'd* gone right into the gutter, not her. She wanted to protest, but the pink tinge on the librarian's face made her shift gears. "Sorry, Frank. I'll behave." She leaned across the desk. "But you do realize that one of the notorious Kilby Catfish is in our humble library. I just hope the patrons are safe. We all know how crazy those ballplayers can be."

"Now that's just prejudice, plain and simple," Mike announced, looking injured.

"I'm a law-abiding citizen here to settle up before I leave town. Frank knows I would never cause any trouble. Unless trouble comes looking," he added, sweeping Donna with a glance that made her skin warm. "I have a few more of these, man. Be right back."

"Thanks, Mike. I'll get started." The librarian reached for the top of the stack. Donna stared, mouth dropping open a bit. Apparently Mike was just as well-known to the staff of the library as to the bartenders at the Roadhouse. Well, well, well.

"Donna, you'd better come with me," Mike added, putting out his hand. "I'm not sure I trust you alone with all those big, thick things."

"Ha . . . ha." The rest of her no-doubt-brilliant comeback evaporated as his big hand enveloped hers in callused strength and heat. She and Mike Solo had been flirting with each other all season, ever since she'd first met him at the Roadhouse. But it had never gone further than that, for various reasons. Her complicated life, for one thing. His Vow of Celibacy, for another. Everyone knew that Solo took a Vow of Celibacy at the start of the season and never broke it.

Hoping her way with words would come back soon, she followed him out of the library into the hot parking lot. It was just so . . . *strange* to see him here, in real life, instead of out on the ball field or partying with the other Catfish. Like one of those "Look, celebrities are just like you" magazine spreads showing movie stars with cups of Starbucks. It made her wonder what else she didn't know about Mike Solo.

He opened the door of a silver Land Rover and reached in for more books, giving her a chance to watch the flexing muscles of his back and a truly spectacular rear end. She averted her eyes before he caught her, fixing her gaze instead on the books he dropped into her arms. On the cover of the top book, the face of Steve Jobs stared back at her. "Do you really read all these books?"

"We have a lot of road trips and I like to keep my brain cells active. I'm a catcher, you know." He extracted himself from the car, burdened with another stack of books.

"So?"

"So, catchers have to be smart. We have to know the game better than just about anyone. Strategy, patterns, human behavior. I have to know what someone's going to do before they even do it. Like you, right now." With a twist of his hip, he closed the door of the Land Rover. It was unfairly sexy, how he did that.

"Me, right now, what?"

"From what I know of Donna MacIntyre, you're going to make a joke. That's your go-to, make a joke. Come on. Tease me, baby. Do that thing you do so well."

She clamped her mouth shut, not wanting to prove him right, though of course he was. Ever since she was little, she'd coped with all the crap in her life by laughing about it. What else could you do?

Lifting her head high, she marched toward the library. Mike caught up with her instantly. "Did I forget to mention I like it?" He leaned down close, so she felt his warm breath on her ear. Shivers raced down her spine. "Don't hide your light for me. Joke away. Bring it on."

"Maybe I'm not in a joking mood. This is a library, after all."

"I keep forgetting that, maybe because I usually see you in a party atmosphere. What brings a wild and crazy girl like you here?"

For a reckless moment she wanted to tell Mike the

truth. The whole story, in revealing detail. But she hadn't even told Sadie, her best friend. Which was all kinds of wrong and had to change, right away. But for now . . .

"Picking out books for the Shark. He's the boy I nanny for."

"Love the nickname."

"Thanks, Priest. I have a knack for nicknames."

"*That's* mine?" The confounded look on his face made her laugh. It was fun getting under Mike's skin.

"Because of the Vow of Celibacy, you know. But don't worry, that's not your only nickname." She winked.

"I shouldn't ask. I really shouldn't. What else?" He shifted his pile of books to one arm and held the door open for her.

She ducked under his arm. "Hottie McCatcher," she told him demurely. "But don't let it go to your head."

"I've got news for you, Red," he whispered, as Frank the librarian put a finger to his lips, urging them to be quiet. "Season's over. The Vow of Celibacy has expired."

Donna's entire body, including her suddenly dry mouth, reacted to that piece of information. With a strangled squeak, she hurried toward the desk.

Mike followed Donna, drinking in the sight of her denim short-shorts and tight T-shirt, which he'd already scoped out as advertising a local zydeco band. Her body curved to a deep indentation at the waist. For about the millionth time he wondered how it would feel between his hands. Sexy, maddening Donna, with her copper-bright hair and changeable hazel eyes. He knew her face was pretty—heart-shaped and stubborn-chinned, with a damn dimple to boot. But to him it went beyond that. He always found himself caught up in the jokes she cracked, her cheeky attitude, her . . . daring.

After all, the last time he saw her, she'd been standing up for her friend Sadie against the entire Wade clan of bullies. That took guts, and he respected the hell out of her for it.

At the desk, they both unloaded their piles of books. Mike pulled out his wallet and extracted two hundred-dollar bills.

Apparently stunned, Frank dropped one of the overdue books—an account of World War I fighter pilots—on the floor. "Oh, I'm sure it won't be that much." The librarian shook his head nervously. "We're only up to five dollars so far."

"Consider it a donation, then. A little something extra for keeping all these books out of circulation. Sometimes the season gets away from me."

Donna was looking at him strangely. "You do this a lot?"

"Check out books and forget to return them? Been known to happen. Road trips. Injuries. Team drama." He shrugged. "I try to make up for it. Are we good, Frank?"

"Good, good. Very good."

"Excellent. Maybe I'll see you next season. Hopefully not, of course. Nothing personal." He winked at the librarian, which seemed to unnerve him, as he just kept nodding in response.

He turned to Donna, who had her hands in the back pockets of her shorts. Lord, she was sexy. And fun. The most fun he'd had with a girl in . . . well, definitely since Angela, and maybe ever. And they'd never even kissed.

Yet.

With a lightning-quick calculation—the way he figured things behind the plate—he did the math.

1. The vow was over.
2. Donna was giving him that sassy look.
3. She was wearing that T-shirt that hugged her gorgeous curves.
4. Tomorrow he'd be gone.

"C'mere a second." He took her hand again and pulled her toward the tall, secluded stacks where the biographies were shelved. He'd never seen anyone in this section, and anyway, there were only two other people in the library, including Frank.

"What are you doing?" she hissed. But she followed him willingly. Maybe she'd had the same thought. It took two to create this kind of chemistry, after all.

When they'd reached the deepest part of the stacks, where dust floated in the quiet sunbeams, he stopped, then turned to face her. The sun lit her hair into a fiery cloud. "I'm going back to Chicago tomorrow. But before I go, I'd like to do something."

"Return your library books. I can see that. You probably have some parking fines to pay too. Disorderly conduct, maybe?"

He ran a hand through the rough curls at the back of his head. "I have to confess something." His Catholic-boy conscience had been tugging at him this whole time. "Only a couple of those library books are mine. Mostly they're my neighbor's. He's house-bound, so I pick up books for him."

She blinked, her eyes a soft heather green in the filtered sunlight. "Your confession is that you don't read big piles of books, and that you go to the library for your neighbor? What else, do you feed his cat?"

"Only when he forgets."

Amusement lit up her little heart-shaped face. "I'm

crushed. I was thinking there was a secret genius hidden inside that ripped body."

She was talking about his body. Looking at it too, her gaze lingering on his chest. That was good. Seize the opportunity.

"Maybe I was trying to impress you. We've been dancing around each other all season. Don't you want to see if there's anything to this chemistry?"

Her eyes widened. "*Here?* Are you trying to add public indecency to all those fines?"

"Just a kiss. One kiss. There's nothing indecent about a kiss."

She seemed to consider that for a long moment, while a pleasant tension rose between them. He meant what he said; he didn't intend anything beyond a kiss. He was leaving the next day, and one-night stands weren't his style. But Donna had been on his mind for months, and damn it, he wanted one taste of those curvy pink lips before he left Kilby.

Finally she seemed to make up her mind. She took a step forward, brushing against him. A fresh fragrance came with her, like a fern unfurling in the woods. "Nothing indecent, Priest? I've got news for you."

"What's that?"

"There is if you do it right." And she lifted her mouth to his.